Free Radicals

A Novel of Utopia and Dystopia

D1568189

Zeke Teflon

See Sharp Press ∿ Tucson, Arizona

For more information contact

    See Sharp Press
    P.O. Box 1731
    Tucson, AZ 85705

    www.seesharppress.com

Teflon, Zeke.
Free radicals : a novel of utopia and dystopia / Zeke Teflon. – Tucson, Ariz. : See
Sharp Press, 2012.
300 p. ; 23 cm.

ISBN 1-937276-05-8

  1. Anarchists—Fiction. 2. Musicians—Fiction. 3. Dystopias—Fiction. 4.
Utopias—Humor.
             813.6

This book is dedicated to

Glossary of Spanish Terms
Used in the Text

AL, phr. An elision of "a" and "el": "to the."

BACANORA, n. Home-brewed tequila.

BOBOSO, n. A drooling idiot.

BUENO, adj. The usual Mexican answer to a phone call. Literally, "good." Corresponds to "hello."

BUENOS DÍAS, phr. Good day.

CABRÓN, n. Asshole. Son of a bitch. Literally "big male goat," which refers to the goat's horns, corresponding to the horns of a cuckold.

CAUDILLO, n. Big boss, chief. (Normally used in a political sense.)

CERVEZA, n. Beer.

CHILAQUILES, n. A breakfast dish. Fried (usually stale) tortilla strips drenched in salsa and sometimes also with melted cheese.

CHINGAR, v. (Mexican slang) To fuck.

CHINGASO, adj. (Mexican slang) Fucked up; messed up. n., A punch.

CHUPA LA VERGA, imp. phr. Suck my dick. Literally, "Suck the dick." (In Spanish, body parts are never referred to with possessive pronouns, always with articles.)

CHUPACABRA, n. A folkloric monster. Literally a "goat sucker," a monster that sucks the blood from and mutilates livestock.

CHUPAVERGA, n. Cocksucker.

CHUY, n. The normal Mexican nickname for "Jesús." Pronounced "Chew-ee," with the accent on the first syllable.

COJONES, n. pl. Balls.

COMEMIERDA, n. Shit eater.

COMANDANTE, n. Commander.

COMITÉ, n. Committee.

¿COMO ESTAS?, phr. How are you?

COMPA, n. Contraction of "compadre"— pal, bud, bro.

COMPAÑERO, n. Comrade. Informally, "bro." Often used in political contexts. A bit more familiar than "compadre."

CON, conj. With.

CONFIANZA, n. Confidence. Trust.

¡COÑO!, int. Shit! A Caribbean-Spanish term.

CORPORADO, n. A company man. (Coined term, not in common use.)

¡CORTA!, imp. Cut! (From the verb "cortar," "to cut.")

CULERO, n. A homosexual who has anal sex. (Derived from "culo"— "asshole")

DEFENSA, n. Defense.

DEL, phr. An elision of "de" and "el": "of the."

DISCURSO, n. Speech.

DOLENCIA, n. Ache or longing.

¿DONDE ESTA?, phr. Where is (it, he, she)?

ESE, n. A contraction of "socio": "associate," but in common usage "bud," "pal." Pronounced almost like "essay."

ESTIMADOS COMPAÑEROS, phr. Esteemed comrades.

GABACHO/A, n. (Mexican slang) A derogatory term for non-Mexicans, especially white people.

GRINGO/A, n. Another derogatory word for non-Mexicans, probably derived from *griego* ("Greek"), as in the Spanish-language equivalent of "it's all Greek to me."

GUARDIA, n. Paramilitary police.

HABANERO, n. One of the hottest chiles on earth. So hot that they can cause physical damage and agonizing pain if eaten raw. Habaneros are normally used only in sauces.

HACE UNA SEMANA, phr. A week ago.

HERMANO, n. Brother.

HIMNO, n. Hymn.

HOMENAJE, n. Homage.

HUEVOS CON CHORIZO, phr. Eggs with highly spiced, usually unencased pork or (less commonly) beef sausage.

HUEVOS FRITOS, n. Fried eggs.

IMPERIALISMO, n. Imperialism.

JUNTANOS, imp. phr. (w/pronoun suffix) Join us.

LANZALLAMAS, n. Flamethrower.

LEVANTATE, imp. phr. (reflexive verb w/pronoun suffix) Get up. Literally, "Get yourself up."

LÍDER MÁXIMO, n. Maximum leader. ("Líder" is pronounced almost like "leader," and is one of the many border Spanish terms borrowed from English. "Troque" [pickup truck], "parquear" [to park], and "lunchear" [to eat lunch] are other examples.)

LISTO, adj. Ready.

LO SIENTO, phr. I'm sorry. I regret it. Literally, "I feel it."

LOCO, adj. Crazy.

MAGNÍFICO, adj. Magnificent.

MALDITO, adj. Damned.

MARICÓN, n. Faggot.

MARTIRES, n. pl. Martyrs.

MÁS, adj. or n. More.

MATERIALISMO DIALÉCTICO, n. Dialectical materialism.

MENUDO, n. Tripe and garbanzo soup. The traditional Mexican hangover recipe.

M'ESTAN MATANDO, phr. ("Me estan matando") They're (it's) killing me.

MIERDA, n. Shit. Often used as an exclamation, as in "¡Que Mierda!" — "What shit!"

MONTUNO, n. A fast, repeating chord pattern played by the keyboard (piano) player in salsa arrangements.

MOTA, n. (Border Spanish slang) Marijuana.

¡MUERTE A LOS CONTRAREVOLUCIONARIOS!, phr. Death to the counter-revolutionaries!

MÚY, adv. Very.

NARCOS, n. pl. A shortening of "narcocorridos," a subgenre of the common Mexican corrido, varying from it only in subject matter. Like corridos, narcocorridos are ballads, story songs, but their subject matter deals with drug dealers, smuggling, the cartels, and murder, invariably in a glorifying manner.

NO HAY NADA MÁS, phr. There's no more.

NOS ESCAPAMOS, phr. We escaped.

NOS LLAMAN, phr. We're called.

NOVIO/A, n. Boyfriend/girlfriend.

NÚMERO UNO, phr. Number one.

OTRA/O, n. Other. Another. One more.

OTRA VEZ, phr. One more time. Again.

PAPAS FRITAS, n. Fried potatoes.

PA' TODOS, phr. "Para todos." For all. For everyone.

PARTIDO, n. Political party.

PELIGRO, n. Danger.

PENDEJO, n. Idiot, moron, dumbshit. Literally, "pubic hair." Very common, but also mildly offensive. Often used as a term of endearment and familiarity, but when used with strangers it is offensive.

PINCHE, adj. Mean, low down, dirty. A mild curse word roughly corresponding to, but not as crude as, "fucking" in the nonsexual sense in English, as in "no fucking good."

PRONTO, adv. Quickly. Soon.

PUTO, n. Male whore.

¿QUE PASO?, phr. What's happening?

¿QUE PIENSES?, phr. What do you think?

QUINCEANERA, n. A coming-out party for Mexican girls at age 15.

REALIDAD, n. Reality.

REGALO, n. Gift.

RÉGIMEN, n. Regime.

REVOLUCIÓN, n. Revolution.

RUSOS, n. pl. Russians.

SABROSO, adj. Flavorful. Tasty.

¡SALUD!, int. The normal Spanish-language toast. Literally, "Health!" Less literally, "To your health!"

SE ME PARO, phr. (Mexican-American slang) I have a hard on.

SIMPÁTICO, adj. Empathetic.

SOCIALISMO, n. Socialism.

SOMOS REFUGIADOS, phr. We're refugees.

SUAVE, adj. Smooth. When used with the article "el," as in "el suave," it functions—like all Spanish adjectives—as a noun: "the smooth one."

TOMATILLO, n. A common Mexican and Southwestern vegetable.

TROQUE, n. (Border Spanish term) Pickup truck.

UN POCO MÁS, phr. A little more.

VAMONOS, imp. phr. (verb w/pronoun suffix). Let's go.

VATO, n. (Mexican-American slang) This term has no exact translation in English. The closest thing to it would be "homey"or "homes." (I once saw a would-be-hip writer spell the word "holmes," as in "Sherlock.") Sometimes misspelled as "bato." ("B's" and "V's" are pronounced very similarly in Spanish, hence the occasional misspelling of words beginning with "V" in border Spanish.)

VECINO/A, n. Neighbor.

VENCEREMOS, v. We will win.

¡VETE A LA CHINGADA!, imp. phr. As commonly used, "Go to hell!" A very strange phrase that literally means "Go to the fucked female." This might refer to the humiliation of Mexican Indian men after their women were raped by the Spanish during the Conquest.

¡VIVA!, imp. Long live!

VOLVEREMOS, v. We will return.

1

I woke up this mornin' and I got myself a . . .
Well, you can see where this is going . . .

Kel Turner was snoring, one arm dangling down from the couch toward the remnants of last night's dinner—nine mostly empty cans of Schlitz Classic Ice and a greasy pizza box, empty but for a cardboard-like wedge missing several bites and resting against one edge of the box. A few roaches were feasting on the half-eaten piece and the hunks of cheese stuck to the bottom of the box.

Kel stirred. He opened one eye. He screamed.

There, on the end of his nose, antennas wriggling, sat a large, brown sewer roach. Kel levitated a meter into the air as he batted the roach away. He ran to the bathroom and scrubbed his face viciously. Three times.

He filled his his hands with water and emptied them over the top of his head. While smoothing back his hair, he smarted as his hand hit a large knot on the back of his scalp. Where had *that* come from? He carefully put his fingertips on the knot and winced, feeling what seemed like an inch-long cut. He pulled his hand back in front of his face and looked at his fingers. Flecks of blood. He washed and dried his hands, pulled his hair away from the wound again, put his fingertips on the cut, and put them back before his face. This time there was no blood. But it still hurt.

As he walked out of the bathroom, he bumped his knee on the handle of the vanity door; he gasped and reached down. His knee, no, both of his knees, were rubbed raw. What in hell had he done last night? He turned back to the sink, splashed more water on his face and hair, and muttered, *"Jesus Festering Christ."*

There were black bags under his eyes, three days' worth of stubble, long, grey, greasy strands of hair hanging in front of his face, crow's feet spreading around his eyes like the cracks in drying mud, and a jello-like pot gut he could hold in both hands and jiggle up and down like a lard-filled beach ball. Once you were off Comp-Med, this shit happened *fast*. Kel was only a hundred and eighty centimeters tall, but he easily weighed a hundred kilos, and all too much of it wasn't muscle.

He grunted in disgust, walked back into the room he called home, and started to pick up empty beer cans. To his surprise, the first one, a can of Schlitz Classic, was almost full; and it would be a shame to waste it. He took a sip. Warm, but not totally flat. It would do.

What the hell time was it? He took a hit of warm beer and blinked a gummy eyelid twice, but his readout didn't come up. Of course not. When would he stop doing that?

His implants had been wiped in the EMP bursts during The Troubles. Then, it had been nukes exploding above the atmosphere, taking out anything with an unshielded chip for hundreds of miles in all directions. Now, any asshole who could build a half-meter parabolic dish, who knew the meaning of "high energy radio frequency," and who could tell one end of a soldering iron from the other, could construct a HERF gun, point it in any direction, and fry all of the electronics in its beam that weren't heavily shielded. So no. No inner-ocular displays.

Kel remembered what it had been like after the first EMP bursts: the feeling of loneliness, of being cut off from the rest of humanity. It had taken him weeks to adjust, and some people never had, like the dust addicts infesting the slumped nano buildings just down the street, shuddering, coughing, staring into space at nonexistent displays. The neuro-stim addicts were even worse, not that there were many still around. The EMP bursts had fried the tissue around their pleasure-center 'trodes, and most who hadn't been reduced to drooling cretins had committed suicide within weeks: no way to feel pleasure, no reason to live. Even a lot of people with ordinary inductive implants and no brain damage had gone bat-shit crazy; some said the abrupt connectivity cut felt like being struck blind. Today, two decades later, all it meant to Kel was that he'd have to learn the time from his wall screen. But that could wait.

He went to the apartment's window, pulled up the blinds, wiped some of the grime from the top pane with the side of his hand, smeared it on the back of his pants, and peered out. The window, so old it wasn't even photosensitive, mercifully faced north, so he was spared the agony of direct sunlight.

At first glance, things looked normal. The huge, 3-D ads floating before the apartments on the opposite side of the street were flashing their usual come-ons, the two most eye-catching ones directly facing Kel's apartment. In the first, a heavily muscled, flak-jacketed Uncle Sam, hefting an M-99 over one shoulder, swept a pair of night-vision glasses from side to side. Its message was simple: "Report suspicious activities. Only those with something to hide need be afraid." The ad had repeated this message endlessly for the past four months.

The second ad showed a gleaming starship blasting off and disappearing into a luminous spiral galaxy: "Your future is in the stars. Live the life *you* deserve!" The flashy emigration board was in stark contrast to its surroundings: dilapidated 20th- and early 21st-century buildings—no arching or branching nano-composite structures here, just concrete, steel, glass, and brick rectangular monstrosities interspersed with debris-strewn vacant lots and, still, the slumped remains of some of the early nano buildings that had been sprayed during The Troubles.

Depending on how much of a dose they got, they'd either oozed into gelatinous puddles or slumped into flattened-skull shapes, their windows gaping like deformed eye sockets. The stench from their entombed—or, worse, partially embedded—occupants had been intolerable for weeks after the rioting ended, and even now the only ones who would go into them were dust or spike heads.

Kel stared at the nearest skull-like ruin as a shivering human skeleton crawled out of an "eye" just above ground level and shuffled down the dirty, potholed street. Kel's gaze followed him as he shambled past shabbily dressed men and women haggling with street vendors amidst the carcasses of graffiti-covered vehicles stranded like beached marine mammals on the street and shattered sidewalk.

As the dust head turned the corner, Kel chuckled when he glanced at the remnants of an airvan buried nose first in the broken glass-strewn corner lot. For perhaps the hundredth time, Kel mused that the driver must have been mighty surprised when his controls and engine went dead. A lot of people in those flying coffins, and on the ground, had died during the EMP bursts. Today, no one in his right mind would even think about getting into one.

Kel shifted his gaze to the right and saw two cops confronting Emmy, a middle-aged, black homeless woman, and an occasional recipient of Kel's pocket change. One cop pushed her to the ground and began beating her with his club as she pulled her filthy plastic coat over her head. Kel was glad the window was closed so that he couldn't hear her screams. The other cop pulled out his club and joined in. Kel shuddered as the second cop's truncheon smashed the hand that covered her face. When the bones in her hand snapped, she reflexively pulled it down, clutching it with her other hand, and the cop connected with her jaw. Her teeth went flying in a spray of red.

The cops stopped. The one who had smashed her face hitched his truncheon back on his belt and stood towering, triumphant over Emmy's cowering form. Kel saw his mouth start to work and, even though he couldn't hear him, he was pretty sure, even at a distance of fifty meters, that he could make out the final word, "bitch." . . . *Fucking cops!* And not a goddamned thing he could do about it.

The cop who had bashed Emmy's face reached into his back pocket, looked up at the nearest power pole's dead surveillance camera, its lens smashed, took something small out of his pocket, and stuffed it into Emmy's coat. Then he activated his helmet recorder and gestured for his partner to search her. The other cop began roughly pawing the huddled figure, and shortly held up something that Kel couldn't make out. But he was pretty sure that he knew what it was.

Emmy must have really pissed them off, because this was not the normal drill. Usually, after kicking the shit out of her, they'd drag her ass downtown, book her, and the following day she'd be hauled in front of a judge on a charge of assaulting an officer or resisting arrest. Six months and out. This time, they'd planted a bag of dust or spike on her and would charge her with possession *and* assaulting an officer.

If they *really* wanted to fuck with her, they'd bypass the dope charge and accuse her of terrorism. But that would be overkill with Emmy, and they usually reserved that charge for politicals. Whatever the charge, conviction was a foregone conclusion.

Kel exhaled noisily and looked away from Emmy. Thirty meters farther down the sidewalk, sub-teenaged hookers were hustling passersby, paying no attention to the cops, and the cops paying no attention to them. Kel took a long sip of warm beer as he watched a blubbery civ-serv in a rumpled, grey business uni approach the kids, haggle for a few seconds, and then waddle past the cops and Emmy with his hand kneading the butt of a garishly made-up 11-year-old in a see-through red mini. No, there was no reason to worry. Everything was normal.

2

MARRIAGE, n. The state or condition of a community consisting of a master, a mistress and two slaves, making in all, two.

—Ambrose Bierce, *The Devil's Dictionary*

MARRIAGE, n. A common means of discouraging sex.

—Chaz Bufe, *The American Heretic's Dictionary*

Kel stepped back, rubbed his eyes, and set his warm beer on the window sill. He picked up his acoustic guitar, which was face down on the no-longer-self-cleaning, varying-shades-of-tan carpet, and set it back on its stand, noticing with relief that it was undamaged. He picked up the pizza box and beer cans, walked to the sink/stove/refrigerator/recycling combo, picked up some additional empties on the drainboard, and fed everything into the recycling chute.

He walked back into the middle of the room and faced the ancient 2-D wall screen, which had activated when he'd started moving. He glanced at the time in the lower right-hand corner. *Jesus Christ!*—1:37 pm. He yawned and said, "Messages?"

"Seventeen. One from—"

"Play 'em."

The screen lit up with the all-too-clear image of Mig, an angry, 40-ish woman with dyed, curly red hair, a complexion like sandpaper, and way too much makeup covering it up.

"You bastard! Do you know what you did last—"

"Stop! Erase!"

Jesus, that was it! That was the reason for the gash on the back of his head and his rubbed-raw knees. He'd gone over to Mig's yesterday afternoon with a bottle of vodka, and she hadn't been there. But her roommate Sally had, and Sally had been only too happy to have a drink while they waited for Mig to come home from work.

An hour later, or was it three?, Mig still wasn't home, the bottle was gone, and he couldn't remember who had made the first move. All that he could remember was Sally's bare legs over his shoulders, the rug burning his knees. Then waking up with a blinding headache, blood dribbling down his face, drunk and naked in the hallway outside Mig's apartment, his clothes next to him. Followed by the painful walk home—and finally the welcome coldness of the first Schlitz Classic Ice after he got there, far too close to sober.

Why had he ever gotten involved with Mig? She was mean, vengeful, and man but she could hold a grudge. She was still sore from a couple of months back when he'd made a joke about getting lockjaw after trying to get her off for fifteen minutes. He thought she'd get it, but she hadn't, even though they'd watched that ancient Woody Alvin? Elvin? 2-D together just a week before with the same damned joke. Even after he explained it to her, she was still sore. God could he pick 'em.

He looked back at the screen and said, "Next."

The All-American Property Management Corporation's logo filled the screen: a golden dragon on a blood-red Viking shield. The dragon had always looked more like a lamprey to Kel. Now, its sucker-like, needle-toothed orifice was flaring out of the screen, its barbed tongue darting menacingly as flames filled the screen behind it and smoke poured from its nostrils.

"Mister Turner, your rent was due on the first. If you don't pay within the next ten days we'll be forced to—"

"Erase!"

Mig's angry face again, close up, taking up the entire screen.

"Answer me, damn it!"

"Erase!"

Mig was replaced by a soothing, robin's egg-blue sky flecked with cumulus clouds. A tiny speck grew into a bird soaring closer, but it faded as it grew in size. As its image vanished, the stylized, cursive logo, "Bank Two, Your Banking Buddy," faded in, along with an all-too-familiar, overly friendly baritone voice:

"Kel, we know that you intend to pay, but don't worry if you can't! We're your *friends* at MDNA's Bank Two, and we have the answer to your financial problems! That's right! *We have the answer!* And we have great news! That's right! *Great News!* You don't need to worry about your bills! That's right! *Don't worry about your bills!* . . . And get cash back! Just report to MDNA's southside organ recycling center at—"

"Erase!"

Dick, a tall, clean-cut man in his early thirties, was next.

"Kel, we have a job Friday night at the Retro. They want really old shit—jazz or blues, and real instruments—so we'll have to practice before then. Bill and Lenny can do it Thursday night. My place. Let me know if that works for you. This could mean regular gigs, so let's not fuck this up. Call me."

The screen went blank and Mig reappeared.

"I know you're there! You—"

"Erase!"

Another second of black, and then Mig again.

"You gutless—"

"Erase!"

Still more Mig.

"I'll get you for—"

"Erase! Next!"

"You ass—"

"Erase! Stop!"

The screen froze. Kel picked up the remote and clicked to the next message. Mig's face came up, open mouthed, looking remarkably like the All-American lamprey. He clicked to erase before she could utter a word. He did this nine more times in quick succession, with Mig's face growing angrier and more contorted with every message, looking almost like 19th-century flash-card animation, until "No More Messages" flashed on the screen.

Kel exhaled, walked to the window, and slugged down the remnants of his warm beer in a single gulp before turning back and staring blankly at the green screen. He walked to the 'fridge combo, grabbed another Schlitz, walked back in front of the screen, and said "UltraRealityBlue."

The screen lit up with his favorite feed, the massage parlor 2-D, showing a well-endowed, nude "therapist" working on a moaning, hairy, potbellied customer lying on his back while the therapist stroked him rhythmically with both hands.

At the moment he started to jerk, the audio feed cut out and was replaced by a voice-over: "Why settle for this? For only a thousand a month you can have full-immersion sex! Anything you want: straight sex, gay sex, group sex, cross sex—be a man, be a woman, be anyone, be any*thing* you want! Ream an altar boy! *Be* an altar boy! Be Catherine the Great! Or Catherine the Great's *horse!* Don't settle for a 2-D or 3-D feed! Get full-immersion for only a thousand a month! Just call us and we'll deliver your senso-lounger tomorrow!"

Kel was none too pleased as the voice-over ended, because the massage-parlor audio remained off as the man under the therapist's hands continued to jerk and his mouth continued to make what looked like moans. Then, finally, the announcer cut back in: "And coming next month, our ultra-max prison channel available in 2-D or 3-D! *Don't miss it!* Sign up now and get your first month free! Here's a taste!"

The feed from the massage parlor cut back in for a second as the potbellied man climaxed, then immediately switched to an overcrowded prison yard. Not much was happening—just prisoners milling around to no apparent purpose, all wearing their standard-issue prison pinks with Bible verses in large block letters on the back of every shirt. A bald-headed Mexican prisoner turned his back to the camera, and Kel read: "And if a man lie with a beast, he shall surely be put to death: and ye shall slay the beast. —*Leviticus* 20:15." Another prisoner turned his back to the camera, revealing: "And I shall take away mine hand, and thou shalt see my back parts; but my face shall not be seen. —*Exodus* 33:23."

Kel smirked, remembering the solemn proclamation a few months ago by Joe Bob Arpayaso, the hopelessly corrupt Secretary of Homeworld Security. When the new prison uniforms were unveiled, Arpayaso had pontificated that constant exposure to random verses of Scripture couldn't help but have a rehabilitative effect on prisoners.

The viewpoint abruptly shifted to a corridor in a cellblock where two black inmates were straining to hold the arms of a heavily muscled, tattooed white prisoner. Another black, his back to the camera, his shirt bearing the verse "Let every soul be subject to the higher powers . . ." was moving toward them, trying to shove a wicked looking shiv into the white prisoner's guts, as he was kicking furiously at the assailant's knife hand. Finally, the would-be murderer found an opening, and struck shockingly quickly.

Kel said, "*Off!*" and drained his beer as the scene cut off in mid-scream. Kel walked to the loudly humming refrigerator portion of his apartment's all-in-one. He stopped for a moment and looked at its well-decorated door, before grabbing and downing half of another Schlitz, while breathing hard. He closed the door and looked blankly at it. The largest thing attached to it was a tattered flyer for the final gig of his last band, the punk-revival group, Brutal Scrotum Attack; they'd done well that night and had pulled in just over $32 apiece. Next to the flyer was a brown printout advertising their sole recording, Colostomy Aroma, with what Kel thought was a classic graphic: a 2-D of a filthy bum in a sleeveless T-shirt with tracks up and down his arms, holding a colostomy bag under his nose, inhaling rapturously. Colostomy Aroma had sold well for a punk-revival burn: 131 loads.

Next to it was a raggedly torn printout showing a boy of two, with a woman's arm sticking into the jagged edge of the print from empty space, and curling around the boy. It was the only print he had of his son, Folky.

After the divorce, all of the other prints and holos of his kid had disappeared, leaving only this one. He would never have another, because Folky, according to Amilee (who'd named him Foucault, and who'd always hated the nickname), had died two years ago. He couldn't bring himself—didn't dare—to ask Amilee for a replacement photo or holo. Not after the last beating.

Seven years earlier, shortly after his discharge from the Peacekeepers, she'd come up to him at a gig at Nimbus. Just looking at her made him want to wrap his hands around her ass and pull her to him, which had happened quickly enough—after the third set.

They'd had it bad for each other, couldn't keep their hands off each other, for months. They didn't talk a whole lot during those months—they didn't need to—and it hadn't worked out too well when they did.

The sex had been great until she'd moved in, they had to talk more, and he'd discovered that there was another side to Amilee, a straight, ambitious side that wanted to make it in academia and was perpetually at war with her sensual side. He'd always figured that although she used a lot of peculiar jargon her heart was in the right place. So he'd kept his mouth shut, hoping things would get better, as they drifted further and further apart.

What had really sealed the deal was their career paths. He'd been gutting it out on the Central-Asian GI bill, studying music theory and comp, not daring to think what he'd do with his degree after he got it. Amilee, whose family had money from cattle operations on the fringes of the Amazon Desert, had been finishing her cultural studies dissertation.

Their contempt for each other's viewpoints—what he considered her "sponge-brained, new-age bullshit" and her contempt for his "simplistic, 18th-century-Enlightenment mechanistic rationality"—hadn't helped, either.

Her respect for him had dropped even further when he'd asked her, during an argument, what the hell The Enlightenment was.

They'd been studiously avoiding talking, having sex less and less often, when she'd proudly shown him the first draft of her dissertation, "Toward an Ur-Feminist Reconstruction of the Epistomological Morphology of Post-Structuralism: A Proto-Ontological, Semiotic Approach," and had basically dared him to go through it.

He hadn't even faked it—he suspected that the people on her committee hadn't, either—and had put her off with ever-lamer excuses. With every week that passed, her contempt for him grew. But by that time she was pregnant, so they'd stayed together for another three years after Folky was born. And as awful as many of the memories from those years were, he found himself smiling at a few of them.

Shortly after she'd started to suspect that he'd never read her dissertation, she'd tested his loyalty by pressuring him to feature her in his cowpunk band, Bubba's Toxic Breakfast, as the lead vocalist. After a few days of badgering, he gave up and allowed her to sit in at a rehearsal. That had nearly led to the breakup of the band. As Duane, the drummer, put it later, "I've heard better sounds coming out of people having hemorrhoid surgery."

But they'd stuck it out for another three years. Why? He still didn't know. Probably habit. Or fear of being alone. The excuse was that it was "for the kid," as if his being around parents who loathed each other was somehow good for him.

But then he thought about Folky. About the first time he picked him up, felt Folky's tiny hand curling around his index finger, and looked into his eyes. When he held him like that, nothing else mattered. Folky's smile was the most beautiful thing he'd ever seen. He was hooked. He'd do anything for his kid. Even put up with Amilee.

It all ended two months after the last time they'd had mutually unsatisfying sex, and two days after he'd had a quicky in his van at a gig—how *could* she have known?! He came home two nights later, after another gig, to find Amilee and Folky gone, and a note on the table saying he was a lying, cheating son of a bitch, and that she never wanted to see him again.

A week later a process server handed him divorce papers.

She got full custody. He didn't even get visitation rights.

The first time he called after the divorce, she said "Don't call again," and had abruptly cut him off. The second time, he got a black screen—no way to even leave a message. The third time, he also got a black screen. And a day later two guys stomped him in the alley. They didn't say a word. They didn't need to. His broken ribs told him everything he needed to know.

Two months after that, he got a terse note saying that Folky had drowned. He dared to call. As he expected, all that came up was a black screen. He ran a search of the public feeds, but he couldn't find anything. He hadn't expected to, but he couldn't have lived with himself if he hadn't tried. When anyone ran a search about people like him, searches revealed all, no matter how horrifying or embarrassing. But when people like him ran searches on people like Amilee and her family, they revealed only what people like Amilee and her family wanted them to reveal. When the government or the mega-corps ran searches, it was, of course, a very different story. But he wasn't the government or a mega-corp.

Then he started thinking about the dirt in the corporate walled-off areas (including that of Amazon Desert Cattle Corp., Amilee's parents' fiefdom) and the news corporations' back channels, and he hired a snoid, a hacker who supposedly could get into anything.

Two days later, the snoid was nearly beaten to death, and Kel found himself lying in a pool of blood, face down on his living room floor, his nose broken, a knee pressing down painfully on his back. The pressure on his back increased as his right arm nearly jerked out of its socket as it was pulled straight up. Then blinding pain as his right pinkie finger snapped. Kel screamed as his assailant threw his arm to the floor. The goon grabbed Kel's left arm, wrenched it up and, Kel felt his pinkie and ring fingers—on his fretting hand!—held in a vice-like grip for what seemed like minutes. When the grip released, he relaxed momentarily. And then he felt his head pulled back by the hair. His face smashed into the floor. And then again. A moment later, the pressure on his back eased, and he vaguely registered, "Knock it off, asshole, don't let there be a next time," before repeated kicks in the guts. As he curled into fetal position clutching broken ribs, he heard retreating footsteps, a slamming door, and then silence.

Now, all that he had left was his bitterness, this 2-D print marred by Amilee's intruding arm, the remnants of his music gear, and the strong suspicion that she'd lied to him about Folky's death.

He was at a dead end: alone, almost penniless, living in a shit hole that he could barely afford, playing any gigs he could get as long as they paid, even when he hated the music, and developing an embarrassingly large beer gut and a major case of depression. He was nursing outright rage toward Amilee, and an aching need to see his supposedly dead son. And he had absolutely no way to do anything about either.

After several moments Kel's anger subsided. He looked away from the printout and opened the refrigerator portion of the all-in-one. What could he do? Nothing.

He had a hangover that would have dropped a water buffalo, and he nearly picked up the traditional remedy on the top shelf of the 'fridge: a liter jar of menudo. But he hesitated, his hand hovering over the jar. Yes, the menudo would taste good, but it had no therapeutic worth, only distraction value; it would be impossible to focus on a hangover while chewing soft, slimy honeycomb tripe. He suppressed a shudder. Worse, this was a jar of street-bought, brown menudo. It'd taste good, but sometimes the brown spices were added for a reason, and Kel really didn't want to think about the nature of some of those flecks floating in the broth. Worst of all, getting the jar out, opening it, emptying it into a bowl, and nuking it seemed like way too much work.

So, Kel pushed aside a clump of green slime that had once been . . . celery? . . . lettuce? . . . broccoli? . . . grabbed another can of Schlitz, wiped the remnants of the green slime sticking to his hand on his pants, sat down on an armless, backless chair, leaned over, picked up his acoustic guitar, popped the top on the Schlitz, took a long slug, played scales for five minutes, and then began running through jazz and blues numbers for the gig at the Retro.

He didn't need to practice, and he didn't need to drink another seven cans of Schlitz. But he did.

3

Stairway to Free Bird

. . . or . . .

MUSIC, n. An area of universal expertise. The less formal musical
training persons have, the more certain they are to know what is
"good," and the more certain they are that their opinions are
just as valid as the opinions of those who have spent
their lives studying, playing, and composing music.

—Chaz Bufe, *The American Heretic's Dictionary*

Kel was setting up the p.a. system, snaking cables around mike
stands, frantically trying to get everything up and ready for the
sound check. Somehow, two of the mike cables had disappeared
since the last gig, and he had exactly enough. If any of them were
bad, he was fucked. What was almost equally fucked was that the
stage lights were off, and that the barkeep had told him that nothing but the brights were working. So, he was working in near darkness.

He sourly pondered the thought that he should have taken up
another instrument as he held a flashlight in his teeth while trying to shine it on the back of the mixer, as he tilted it up with one
hand while attempting to insert a cable with the other. Jesus. What
a gig. Guitar players were a nickel a dozen. If you wanted to play,
you'd better have a p.a. system, be willing to lug it around, set it
up, maintain the vid presence, and more often than not do the
booking, too. Kel inserted the cable, took the flashlight out of his
mouth, turned it off, and grabbed another cable.

Shitty sounding, loud, canned neo-rap music assailed Kel from
the club's system as he fussed and stewed. Outside, huge holos
hung in a grey, drizzly sky, almost eclipsing the skyscrapers behind
them, with the tracks from elevated mag-lev tracks vanishing into
and jutting out of the ads.

The ads were for the usual: virtual sex (anything your sick little imagination could desire—virtual sheep? no problem, no extra charge) Maui Wowees, emigration to any of a dozen recently opened stellar systems, Black Mamba Malt Liquor ("When You Want a Deadly, Aggressive Bite"), and, of course, the omnipresent, body-builder Uncle Sam, sweeping his field glasses endlessly along the horizon.

Below, an orange neon sign reading "The Retro," hung from rusty iron brackets on the corner of an ancient, two-storey brick building, reflecting off rain-soaked, faux-cobblestone streets in a rundown commercial district of two-and three-storey converted warehouses. Canned blues music replaced the neo-rap and drifted out the bar's door, growing louder and softer as people walked in and out dressed in flapper clothes, zoot suits, disco outfits, punk gear, grey, severe, youth-for-truth unis, and unclassifiable outfits such as the one on the rail-thin 20-something with a sculpted, narrow black beard, shades, black skull cap, wearing a cheap black synth suit with white vertical stripes, a good ten centimeters too short at the wrists and ankles, all set off by cheap, shiny, black patent leather shoes without socks, and with fluorescent green tattoos of barbed wire wrapping themselves around his shins just above his ankles.

As he set up, the scene facing Kel was dismal. The Retro was modeled on a twentieth-century rock club: dimly lit, tiny round tables scattered randomly around the interior; uncomfortable, high-backed, wrought iron chairs crowding the tables; grimy red shag carpeting on the floor; black velvet on the walls; a sequin-spangled ceiling with discolored strips of paint hanging down—no one ever noticed; no one ever looked up—and halter-topped, slit-skirted waitresses shivering from the frigid air conditioning, lugging around trays of overpriced, watered-down drinks.

Kel was still running cables, but glanced up as a pair of diesel dykes—at least that's what they looked like; at the Retro, you never knew—walked in and found their way to a table off to the side of the stage: sunglasses, fake piercings, fake brands, fake tattoos, motorcycle boots, leather vests over too-tight black T-shirts, with too-ample stomachs bulging beneath the shirts, black men's jeans with keys jangling down on chains, and pancake make-up heavy enough to hide the pallor of a corpse. Kel did a double take. Even beneath the disguise, Kel was pretty sure it was Mig and her best friend Melly. What the fuck were they doing here? Nothing good, no doubt of that, but what?

He stared at them, but they didn't even glance at him as they ordered drinks from the slit-skirted waitress and then turned toward each other and started talking. Kel returned to his task in an even fouler mood.

The house was half full as the band did the sound check, a verse of "Messin' with the Kid," and then launched into the first number, as the overhead lights flared on, blinding them. It was so bright on stage that it was almost impossible to see if anyone was dancing. But Kel could tell by the near-silence between songs that no one was.

Forty-five minutes in, the band was finishing "Shotgun Blues," while a drunk at one of the front tables shouted, "Play Free Bird!"

Kel and the other musicians ignored him and broke into a fast, jazzy version of the "T-Bone Shuffle," with Kel taking an extended guitar solo and Lenny, the bassist, playing inspired walking bass throughout the entire song. The false ending and reprise were killer, but no one noticed. Almost no one applauded; and, still, no one had gotten up to dance.

Kel leaned into the mike and said, "Here's one for all of you who've ever had a close encounter of the fourth kind. It's called 'Abductee Blues.'" Dick looked at Kel with a cocked eye, and nodded toward the near-invisible table where his girlfriend, Teena, who had always hated the song, was sitting. Kel looked at Dick and silently mouthed the words, "Come on!" After a few seconds' hesitation, Dick shrugged and muttered, "What the fuck. Let's do it," and Kel began playing the fast, jazzy eight-bar intro, with the bass and drums joining him on the second verse. After another eight bars, Dick's vocals kicked in.

Two verses later, no one was dancing, as Dick sang the third verse:

They jabbed me, they stabbed me
They stroked and they poked
Until my mind
Was very nearly broke
I'm telling you man
You need the patience of Job
Just to survive
That rectal probe

Kel took a short solo, and they went into the bridge:

The gray said
Don't worry bro
It's no big thing
(instrumental fill)
Don't worry bro
It ain't all that big
Now just . . . bend over . . .
And squeal like a—

Kel pulled off a glissando that sounded reasonably like a scream-ing hog. He then launched into a prolonged solo, and came out of it into the final vocal verses:

Now I got chips in my head
And chips in my bones
This ain't about no E.T.
Tryin' to call home
They flew all the way
To our pretty little globe
Just so they could use
That rectal probe

Rectal probe
Rectal probe
Nobody wants a
Rectal probe
Don't have to be
No homophobe
To live in dread of an
Alien rectal probe

They vamped on, with Kel taking another solo. Finally, since Dick wouldn't do it, Kel went back to comping and leaned into the mike yelling, "No! No!! Oh my god, *no!!!* That thing's got *spines* on it! Aaaagh! No! Please No!! Use some Astroglide!! 30 weight!!! WD40!!!! Tabasco sauce!!!!! Anything!!!!!! Aaaagh!!! Aaaagh!!! Aaaaaagh!!!!!! *Anything!!!!!!*"

When he stopped shrieking, he played the first few bars of "Dueling Banjos." A good five seconds after the final note faded, and with all the other players silent, Kel leaned toward the mike and yelled, "soooooooooo—eee!!"

There was virtually no response, not even the usual scattered applause from the one in ten people who "got" the song, and not even the usual yells of abuse, to which Kel invariably replied, "Thank you, glad y'all liked it!" while holding his Strat by the neck in case he needed to use it as a club. Now, the only response was nonverbal: Teena was looking daggers at both him and Dick.

As the lights faded to black, an audience member shouted, "¡Una más!" Kel caught Dick's eye and mouthed the words, "Crazy Woman"? Dick nodded as the lights came halfway up. He picked up his acoustic guitar, pulled the strap over his shoulder, bent down toward his mike, and said: "Here's an old cow-punk tune called 'I Love a Crazy Woman.' We hope y'all like it."

They finished the song to dead silence. No one had laughed at all, not even at what Kel thought were its funniest lines: "She's in deep psychosis, but I'll tell you boys she's fine. She's on a dozen medications, and I'm proud that she is mine."

And, still, no one had gotten up to dance. Dick looked at Kel, and asked, "Bad News Blues treatment?" Kel nodded. Bill and Lenny quickly fell in behind them as they broke into "This Guy's in Love," in an even slower and schmaltzier version than the original.

A young, neo-Goth couple, with so many facial studs and piercings that they reminded Kel of porcupines, got up and slow danced, rubbing their bodies against each other, but keeping their faces well apart. As Kel strummed the major 7th chords characteristic of the song, he couldn't keep his eyes off the couple, and he couldn't help but wonder how they managed oral sex.

When the song ended and the meager applause died out, Dick bent toward his microphone and opened his mouth, intending to say, "That was supposed to be punishment. Want more?" but before he got the first word out he was interrupted by a raging drunk: "Play Free Bird! This is the goddamned Retro! *Play Free Bird!*"

Dick stood gaping for too long, while a few other drunks took up the call, sounding as if they were mocking the first drunk, and the band.

"Yeah, Play Free Bird!"

"Free Bird!"

Kel gave the traditional reply, saluting them with his middle finger while yelling, "Here's your free bird!" But the drunks were into it by then, yelling one on top of the other:

"Proud Mary!"

"Mustang Sally!"

"Black Cat Bone!"

"Free Bird!"

"Stairway to Heaven!

"Hoodoo Love Thang!"

"Margaritaville!"

"Free Bird!"

"Love Bone Boogie!"

"Taking Care of Business!"

"Rock and Roll All Nite!"

"Brown Eyed Girl!"

"Martian Mojo Man!"

"Old Time Rock and Roll!"

"Sweet Home Alabam'!"

Kel shuddered. That was it. "Sweet Home Alabama" was the last straw. An ode to the state whose official motto was "*Incestum, Tentoria, Obesitas Morbidus*": "Incest, Lynchings, Morbid Obesity."

Worse, while he was gritting his teeth, he noticed Dick holding up his hand to the crowd, palm out, grinning at him with a demonic gleam in his eye. The fucker had always had a perverse streak, and a few months ago had even forced him to play "Brown Eyed Girl" at a gig. That had been bad enough, but "Sweet Home Alabama"? Finally, Dick lowered his hand, looked away from Kel, bent over his mike, and said: "Thanks so much. We'll take a short break and be right back." Kel exhaled to the frenzied but pro forma cries of "Play Free Bird!" and "We want some Skynyrd!!!"

As the lights went down and the canned music came up, Dick, Bill, and Lenny walked off stage, carefully avoiding eye contact with the drunks. Kel reached to the back of his amp and flipped the switch. He put his guitar on its stand, emptied what was left of a pint of stout and, empty glass in hand, headed to the table where his bandmates and their girlfriends were sitting.

Still blinking away the after-images from the brights as he came off stage, he snuck a glance at the apparent dykes three tables over. Mig looked up and waved. Kel turned away without acknowledging her. This was almost too strange. Mig had always loved frilly, ultra-feminine dresses that would have looked great on a chick twenty kilos lighter. So, diesel dyke gear? She had to be fucking with him.

As he sat down next to Dick, he motioned to a waitress, held up his empty glass, and pointed to it.

Dick turned toward Kel and said, "This is a fucking morgue. Don't these fucking people know how to dance? Are they fucking paralyzed?" He took a sip from his drink and turned back toward Kel. "What the fuck do we have to do to get them up?"

"Play Margaritaville?"

"Seriously."

"Free Bird? Mustang Sally?"

"Fuck off, Kel."

"Stairway to Free Bird? Love Bone Sally?"

Dick grunted disgustedly, not deigning to reply.

Kel wasn't deterred: "Free Mary? Proud Margaritaville?"

Dick glared at Kel for a few seconds, pulled out the set list, and he and Kel began to pore over it. The waitress arrived with Kel's pint of Terminator Stout, and he downed half of it, in all its 7.2% glory, in a single gulp.

While they were going over the set list, three Homeworld Protectors swaggered into the club. They were typical federal bulls: steroid-, gene-mod-enhanced slabs of beef wearing black uniforms, mirror shades, ceramo-helmets, slim-kev body armor, flechette and stun pistols, gas canisters, shiny, knee-high poly-leather boots, and in a seeming tribute to cops past, black truncheons with lead tips.

Kel and Dick, absorbed in planning their next set, didn't notice them, but almost everyone else in the place did, and immediately developed an intense interest in their drinks.

One of the Protectors started walking toward Mig and Melly. They looked down at their rum and cokes, shaking, but the bull stopped well before them. He hovered over a bearded zonie, who was smoking and was so spaced out that he hadn't even noticed the cop's approach.

The Protector tapped his baton on the table and drew it back. The zonie looked up, startled. The cop smashed him on the temple as his head came up. The bar went silent as the sickening sound of shattering bone echoed across the room. As the man slumped to the floor, his body spasming, the cop walked away, spitting out the words, "Tobacco's illegal, asshole."

The other two Protectors walked toward the stage, searching. Their necks stopped swiveling as they neared the band's table and rushed Kel. As he began to rise, one of the cops rammed his baton into Kel's solar plexis. Kel doubled over as the other one slammed his truncheon into the back of Kel's head, splitting his scalp open and showering blood over Dick, Bill, Lenny, and Teena.

As he was being hauled out, his bleeding head hanging down, the last thing Kel registered was Mig's loud, cackling laugh.

4

JUSTICE, n. A term of vicious mockery,
as in "equal justice under the law."

—Chaz Bufe, *The American Heretic's Dictionary*

Kel's arms ached. Two black-helmeted, black-uniformed jailers, faces invisible behind blackened visors, held his biceps in painfully tight grips, as they dragged Kel's bedraggled figure before a judge. A week after they'd hauled him in, his hair was still caked with blood from his untreated scalp wound, and his midsection still ached intensely.

His eyes winced in the light of arctic-white illumination strips, their cold glare bouncing off the grimy white tiles on the floor of the seedy courtroom. The door in the back of the room opened, and a balding, round-shouldered man, wearing a judge's robes, entered. Given that he was probably on Merit Med, he could have been anywhere from his apparent thirty-five up to ninety.

Kel looked up, his eyes pinning, searching for some sign, any sign, of where he was, even a name plate on the podium. His heart rate doubled as he looked at his surroundings and realized that he was in a special terrorism court, a secret court with a no-name judge, no defense witnesses, no defense attorney, and no recourse. To be charged was to be guilty.

The judged frowned at him. "Kelvin Edwa'd T . . . Turna. You have admitted to associatin' with known subversives, assaultin' t . . . t . . . two federal police officers with intent to kill, and bein' a member of the illegal, terroris' organizations, The People's Will and Food Not Bombs."

"What!!??"

The jailer on his right viciously twisted Kel's arm. Kel screamed in pain, but tried to continue.

"I didn't—"

The jailer twisted his arm even harder as the other jailer slugged him in the kidneys. Kel screamed again and dropped to his knees. The judge tensed, the muscles around his left eye contracting convulsively.

"Y . . . you were s . . . sayin', Mistah . . . T . . . Turna?"

Kel, grimacing in pain, gasping, didn't even raise his head.

The judge continued, his face twitching. "You're wise to show proper respect to th . . . th . . . th . . . this court, Mister Turna. Do you have anything else to say in y . . . your defense?"

Kel glanced fearfully at the guards and remained silent.

"V . . . v . . . ver . . . very well. You are hereby ordered to be de . . . de . . . ported to Extrasolar Penal Colony Number Three on the next available transport. Until th . . . that time you will be con . . . con . . . con . . . conf . . . conf . . . . . . held at the Coulter Cryogenic Correctional Facility."

"No!—"

The guard on the left slugged Kel in the kidneys again, harder. Kel crumpled, writhing in pain.

The judge looked down at him. "M . . . m . . . m . . . mista' Turna, you should have th . . . th . . . thought of the consequences before assaultin' peace officers and engagin' in t . . . t . . . t . . . t . . . t . . . terrorism."

5

EXILE, n. One who serves his country by residing abroad, yet is not an ambassador.

—Ambrose Bierce, *The Devil's Dictionary*

After a high-G deceleration, made possible by cold sleep and the cushioning gel encasing the bodies of prisoners and crew, the AI controlling the prison-transport, the Rush, woke its crew members for the final two weeks of its journey. At the end of it, the huge, bloated ship slipped smoothly into a parking orbit above Extrasolar Penal Colony 3, a blue-green planet with a single small, narrow continent just north of the equator, and smaller islands in scattered patches. Although it was moving at thousands of kilometers per hour, the Rush seemed to float in place above the sole continent's west coast.

A shuttle, tiny in comparison with the Rush, slipped out of a hatch and headed down toward the surface. Inside the shuttle, row upon row of coffin-pods, stacked three deep, lay in the cargo hold; Kel's was among them. As the shuttle's skin glowed red with heat, another shuttle emerged from the Rush and began its descent. And after that, still another.

Kel's shuttle swept down toward an amalgam of airport and gulag set at the western edge of a sprawling city of one-and-two-storey buildings—long runways leading to grey, blockish structures, with a high wall running all the way around the entire compound, and ramshackle buildings fading into the distance beyond the walls.

The shuttle landed and taxied close to a building near the edge of the runway, coming to a full stop when electro-magnets buried in the concrete locked onto those in the belly of the shuttle. A panel in the taxiway slid to the side, and a hydraulic hoist began to rise. As it did, doors in the bottom of the shuttle retracted, allowing the hoist to enter. The hoist platform was a half-meter narrower on all sides than the shuttle's bay, but, once it was even with the shuttle's floor, panels slid out from the sides of the bay, closing the gaps, and the crew began loading pods onto the platform.

Within five minutes, the panels retracted and the hoist began to descend, bearing two dozen pods. It passed below the surface of the runway and came to a stop six meters below ground, where forklifts plucked the coffins off the lift and sped them down a dimly lit tunnel to an immense, bare-concrete room, depositing them in neat rows, as the lift and others like it rose and descended again and again, bearing their human cargo.

After dozens of landings and departures, all five thousand of the prisoners' pods rested in a huge concrete sarcophagus. Pneumatic ratchets echoed off the dank cement walls. The blur of sound continued well into the night, as technicians opened coffins, pulled out tubes, plugs, and wires from bodies, and lifted those still alive, men and women alike, naked, shivering, and groggy, out of their slimy coffins onto green gurneys bound for "the car wash."

When they reached it, more techs, former prisoners themselves, hosed down the new arrivals. Then, still more techs wheeled the wet, violently shivering prisoners to the revival bay; they lifted them from the gurneys and flopped them down on row upon row of stained, sheetless mattresses, and threw filthy blankets over them.

Back in the receiving area, the transfer technicians pulled out the tubes, plugs, and wires from those who hadn't survived and lifted them onto other gurneys: those brain dead but with salvageable parts onto red gurneys, and the few so ripe they were clearly worthless, except as biomass, onto black gurneys bound for the city's rendering plant.

In the revival bay, technicians injected Kel and the other survivors with restorative nanobots, nutrients, and time-release stimulants that would kick in the next day.

Hours later, when he wasn't preoccupied with dry heaving, or with clutching the painful places where tubes, needles and wires had been withdrawn, Kel looked at the grey, windowless walls, and concluded that his worst nightmare had come true: he was still in prison on Earth, being tortured while under the influence of drugs.

6

Capital punishment is our society's recognition of
the sanctity of human life.

—Senator Orrin Hatch

The next morning, Kel trudged leadenly down a dim, concrete hallway toward a blinding, white rectangle, occasionally stumbling against other trudging prisoners. His veins, orifices, and urethra ached, his mouth tasted like gun metal, and his long-unused guts churned. As he dragged himself through the painfully bright opening at the end of the corridor, he raised his hand to shield his eyes, and tripped over another prisoner's foot. He stumbled to the ground and his body spasmed at the sharp sting of a shock baton. A loud voice growled, "Get up, asshole. Keep moving." Kel staggered to his feet and stumbled forward, nearly tripping again with his first step.

After more stumbling and more shocks, he took his place in the ranks standing in the sand. Kel looked around. Jesus. What a motley looking bunch. Then he looked at himself. Like all of the other prisoners, Kel was dressed in a work shirt and dungarees, and had a dull green duffel bag at his feet. He'd been so out of it that he hadn't even looked through it when he'd received it.

After more persuasion from the shock batons, the prisoners stood sullenly in quasi-military formation, swaying, some collapsing, as still others were herded into rows behind them. Those who collapsed were quickly and painfully rousted back to their feet.

Kel closed his eyes and concentrated on staying upright. To steady himself, he began breathing deeply and slowly, visualizing himself standing. After what seemed like hours, he rubbed his stubbly cheeks, opened his eyes, and looked around. He was in the third row from the front in a barren, rectangular courtyard surrounded by windowless two-storey buildings. The structures formed two sides of the square. The third was dominated by a two-storey-high wall with a huge gate in its center; on the fourth side, facing him, was another high wall, this one bearing gun-toting guards, with a gallows before it.

Kel wiped his brow; it wasn't even close to noon, but he was already sweating in the deadly still air and strange light. He looked up, and the sun was wrong—too orange. It was nearly straight overhead, but had the color of the sun near the horizon back on Earth. He turned his head and looked at the doorway where he'd entered the square. A few prisoners were still coming through it, stragglers being nudged along none too gently by the guards.

After the final few were herded into ranks at the back of the courtyard, they and all the rest of the sweating, terrified prisoners waited. And waited. Finally, a door in the building to Kel's right opened, and a round, balding man in full dress uniform, with a pencil-thin mustache, stepped through it and strode rigidly to the gallows, which dominated the courtyard. He mounted the platform with remarkably mechanical steps, rhythmically slapping a riding crop into the palm of his black-gloved left hand. Once on the platform, he put his hands behind his back, rocked on his heels, and stared at the prisoners for several seconds. A few guards carrying projectile assault weapons, obviously enjoying the show of dominance, stood facing outward below the man on the platform; a few others stood by the heavy, locked gate; and still others looked down from the top of the wall.

"Welcome to Extrasolar Penal Colony 3, or as we call it here, Tau Two. I am Colonel Corona, the commandant of this planet. Your commandant. Remember that. And remember this. This is simple enough that even scum like you should be able to remember it. There are only two rules here: don't rebel, and don't fuck with us. That's what this is for."

He patted the gallows with his riding crop and then abruptly slapped the crop into his hand. He looked out over the prisoners, waited until the silence became uncomfortable, then unbearable, and finally released the crop and gestured with it to an officer standing at the door of the building to his left. The man opened the door and stepped back.

Kel gaped in horror as two beefy guards pushed a struggling, hooded prisoner—a grotesquely fat, dead-fish-colored white man, naked above the waist but for the hood—through the door. Once through it, they released the man's hands, and he began frantically trying to pull the hood off of his head. As he was clawing at it, one of the guards ducked below his flailing arms, pressed his shock baton into the man's chest, and pressed its activation stud.

The hooded man fell to the ground writhing. Corona and most of the guards laughed. Kel felt physically sick. They had released the man's hands to give him hope, only to snatch it away.

After the guards stopped laughing, and the prisoner stopped writhing, the guard with the shock baton adjusted its handle, stuck the baton into the folds of flesh on the prisoner's back, and pressed the stud again. The prisoner jerked, but not as violently as with the previous jolt. As he was still shuddering, the other guard leaned over him. "Get up, scumbag!" The man rose slowly, unsteadily, and once he was on his feet the guard with the baton prodded him almost gently, without shocking him. But then he did, and the man lurched forward. With the aid of several more jolts, the prisoner staggered to the scaffold, where he stumbled on the steps and fell forward, smashing his hooded face on the edge of a step. Again, Corona and most of the guards laughed.

The two guards conducting the prisoner pulled him to his feet and, with effort, dragged him up the steps. Once on the platform, the smaller of the guards forced the prisoner onto the trap with one final, gratuitous jolt from his shock baton. The hangman, wearing a captain's uniform, his hatchet face unconcealed, put a noose over the hood and around the prisoner's neck, and pulled it tight, as the larger guard bound the man's hands behind him.

Corona stepped forward and addressed the crowd, as the prisoner trembled and the hangman stared out at them.

"This man is a common criminal. We don't care about that. But he made the mistake of counterfeiting currency. He thought that he was one step ahead of *us.*" Corona paused, smiled, and said: "But obviously he wasn't." He gestured to the hangman.

The hangman sprang the trap. The prisoner dropped, and when the rope snapped taut the prisoner's 200-kilo body continued plummeting toward the earth, but his hooded head didn't. It separated from the body, rebounding upward from the noose, spewing a rainbow of blood. The headless body slammed into the earth, spasmed momentarily, and then lay still, blood pumping from its neck, as its loosened bowels and bladder stained its pants.

After a moment staring hard at the stunned prisoners, with the stench of shit, blood, and piss gradually spreading outward in the nearly still air, Corona spoke again.

"Remember this. Remember what happens if you cross us. Remember this simple rule and you might live: don't screw with us. Other than that, do what you want. And don't come crying to us if you get in trouble. We don't give a damn about what you do to each other."

He paused and then turned his head to survey the prisoners, tapping the riding crop into his gloved hand. After he'd stared at the crowd for several seconds, he stopped tapping and said, "You'll be issued five hundred credits each. Do with them as you will. Get the hell out of my sight!"

Corona turned away from the prisoners, descended from the gallows, and walked stiffly into the nearest building without looking back.

7

"... and who are you?"
"I—I hardly know sir, just at present—at least I know
who I was when I got up this morning, but
I think I must have been changed several times since then."
—Lewis Carroll, *Through the Looking Glass*

The shocked, confused prisoners, prodded by the baton-wielding guards, queued up in lines before paymasters near the main gate, who handed them their five hundred credits. It was odd-looking money—the hundred-credit notes were not only pink, but they bore the smirking, chimp-like visage of the most hated and corrupt *caudillo* of the twenty-first-century American empire, the idiot non-savant who had ushered in the new homeworld order; and the fifty-credit yellow notes bore the visage of his more photogenic, more persuasive successor and accolyte

The paymaster handed Kel his banknotes, and Kel counted them, stuck them in his front pocket, and headed for the gate. As he walked through it, starting to feel surprisingly good as the time-release stims kicked in, he spotted a faded, painted wooden sign to the right reading, "Welcome to Novaya Moskva."

Kel muttered "some fucking welcome," looked left and right, and after a few seconds arbitrarily turned to the right and started walking north on Korolev, the long gravel street onto which the compound's main gate opened. Within seconds, hustlers approached Kel and many of the other newly released prisoners. A gimpy hustler with bad teeth, ten o'clock shadow, and a brown, pebbly patch on one cheek approached Kel and told him to stop. Kel turned his head, looked at him, turned his head back and kept walking as the hustler limped, trying to keep up with him.

"New here?"

Kel continued walking, without looking at the man.

"You need someone to show you around."

Kel didn't turn his head. "No thanks."

"It can be dangerous—"

"I can take care of myself."

"You don't look like you can. Listen—"

Kel turned toward the hustler. "Fuck off."

"Look—"

"Fuck off!"

Kel, fighting sudden lightheadedness—god it felt hard to breathe—stared grimly at the little weasel, who returned the stare a bit too long before turning his gaze toward Kel's duffel. But after glancing at the other nearby former prisoners, some of whom were looking at them, he turned and limped away. Kel watched as the gimpy hustler retreated; then he resumed his walk down Korolev.

Despite the unnerving, orangish light, Novaya Moskva was strangely, depressingly familiar. There were power poles, ugly, 2-D wooden billboards, and what looked like prickly pears, manzanitas, and mesquites in the vacant lots dotting the street. But there were also patches of an unidentifiable purple-black, fern-like ground cover with tiny, elliptical leaves, and a strange, reddish-brown succulent with huge, bloated, finger-like extensions. Strangest of all, there were purple palo verde analogs minus the spines on the branches, and a few tall, slender trees with dull green foliage spiraling up around them in a helix, hugging ever more closely to the trunk, and coming to a point at the top. Except for the helix-shaped trees, all of the vegetation was low to the ground, with the manzanitas, mesquites, and palo verde analogs being little more than shrubs.

Kel walked on. The buildings were all ramshackle, one- or two-storey affairs, most built of unpainted, rough-hewn wood, with the rest built of cinder blocks, adobe, bricks, or concrete. There wasn't a nano-composite structure in sight, except occasional re-cycled composite cargo containers serving as small shops or food stands.

As pedestrian as the buildings were, most of them, except those sandwiched between other buildings, had angled west walls that merged seamlessly with their roofs. Despite this peculiarity, the strange, too orangish light, and the weird native plants, Novaya Moskva reminded Kel of a place familiar from the vids: a 20th-century, western American mining boomtown. All that was missing were the double-wides, pick-ups, American flags, Bud Light signs, vehicles up on blocks, and roaming packs of semi-feral dogs. It seemed like the type of place that, once the ore or coal ran out, would have been abandoned within a week. But the resemblance only went so far. Novaya Moskva was huge, and there were a lot of jitneys and small trucks in the street—all evidently electric, for all were silent. There were no internal combustion behemoths in sight.

The city—well, at least Korolev—was appallingly ugly. The street was dominated by billboards and signs painted on the sides of buildings. Most of the ads were for the usual—beer, condoms, cocaine—though, strangely, there were none for full-immersion sex, not even for vanilla full-feel sex, let alone for the more popular types no one would admit to wanting, let alone paying for.

And there were no holo-ads. No 3-D boards. Instead, there were only flat, ugly, 2-D billboards urging newcomers not only to stupefy themselves with booze and other drugs, but also with politics and religion: "New Havana: The People United Will Never Be Defeated"; "Baghavad: Outer Peace Through Inner Peace"; and too many others to keep track of.

All of the boards had prominent contact numbers inviting Kel to call his "new home." It was tempting. Really tempting. Kel was starting to feel like shit, and he could feel a crash coming on—they'd evidently pumped him full of bots or stims at the revival facility, and the edge was beginning to wear off. Worse, it was hot, the duffel bag felt heavier than hell, it was still hard to breathe, and the damned long-sleeved, blue work shirt he was wearing stuck clammily to his sweaty skin.

On a whim, he turned left off Korolev onto another main drag, Gagarin. It was more of the same: billboards, one-storey shops, traffic kicking up grey-brown dust from the unpaved street, and the weird mix of native and Earth vegetation. Kel stopped and looked down the street in the direction he thought was west. In the distance there were, yes, actual purple mountains.

He trudged on for several more blocks, gazing curiously at the jitneys, trucks, and other people in the street, until he walked into a small packing-container store, attracted by the garish clothing displayed in the window cut into its side. He walked out a few minutes later minus his duffel bag, and wearing a neon-orange and white Hawaiian-style shirt replete with pineapples, and sporting a canvas backpack, unhappy over what had seemed like a reaming by the store owner.

Still, had it just been his imagination or had the almost cute, somewhat-the-worse-for-wear blonde at the back counter been checking him out? She'd smiled in his direction. But then, halfway through the smile, she'd glanced toward the door and had shrunk back. Kel had followed her gaze, but all he saw was a heavily muscled leg in a black leather boot, with straps attached to a circle of brass at the ankle, disappearing from the door as its owner strode down the plank walk that fronted the store.

What had her name badge said? Sarah? Sue? Susie? Sandy? He couldn't recall and it didn't matter. How many years had it been since a woman, any woman, had smiled at him? Forty? Sixty? Eighty? Kel smiled, adjusted the straps on his new backpack, and stepped back onto the street.

He continued on in the direction he'd been walking, feeling cooler, becoming more and more conscious of the sound of his boots crunching on the gravel as the pounding in his head continued its thumping beat. He trod on, feeling increasingly lonely, weary, and vulnerable among the passing strangers.

What would happen if he passed out on the street or simply crawled into a corner to sleep?

He walked on.

He stopped at a corner, wiped his brow with his hand, rubbed his eyes, and looked up at a billboard touting New Havana, bearing the image of an attractive young latina, her breasts nearly bulging out of her half-buttoned red blouse, as she raised her arm in a military salute. He pulled out a pad and pen from his backpack and started to write down the contact number, when he was interrupted by a familiar voice.

"Hey *ese! ¿Que paso?*"

Kel turned and saw Chuy Andrade, a plump but handsome man in his mid 40s with a soul patch triangle beneath his chin, and wearing a black fedora—a long-missing friend he'd played music with ages ago, who was one hell of a bass player and vocalist, and who could drink like a fish without ever showing it.

"Chuy!"

They embraced in an A-frame hug.

Kel asked him, "What in hell are you doin' here?"

"Probably the same thing you are, *ese*."

Kel looked at him quizzically.

Chuy paused for a second before continuing.

"You were doing political shit, weren't you, *compa*? You had to be." Chuy cocked his head slightly to the side. "That is what you're here for, isn't it?"

"No, man. I wasn't doing that kind of shit. I got set up. At least I'm pretty damn sure I was."

Chuy raised an eyebrow and Kel continued: "I wasn't doing shit. I was married and working this day job, but got divorced and was just playing music for the last five years. . . . My ex hates my guts and has the connections to set me up, but we were done years ago . . ."

Chuy paused a few seconds before responding. "So who did it?"

"I had this crazy girlfriend . . . well, sort of a girlfriend. She was out of her goddamned mind, crazy jealous. She was at the gig where I got busted, and she was laughing her ass off when they grabbed me, so I'm pretty sure it was her."

"You're 'pretty sure'?"

"Yeah. They were working me over but good, and I was half lit even before that. So I wasn't watching her real close. Hell, I wasn't watching her at all. But, yeah, I'm pretty sure she did it."

Kel grimaced in disgust and said, "Screw it. Let's go throw down a few."

8

PROGRESS, n. An uplifting term used by Chamber of Commerce types
to refer to deleterious change. The more deleterious
the change, the greater the progress.

—Chaz Bufe, *The American Heretic's Dictionary*

Kel and Chuy sat across from each other at a rough wooden table, with a half-full pitcher of Implant Ale on it, on the patio of The Grey Ale Inn, a local dive whose wooden marquee bore the iconic figure associated with cattle mutilation, cornfield decoration, and anal probe implantation in the popular mythology of the late 20th century. Trellises covered with reddish-purple vines shaded the patio, lending the Grey its only trace of charm. Although it was early in the afternoon, one of the other patrons had already passed out and was slumped over a neighboring table, snoring noisily, his head resting in a puddle of stale beer, one arm dangling down nearly to the floor.

Kel had revived with his first drink, even though he'd shuddered at the taste, and was firing so many questions at Chuy that neither of them paid much notice to the drunk, the ugly surroundings, or anything else on the patio.

"What's with this place? It seems like home, but it feels wrong. The sun doesn't look right, and even the clocks are weird." He pointed through the bar's open door toward a clock—circular, with hands!—on the wall, with its second hand racing around its face. What's up with that? Why so fast?"

Chuy sighed. "Okay, man. Tau II is about the same size as Earth, but it rotates faster. They kept the 24-hour day, thought it would make it easier to adjust, but they had to speed everything up. So, an 'hour' is only 49 E-minutes long, and a 'minute' is only 49 E-seconds long."

Warming to his subject, Chuy continued, "The reason this place seems like Earth is that there was a lot of parallel evolution. There are advantages to photosynthesis and to having a head, arms, and legs—or fins and gills or wings—so it's not quite as alien as you'd expect. Tau's spectrum is pretty close to Sol's, so most of the plants are green. And most of the plants here *are* Earth plants. So are most of the animals. The native ecosystem was just a few million years past an extinction event when—"

Kel cocked his head to one side and squinted.

"Yeah. An extinction event. Tau has a cometary disk with a ton more debris than back home, so this place gets whacked every few million years.

"When the first assholes got here, the native ecosystem was only a few million years past the last impact and was just starting to redevelop. But they just couldn't leave it alone.

"It's a total mess. There are major problems with introduced species, and here in New M, air and water pollution. And it was all entirely predictable. They didn't even have to use the old bullshit line, 'Trust us. We know what we're doing.' The *pendejos* just went ahead and did any damned thing they felt like. Didn't have to justify it to anybody. It was like the Wild West. Hell, it still *is* the Wild West."

Kel, who had been listening, glass in hand, while Chuy ranted on, took a long slug before replying. "Come on. Why the hell would they waste a sun-type star and an Earth-type planet on a prison? Even back on Earth I never understood that."

"Okay, man. This is a sun-type star, sort of, but Tau has more flares than the sun. And with the weak magnetic field we get a hell of a lot of radiation whenever there are flares. Hell, every goddamned day, even without flares, it's worse than on Earth. And this ain't no Earth-type planet. Not much land mass, not much in the way of heavy elements, way too many asteroid and comet impacts, a weak magnetic field, and no moon."

Kel looked puzzled. "No moon? Then what the hell is *that*, and why in hell does it look like that?" Kel gestured toward a tiny, potato-shaped object, barely visible in full daylight, noticeable only because it was just above the tip of one of the drill bit-like, dull green trees at the edge of the courtyard; the potato's apparent size was about that of Earth's only natural satellite.

Chuy repeated, "No moon. At least nothing like The Moon. Sure, we have two small ones. The *rusos* in the first expedition named 'em Boris and Arkady for some reason. They're probably just captured asteroids. And probably too damned small to stabilize Tau Two's rotational axis; it could be at one of the poles in another million years. Those moons are so damned small gravity won't even compress 'em into disks. Boris—that's the one up there"—he pointed at the small, barely visible, irregular shape skimming the treetops— "is only about 600 klicks in diameter and it's 60,000 klicks out, and Arkady's only about 400 in diameter and it's 90,000 out, so they don't exert much gravity. Some, but not much, so there's not much in the way of tides to slow us down, and we spin too damn fast. Makes the weather a bitch—the faster the rotation, the worse the storms. And it's hell getting used to the short days."

"Jesus!"

"Yeah, Jesus. What we got here is almost no land mass, too short a day, and not much in the way of resources. No oil or coal and not much in the way of minerals. It's a real fucking prize. And then there's the weak magnetic field and solar flares. Chances are the cancer rate is a lot higher here than on Earth, not that anybody's keeping track. Some of it's pretty obvious, though." He gestured with his head toward the passed out drunk at the next table, and said, "Look at his arm, down near his wrist."

There was an irregular rough brown patch, similar to the one he'd seen earlier on the hustler's cheek. Cal looked back at Chuy.

"Skin cancer."

"Jesus. Is there anything good about this place?"

"Well, yeah. Actually, a bunch. We can breathe, and we don't freeze or fry. There're some iron and copper deposits on this "continent"—which is weird, given how depleted this system is—and there's one other thing. We can eat some of the native plants and animals, not that there's a whole lot to eat. . . . But at least the chickens, pigs, and other critters aren't starving. A lot of 'em have problems with mineral deficiencies, but at least they aren't starving."

Kel stared at his beer for several seconds before replying. "Okay, I can see why we're here, but why would the screws and military come here?"

"The military? They love to push people around, and this is one sweet set-up for 'em. The screws? No choice. For most of 'em it was either come as screws or come as prisoners. Most of 'em were common criminals before they became screws."

Kel looked at him quiizzically, again.

"Yeah. Who better to keep down the politicals?"

"But what about the ships, what about the crews?"

"Big time pay. If you don't have much in the way of friends or family, a hundred-, hundred-and-twenty-year round trip doesn't matter much, especially if you're out cold for almost all of it and your pay is getting compound interest."

Kel rubbed his chin and asked, "But what's with the buildings? Nothing but wood and cement. No 3-D shit either. And I'm seein' *light bulbs* and fluorescent lights. This place looks like it's straight out of the 1980s."

"It is. And it's deliberate. They keep things primitive so it's easier to control us. They have some high-tech shit, but nobody else has jack. What's worse is that if we ever get cut off from Earth for any length of time, this place will really go to hell. Not enough of an industrial base and not enough resources. We'd be lucky if we only fell back to the 1880s. The 1780s might be more like it."

Kel drained his beer, made a face, said "Jesus Festering Christ! This is worse than Schlitz!" and immediately reached for the pitcher. As he filled his glass, he glanced up at two skinheads and a grossly obese bearded biker type marching past The Grey on the street. All three were wearing denim vests with identical symbols on their backs: three green lightning bolts radiating out an even 120 degrees apart from a red star at the center to an enclosing red circle. After they'd passed, Kel asked, "Who are those assholes?"

"Them? The goddamned Eco-Aryans. Nazis with pretensions. But don't let 'em bother you. There are a bunch of 'em here, but they're smart enough not to start shit when they're outnumbered, which is all of the time, what with all the brown and black folks around here. Most of those *pinche putos* are hundreds of klicks away, and Earth-gov keeps real close watch on 'em. They're a bunch of fucking *cabrones*, but they can't do shit. Earth-gov can track 'em real easy. Hell, they can track all of us real easy."

He reached under the table and squeezed Kel's right shin just below the knee. Kel shrieked, drawing looks from the other conscious and semi-conscious drinkers on the patio.

"As soon as you arrive here, while you're still out, they shoot an arfid chip into your shin bone, along with an antenna, a micro-battery, and a piezo generator—you move, it generates current. Only puts out a few microwatts, but that's enough. And it'd be real painful to dig it out."

Kel gestured toward a billboard for New Havana. "What about that?"

"New Havana? Come on, man. It's pretty obvious."

"To you maybe. Not to me."

"Okay. New Havana? That's the commies. Earth gov has been shoveling all of us up here: Nazis, commies, islamists, anarchists, career criminals, anybody they want no part of. It's a nice, neat way to get rid of us. Put us in cryo, and they have to let us out eventually. Kill us, and thousands of dead bodies every year tend to cause resentment. . . ."

Chuy excused himself to go to the head, and Kel took a slug of beer. He glanced at the passed-out drunk at the next table, and was silent for a moment, thinking about the last time he and Chuy had been really drunk.

9

MOTORCYCLE, n. An indication of arrested emotional development sometimes misidentified as a means of transport.

—Chaz Bufe, *The American Heretic's Dictionary*

Their five-piece, The Axel Mars Blues Band, had played eight sets over ten hours at an outdoor, one-per-center biker gig in Cascabel. It was December, and a cold wind was whipping through the mesquites behind the stage as they set up around eleven. But at least it had been sunny, and, while they were setting up, Fat Freddy, the concert promoter, had delivered an ice chest filled with two cases of Sun Lik beer. They'd called for a refill at three, and another at six. Chuy had drunk at least a third of the beer.

Kel remembered looking over at Chuy when they'd gone on an hour after sunset for the seventh set, wondering how much longer Chuy would be able to keep it together. He was nearly staggering, but when they broke into their first number, an ancient, driving blues anthem called "I'm Leavin' Your Town," he'd been spot on.

Two hours later, after he'd drunk four more, and Chuy six more, beers, it was so cold that they couldn't feel their fingers. So, they'd put down their instruments, picked up their beers, and Chuy had lurched off the stage and had almost stumbled into the bonfire. Two nearly as drunk bikers grabbed his arms before he fell in, and hauled his drunk ass back to Kel's van, where they laid him out in the bed, putting another beer in his hand before they left. A few minutes later Kel staggered over to check on Chuy who, when he saw Kel opening the side door, had pushed himself up onto his elbow, raised his beer in a toast, slurred, "¡Ese! ¡Salud!," had taken a long slug, and had then immediately passed out, spilling beer all over his chest, pants, and the carpet-lined van bed.

Kel looked down at his passed-out friend and raised his own bottle in salute. He set his bottle down, reached in, dug out the well-worn, dirty blanket under the passenger's seat, and covered Chuy with it, hoping that it would keep him from freezing. He closed the van's door and walked over to the bonfire, the relatively friendly bikers, and another beer.

It was just as well that Chuy had passed out. On the way to the gig, while passing around a bottle of tequila—well, the agave-less synthetic shit that passed for tequila—Chuy, who had a deep suspicion that all white bikers were racists under the surface, had been making comments about "fake ass bikes" and "fake ass bikers," referring to the only legal type of "motorcycle": all-electric, fuel-cell bikes with the mandatory anti-terrorist tracking/control circuits, but which also had circuits to mimic exactly the sounds of vintage Harleys, sounds which even rose and fell in pitch and volume, emerging from fake exhaust pipes as fake gears were fake shifted. That was what mattered to most bikers—the look and the sound. Never mind that the Protectors could track the bikes anywhere and take control of them in a heartbeat; what mattered was that the bikes looked and sounded *bad*.

During the gig, Chuy had it together enough to keep his mouth shut, but the longer it went on, and the drunker he got, the more likely he was to make a comment that would get him—hell, all of them—stomped. So, it was just as well that he was out for the count, totally *chingaso*.

Chuy might have been more impressed if he'd been awake two hours later to witness the brief, bonfire-lit appearance of two highly illegal, alcohol-burning two-wheeled monsters—monsters whose lack of tracking/control circuits would have gotten all of the bikers, and probably the band, busted for terrorism in a heartbeat if the Protectors had shown up.

* * *

Kel recollected that it hadn't all been that one-sided. Not by a long shot. He'd done some really fucked up shit, too. Shit that he could barely remember and that Chuy had to tell him about later.

There'd been that incident after he'd really started going downhill and had called Chuy three times in one evening. The first two times he called, Chuy said that he'd blocked the video signal, just sent a blank screen, audio only. Even so, Chuy'd told him he'd answered, as he was expecting a call from some chick. Kel grimaced and took a long slug as he recalled Chuy's description of the call:

Chuy: "Hello? . . . ¿*Bueno?*" No answer, drunken noises in the background: male and female laughter, random indecipherable shouts, glasses clinking, glasses breaking, unidentifiable thuds, crashes, and shrieks.

Chuy said he'd hung up at that point. But from the noises and slurred voices in the background, he'd been pretty sure it was Kel. So he answered the second call, expecting either the hoped-for female voice or Kel. The "conversation" had been virtually identical. The third time Kel called, Chuy said there was still no video and no i.d., but the conversation had actually been a conversation. Of sorts:

Chuy: "Hello?"

Kel: (in a hushed, slurred voice) "Hey man, I'm trashed."

Chuy: "No shit. I'd never have guessed."

Kel (even quieter): "I'm in the bathroom and can only talk for a minute."

Chuy: "Okay, man. What's happening?"

Kel: "My neighbor came over. She's this hot, kinda dykey 22-year-old. She's trashed too, and she wants to fuck me. But I'm really trashed, I whacked off twice earlier today, and I don't think I can get it up. What should I do? Go for it or go straight to oral?"

Chuy laughed: "Go straight to oral, man. She'll come back for more."

Kel: "Thanks dude." (click)

That might have been the funniest incident, but it wasn't the worst.

*   *   *

Kel shook himself from his revery, his eyes landing on the drunk who'd passed out at the next table and was now sprawled on the floor. Kel thought about helping the guy up, but stopped himself. The old motto was all too true: no good deed goes unpunished.

He lifted his head and looked at where Chuy had been sitting. *Christ! Where the fuck was Chuy?* He took another drink.

How—more precisely *why*—had he ever hooked up with this dude? And why, more to the point, had Chuy taken him on?

They'd met at Chuy's mom and dad's place in Tucson shortly after Kel had gotten back from Khyrgistan. He'd moved into a dive triplex in the Keeling barrio (motto: "The Keeling Neighborhood: It's not as bad as it looks") and had gone over one Friday night to the neighbors' weekend get-together: everyone totally fucked-up drunk—Chuy's mom, dad, brothers, sisters, aunts, uncles, cousins, second cousins, their wives, boyfriends, girlfriends. He'd invited himself over, this long-haired, chunky, white dude, the new neighbor, sitting there talking to everybody over the banda, norteños, grititos, perricos, corridos, rancheras, etc., trying out his bad Spanish, until Chuy's mom had said, "Let's talk English." He'd been a little offended, but had said, "What the fuck!? Okay," and had reached for another Bud Light upon hearing this death sentence upon his gringo Spanish.

Then Chuy's mom had called Chuy over and said, "This is Kel, the new neighbor. He's a musician, too." And Chuy said, "Yeah?" After several more beers, a couple of joints, a couple of hits from a liter jar of *bacanora*—the homebrew tequila common to northern Mexico, one of Chuy's cousins had brought up from Agua Prieta—and two hours of talking music, he'd ended up going down with Chuy to The Rooms. More specifically, the room Chuy shared with the other members of his loose group, Apocalipso Aztlan, in the old telephone exchange building. The equipment was long gone, and all that was left was filthy brown carpets, grey concrete walls with layers of stains, the reek of spilled beer, tobacco, and pot, and room upon room upon nearly identical room, separated by cheap partitions, of drinking, doping, nonstop partying, and reeking, beer-soaked couches, the occasional bizarre, frightening or erotic holo image oozing out of the walls—this particular night some asshole had loosed all-too-real-looking holo cobras in the halls—and 3:00 a.m. practice sessions, insanely loud rehearsals and insanely loud jams. It normally didn't start to quiet down until 6:00 or 7:00 in the morning.

And Kel had done fine. He'd shown up with Chuy at midnight with a 12-pack of Schlitz Classic Ice, a dinged-up Stratocaster, and an ancient, off-brand, tube-emulation amp. No effects at all. Just the guitar and amp. And he'd blown them away. "Them" being the usual gang on a Friday night: Arturo, sitting behind his rack of drums: hi-hat, seven other cymbals, eight toms, two snares, and two bass drums (disturbingly, both 24-inchers), normally the sign of a real shitty musician (the more drums and cymbals, the worse the drummer), but in this case the armory of a 150-cm-tall, 55-kg motherfucker; Rita, the round, middle-aged, heavy drinking Yaqui jazz player tearing it up on tenor sax; Joey, the even more alcoholic Tohono O'odham guitar player, who tended to fall apart in the second or third set, and Chuy laying down walking lines on an ancient, real P-Bass. And it worked.

Everybody had been pretty fucked up that night, and Joey hadn't been too thrilled about another guitar player showing up. But he was a lot drunker than Kel and had really screwed things up on the first number. Then, he'd gotten pissed off and had left when Arturo suggested that he sit out a song or two. After Joey split, they'd played for four or five hours, between dope and beer breaks, and it had sounded pretty good considering. Even his and Chuy's vocals hadn't been all that bad. They'd ended after dawn and had agreed to get together on Sunday, giving themselves a full day to recover.

He'd ended up playing with Chuy off and on—mostly off—for nearly seven years, playing everything from rock to strut to cow-punk to Blue Latin, their last band breaking up a few years before he'd gotten busted and deported.

But where the hell was Chuy now?

* * *

Chuy walked out of The Grey's unisex restroom. Kel, trying not to look too relieved, took a slug of beer, and then another. As Chuy settled into his seat, Kel asked, "So tell me, what do people do after they get here? How do they get by?"

Chuy smiled, one corner of his mouth twisting downward. He said, "Most of 'em stick around New M and work for somebody else, or they go back to what they were doin' on Earth—stealing, robbing, or whoring. A lot of 'em love it here. It's familiar—the same old shit. Most people love it, no matter how bad it is. They fucking love anything familiar . . . Anything. Absolutely *anything*. Take music: 'Stairway to Heaven,' 'Proud Mary,' 'Free Bird,' 'Alien Angel,' 'Margaritaville,' 'Martian Mojo Man,' 'Gloria,' 'Love Bone,' 'Sweet Home Alabam.'' Those songs sucked when they were new, they still suck, and people *still* want to hear them. It's the same with everything else.

"They get here, see the dog-eat-dog shit going down in this fucking town, and the assholes stick around because it's *familiar*. They feel at home. They burrow right into it. Fucking wallow in it.

"But not all of 'em do. Some head for the hills and set up their own little utopias, or head to one of 'em that's already out there."

Kel prodded Chuy on: "Really?"

"Yeah, really." Chuy nodded his head to the left and raised an eyebrow. "Look at those billboards. Those are all real places. Most of the time I live in one of 'em, New Harmony. It's the anarchist place. Beats the hell out of living in this shit hole."

"So why the hell are you here, then?"

"It's my turn on the shit detail. My turn at the outreach house. My turn"—he pressed his index finger into Kel's chest—"to recruit assholes like *you*."

10

HOPE, n. The carrot dangling at the end of life's stick.

—Chaz Bufe, *The American Heretic's Dictionary*

Kel woke with a splitting headache and cramps throughout his body. He was lying on a sheetless single mattress, and was clutching a brown, scratchy blanket. He managed with effort to lift himself up on one elbow, glanced at the unfamiliar surroundings, and nearly panicked. He had no idea where he was.

A dim incandescent bulb dangled at the end of wires hanging down from the exposed rafters at the far end of the unfinished room. Dented screens ran to the ceiling along three walls, interrupted in the middle of the longest one by a screen door, with a wooden door opposite it in the solid fourth wall. Outside the screens it was pitch black.

Kel listened closely and heard muffled voices coming through the wooden door, though he couldn't understand any of the words. He put a hand against the wall next to the mattress and painfully pushed himself to his feet. Once up, he walked shakily across the room and pushed opened the door. Chuy was talking softly with two women: another former prisoner, a short Mexican woman in her twenties, still dressed in a prison shirt and dungarees, and a thin woman in her early 40s with finely chiseled features and luminous dark eyes. Chuy turned to face the older woman.

"*Sonia, ¿que pienses—*"

When he saw Kel, Chuy immediately switched to Spanglish. "Hey *ese! ¿Como estas?*"

Kel groaned. "I feel like shit."

Chuy laughed. "Really? Want some breakfast?"

Before Kel could reply, Sonia looked over at the stove, then at Kel, and said, "*Lo siento. No hay nada más.*"

Kel rubbed his face and was saying, "That's okay, I don't need—" when Chuy interrupted him.

"Yes, you do. Let's go to the Grey. I'll buy. They have a good breakfast."

"I really don't—"

"Yes you do. *¡Vamonos!*"

Kel resisted the suggestion. He slumped against the door frame and asked, "They serve breakfast in the middle of the night?"

"Yeah, they do. A lot of places do."

Kel raised an eyebrow.

"They're always open because a lot of people are on weird-ass schedules."

Kel yawned and rubbed his eyes. "Why?"

"Some people never adjust. They still need to be on something close to a 24-hour day, but that doesn't fit with the 'day' here, so it's kind of chaotic. Most people adjust, at least sort of, but some are on pretty weird schedules. . . . So, yeah, they'll be open."

He got up, walked by Kel through the door, paused and said, "Come on." Kel followed him through the unfinished porch, and down the walkway behind it toward the street.

When they arrived at the Grey, they sat down at the bar and Chuy ordered coffee for both of them, house special *Número Uno, El Lanzallamas*, The Flamethrower, for himself, and house special *Número Dos, El Suave*, The Bland One, for Kel—*Huevos con chorizo:* scrambled eggs with tomatillos, green onions, garlic, mild yellow chiles, and pork sausage, served with flour tortillas.

Ten minutes later, Kel bit in. He shook his head, quickly took a drink of coffee, swallowed it, and said, "Damn!"

Chuy chuckled and said, "Come on. Didn't you ever get used to hot shit back in Tucson? I told them to make it *gabacho* style. Let me have a bite." He took the spoon from his coffee cup, scooped up some of the eggs, and stuck the spoon in his mouth. After a few seconds, he swallowed, forced back a laugh, and said, "You think *this* is hot? Have a taste of *this*!" He pushed his own plate, scrambled eggs covered with *habanero* sauce, and filled with onions, garlic, and minced cayenne and *serrano* chiles, toward Kel, who recoiled from it as if it were a rattlesnake.

"Fuck you, Chuy. You think I'm gonna eat *that*?"

"Have a beer. After one or two you'll start to like it." Chuy laughed and pushed his own plate farther toward Kel, who backed farther away from it. As Kel was still retreating, Chuy motioned to the barkeep and ordered a pitcher of beer.

Kel waited until he had taken a long slug before diving back into his own eggs. After he finished eating, he belched and pushed the plate away. Chuy looked up from the last of his eggs and tortillas and asked, "Feel better?"

"A little."

"Don't worry. The first couple of days are the worst. Have another beer."

He reached for the pitcher and refilled Kel's mug. They sat for a moment before Kel asked: "So you really like it there, at that anarchist place?"

"You remembered!"

"Come on, I wasn't that fucked up."

"Oh yes you were. And yeah, I do like it."

"Why?"

"Well, there are a lot of things . . . Not having to watch over my shoulder all the time like I do here . . . Running into people I know all day long . . . Having people watch out for me, for each other . . . Not having sex all messed up by money and power trips . . . Not having some asshole leaning over my shoulder telling me what to do, and not being able to tell him to fuck off . . . Knowing that if I work a few hours a day I'll have enough to eat and a place to stay . . . Not walking down the street at night and scaring some poor woman shitless just 'cause I'm there . . . More than anything else, feeling free to do any goddamned thing I want as long as I don't fuck with anybody else."

Kel hesitated a few seconds. "Sounds nice."

"It is. But don't take my word for it. It's one thing to hear about it, another to see it. Do you want to?"

Kel shrugged and said, "Yeah. Why not? My kid is probably dead and there's nothin' for me back on Earth but jail, my asshole ex-wife, and that asshole chick who set me up. I've got scores to settle, and I want to find out what happened to my kid, but how am I gonna get back? And I can't do shit even if I could." He shook his head. "And there sure ain't shit for me here."

Chuy cocked his head and asked, "Your kid is *probably* dead?"

"Yeah, my ex won custody, and her story was that she was screwing around with him like she always did—taking a five-year-old kid on a whitewater rafting trip in Borneo!—and managed to get him killed. But no body. No funeral. At least none that I heard of. I think it was all bullshit. She hated my guts. Didn't give a damn that Folky would never know his dad. Fuck! She didn't *want* him to know me! She hated me so much that she had me stomped twice when I tried to find out about him."

Chuy tilted his head even more.

Kel insisted, "She did! The really fucked up part is that I think she didn't even want him. She just wanted to keep *me* from having him.

"What's *really* fucked up is that he might be dead or older than I am. If he pissed her off she probably cut him loose. If he ended up on Basic Med, he's either older than I am or dead. If he was on Merit Med, he might be younger than I am. Or if he sucked up to her he might be on Comp Med and be twenty-five damn near forever. Not knowing is driving me nuts."

Chuy, looking lost, paused before speaking. "There's no way to know, man. And nothing to do about it."

Kel didn't respond.

Finally, Chuy asked, "So what do you want to do now, Kel?"

"I want to find my kid. . . . But for now, I just want some place to call home."

"I can help with that. But the other stuff . . . Sorry to tell you this, man, but your ex and is probably dead. So all—"

"No. Her family has money up the ass and you can bet that she'll still have Comp-Med, the whole nine yards. Telomere repair, gene therapy, stem cell organ regrowth, nano repairs, and anything new they've come up with."

Kel glared for a second at Chuy, downed another half pint of beer in one gulp, shuddered, and immediately refilled his glass, exclaiming, "Christ! This is worse than horse piss!"

Chuy refrained from asking the obvious question, took a sip from his own beer, and said, "She probably is dead, man; and sorry *ese,* but your kid probably is, too. Radio traffic from Earth went dead eight years ago, and there's no good explanation for that."

"What happened?"

"Who knows? All I know is that eight years ago radio traffic died."

Kel gaped at him.

After a long pause, Chuy said, "You can't go back to Earth, but I can take you with me when I go back to New Harmony. You can stay at the house until we catch a shuttle."

Cal paused. "When do we leave?"

"We just missed a shuttle, but we can probably hop the next one in a couple of weeks."

"They have shuttles here? Earth-gov doesn't have them all?"

"No, they don't. There's a commercial fleet that uses old shuttles from some of the parked ships. Since radio traffic went dead, nobody's gone back, and all the ships that arrived since then have been piling up, and the crews need to make a living."

Kel paused and then said, "Have you been doing much playing lately?"

"Not much. Not here anyway. It's a pretty depressing scene . . . at New Harmony, yeah. But here, no. I know a few guys who are all right, but I haven't met anybody I really want to play with . . . What did you have in mind?"

11

JEALOUS, adj. Unduly concerned about the preservation of
that which can be lost only if not worth keeping.

—Ambrose Bierce, *The Devil's Dictionary*

After Chuy hauled him back from the Grey, Kel spent three-
and-a-half days sleeping, getting up only to relieve himself and
shovel down food. Chuy shook him awake late in the afternoon of
the fourth day, and half an hour later he dragged a much-improved
Kel and a truckload of gear, including a guitar amp, a bass amp, a
drum kit, and an antiquated small p.a. system, to The Bandit, one
of the local dives. Once there, he and Kel went on autopilot, pulling instruments, mikes, mike stands, cables, amplifiers, monitors,
speaker stands, speakers—thank god! at least the nearly weightless, flat-radiator type!—out of the back of the ancient, squat, solar/
electric truck Chuy had rented. They had everything set up, cables
snaking everywhere, and the sound check done within forty-five
minutes.

Kel felt more alive than he had in ages. He was back in his ele-
ment: a dingy tavern with a long, U-shaped bar, a dozen cigarette-
burned wooden tables coated with yellowing, bullet-proof resin,
a dart board mounted on a large piece of protective cork board,
with dart holes in the wall for a good meter on either side of the
board, two pool tables with beer-stained, ripped felt, and a small
stage at the back of the room, maybe a foot above the dance floor.
The lighting was dim, the cement floor sticky, and the low, crumbling ceiling mercifully unobtrusive. Kel luxuriated in the familiar atmosphere: smoke-stained, wood-paneled walls, garish neon
signs, and the reek of spilled beer and stale tobacco and marijuana
smoke. Kel pulled out a joint, lit it, inhaled deeply, coughed hard,
and exulted: "Damn! Feels like home!"

Chuy grinned.

Kel took another hit, coughed again, and continued, "It's gonna
feel damn good to play again!"

"It should. What's it been, forty, fifty years since you were on stage?"

Kel laughed and handed the joint to Chuy. "Yeah, and forty or fifty since I gave up smoking this shit."

He raised his glass and clinked it against Chuy's. They said "*¡Salud!*" simultaneously and drained their beers.

Kel's smile faded as he looked up and saw, at a back table, staring at him, the weasely hustler who had approached him the day he arrived. He gestured toward him: "Who's that asshole?"

Chuy stared at the hustler for a second before turning back to Kel, saying, "Who knows, and who cares? That guy's just a punk. Fuck him."

Two refills later, they grabbed their beers and walked on stage with Toad, one of the local mercenaries, a very fat but solid drummer Chuy had lined up for the gig. Kel picked up his borrowed Strat copy, took a puff, and wedged his smoldering joint into the strings of the headpiece. Chuy picked up his bass, and they played for an hour, starting with the Jonny Chingas doo wop tune, "*Se me paro*," following it with another Chingas tune, probably the filthiest song ever written, "*La dolencia*," following that with a string of blues classics, and ending with a latin rock tune which Kel introduced: "Here's one of our originals. We wrote this together a long time ago. It's called 'Pinche Blues.' We hope you like it." With that, he began hammering and arpeggiating minor blues chords in a syncopated latin rhythm as Chuy began singing.

Wakin' up at five a.m.
Sleep still in my eyes
With the smell of Jack Daniels hangin' 'round
Can't get up I'm so damn tired
I feel half dead
I should have stayed in my bed . . .

Three minutes later, after the final line of the final stanza, "*Los pinche blues, m'estan matando . . .* " Kel played the tag to scattered applause, and Chuy immediately said, "Thanks. We'll be back shortly." Kel turned off his amp and the p.a., took off his guitar, and put it on its stand.

As they were walking off stage, Kel spied a tall, leggy, weather beaten but still good looking blonde sitting at the end of the bar, sipping a drink, and giving him the eye. Was it? Yes, it was the blonde in the store who'd been checking him out the day he arrived. But—*shit!*—she wasn't looking at him, she was looking at Chuy. Chuy gave her a smile, and she nodded toward him.

Chuy headed for the bar, looked over his shoulder, and said, "I'll be back in a few."

Kel called after him, "Hours? Days? Weeks?" Chuy ignored him and kept on walking.

Toad went into a fit of high-pitched giggling. Chuy continued to walk toward the blonde without acknowledging either of them. He grabbed the bar stool next to her, pulled it well into her personal space, and sat down. She didn't back off, and faced him, drink and cigarette dangling from the fingers of the same hand, obviously liking what she saw.

Kel tried to lip read what they were saying, and managed to pick up Chuy's first question: "Hi. What's your name?" as well as the woman's reply, "Sue"; two questions later, she reached out, took Chuy's hand, turned it over, and pretended to read his palm, stroking it as she did so.

Two minutes after that, as Kel continued to stare enviously, their stools were close enough that their legs were touching. Sue reached out and slid her hand up Chuy's leg. He covered her hand with his, leaned forward, and kissed her. Kel watched, half-envious, half-appalled as Chuy ran his hand up the blonde's leg, as she slid her hand further up his, stroking his thigh.

When the kiss ended, Kel saw Chuy ask what had to be "You want to get out of here?" as he tilted his head toward the side exit. The blonde glanced over at Kel and Toad, turned back to Chuy, and whispered a question. In reply, Chuy jerked his head toward Kel and Toad, then back toward the blonde, and muttered something indecipherable.

The blonde began to massage Chuy's thigh even harder. Within seconds he was rising awkwardly.

They headed for the side exit, grabbing each other's butts. Chuy walked stiffly, with his right hand cradling and massaging one of her ass cheeks, with her hand massaging one of his, making his every step more awkward.

Kel was so intent on watching them that he didn't notice the hustler at the back table get up and scurry out the front entrance.

After Chuy and the blonde exited, Kel looked at Toad, who was still giggling. Kel said: "What the fuck?! We're supposed to be on in ten minutes. What are we gonna do? . . . Jesus!"

Toad kept on giggling. Finally, he said, "Cool out, man. She's probably just gonna blow him. He'll be back in ten. Have a beer."

Fifteen minutes later Kel grabbed his third beer of the break, drained it, and nearly slammed it down on the table. "Fuck it. That asshole's been doin' this kind of shit ever since I've known him. . . . We can fucking play without him. I can cover the goddamned bass lines."

Toad broke into more high-pitched giggles before squeaking out, "Yeah, but should you?"

Kel scowled at Toad, motioned to the waitress for another pitcher and, after she'd delivered it, he downed a third of it over the next five minutes before dragging Toad back on stage.

Once Toad was behind the kit and Kel had slung the strap over his shoulder and turned on his amp, he cranked up the volume, turned up the bass EQ so that he could play decent sounding bass licks with his thumb, and began to wail.

Forty minutes later, Chuy and the blonde walked back in the side entrance and over to the bar, where she climbed up on a stool. Chuy squeezed her leg, and walked back to the stage just as Kel was starting to announce the next-to-the-last song of the set.

When Chuy stepped on stage, Kel stopped in mid-sentence as Chuy picked up his bass. Kel looked at Chuy and asked, "Chuy, you remember that old Little Charlie and the Nightcats tune?"

"Which one?"

Kel didn't reply, but instead turned away and broke into the percussive, comping riff that was the signature for "Thinking with the Wrong Head," and within seconds he was singing about "that two-legged dog syndrome, that two-legged dog mentality."

After they finished the tune, Kel announced, "We're gonna downshift now." He switched to an exaggerated western accent.

"Do y'all like cowpunk? Here's one we could never play back home. It's an old one called 'I'm Gettin' Drunk with Jesus.'"

After Kel played a short instrumental intro in C major, Chuy started singing. It was a standard country tune that was odd only in that it started on the chorus:

I'm gettin' drunk with Jesus
'Cause Satan's well ran dry
Jesus likes to get on down
That boy knows how to fly
He likes to get all messed up
On whiskey, gin or rye
I'm gettin' drunk with Jesus
'Cause Satan's well ran dry

I'm gettin' down with Jesus
He loves a line or two
He only digs the pure white rock
That cut stuff will not do
He's freakin' and a tweakin'
He don't trust me or you
He's peekin' through the curtains
And he's droppin' out o' view

Kel took a solo, then Chuy continued after a second chorus:

Now Jesus likes to get laid
He's got a ten-inch dick
When the women look at it
They say "Oh God it's thick!"
He walks into a barroom
You know he's got his pick
'Cause when they're lookin' at his fly
They think they see a brick

At the end of the final chorus, Chuy hung on the final word, "dryyyyyyy" as Cal joined him on backup vocal. They shifted up to F as they intoned "ey-ey-ey-ey," paused, and then dropped back to C for the final, drawn-out "ey." It had been a classic "amen" ending. Still effective after all these centuries.

When they had milked the ending for all it was worth, Toad put down his drumsticks, Kel and Chuy put down their instruments, and Chuy headed straight for the blonde at the bar. As soon as he sat down, the woman flinched and looked up open-mouthed past Chuy's shoulder. Chuy, following her gaze, turned, and his head snapped back violently. As the fat, heavily muscled biker's fist connected with Chuy's nose, Chuy's barstool tipped over and he fell with it to the floor. The biker turned toward the woman, his fists clenched, as Chuy got up. The biker smashed him in the face again, sending him back down, blood spurting from his nose and mouth.

As Chuy lay on the floor, the biker turned toward the woman. "You bitch! I'll deal with you later!"

He turned his attention back to Chuy, who was grabbing the leg of his bar stool, trying to get up. The biker reached down, grabbed Chuy's shirt with one huge paw, pulled him up, and raised the other, taunting him, waving his fist in front of Chuy's face. "Check it out punk! You gonna die!"

Kel, who was heading for the band's table with Toad, looked toward the bar and saw the biker's fist descending. He ran toward the fight. His military get-a-weapon-any-weapon training kicked in, and he grabbed a pool cue on the way.

The biker was so intent on beating Chuy to a pulp that he didn't notice Kel until Kel was nearly on him, raising the cue, clutching its narrow end. At the last second, the biker half turned and ducked, so the cue caught him on the side of the head. Although it was a glancing blow, the biker dropped like a box of rocks. But even after he was down, Kel, eyes dilated, breathing fast, raised the cue again.

"You motherfucker!"

He smashed the cue into the biker's ribs, grunting with satisfaction at the cracking sound and the resulting screams. The biker curled into a ball.

"You fucking asshole!"

He smashed the cue onto the man's side again. More cracking.

"You don't have a fucking license . . ."

He smashed the biker again, this time on the forearm, as the biker raised it trying to shield his head. The arm shattered with a satisfying crunch.

". . . to fuck people over!"

The biker pulled in his mangled limb. Kel raised the cue again, swung, aiming for the biker's head, and smashed his collar bone when he rolled away. Kel raised the cue yet again, intending to cave in the biker's skull, but a large hand grabbed the cue, whipped him around, and he was face to face with the barkeep, the end of Kel's cue grasped in one meaty hand and a baseball bat in the other.

"Knock off the shit, asshole! You'll fucking kill him!"

"So fucking what!"

Kel tried to shake off the bartender, who kept his grip on the cue and pulled his bat back a few centimeters.

"I fucking mean it! Knock it off! Nobody's gonna kill anybody in here!"

Kel struggled to free the cue, but the bartender held on, raising the bat even higher, his arm tensing, screaming in Kel's face: "Knock it off, asshole!"

Kel stopped struggling and let go of the cue at about the same time that Chuy pulled himself to his feet. They stared down at the ruined biker, curled into fetal position, clutching his broken arm and ribs, whimpering and groaning, and bleeding from the gash on the side of his head.

Sue, who had been watching open mouthed, backed away and ran out the bar's front entrance without looking back. Toad was right behind her.

The barkeep dropped Kel's cue to the floor, and still holding the bat gestured with it toward the biker and the green lightning-bolt logo on the back of his vest.

"Do you know who that is?"

Kel shook his head.

"It's Miller, the Eco-Aryan honcho. Get the hell out of here. That Nazi piece of shit's asshole buddies will kill you when they hear about this. And there's a fucking ton of 'em."

Chuy looked toward the gear on stage. "Will you watch this shit?"

"No."

12

INTELLIGENCE, n. The human faculty that allows us to worry about the future . . . and the present . . . and the past . . .

—Chaz Bufe, *The American Heretic's Dictionary*

Kel was coming off his adrenaline rush, but he was still jacked. As he helped Chuy toward The Bandit's front door, he asked, "What about the gear?"

Chuy blotted up the blood flowing from his right nostril and lip with his sleeve. He shook off Kel's arm and kept on walking. "Screw it. I'll call Hydro. He'll pick it up."

"Hydro?"

"Yeah. The real straight looking young dude at the outreach house. He'll pick all this shit up."

"What a weird-ass name."

"Hydro?"

"Yeah."

"He doesn't drink."

"Oh . . ."

"It takes all kinds." Chuy continued mopping his nose with his sleeve. "Let's get out of here."

They walked through the door, turned right, and went to the jitney stand on the corner. Kel looked up and down the dimly lit street and at the scant people scuttling along it, and wondered what in hell he'd gotten himself into. A minute later, as Chuy was still attempting to clean himself up, Kel nervously asked, "What the fuck are we gonna do?"

"Get the hell out of town. Nobody is gonna back us on something like this. We've gotta get out of here."

"Where? New Harmony?"

"You got it."

"Cool. But how are we gonna get there? You got a vehicle?"

"No, and it wouldn't do much good even if I did. It's over two hundred klicks and the roads are so bad that probably nothing in this town, at least nothing we could get our hands on, would make it."

He wiped some more blood from his nose onto his sleeve as Kel asked: "So how do we get there?"

"We can probably hop a shuttle."

"Probably?"

"Probably."

A jitney rounded the corner and stopped. They started to board, but the driver said, "Well?" and held out his hand. Kel looked at the rate sheet posted above the driver and handed him a banknote Ten minutes later, they were at New M's civilian shuttle port and Chuy had called Hydro.

After marching in the glare of blinding blue-white lights past several dull grey shuttle hulks missing windows, with hatches half open at awkward angles, they walked into the cargo hold of a shuttle, and began talking with Bud, a buzz-cut, bookish-looking pilot with a thick Texas accent and wire-rimmed glasses, who wasn't letting them get a word in edgewise. As he vented, Bud was checking readouts and controls in a dirty, weather-beaten shuttle loaded with crates, cartons, barrels, and objects Kel couldn't even guess at. Bud was moving quickly, darting to and fro through the shuttle's teardrop-shaped interior while he shouted at them, mostly at Chuy. He interrupted his tirade to bang his fist on a panel with a dead readout. When it glowed back to life, he looked at its flickering digits, grunted, and continued: "New Harmony? No fucking way. I'm goin' to Baghavad, and then I'm goin' straight back. It's bad enough flying this piece of shit without making extra stops. I ain't goin' to New Harmony!"

Chuy was aghast. "Christ Bud, Baghavad? That's at the ass end of the continent."

"Yes 'tis. Take it or leave it."

"Bud, you owe me."

"Take it or leave it."

"Bud—"

"Take it or fucking leave it!"

Chuy paused before asking, "Is anybody else flying out of here tonight?"

Bud smiled. "Not tonight. Derek might be going to Xenadu or just maybe Serenity Two tomorrow, but nobody else is going out tonight. And why should Derek do you any favors? Somebody else might show up, but I wouldn't bet on it."

* * *

Five minutes after the shuttle took off, Chuy was sitting in the co-pilot's seat, Bud was in command mode, and Kel was crouching on his haunches on the floor between them. They'd said almost nothing since takeoff. Chuy finally spoke in a conciliatory tone.

"Come on, Bud. New Harmony ain't that far off course."

"Forget it."

"Come on Bud.

"No fucking way. Drop it."

"Please. Give us a break."

"A break? I haven't forgotten how you aced me out of that Bonnie chick a couple of years back. That was fucking low. . . . And even if you hadn't o' done that, I really don't want to fly this shit can any further than I have to. I'm goin' to Baghavad, then I'm headin' straight back. Full load both ways."

Kel, crashing after the adrenaline high of beating Miller half to death, and still blasted from all the beer he'd drunk, asked, "What's it like in Baghavad? Do they have any booze there?"

Bud laughed. "Yeah, but I doubt that you'll be gettin' any."

"Why not?"

"It's only for the real spiritual types, the real enlightened types, and that ain't you." Bud laughed again. Disturbingly, Chuy joined him.

An hour later they were still heading east in total darkness. Kel, who had been fading in and out, spoke again, unconsciously lapsing into an exaggerated version of his normal drawl, imitating Bud. Fortunately, Bud didn't notice.

"Bud, y'ever think about goin' back t' Earth?"

"Nope. And why in hell would I want to do that? There's nothin' for me there. Everybody I know's dead. Hell, it might not even be there anymore. . . . And besides," he smiled crookedly, "I kinda like it around here."

Kel wasn't put off. "C'mon Bud. Don't you wanna know what's goin' on back home?"

"No I don't. I don't give a flyin' fuck about what's goin' on there. . . . I ain't goin' back to Earth. I ain't goin' to New Harmony. And I ain't gonna help you get there. So shut up and lemme fly."

Kel winced and shut up. A few minutes later Chuy asked, "What's Baghavad like, Bud? You've been there. I ain't."

Bud chuckled and said, "You'll see. But don't worry, they're pretty harmless . . . mostly."

After four more hours of thrumming engines, darkness, and, for Kel, fitful sleep, the shuttle began to descend just after dawn broke. It hit an air pocket and dropped sickeningly. Kel woke instantly. After he stifled his gag reflex, he looked down and thought he was dreaming or hallucinating, as a mottled purple, brown, and green landscape, crisscrossed by streams, unfolded in slow motion below. As the shuttle descended further, with more gut-wenching drops, the rolling, wild landscape gave way to a coastal plain bearing a semi-regular pattern of rice paddies dotted with microscopic water buffaloes pulling wooden plows, with tiny, straw-hatted workers clutching the handles of the plows. It looked like a dream sequence from a 2-D of Vietnam atrocities. All that was missing was the napalm.

The vista became more distinct as the shuttle dropped even further, and the procession of paddies petered out into a spread-out compound of mostly single-storey buildings set on a plain abutting low, wooded hills, with the sea in the distance. The sun glinted off the largest building, a huge, partially completed structure with an ornate, gilded dome, which looked at first glance like a Hindu or Buddhist temple, with ant-size workers scurrying about its unfinished portions. Bud circled the building twice before setting down on a rough shuttle pad a klick to its north.

As soon as he landed, emaciated, bald headed men and women wearing identical baggy, off-white uniforms appeared and began to silently unload crates and cartons from the back of the shuttle, placing them in ox carts.

Bud climbed out of his seat, walked to the back of the shuttle and down the loading ramp without saying a word, as Kel and Chuy followed him down the ramp. At the bottom, Bud told them "Wait here," and walked off.

They stood to one side of the ramp, avoiding the coolies hauling out the shuttle's cargo and loading it onto carts, as others walked into the shuttle, bent nearly in two by the huge bags of rice they were toting up the ramp.

Kel found his voice first. "What the hell is this? And what the hell are we doing here?"

"You didn't want to die. Remember?"

Kel didn't reply. They mutely watched the pantomime unfolding before them until Bud returned.

Bud cheerfully told them, "Everything's cool. Just keep your mouths shut and you oughta be okay. I'll be back in a few weeks, maybe a month. I don't think there are any other shuttles due before then. I can probably get you out when I get back."

Chuy gulped. "Probably?"

"Probably. Right now, I'm heading to The Iron Dream, and, trust me, you don't wanna go there." Chuy started to speak, objecting to the apparent lie Bud had told him about heading straight back to New M, but Bud cut him off. "Then I'm headin' straight back to New M. What with that shit you did you're lucky I'm droppin' you here. If it wasn't for your buddy," he nodded toward Kel, "I'd have dumped your sorry ass at The Dream. . . .

"And don't try to take off before I get back. These guys're like the goddamned Loonies back on Earth. Do what they say, you're okay; buck 'em and you're fucked. And they think you're here for life. They'll probably have you sign trillion-year contracts."

Chuy sputtered, "A trillion-year contract?!"

"Yup. Reincarnation, y'know?"

Kel and Chuy gaped as Bud took off his specs, put them to his mouth, breathed on both lenses, and polished them carefully with his shirt tail. He put them back on before continuing. "If you can't stand it here, Serenity is about a hundred clicks west o' here, and New Havana is another two or three hundred past that. You can walk if you have to, but make damn sure you get away. . . . The roads, well, what passes for roads, should be okay for walkin'. You might get lucky with the weather, and the animals ain't too dangerous." He chuckled and then continued, "Well, most of 'em ain't."

After several seconds, Chuy croaked out, "Thanks. I guess."

Bud's face lit with a half-smile as he turned away from them and walked back into the shuttle. As it was lifting off, a well fed, middle aged monk with a shaved head approached them from the direction of the temple. His jowls quivered as he addressed Kel and Chuy:

"I am Brother Sand. Bud tells me that you are seekers after The Truth."

Chuy quickly replied, "We are."

Sand bowed. "Welcome to The Family."

13

RELIGION, n. 1) The first refuge of the desperate; 2) A convenient means of avoiding such unpleasantries as reality and independent thought.

—Chaz Bufe, *The American Heretic's Dictionary*

The ascetic makes a necessity of virtue.

—Friedrich Nietzsche, *The Anti-Christ*

Kel and Chuy followed Sand to one of the men's barracks. Once they walked inside, Sand half bowed, quickly straightened, smiled, and addressed them: "Welcome home."

Kel was appalled. The barracks was spartan: a mud floor, no interior walls, no insulation, bare rafters, ill-fitted rough-hewn boards nailed to studs for exterior walls, a few tiny windows casting forlorn patches of reddish light on the floor, bunks, and a few bare bulbs dangling from the rafters at the ends of twisted wires.

Even though it held over fifty bunks, the barracks had only a single door, with a desk and chair immediately adjacent to it.

As Kel and Chuy gawked at their new home, Sand bowed again, then turned and walked out the door before they could ask any questions. As they were gaping after him, a figure approached from the interior gloom: Brother Luna, a saturnine, bald-headed, rail-thin monk who might have been middle-aged or elderly; the shaved head and lack of facial hair made it hard to tell. He was dressed in a plain, baggy uniform of threadbare drawstring pants and loose-fitting top, both of which were a light, uneven tan, and a pair of sturdy sandals.

He beckoned with his hand and led them through a door to a small room which was bare but for two wooden benches. Luna gestured toward the benches and said, "Sit." As soon as they did, he walked to the other door, opened it, and another monk entered carrying a large scissors, a straight razor, and a bowl of soapy water.

Kel flinched as he felt the cold, sharp scissors begin their work. Worse, his clipped hair was sifting down through his collar, tormenting his back and chest. He felt pissed off and helpless, and was becoming thoroughly enraged, when his head was drenched with cold, soapy water. He sputtered and began to rise, fists clenched. Luna's hand pushed him down, and he saw a straight razor before his eyes in the hand of the barber monk. It was hardly necessary, but Luna said, "Sit very still," as the straight razor put the finishing touches to the clip job. Chuy was next.

Once the barber concluded his work, Luna handed Kel and Chuy rags to mop the blood from the nicks on their heads, and clothing almost identical to his own. The difference was a large, black ideogram on the front of their tunics.

Luna then led them into the shower room. They hung their new clothes on pegs sticking out from the wall, took off their soggy clothes, hung them on other pegs, and stepped in under the shower heads. Kel yelped when he twisted the handle on the "hot" faucet and was blasted with a spray of cold water.

Chuy, who had held back, said "Fuck it," turned the handle, and stepped in under his own needle-sharp spray.

They emerged from the shower room five minutes later dressed in their new baggy uniforms, each holding his old clothes in one hand and his few personal effects in the other. Luna reached for Kel's clothing. Kel pulled back from Luna.

"Hey! These are mine!"

"You will not need these unholy things."

Kel glanced down at his Hawaiian shirt. Then at the pants containing his wad of cash.

"What about my money?"

"You will not need that, either. You are now free of material bondage. Father provides."

Chuy nudged Kel as he began to speak again. Kel glanced at Chuy, saw the look in his eye, and shut up. With that, Luna took their clothes and other possessions, and walked into his office, a room at the far end of the barracks. They stood silently, Kel seething, Chuy stoic, until Luna returned with clipboards and a pen.

As Chuy took the first clipboard, Luna muttered, "Your contracts."

Chuy signed without looking at the form. Kel did, and gave a start at the provision promising a trillion years of unpaid labor, but signed when Chuy nudged him, and handed the contract back to Luna, who retreated into his office.

When Luna came out, he handed each of them a thin, rough blanket and led them to their bunks, which consisted of three-centimeter-thick, sheetless straw mattresses resting on frames of rough-hewn lumber. After Luna walked off, Kel pushed down on the mattress with his index finger. It left a dimple where it pushed through to the board. When Luna returned a few minutes later he motioned for them to follow him, as he headed for the barracks' single door.

As they walked away from the building, Kel smelled acrid smoke. He turned and saw a wispy black column, presumably the remains of their clothes and shoes, rising from a chimney above Luna's office. Luna led them along a winding path through the same purple ground cover Kel had noticed in New M. As the path twisted around dilapidated one-storey buildings, the golden dome of the partially finished temple loomed ever closer. Once they were at the temple construction site, Kel and Chuy, sleep deprived, hungover, and hungry, found themselves facing mounds of sand, gravel, and cement, with shovels in their hands.

After very brief instructions from the foreman—at least that's what Kel thought he was; he looked the same as all of the others—they began shoveling the sand, gravel, and cement into a mixer. It was hot, and several of the other workers had taken off the top half of their uniforms revealing protruding ribs, thin arms, and deep, crisscrossing scars on their backs. After a few moments, Kel and Chuy, sweating profusely, looked at each other nervously. Kel said, "Screw it," and they both pulled off their tops.

When the first hod carrier approached to get a wheelbarrow of "mud," Kel, sweat streaming down his face, asked him, "What's your name?" The alarmingly thin man didn't respond. He simply stared vacantly while they poured concrete into his wheelbarrow, repeating nearly inaudibly the phrase he'd been chanting as he approached: "Father is good. Father knows all. Father provides. Father is good. Father knows all. Father provides . . ."

Kel tried again with the next hod carrier, and received an identical nonresponse: "Father is good. Father knows all. Father provides. Father is good. Father knows all . . ."

They worked until sunset without a break and without lunch, and well before dusk their palms had blistered. They were exhausted when they and the other worker-monks returned to the barracks in an eerily silent procession, after a single bash from a gong somewhere high above them in the unfinished temple. None of the other men spoke with them, or to each other, even after they were in the barracks; nearly all sat down carefully on their bunks, crossed their legs into the full-lotus position, and began swaying backwards and forwards, chanting. All of them ignored the sacked-out figures of Kel and Chuy, who had fallen asleep within seconds of hitting their mattresses.

After a few minutes, a bell rang and the other monks got up mechanically and headed for the door. Kel and Chuy were still sleeping when Luna jabbed them repeatedly with a dowel. While cursing him—he didn't deign to even acknowledge their curses, just kept on jabbing—they sat up sluggishly.

Luna stopped jabbing and said, "Get up!"

Kel forced himself up from the bunk, and with Chuy stumbling after him followed the last stragglers out the barracks door. Two minutes later they found themselves in a food line in the next building, a large, ramshackle, one-storey mess hall, wooden bowls and chopsticks in hand, with brother Luna behind them, dowel in hand. Kel was in front, and when he reached the servers he received a single ladle of rice. He stopped, looked down at it, and then looked at the server and held up two fingers, mouthing the word "two." Everyone in front of him had received two ladles of rice. The server pointed at the ideogram on his tunic, shook his head, and looked down. Luna, looming behind Chuy, stepped around him and poked Kel in the back.

Kel shot a deadly look at Luna, while fighting down the urge to take the dowel and shove it up Luna's ass. After they stared at each other for several seconds, Kel turned wordlessly and walked to the next server, who doled out a single ladle of grey gruel over the rice, with semi-solid, gelatinous chunks poking up through the ooze. Chuy also got half rations.

Luna, who had gotten two scoops of rice and two scoops of gruel, led them to a long, low table in the back, separated from the other tables, where perhaps fifteen other grimy workers squatted cross-legged as they waited to eat their identical meals. All had ideograms on their tunics, though different from the ones on Kel's and Chuy's. But, like Kel and Chuy, they all had half-rations. As soon as Kel and Chuy sat down, Luna walked away without a word.

There were dozens of other tables, and there were hundreds of men in the mess hall. There was not a single woman present.

Kel looked with loathing at the skimpy amount of slimy gunk in his bowl and whispered to Chuy, "What slop!"

"Yeah. What fucking shit!"

Kel hesitated a moment, then gripped his bowl with both hands, raised it to his face, and emptied almost half of it in one long gulp. He shuddered with revulsion and wiped his mouth with the back of his sleeve.

"Jesus!"

When Chuy didn't reply, Kel looked up, suddenly aware that they had been the only ones talking. All of the other workers within earshot were staring at them. So, they bent over and buried their heads in their bowls eating awkwardly and silently, fumbling with their chopsticks, grimacing with every sparse, slimy mouthful.

What made it even more painful was that at the far end of the hall, on a raised platform not forty meters away, cringing white-robed kitchen workers were serving Sand and a dozen other saffron-robed, well-fed monks heaping portions of white rice and what might have been Chinese or Thai food. A painted motto on the curtains behind them announced, "Father's bounty flows to those who most deserve it."

14

MYSTIC, n. A man or woman who wishes to understand the mysteries of the universe, but is too lazy to study physics.

—Chaz Bufe, *The American Heretic's Dictionary*

The cosmos is a gigantic fly wheel making one thousand revolutions a minute. Man is a sick fly taking a dizzy ride on it. Religion is the theory that the wheel was designed and set spinning to give him the ride.

—H.L. Mencken

Half an hour later the tables were empty, and Brother Sand was standing behind a podium on the now-empty raised platform where he and the deserving others had gorged themselves. The lights went down, and, illuminated from below by floodlights, a gigantic portrait of an oily skinned, pudgy, late middle-aged Asian man in a business suit loomed above Sand. The only other light was a spotlight directly on Sand.

"Praise be to Father. Father provides."

The crowd responded in unison: "Praise be to Father. Father provides."

Sand and the devotees repeated the call and response twice more before the spotlight on Sand cut off. On that cue, Sand and the rest of the worshippers prostrated themselves before the portrait of Father, Sand on the floor of the platform, and the workers with their upper bodies face down on the tables, their eyes closed and their torsos twisted so as to face the portrait. Kel looked at Chuy for a second before they reluctantly bent over. After a full minute of prostration, a tinny bell rang, and the workers straightened and looked toward the front of the room. As the spotlight flicked back on him, Sand was already standing behind the podium, leaning forward, both hands gripping its sides.

He boomed: "The Divine Principle of the Eternal Return has been proven by quantum physics. We live in an uncertain universe, but we have certainty. Matter can neither be created nor destroyed. Energy can neither be created nor destroyed. Nor can consciousness be created or destroyed. It recurs. It persists. It remains. Eternally. As does matter. As does energy. As does Jesus. As does Buddha. As does Father. Consciousness recurs. In this turn of the wheel, the consciousness of Buddha and Jesus Christ have returned to us in the One, the One Father, the One Perfect Master, Byung Hyung Fung.

"But just as consciousness recurs and just as the wheel turns, so recurs sin and its need for expiation. Just as Jesus has returned as Father, and as Buddha has returned as Father, so has sin and the need for expiation returned. As you. As us. As the unworthy.

"But on this turn of the wheel, Father has freed us of the obscene sacrifice of the innocent for the guilty. We are not worthy of Father's sacrifice, so Father has not sacrificed himself. This time The Innocent, The Perfect, will not suffer for the sins of the guilty, for the sins of the imperfect. For you. For me.

"Father has delivered something greater than sacrifice; father has delivered justice. This time, this turn of the wheel, we, the guilty, will suffer as we deserve to. Our time for expiation is here. Our time to free ourselves through suffering is here. If we but suffer enough, we will free ourselves. We will break the wheel of samsara! Freedom through pain! Freedom through suffering! Freedom through suffering is God's gift! Freedom through suffering is Father's gift! Every second of agony is a step toward freedom!"

The entire crowd stared glassy-eyed at Sand. Kel snuck a look at Chuy and then turned back and gazed at the madman. Sand continued in similar vein for three more hours, and Kel and Chuy were awakened several times during the sermon with hard prods to their backs. Fifteen or twenty minutes after the final prod, Sand finally ended with, "Praise be to Father! Father is good! Father knows all! Father provides!" The light on Sand abruptly extinguished, leaving only the glowing image of Father on the wall at the back of the platform. When the overhead lights came back on, Sand was gone and the workers uncrossed their stiff legs, got up, and shambled toward the exit.

When Kel and Chuy returned to the barracks, the dim overhead bulbs were on, and most of the other workers stripped off the tops of their uniforms and reached in under their bunks, hauling out short leather whips. Kel looked under his own bunk and, shuddered with revulsion as he saw a similar instrument of self-torment. The lights went out within seconds, and the place was soon filled with the wet sound of leather striking flesh, followed by grunts of pain that started out subdued but quickly became frenzied and then orgasmic. Kel and Chuy were both so tired that they were asleep within two minutes, amid the sounds of whips and cries of pain and pleasure.

The next morning, Kel, against Chuy's advice, approached Brother Luna.

"Why do we get less food than the others?"

"It is the same for all newcomers. It is a purification process, an aid to you in receiving Father's wisdom."

"For how long?"

"A month is sufficient."

"A month!?"

"A month."

"What about the others at our table? Are they newcomers, too?"

"Satan has tempted them. They, too, need purification. Now go to work."

With that, Luna turned and walked away.

The following days were a blur of sunrises and sunsets, hour upon hour of feeding sand, gravel and cement into the mixer, and feeding gruel—never enough! and never any meat or fish!—into himself. Kel even began looking forward to dinner: lovely, lovely grey gruel caressing a mound of scrumptious rice, with only a little bit of sand in it, and, most nights, the only protein in his diet: one or two, sometimes, if he was really lucky, three, large, dead cockroaches.

After dinner, the pattern continued with Sand at the podium every night, sometimes speaking until midnight. And then the sound of whips, cries of agony and ecstasy, and blessed, blessed sleep. Four hours later the lights would come on and the whole pattern would repeat itself. Sand said that this mind-numbing sameness was a good thing—"letting the samsara of existence, the physical consciousness of eternal recurrence, seep into one's bones."

A little over a week after they arrived, Kel and Chuy had eaten their sparse evening meal, were sitting cross-legged at their meal table, and Sand was droning on.

"Just as the electron revolves around the proton, the moon revolves around the Earth, and the Earth revolves around the sun, human consciousness revolves around God consciousness, and our fallen consciousness revolves around Father consciousness. Just as fallen female consciousness revolves around pure male consciousness, our weak, impure consciousness revolves around the great pole of Father consciousness. But there is a demonic force which seeks to destroy this great symmetry.

"This great destructive force, this great enemy of God consciousness, this great enemy of Father consciousness, is Satan, the great enemy of Father, the great enemy of Truth. And just as Satan is the enemy of God consciousness, your consciousness is the enemy of God consciousness, your consciousness is the enemy of Father consciousness. You, through the very act of using your mind, betray God, betray Father.

"As God speaks to you through his perfect instrument, Father, Satan speaks to you through his imperfect instrument, your mind. Your mind is an instrument of Satan. I repeat, your mind is an instrument of Satan! To be saved, you must not use your mind! To be saved, you must surrender this imperfect instrument! You must not use this imperfect instrument! To be saved, you must not use your imperfect mind!!

"Surrender! Surrender your fallen consciousness to God! Surrender your fallen consciousness to God's perfect instrument! Surrender your fallen consciousness to Father! Surrender! . . . Surrender is the road to enlightenment! Surrender is the road to freedom!!"

And so on, for three more hours.

After the sermon, as they walked back to the barracks in near-total darkness, Kel heard Chuy whispering to him, "Hang in there. Bud will be back in two or three weeks." Kel was so tired he didn't reply, didn't even acknowledge Chuy. A few paces later, he felt Chuy grab his arm, shake him, and whisper something incomprehensible to him. Kel was so fatigued he didn't acknowledge Chuy except to stop, and when Chuy released his arm he continued to plod silently toward the barracks. Once on his bunk, he was asleep within seconds; the whips and cries, now as familiar as the sound of cicadas, had become simple background noise.

* * *

Three days later, Kel was sitting cross-legged next to Chuy, listening to Sand after dinner. Both had lost a lot of weight in the week and a half since they'd arrived. Chuy had lost his beer gut entirely and was on the verge of starting to lose muscle. The hard work, no-protein diet, and inadequate sleep were wearing him down. Kel was in even worse shape; he'd barely recovered from his years in cold sleep when they'd fled New M; now he felt half dead. Could he even last until Bud returned? He felt his head sagging, felt his mind drifting down, sinking into Sand's soothing words.

"Your mind is fallen. Your mind is God's enemy. Your mind is *your* enemy. Your mind allows Satan to sow the seeds of doubt and to destroy the beauty of God's truth. Your mind is Satan's seed bed of doubt. Cast out that foul seed. Cast out that demon seed. When your mind questions God's holy truth, it isn't *you* that is doubting, it is *Satan* that is doubting through his foul instrument—your mind. Doubt is satanic and those who succumb to doubt are satanic. Purge your mind of Satan! Purge your mind of doubt!

"Yes, this is difficult. But Father has given us tools, perfect tools, with which to defeat Satan. When you hear the whispers of Satan, drive him back into the pit, drive him back into the blackness from which he came with God's Word, with God's Mantra: 'Father is good. Father knows all. Father provides.' Simply repeat this mantra until you have defeated Satan. 'Father is good. Father knows all. Father provides.' Repeat it for hours if you must, but do it! 'Father is good. Father knows all. Father provides.' Your immortal soul is at stake! This perfect tool will save your soul—but only if you use it!"

After the sermon, on the way back to the barracks, Kel didn't respond when Chuy asked repeatedly if he was okay.

The next morning, after a cup of gruel and ladle of rice for breakfast, Kel trudged with the hundreds of other silent devotees to the construction site. While he was feeding sand into the mixer, he observed, as if from a great distance, his mouth working nearly silently, apparently of its own accord: "Father is good. Father knows all. Father provides. Father is good. Father knows all . . ."

15

RELIGION, n. A daughter of Hope and Fear, explaining
to Ignorance the nature of the Unknowable . . .

—Ambrose Bierce, *The Devil's Dictionary*

Kel tried to scream as a hand clamped his mouth shut and he felt a stinging slap to his face.

Someone was whispering insistently, "Get up! Get up!" Kel struggled feebly in the total darkness. More slaps stung his cheeks. The whispers grew more urgent. "Get up you son of a bitch!" More slaps. And harder. "Get the fuck up!"

The whisperer removed his hand from Kel's mouth, and Kel said the only thing in his mind, "Father is good. Father knows all. Father pro—"

A really hard slap stopped him. "Get up, asshole!" An even harder slap and a more insistent whisper followed, as his assailant shook him by the shoulders: "Get up, motherfucker! Father wants you to come with me! Father wants you to come with me *now!*"

The abuser released Kel, and when he saw that Kel was quiet, he took Kel's arm and pulled him up on the side of his bunk. Then he pulled Kel to his feet, saying, "Put on your sandals. Father commands it." After Kel shuffled into them, in what felt like slow motion, he felt himself being dragged by the arm through the barracks door.

He floundered several times, and tripped, as he was dragged across the open space between the barracks and the wooded hill behind it. After ten minutes of stumbling up an animal track, as he gradually emerged into a semi-conscious state, the hand holding Kel's arm in a vise was suddenly gone. Seconds later, he found a piece of bread stuffed into his hand. A subdued but familiar voice said, "Eat it." Kel slowly raised it to his mouth, but once he'd tasted it he gulped it down within seconds and found another piece thrust into his hand. Then he felt a grip on his arm and he was being pulled again, stumbling, along an endless trail, as he recited the sacred mantra: "Father is good. Father knows all. Father provides."

An hour and a painful kilometer later he jolted near-awake as his feet plunged into cool water. His abductor pulled him down an ankle-deep stream, both of them slipping and falling on the round, smooth stones. Twenty meters down the stream bed, Kel felt himself being pushed into a hole in the thicket along the bank, while the familiar voice told him, "Father wants you to crawl in here." So Kel crawled in, ignoring the thorns tearing at his arms and face. A few seconds later he found himself in an empty space. Then a hand pushed him down, and the familiar voice told him to sleep.

* * *

The sun was well up when an insect scurrying across his face woke Kel. He rubbed his stubbled, sweaty cheek, knocking off the insect. He opened one eye and stared dumbly down at it. It was like nothing he'd ever seen: about two centimeters long, vaguely beetle-like, but fluorescent red with eight legs, multi-faceted eyes, and a needle-tipped proboscus. Kel looked sluggishly around. Another monk was sacked out, snoring noisily, his head on a burlap sack. Kel rubbed his cheek again, sank down, looked up through half-closed eyes at the branches above him, and fell asleep almost instantly.

Two hours later, Kel was still snoring when Chuy sat up groggily and reached into the burlap sack. He pulled out the loaf of bread they'd started on the previous night, and a large sausage. He pulled off a piece of bread and cut a piece off the end of the sausage. And then, eating them as fast as he could, another and another.

As Kel stirred, Chuy reached back into the sack and found a brown, unlabeled half-liter bottle that he'd taken the previous night. He unscrewed the lid, took a hit, and immediately spat it out, wiping his mouth with his sleeve. Cooking oil. He screwed the lid back on, reached into the bag, and found another bottle. He opened it and sniffed suspiciously. Brandy.

He took a long slug, then bent over and poured half a shot into Kel's open mouth. Kel jerked upright, sputtering.

Chuy immediately asked, "Who are you?"

"I am de—"

Chuy grabbed Kel's shoulders and shook him.

"Kel. You're Kel. Kel Turner."

"I am de—"

"You're Kel. Kel Turner."

"I—"

Chuy shook him even harder. "You're Kel! Kel!"

Kel pushed Chuy away and mumbled, "Father is good. Father knows—"

Chuy slapped him hard across the face and shook him again. "You. Are. Kel. Kel. Fucking. Turner. Got that motherfucker!? Got that *pendejo*!? Kel. Fucking. Turner!" He slapped him again and shook him hard for several seconds, finally asking, "Who . . . Are . . . You?!"

Kel tried to reply, but nothing came out but a rasp. Chuy repeated, "Who are you?" Kel started to mumble, "Devo—," but upon seeing Chuy raise his hand again, he croaked, "Ke . . . Ke . . ." Chuy finished for him. "Kel." He released his shoulders, and Kel slumped. A few seconds later he looked up, still half-dazed, and asked, "Wh . . . Where . . . ?"

Chuy blew out some air through pursed lips and said, "Here. Eat something." He handed Kel the bread heel and began slicing off hunks of sausage.

Kel ate greedily for several minutes as Chuy took nips off the bottle of brandy. Kel had just started to reach toward it when the silence was broken by thrashing sounds and voices in the distance. Chuy set down the bottle and put his index finger to his closed lips. Kel, looking confused, opened his mouth, but Chuy put his hand over it while continuing to signal silence. The thrashing came closer, as Chuy continued to signal Kel to be quiet. The flailing stopped abruptly, and the far quieter sounds of the forest filled the air. Finally, the thrashing started again, this time moving away from them, farther up the hill into the woods. As he continued to sit stock still, Kel heard another familiar voice, Sand's, fading but distinct.

"We'll find them, and then we'll get that bastard Bud for dropping those two ringers on us."

When the sound of the searchers had faded to nothing, Chuy withdrew his hand and spoke in a low whisper.

"Kel?"

"Yeah . . ."

They sat silently for several seconds before Kel rubbed his stubbled face and stubbled scalp. Chuy handed the bottle of brandy to Kel, who took a small gulp before Chuy took it from him. Another moment passed before Kel mumbled, "What . . .?"

Chuy didn't reply.

They sat silently, both too tired to move. Chuy was staring vacantly down at the sand when Kel spoke again.

"Where . . . are we?"

"Baghavad. . . . Here, have a hit." Chuy took a long slug off the bottle and handed it to Kel. Ten minutes later they were both asleep.

16

The Invisible Hand at Work

. . . or . . .

This American system of ours, call it Americanism, call it capitalism,
call it what you like, gives each and every one of us
a great opportunity if we only seize it with
both hands and make the most of it.

—Al Capone

Once you give up integrity, the rest is a piece of cake.

—TV character J.R. Ewing, *Dallas*

Kel awoke. He felt the warm sand beneath him, then looked up at the orangish sun poking nearly straight down through the branches of the tree above him. The tree had what looked like dozens of brown fingers reaching up on all sides into a nearly perfect dome of purple-red needles. He put out a hand toward its trunk and winced as he felt the hard, sharp protrusions of its alligator-like bark. After he pulled his hand back and sat up, he looked over and saw Chuy's passed out form, with a steady stream of fluorescent red beetles marching across Chuy's legs. Kel looked up at the brown fingers of the purple-crowned tree, lay back, closed his eyes, and lied still for several minutes, trying but failing to go back to sleep. Finally, Chuy stirred, brushed off the red insect-like marchers, and sat up.

As Chuy was still yawning, Kel sat up and opened the bag of food. He pulled out a knife and then cut up hunks of bread and dried fish, which he handed to Chuy as he was stuffing his own face. After they finished, Kel put away what was left of the food, and they sat nearly motionless. After an eternity that could have been two or twenty minutes, Chuy looked at Kel, glanced up through the tree at the noonish sun, and said, "Screw it." He reached into the food bag, grabbed the bottle of brandy they had half-emptied the previous day, settled back down on the sand on his elbows, screwed open the top, took a long pull, and handed it to Kel, who took an even longer pull. After handing it back, Kel reclined again on the sand and was asleep within a minute. As Kel was crashing, Chuy took one more small slug, capped the bottle, laid down flat on his back, and fell asleep almost as quickly.

* * *

When Kel awoke early the next morning, it was barely dawn and tiny purple-red bits were raining down on his face. He brushed them off as he shielded his eyes with his cupped hand. He looked up, squinted, and couldn't see what type of insect or animal was ploughing through the branches. All that he could see was the shower of shredded needles drifting down. He shook Chuy awake, and they had what was left of the bread and sausage, and also two bananas.

When they'd finished, Chuy took off his sandals, and said, "*¿Listo?*" Kel said, "Yeah, I'm ready, but how'd you do it?"

"Do what?"

"Get us out of there?"

"It wasn't all that hard. When we were back in the barracks after the sermon, I put a rock under my back, waited until everyone else was asleep, got up and told that son of a bitch Luna I needed to take a piss. He was at that desk by the door. When we went outside, I knocked him down, smashed his head on the ground, grabbed his keys, dragged his ass inside the outhouse, whacked him in the head again, and wedged the door shut.

"I almost felt sorry for the poor fucker. When he came around he must have been suffering." Chuy chuckled. "Especially having to breathe that stench until somebody found him. Christ. He probably still stinks."

Kel, who had always hated Luna, chuckled and then asked, "Why the hell did he go outside with you when you went to take a piss? I never understood why they do that."

"It's a control thing. Never give you a moment by yourself. Never give you a moment to think. Not even when you're taking a piss or a shit in the middle of the night."

Kel gestured toward the sack. "Where'd you get that?"

"I went to the mess hall. It was locked, but one of Luna's keys worked. I found some bags of rice and beans, then found these locked cabinets along the back wall of the kitchen. And all of the good shit. All the shit that Sand and those other assholes were eating in front of us."

He grabbed the food bag and said, "Let's get out of here." Chuy took off his sandals, slung the bag over his shoulder, got down on his knees and crawled through the hole in the thicket. Kel took off his sandals and followed him. They stumbled upstream on the smooth rocks until they were back on the path. It was odd. His soles had become so hardened that he only felt the wetness of the stream on the tops of his feet. The bottoms were almost numb.

They sat down, dried their feet on their trousers and sleeves, put their sandals back on, looked up at the sun hanging above the ocean to the east, and began walking away from Baghavad.

After trudging a few minutes, Kel asked, "Where are we headed? New Harmony?"

"Eventually. For now, Serenity."

"How far is it?"

"Longer than we want. Four, five, six days. In the shape we're in, probably six days. But we'll get there."

"What about animals?"

"Hey *ese*, don't worry. That lying asshole Bud was just fucking with you. There's nothin' to worry about, no large native predators, and Earth-gov ain't been crazy enough to introduce any."

"Then what made this trail?"

"Deer, probably."

"Deer?"

"Yeah, deer. A lot of the Earth-gov assholes like to shoot things, damn near anything, as long as pain, death, and dominance are involved. The same old shit as back on Earth. Pretty much as soon as they got here, forty-five, fifty years ago, those *comemierdas* decanted a dozen deer embryos and let 'em grow. When they were a year or two old, they hauled 'em out to a ranch a couple hundred klicks from here near Mount O'Reilly. It's an old volcano that's erupts every now and then—doesn't do any real damage, just spews noxious gases. But the area around it is still the nicest place on the planet, and this is what they did with it. Turned it into a fucking slaughterhouse. Totally enclosed part of it with barbed wire so there was no escape, and turned the deer loose. Then they flew in and were gonna shoot those poor goddamned animals like those rich *chupavergas* do on those 'safari game hunts' they still got goin' down in Texas and what's left of Florida."

"Safaris?"

"Yeah. It's been a big thing since . . . Oh Christ, forever . . . You don't hear much about it because it's so politically incorrect, so fucking disgusting, just for the rich, for the *pinche* Comp-Med types. And the *culeros* who run it get most of their clients through word of mouth. The corporate fuckheads who do this shit can't resist bragging about getting it on with man-eating beasts. So, they brag about it, their asshole buddies hear about it, and they can't fucking wait for their turn to blast the shit out of those poor goddamned animals."

He stopped and turned toward Kel. "It's basically the same shit as it was a hundred, two hundred years ago. I read about it in this novel by some guy who lived in some submerged part of Florida. It was funnier than hell. I think it was called "Sick Doggy." Anyway, they used to go to circuses, wild animal parks, zoos—"

Kel shot him an open-mouthed glance.

Chuy continued before Kel could speak: "Yeah, it happened. They're that sick. They'd take old, lame lions, tigers, elephants—whatever the fuck those assholes wanted to shoot—dope 'em up so heavy they almost had to screw eyelets into their backs and hang 'em from cables, and then these corporados would blast the shit out of 'em at point-blank range. The really sick motherfuckers would sit in their goddamned cars, drunk on their asses, and shoot birds released from traps. What a bunch of fuckwads.

"But it's more high end now, except for the real bottom feeders. Mostly it's custom jobs. Some asshole has the money and wants a wildaroo or Kimodogator, they'll find a gene-splicer to do the job.

It costs a mint, but those assholes have a mint. And if they can't live without blasting the shit out of a rhinophant or buffazelle, they'll pay whatever it takes to do it, even if they have to wait a year or three for the fucking abomination to reach trophy size. It doesn't even matter if the poor goddamned things are sick, sterile, or terminally fucked up. All they have to do is live long enough to get decent sized and get shot."

"Jesus!"

"Yeah. Another of the multi-fold blessings of capitalism. . . . Another of the multi-fold fucking blessings . . . Another example of the invisible hand at work."

"Invisible hand? What—?"

"You never heard of it? The invisible hand? Goes back to the nineteenth century. Adam Smith. Said that the unbridled pursuit of individual profit produces the greatest common good."

"People actually believed that shit?"

"Yeah. Some still do. I remember a story on the 2-D years ago about some unlicensed dental outfit two assholes set up in their garage in Phoenix. Catered to *indocumentados* who didn't even have Basic Med. *Indocumentados* from such a fucked up part of Mexico that they still had dental problems. They made a lot of dough, but they screwed a lot of people over. Real gruesome shit. Didn't even know how to use anesthetics; didn't even follow basic sanitary practices.

"What got 'em busted was that they accidentally fused this chick's jaws together. They didn't have the heart to kill her, so they let her go and she went to the emergency room. The desk jockey there took one look at her and called the cops. They scanned her implant—fake, of course—and then forced her to talk." Chuy choked off a chuckle. "Well, forced her as soon as they were able to pry her jaws open.

"That's just one example, but it's a good one, of the invisible hand. Those fuckwads were doing what they were doing purely for private profit. Some fucking public good it did . . . And don't even get me started on the environmental shit."

"Yeah, but that's just one example. What about things on a bigger scale?"

Chuy laughed. "You want to talk about the climate meltdown? The 'scientific' whores the energy corporations paid for? The lying ass scum who covered it up for a few more years of oil profits before two centuries of misery? What more proof do you need? Give me a fucking break."

They walked on. Eventually, Kel asked: "But what about the deer? What about these trails? Didn't they shoot all of 'em? Why is this here if they shot all of 'em?"

Chuy laughed. "It's about what you'd expect. According to what I heard, when they went 'hunting,' they didn't dope up the deer quite heavy enough, and before they passed out those Earth-gov shitheads were so drunk they only managed to shoot six or seven of those poor goddamned animals. The rest of 'em found a hole in the fence, or jumped over it, after the drugs wore off, and escaped. Now they're like the goddamned rabbits in Australia—no natural predators and they eat everything in sight.

"And that ain't the worst of it. Five or six ain't an adequate breeding population, so pretty soon we're gonna start seeing deer crazier than shithouse rats. Deer with more congenital idiocy than the British royal family."

17

Your best thinking got you here.

. . . or . . .

Belief means not wanting to know what is true.

—Friedrich Nietzsche, *The Anti-Christ*

The next day, Kel and Chuy hit the main "road." Three days later, after trudging every day down the sun-baked, rutted mud tracks for as many hours as they could stand, not a single vehicle had approached them from either direction, and not a single shuttle had flown over them. The landscape had changed little from the countryside above Baghavad, except that it was drier and a bit sparser—rolling hills covered with primitive native conifers, interspersed with pines, the short, dome-shaped, purple-red trees with slender, finger-like branches supporting a nearly perfect domed top, and introduced grasses mixed with and driving out the purple native ferns and iceplant-like ground cover. From time to time, shallow streams rolled lazily along the side of or across the road. There were no fish in the streams, only purplish fungus-like mats floating just under the surface, and occasional small, red, newt-like swimmers with two tails darting in and out of the mats. On the land, thanks to the extinction event, there were almost no animals except for introduced species, birds most obviously.

Alien as it was, the landscape was monotonous. But just when it appeared that nothing would ever change, Kel would look down and see a turquoise, beetle-like creature with only four legs with black trapezoid patterns on its back, or look up and be startled by a nightmarishly large cyan dragonfly with a needle-sharp, tarantula hawk-like proboscus. And then it would be gone. And then, again, hour after hour of marching until Tau was nearly on the horizon or they were too tired to go on, pitching camp, starting a fire, eating the ever-diminishing rations, and then doing it all over again the next day.

On the afternoon of the sixth day, as they tramped on, Kel asked, "If all of those ships are out there and so many people know how to fly 'em, why doesn't anybody head back to Earth?"

"You've gotta be kidding. I already told you: no radio traffic. Earth might not even be there. It might be a ball of grey goo—nanobots eating everything. They might have let Von Neumanns loose and it's nothing but machines cannibalizing each other, for-ever. Or, if they were lucky, some gene-spliced plague wiped out humanity or came so damned close to it that they're back in the Dark Ages. . . . And that's the up side."

They marched on.

The following morning, shortly after they broke camp and start-ed walking, Kel saw a faded, hand-painted sign next to the road reading, "Serenity 3 km," with an arrow pointing straight up and then bending to the right. After he'd pointed the sign out to Chuy, Chuy immediately started walking into the woods to the north of the road, and said, "Come on."

Kel stayed put and called after him, "Where are you going? Why don't we just follow the road?"

Chuy stopped and turned to face Kel.

"Come on, man! We need to check this out. You don't know how crazy these *pendejos* are."

Kel didn't reply and didn't move.

Chuy yelled again. "Come on! Nobody I know has been here for years, and by now they could be flogging people or crucifying 'em in public. Literally. I mean it. They're out of their goddamned minds. We've gotta be careful."

As Kel hesitated, Chuy turned his back on him and started walking into the woods. After a few seconds Kel fell in behind him. An hour later, they were on a trail in the pines hugging a ridge overlooking the valley that cradled Serenity. Even though they were high above it, they could see gravel roads connecting scattered buildings and fields, with ant-like figures scurrying about. There were no signs of public mayhem. No gallows. No crucified corpses. No whipping posts.

After a couple of minutes of careful scrutiny, Chuy said, "This looks okay. Let's stash our gear and check it out."

"I told you. We should have just walked—"

"No, man. We need to check this out. You have no idea what you're getting into."

"And you do?"

"I was in one of these goddamned places for a year after I got busted for spike! It was almost as bad as Baghavad: One Correct Way of Thinking, and you damn well better toe the line. When I was in their New Life Center back in Losanfrancisco, they locked me up in a basement room for a fucking month. Almost no light, just a few of those goddamned glass blocks set up high in one wall, a mattress on the floor with no sheets, a blanket that smelled like piss, and a chamber pot they made some poor asshole on punishment duty empty every other day. And seven fucking squares of toilet paper a day—seven! I fucking counted!—not that I used all of 'em, because all I had to eat was macaroni and cheese twice a day for a goddamned month. I'm lucky I didn't die of an intestinal blockage. I was lucky to get off with hemorrhoids. . . .

"When we get down there, let me do the talking. Don't argue with me. And keep your mouth shut."

Kel shrank back and didn't reply. This was not like Chuy.

After a short pause, Chuy said, "Sorry, man. That ain't a good memory. . . . Anyway, if it's anything like what I went through, it'll be a lot like Baghavad. Slogans, dogma, bullshit, orders—always more damn orders—and some guy they call Father lording it over you. Here, I think it's some fucker they call Clancy. Back on Earth, they have a dead saint named Will and a bunch of assholes who are more than happy to 'channel' him.

"But basically it's the exact same shit as Baghavad. Exactly the same. You remember that slogan, 'You think too much'? It's the same here: 'Accept, don't reflect'; 'You are your own worst enemy'; 'Do, don't doubt.' That sort of crap. It's the same damn thing as with every other religion: 'Trust us; don't trust yourself. We have a direct line to God.' The only real difference between this and Baghavad is that, probably, you get a little, and I mean a little, more privacy, the food's better, and you get almost enough sleep. Almost."

"How do you know all this shit?"

"I just told you! Before I got busted for the political bullshit and got shipped here, I got busted for dope and had to go through one of their treatment centers. I was there almost a year.

"They have all these fucking rules. Rules about what you can say, what you can read, who you can hang with, how you can dress, how you can take a fucking shit.

"The worst part is that the fucking *cabrones* ratpack you. They call it therapy, and the motherfuckers think you should *thank* them for it. They single you out and then close in on you like a pack of hyenas. The goddamned *chupavergas* never let up. They fucking *enjoy* it."

Kel took several seconds to reply, a malicious smile playing on his lips: "Come on. Don't they have to do that? They're dealing with addicts. Don't they have to break through their denial?"

"Coming from *you*, that's rich. You know me. I was never an addict. I just got caught with some dope. Same as most of the other poor bastards in that goddamned place. And don't give me any crap about that 'denial' bullshit. If you admit you're an addict, you're an addict. If you deny it, you're 'in denial,' which is *proof* that you're an addict. It's like being accused of witchcraft in the Middle Ages. The accusation is its own proof."

"But why would they do that? Why would they screw with you like that?"

"Other than that they're a bunch of sadistic, power-drunk assholes who get off on screwing with people? They say you need to get spiritual to beat an addiction, and they have the only way to do that. To get as humble as they are. They beat you down to build you up—the way they want to build you up." Chuy turned and stomped ahead. Kel had to hurry to catch up.

They continued walking with the silence hanging heavy before Chuy stopped, turned his head, and spoke again. "Screw it. We need to get into Serenity, see if we can radio Bud not to go to Baghavad, and get the hell out."

"Why the hell should we give a shit about that bastard Bud?"

"You want to walk twelve hundred klicks to New Harmony or get stuck in one of these religious gulags? Christ. Do you think you *can* walk twelve hundred klicks? We barely made it here. If we warn Bud, there's a pretty good chance he'll pick us up. He's not a complete bastard; he's just pissed at me, has this perverse sense of humor, and likes to fuck with people."

With that, Chuy charged up the path again, not slowing until he reached the crest of a ridge. A few dozen meters later the trail intersected with another heading down toward Serenity. Chuy stalked into the undergrowth next to a large pine three meters off the trail and flung the bag with their remaining food and cooking gear over as high a branch as he could reach. Then he made a cairn at the intersection of the two trails and started walking down toward Serenity. Kel followed.

After walking several hundred meters down the path, they emerged from the trees into a clearing with an overgrown shuttle pad in its center. They walked onto the pad, looked down at its shattered concrete surface, grass and weeds poking through the cracks, then looked up at its overgrown light poles bearing scum-encrusted lights and cameras, with purple creepers snaking over and through them.

Kel said, "Shit. It's been years since a shuttle landed here. We're gonna have to walk out unless Bud wants to land in broad daylight in the town square or they have another shuttle pad."

"No shit, man. Tell me something I don't already know."

Chuy turned his back to Kel and started walking down the now nearly flat trail through shoulder-high grass. Seventy-five meters later they walked into a clearing with two abandoned, decaying frame buildings and two shattered concrete slabs, rusted bolts jutting up along their edges. Rusty nails, bits of concrete, plaster, wood, and broken glass littered the path.

They stopped. Kel gaped at the ruins and asked, "What in hell happened here?"

Chuy replied, "Who knows?" and resumed the trek into the shoulder-high grass on the other side of the clearing.

A hundred meters on, as they emerged from the grass, Chuy grazed his shin on a boulder hidden by low weeds. While he was rubbing the bruise, Kel stepped past him onto one of the village's main gravel streets. It was near a "T" intersection, where a neatly lettered, hand-painted sign on a pole identified the road leading to the left as Shoemaker Court and the one they were on, heading straight toward the main cluster of buildings, as Oxford Way. They started down it toward the center of the village. As they reached the first building, a single-storey frame structure, a few pedestrians approached from the opposite direction: blank-faced men and women in plain cotton clothes, many sucking on cigarettes. They stared at Kel and Chuy, but otherwise ignored them when Kel and Chuy returned their gaze. A few others, slowly working their jaws, some with purple drool running down their chins, shuffled past without even looking at them.

Kel whispered, "Jesus!" Chuy shrugged.

After they'd walked a hundred meters farther into the compound, a fat, late middle-aged man with a grey ponytail, grey Van Dyke, heavy five o'clock shadow, and a smoldering cigarette hanging from the corner of his mouth, stepped onto the road twenty meters in front of them. He was wearing motorcycle boots, low-slung black jeans with a thick leather belt, and a heavy chain attached to his left-front pants pocket with keys dangling from it.

The finishing touches were wrap-around shades, a bejangled black leather vest, and a black T-shirt that didn't quite cover his ample gut, which hung down, froglike, over his massive belt buckle, and which nearly hid the name engraved on the buckle, "Jimbo."

As he walked toward them, Jimbo was grinding two dice together in his right hand. He stopped just short of them and coolly surveyed their near-shaved heads, stubbly faces, and grimy coolie clothing. He took a hit off his cigarette, exhaled smoke in their direction through his nose, turned his head to the side, spat on the road, turned back toward them, and spat out his first question:

"Who the hell are you?"

Chuy answered immediately: "We're friends of Father." Kel winced, but Jimbo didn't notice.

"Father? Jesus H. Christ are you in the wrong place! This ain't Baghavad."

"No, man. We're friends of Father, friends of Will B."

Jimbo's eyebrows rose, and he looked at them more closely.

"Friends of Will? From Baghavad?"

"Yeah. We escaped."

"Really? . . . . Tell me . . . The more helpless you are—" He stopped in midsentence.

"—the more helpful you are."

"War upon self-will—"

"—is peace with God's will."

"Freedom to indulge your desires—"

"—is slavery to your desires."

"Ignorance of evil—"

"— is strength to do good."

"Heavenly ends—"

"—justify earthly means."

Jimbo grunted, "Come on." He turned, and motioned with his meaty hand for Kel and Chuy to follow, but he dropped one of his dice as he was gesturing. When he bent over to pick it up, his pants slid down, revealing plentiful butt cleavage. Kel averted his eyes. After a couple of seconds Jimbo grabbed the die with his sausage-like fingers, straightened up, and began walking again, grinding the dice in his right paw. Kel and Chuy fell in behind him.

As they approached a playground, Kel, despite his exhaustion, couldn't help but stare at the well-stacked blonde teacher wearing a tight, long-sleeved yellow top, who was supervising a group of what looked like kindergartners or first graders. But when he got closer, he couldn't help but stare at her yellow-stained fingers and teeth, the crow's feet around her eyes, and her yellow-green complexion, all of which was partially hidden by the smoke she was exhaling through her nostrils.

Several of the children were also engulfed in smoke from their clumsy, hand-rolled cigarettes, with most of them pausing occasionally in their play to wheeze for breath or to cough and hack up phlegm between drags. One tow-headed, running boy slipped and fell on a patch of grey mucous, and came up making a face while wiping it off his hand and onto the grass. The other kids taunted him and laughed at him for several seconds before the teacher shushed them, coughed, spat, and pointed out that the same thing could happen to any of them, and probably would before long.

Kel started to say something, but Chuy nudged him hard in the ribs, and they continued following Jimbo. A few minutes later they came to a barracks complex. Jimbo stopped, pointed to the left, and spoke: "The showers are over there, next to the barracks." He turned and pointed to the right. "That's the mess hall. Take a shower and then go grab a bite. I'll meet you in the mess hall in half an hour. We'll get you stowed away and workin' after you've ate. There are book studies at seven and meetings at eight. The book studies are optional." He turned and started to walk back along the path toward the village center. After a few paces, he turned back toward them. "Hey! What are your names, anyway? How the hell did you end up in Baghavad? And, oh yeah, welcome home. You look like death warmed over." He laughed, turned, and resumed walking, the dice grinding, before they could say a word.

18

Fake it until you make it.

. . . or . . .

"Salvation of the soul"—in plain words, the world revolves around *me*.
—Friedrich Nietzsche, *The Anti-Christ*

Thirty minutes later in the mess hall, Chuy was feeding Jimbo a highly edited version of their escape from Miller and company in New M and their subsequent flight from Baghavad. It was between mealtimes, but Mary, one of the kitchen crew, had hustled up a meal of apples, cheese sandwiches, glasses of milk, and packs of matches and machine-rolled cigarettes. Both Kel and Chuy were thoroughly enjoying their meal, and Chuy's virtuoso bullshit performance, when they heard Mary, through the closed kitchen door, begin to cough, followed by a long, juicy hack, the sound of spitting, and the momentary gush of a spigot splashing into what must have been a wash sink. Kel turned green, looked down at his plate, paused, and resumed eating, as Chuy continued his stream of bullshit without missing a beat.

When they'd finished their meal, Jimbo led them to the barracks opposite the mess hall, where he gave them white T-shirts, work shirts, blue cotton coveralls, black leather boots, and packs of smokes. Jimbo sat down on one of the bunks, motioned for them to do the same, pulled out and lit a cigarette, took a long hit, lifted his head and blew a smoke ring into the air.

Chuy, as soon as he sat down, pulled out a cig, put it in his mouth, lit it, and sucked heavily, barely managing to stifle a cough. While Jimbo was looking away, Chuy nudged Kel with his foot, and Kel hesitantly took out a cig, lit it, inhaled tentatively, and broke into a coughing fit. Chuy laughed and apologized to Jimbo, saying, "It's been a few weeks since we had any; they don't allow it at Baghavad."

Jimbo didn't deign to reply. He rose to his feet, walked toward the door and said "C'mon, let's go." He added, "You look like shit, but workin' out in the sunshine should do you some good. Don't push it too hard today."

They followed him out the barracks door and down a gravel path toward a construction site next to the fields at the edge of the village. Along the way, Kel recognized tobacco, corn, chiles, tomatoes, eggplants, what he thought was coffee, and squash; but there were also carefully cultivated rows of dwarf trees bearing bulbous purple fruit, similar to grapes but twice the size.

As they were nearing the site, Chuy asked, "Jim, we need to warn a friend of ours not to go to Baghavad. Can we use your uplink?"

"The name is Jimbo. And why would you want to do that? What's goin' on?"

"They think he helped us escape from Baghavad. They could mess with him real bad. We've got to warn him. It's our Christian duty."

"No, you don't gotta warn him. And it ain't your Christian duty. If God wants him to go to Baghavad, he'll go to Baghavad."

"Jimbo, please. They'll screw him over. He's a friend of Will's. Please."

"No. Don't question God's will."

Chuy fell silent as Kel broke in.

"We're not questioning God's will. We just want to save Bud's ass."

Jimbo looked at him disdainfully, took a hit off his cigarette, flicked off the ash, and kept on walking.

Kel didn't give up. He addressed Jimbo's back: "Please . . ." Chuy nudged him. Kel ignored the nudge. "Is there anyone else we can talk to? A communications officer?"

Jimbo turned toward him with an evil grin. "I *am* the communications officer."

Ten minutes later they arrived at the edge of the construction site. Jimbo walked into a tool shed and emerged with a pair of shovels. He handed them to Kel and Chuy, and led them to the partially dug footers for the foundation of a large building.

"Here 'tis. You can see what to do. Get to it."

He walked away, grinding his dice in his right hand, blowing smoke out his nose. Kel and Chuy began digging slowly. No other workers were anywhere near, and it looked like the trench hadn't been worked on since the last rain.

After Jimbo was out of earshot, they put down their shovels and Kel spoke.

"What's with the tobacco? I've never seen anything like it."

"Get used to it, *ese*. It's one of their sacraments."

"Jesus. . . . What a sacrament! . . . Anyway, things seem pretty loose around here. Can we get to the transmitter tonight? Can we even find it?"

"That's not the problem." Chuy pointed toward a tower topped by a dish antenna jutting above the trees on the other side of the compound. "There it is. But we're s.o.l. Things may look loose around here, and in some ways they are. But in some ways they ain't. How they control shit is that they control information tight. It's their whole trip. That and mindfucks. Knowing these assholes, they'll have the transmitter and receiver locked down, and access will require at least two passwords."

"Let's split, then."

"Not now. Things seem cool. We should wait a few days and rest up. If we split, they won't come after us." Chuy paused for several seconds. "Well, probably."

Kel picked up his shovel and began going through the motions of digging, occasionally tossing a thimbleful of dirt onto the pile at the side of the trench. An hour later, Kel looked up from his work and saw, seventy-five meters away, a well-built young blonde wearing a tight, white nurse's outfit—short skirt, body-hugging top and, yes, high heels—pushing a shrunken, green-complexioned man in a wheelchair, wearing a grey business suit. Kel nudged Chuy, who joined Kel in staring at the odd couple. They were traveling slowly down a well-groomed path leading away from a large, two-storey brick house set back in the trees, and were far enough away that Kel and Chuy could see but couldn't hear the nurse or the man; and they could stare at her gorgeous, hour-glass figure without being too obvious about it, as long as they kept up the appearance of digging. Despite the distance and their pretense of working, the blonde picked up on their admiring stares and shot back a quick smile. The man in the chair, who was breathing from an oxygen tank strapped to the back of it, didn't notice.

He turned and put his withered fingers on one of the nurse's hands, squeezed it, and she stopped pushing. She locked the wheels with her foot, moved to his side, and removed the oxygen tubes from his nose. She reached into her purse, drew out two cigarettes and a lighter, put both cigarettes in her lips, lit them, took a long drag off both, exhaled, and put one of them in the man's mouth. He eagerly sucked on it before starting to cough uncontrollably, hacking up blood and phlegm into an already soggy handkerchief which the nurse placed before his mouth. When his body had stopped shuddering, the nurse wiped his mouth with the hand-kerchief, put it back into its pocket in the back of the chair, and put the cigarette to the man's lips again. He took a short, tentative drag, exhaled the smoke through his nose with a blissful look on his face, took the cigarette from the nurse with a trembling hand, and took several more rapturous drags before beginning to cough violently, dropping the butt to the ground.

When he stopped hacking, he wiped the drool from his lips with the back of his hand, and then patted the nurse's ass with the apparently dry palm of the same hand. She took a final hit from her own cigarette, pulled a bulbous purple fruit from the wheelchair's other pocket, and placed it in the man's mouth. He began chewing contentedly. After he finished the fruit and spat out the rind, she wiped a ribbon of purple drool from his chin, and replaced the oxygen tubes in his nostrils. As she wheeled him off toward the village, Kel, who had been staring open mouthed, managed to speak.

"Jesus Festering Christ! Who was that?"

Chuy laughed. "Father."

Kel looked at him quizzically.

"Father. Clancy. *El mensajero de dios.*" He laughed again. "God's chosen messenger."

19

Let us love you until you learn to love yourself

. . . or . . .

If today persons are still to be found who do not know how *indecent* it is
to be a "believer"—or in how far it is a symbol of *decadence,*
of a broken will to live—they will tomorrow.

—Friedrich Nietzsche, *The Anti-Christ*

When the sun was low in the west, the whistle blew and work
stopped dead at the construction site and adjacent fields. Those
who weren't already smoking lit cigarettes, taking long, hungry
drags off them, before starting to walk back into the village. Kel
and Chuy also lit up, but only faked inhaling, as they were a good
distance from the other workers. Then, smoldering cigs in hand,
they fell in behind the others, who were heading for the mess hall.

Whenever anyone nearby glanced at them, Chuy—and Kel, as
soon as he caught on—acknowledged the person with "One day
at a time," sometimes varying the greeting by tacking "brother" or
"sister" or "Praise be to Father!" or "Praise be to Will!" onto its end.
When they were greeted in like manner, Chuy sometimes returned
the greeting and sometimes just nodded or grunted, as did Kel as
soon as he'd figured out the drill. At the mess hall, it was more of
the same: nods and "One day at a time"; "Let go and let God"; "Expect a miracle"; and, most popularly, again as at Baghavad, "Father
knows best."

Being newbies, Kel and Chuy were spared the company of those
with more "time" at dinner, and ate by themselves. Kel felt acutely
self-conscious as he and Chuy sat alone at a table in the rear, after
being studiously ignored while standing in line. But at least the
food was good—fried chicken, snow peas, and mashed potatoes,
with coffee and apple cobbler for dessert—even though they had

to eat it in a dense haze of tobacco smoke, their own included, for fear of looking out of place.

After dinner, they went back to the barracks, their clothes reeking of tobacco smoke. Kel sat on the edge of his bunk, sniffed his shirt, and recoiled in disgust before lying down. But even the stench couldn't keep him awake. He was so tired that he managed to sack out for over an hour, until the whistle blew fifteen minutes before meeting time, as the last lingering afterglow from Tau disappeared in the west. He forced himself to sit up, then shook Chuy awake; most of their barracks mates were already walking out the door, looking eager. Kel got up and, with Chuy following, walked outside with no idea where to go. People streamed by in all directions, paying no attention to them.

After a moment, Chuy hailed a skinny, shaven-headed, Mexican-looking barracks mate hurrying out the door and asked him, "¿Donde'stá el mitín?" The man looked closely at Chuy and Kel, jerked his head, and replied, almost as if annoyed, "Follow me," and began walking rapidly down a gravel path through the trees without a backwards glance.

A few minutes later they arrived at another barracks building, but one without bunks, partitions, or other amenities. It was empty, save for buzzing fluorescent lights hanging from bare rafters above a grimy cement floor, with at one end a lectern set on a table facing several dozen wooden folding chairs arranged in widely spaced rows. Other than the lectern, there was nothing on the table except a large glass bowl filled with the globular purple fruit Kel had seen growing on the dwarf trees in the fields.

The other furnishings were sparse: a huge coffee urn, cups, napkins, and cookies on a rickety table set toward the back of the room against one wall. About twenty people were milling around the table, siphoning down coffee and wolfing down cookies, while another forty or so, ranging from teenagers to grizzled oldsters, milled about the room talking to each other in pairs or in small groups, with a few hanging back alone. Almost all had coffee cups in hand and were chain smoking cigarettes. Framed slogans adorned the walls: "Alone—In Bad Company"; "Helplessness is Helpful"; "World Changing through Life Changing"; "When Man

Listens, God Speaks"; "Better Than Well"; "Humbly Proud"; "Utilize, Don't Analyze"; "A Mind Is a Terrible Thing"; and "Keep It Simple Shithead."

Chuy wandered over to the table along the wall, poured himself a cup of coffee and picked up a few rock-like cookies. Kel followed and recoiled when he tasted the coffee: it was so black and bitter that it could have dissolved pencils. That was bad enough, but none of the people milling around the table said anything to either of them. Kel, nervous and trying to look as inconspicuous as possible, followed Chuy to the last row of chairs. He needn't have worried; no one was paying the slightest attention to either of them. But even though no one was, Kel's heart was pounding and he had to force himself not to fidget.

After several long minutes, a short, handsome man in his mid-thirties walked in the door. He had longish, greased black hair that looked as if it had been painted onto his head, a pencil thin mustache, and one gold ear ring. He was dressed in black jeans, black cowboy boots, and a black cowboy shirt with pearl buttons. The man surveyed the crowd and then walked to the lectern. He puffed out his chest but remained silent, and looked slowly from side to side until the crowd began to fill the seats, which were in short supply.

Kel and Chuy, despite their newbie status, were soon surrounded. On the left, a nervous, acne-scarred teenager sat down next to Kel, and on the right, a fiftyish, one-hundred-kilo woman, wheezing and coughing as she sucked on her cigarette, collapsed into the chair next to Chuy. Their skinny Mexican barracks mate and a jockish, buzz-cut white guy in his early twenties, with a pack of cigarettes rolled into the arm of his T-shirt, sat down directly in front of them. As the last stragglers settled into their seats, the talking gradually ceased.

The man in black looked around the room, flashing a toothy smile. The crowd became even quieter. The man paused for several seconds, and then boomed out:

"Hi. I'm Rollin. I'm helpless!"

The crowd roared back: "Hi Rollin!"

Rollin stood beaming, and looked at the man at the right end of the front row, who took the cue and said, loudly, "I'm Dave. I'm helpless!"

"Hi Dave!"

The schoolteacher Kel had eyed on the way into the village was next. She was only about thirty, had a to-die-for body, and would have been gorgeous but for her yellow-stained teeth and fingers, and the crow's feet beginning to appear around her eyes.

She started to speak, coughed, recovered, and said "I'm Karen. I'm helpless!"

"Hi Karen!"

"Bob. I'm Helpless."

"Hi Bob!"

"Zita. Helpless!"

"Hi Zita!"

And so on.

Finally, the introductions worked their way to the back of the room and to Kel. Kel had steeled himself and was ready to utter the magic words when Rollin interrupted, looking first at Kel and then at Chuy. "We have two new members of the family, and they're already friends of Father!"

The crowd turned, looked expectantly at them, and then applauded vigorously. Rollin nodded his head at Kel, who managed to fake an enthusiastic: "I'm Kel! I'm helpless!"

"Hi Kel!!!"

"I'm Chuy! I'm helpless!"

"Hi Chuy!!!"

After the others in the back row had introduced themselves, Rollin paused. Milking the dramatic silence, he looked down, pulled out a cigarette, lit it, took a long drag off it, and exhaled the smoke through his nose. He surveyed the crowd, moving his gaze from one face to another. Finally, he began to speak:

"Tonight we're going to talk about freedom. The freedom that we have here. The freedom that was denied to us back home. Back on Earth. We were slaves to alcohol, smack, spike, dust, ice, meaningless sex, and neuro-stim . . . But here we're free, free of those addictions, free to love God, free to follow God's commandments, free to take God's sacraments, free to follow God's prophets . . ." He looked back at the huge, idealized portraits of Will B. and Clancy on the wall behind him—no wrinkles, no liver spots, and plenty of thick, dark hair—before turning back toward the worshippers. "Free to . . ."

Twenty minutes later he was concluding: "Free to be free of self-will. Free to be free of the illusion of freedom. Free to be free of ourselves." He paused, staring over the heads of the crowd, "And free to eat the sacred Kuru, the sacred fruit that God provides, the sacred fruit that provides the quiet time that is the key to God-consciousness. When man listens, God speaks. And when man eats the sacred fruit, God speaks loudly."

He took one of the purple fruits from the glass bowl, popped it into his mouth, and began chewing. He picked up the fruit bowl, clutching it to his midsection with his left hand as he continued chewing, and began walking along the rows, reaching into the bowl with his right hand and placing a fruit into every communicant's open mouth. When the acne-scarred teenager next to Kel received his fruit, the kid immediately began chewing and accidentally squirted purple juice onto Kel's shirt.

Kel recoiled in disgust, but didn't say anything. When Rollin offered an oozing fruit with a torn skin to Kel, he took it, but held it on his tongue and only mimed chewing it, as he looked questioningly toward Chuy. Rollin's eyes were almost rolling back into his head, and he didn't notice. After Chuy had mouthed one of the fruits, he looked at Kel sharply and mimed, mouth still closed, "No!"

Ten minutes later, Kel and Chuy were the only ones still in anything approaching a normal state of consciousness.

20

The more powerless you are
The more powerful you are

. . . or . . .

People to whom their daily life appears too empty and monotonous
easily grow religious; this is comprehensible and excusable, only
they have no right to demand religious sentiments from those
whose daily life is not empty and monotonous.

—Friedrich Nietzsche, *The Anti-Christ*

As Rollin and the others were all moving sluggishly, gradually coalescing into a ball on the floor of the barracks, holding and stroking one another, Chuy stood up. Kel woozily followed him out the door. Chuy spat out the fruit into some bushes by the side of the path, and Kel did the same. Then Kel felt it really hit—a wave of well-being, a wave of peace, of being one with his brothers and sisters. He reached toward Chuy.

Chuy pushed Kel's hand away and said, "Shit! You didn't chew that fucking thing, did you?" He grabbed Kel by the arm and pulled him, almost staggering, to their barracks. When they arrived, Kel dropped onto his bunk. Chuy watched over him anxiously for the next half-hour as Kel stared dreamily toward the ceiling.

When he started to come out of it, Kel ran his hand through his hair, raised himself on one elbow, and said, "Wow!"

"Yeah man, 'wow.' You want to stay here forever?"

"Uhhh . . ."

"Do much more of that shit and you will. We should get the hell out of here, now. But look at you. Hell, look at me. Are you in any shape to walk two or three hundred klicks?"

Kel didn't reply. Just kept resting on his elbow, staring in Chuy's general direction.

"Neither am I. And it ain't like they're gonna fuck with us. Back home, first thing. They'd have ratpacked us already. Had us confessing to being lying, thieving, son-of-a-bitch drug addicts who have sex with animals. Here it seems a lot looser. Let's rest up a few more days and then take off."

Kel barely heard a word Chuy said. He sank back onto his bunk, staring at nothing.

Chuy lied down on his own bunk and said, "Come on *socio*. Let's get some sleep."

Kel continued to stare dreamily at the ceiling.

* * *

Three nights later, Rollin walked behind the lectern at the nightly meeting, and after the ritual round of "Hi, I'm helpless!" introductions, said, "Tonight we have a guest speaker." He gestured toward the open door. "Chuck B.!"

Kel was taken aback by the contrast between the enthusiastic introduction and its object: a bald, elderly man dressed in a threadbare dark blue suit and matching tie, who had just walked through the door smoking a cigarette, his head held high. Rollin walked to a seat in the front row and sprawled down on it, looking expectantly toward the guest speaker.

Chuck B. walked behind the lectern and paused, before loudly stating: "Hi, my name's Chuck. I'm helpless!"

"Hi Chuck!!!"

Chuck hesitated, and then dove into his sermon: "I used to think I was hot shit. Really hot shit." He paused as the crowd chuckled politely in self-recognition. "I had it all. A beautiful wife, two great kids, my own house, my own business, and at night I was a jazz musician, a sax player. Virtual sax and real sax. I was making tons of money, doing whatever the hell I wanted, and thought I was really the shit.

"Sure, I used to drink some, but I could handle it. Hell, I took pride in it. If Churchill could handle it, I could too. If Nixon could handle it? Keith Richards? Buddy Gowarski? Billy Ishikawa? George Jones? Come on! So could I!

"I remember reading an old book about Miles Davis. When Miles was sixty fucking years old he was doing an interview while he had pneumonia. And he was smoking a cigarette and drinking a beer during the interview. I thought that was the coolest thing I ever heard of.

"So I was doing fine. I kept on drinking, doing a little more every year, and a little more dope. But yeah, I could handle it. I could handle it just fine." Chuck paused to light a new cigarette off the stub of the old one. He inhaled deeply and blew smoke through his nose.

"And then one night at this bar I was playing, this chick asked me to go out to the parking lot between sets. After she blew me, she pulled out this little metal case, opened it, and spilled out this blue shit onto her hand mirror, pulled a razor blade out of her bag, chopped the shit up, and swept it up into two lines. I said, 'What the fuck is that?' and she said, 'Don't give me that shit!' and started to laugh. She rolled up a Cheney, handed it to me, and I snorted one of the lines. I was off and running."

Half an hour later, Chuck concluded, "I was down on my knees in an alley, all fucked up, vomit all over my shirt, my pants around my ankles, trying to fuck some orange cat I'd grabbed, when I heard this chick screaming, 'No! Not Tinkerbell!! Not Tinkerbell!! You bastard!!!' A couple minutes later I looked up, saw flashing lights, and some cop standing over me with a club in his hand. I let go of the cat, and my head caved in.

"I woke up in jail the next day. I felt like shit. My head was pounding like someone was banging on it with a sledgehammer. I had blood and vomit all over my face and shirt, scratches all over my arms and dick, and shit in the seat of my pants. I'd hit bottom.

"A month later, they offered me six to nine for possession and bestiality or rehab at New Life and deportation. It was the easiest choice I ever made. And the best choice. I've been clean and sober for thirty years!"

The crowd cheered, whistled, and applauded. After milking the ovation a few seconds too long, Chuck B. bowed his head and walked to the only open seat in the front row. As he sat down, Rollin got up and walked to the podium.

"There's really nothing to say after that except, 'Praise be to Father!'"

The crowd loudly echoed, "Praise be to Father!"

* * *

Two nights later, after the introductions, Rollin looked toward the back of the meeting room and said, "Tonight we'll hear from one of our new brothers: Kel and Chuy." He looked toward Chuy. "Please, tell us your story, tell us how you got here."

Chuy got up, and to Rollin's surprise walked quickly to the lectern, nearly pushing Rollin out of his way.

"Hi! I'm Chuy!"

"Hi Chuy!!"

"I'm helpless!"

Chuy paused and then launched into his tale: "I used to think I was really hot shit. The baddest *vato* in the 'hood . . ."

Twenty-five minutes later, Chuy concluded, "So it was either thirty years or New Life. It was the best choice I ever made. I've been clean and sober for fifteen years!"

Following communion, and with all of the other attendees out of it, Kel followed Chuy out the door. Chuy was agitated. "We've gotta get outta here. I bullshitted them tonight, but they'll be after you tomorrow night. You might be able to bullshit them, but I wouldn't bet on it."

"Fine. Let's go."

Kel followed Chuy back to the barracks, where they pulled the wool blankets off their bunks, stuck them under their arms, and headed toward the mess hall. They walked just slowly enough that their pace wouldn't attract suspicion if anyone was observing them. As they hoped, it was vacant, the crew undoubtedly stoned out of their minds at one of the meetings. Kel targeted the loose food and supply cabinets as Chuy tore into the food cabinets. Kel's two real prizes were a box of wooden matches and a flashlight, which he piled with the rest of his take onto his blanket, and then tied its ends into a bundle.

Kel took a quick glance around, and stepped out the door. He led the way along the path through the barracks buildings and then up Oxford Way toward the trail on which they'd walked in. It was very dark. Serenity had no street lights, and once they were beyond the barracks paths with their dim solar-powered lights at ankle height, only starlight and a descending, crescent Arkady lit their way.

Five minutes later they still hadn't found the trail, and an increasingly nervous Kel heard slurred voices and hoarse shouts in the distance from the various meeting halls, the shouts and cries blending into one another. But that was normal after the taking of sacrament; it would be an hour before the communicants were fully conscious. Kel increased his pace and quickly found the boulder that marked the beginning of the trail by smashing his shin into it. He stifled a scream, grabbed his leg, and nearly fell over.

As Kel was hopping up and down, grimacing, Chuy reached down, felt around the boulder, found the gap in the weeds next to it, and grabbed Kel's arm. He pulled him, limping, into the darkness. Once they were a few dozen meters into the high grass, Kel pulled out the flashlight, pulled his shirt tail over its lens to dim it, and pointed it at the ground. He stepped in front of Chuy and very shortly his feet were crunching broken glass and broken concrete as the path led upward through the ruins into near-total blackness. Even with the flashlight, the going was slow; Kel tripped seemingly every tenth step, fighting back the urge to scream when he hit his shin again, and yet again.

Despite his pain, Kel was replaying in his head, over and over, Chuy's bizarre confession at the meeting that night. It was hard not to focus on it, because of the ever-present reminder provided by the stench of stale tobacco smoke on his clothes, a stench that was an anchor to Serenity.

As he was going over Chuy's testimony at the meeting for maybe the twentieth time, Kel noticed a bulge in the back pocket of his coveralls. He reached down and felt a three-quarters-full pack of cigarettes. He pulled it out and was going to throw it to the ground, but he hesitated while he resisted the urge to take one out, light it, and suck on it. He stopped, muttered "Jesus Festering Christ," threw the pack down, ground it in with his heel, and then had to hurry to catch up with Chuy, who had passed him.

When they reached the intersection with the main trail, Chuy reached down, found the cairn he had left, and turned onto the path up the ridge. He counted off five paces, walked to the tree where they'd hung their bundle, and hauled it down.

Once they were over the top of the ridge, Kel, using the flashlight unshielded, led the way down the trail toward the main road for another hour. They hit it and headed west, but got off on the first path to the south. Twenty minutes later the trail turned west, more or less paralleling the road. Chuy was still following Kel two hours later when Kel stopped under a clump of pines next to a stream and said, "I'm done." They were both so exhausted that they immediately fell asleep after collapsing on a patch of bare earth, using their bundles as pillows.

Kel awoke when the sun was already high in the sky and beams of sunlight wove through the branches of the sheltering trees, as green insects with the hard carapaces of cockroaches and the microscopic feet of millipedes scurried across his arms and legs and through his clothes. Kel jumped up, scratched frenziedly, and was on the verge of leaping into the stream fully clothed when a feverishly clawing Chuy yelled, "Take off your boots!"

After he frantically pulled them off, Kel jumped into the stream and stayed under long enough (he hoped) to drown the insects. Chuy did the same. With only his head sticking above water, Kel pulled his clothes off, tossed them onto rocks along the bank, stuck his head under again, stayed submerged as long as he could stand it, and resurfaced and floated in the cool water. When he and Chuy got out five minutes later, they wrung out their clothes, spread them out on rocks, and sat with their backs against a boulder that was in full sun. It was warm enough that their clothes were half-dry in twenty minutes.

After they dressed, Kel opened the food bundle they'd ripped off at Serenity, found a loaf of brown bread and some hard cheese, broke off a couple of large chunks of each, and walked back to where Chuy had settled back against the boulder, eyes closed. Kel nudged him, handed him his share of the food, and sat down, putting his back against the sun-warmed stone. As they were eating, Kel mumbled, mouth full, "Was all that shit really true?"

Chuy mumbled back, "What shit?"

"What you were talkın' about at the meeting last night. Did you really do all that shit?"

Chuy half-laughed, half-choked. "You *pendejo*! Do you really think I murdered all those guys? Raped all those women? Do you really think I fucked a goddamned *dog*?! It's a contest, man! The worse shit you did, the badder you are now that you're clean and sober! Everything, and I mean *everything*, is grist for the goddamned mill. You fucked a horse? I fucked a *snake! With some asshole prying its jaws open!* Those guys lay awake nights thinking up ways to top each other!"

"You're shitting me!"

Chuy laughed. "No, man. I'm not. You don't actually believe all that shit you heard back there, do you?"

Kel didn't reply, and Chuy continued to laugh. "You goddamned moron! How could you believe that shit!?" He started laughing uncontrollably.

A moment later, Kel joined him. Mostly in embarrassment.

Once they were dry, they put on their boots, slung their bundles over their backs, and started down the trail, which quickly turned nearly straight south. They walked for a few minutes, with Kel in the lead, before he turned his head and asked, "Why do they put up with that horseshit?"

"What horseshit?"

"All of that horseshit. Calling Clancy 'Father,' hearing the same shit night after night after night, the goddamned tobacco, the self-downing, getting fucked up every damned night."

Chuy shot him an amused glance, but didn't reply.

Kel repeated, "Why do they put up with it?"

Chuy stifled a chuckle and said, "Because they think they have to. Those poor bastards really think that their only alternative to all that bullshit is death. Back on Earth, they called it jails, institutions, cryo, or death. Here it's just plain Clancy or death. They've been bullshitted into thinking that they're totally out of control and will self-destruct without Clancy and his goddamned 'program.' It tells 'em how to think, how to act, how to live their entire goddamned lives. They all believe that they'll die if they leave. That their only lifeline is Clancy, the 'program,' and, here, that fucking Kuru. That's the reason things are so loose: they're scared shitless.

"They're so afraid of themselves and those 'potent, bewildering' substances they love so much that they don't even keep grain alcohol in the infirmary. They think it'll force 'em to drink it. So, they only keep wood alcohol around. And one or two of 'em probably go blind every year or two from drinkin' it.

"They really think that drugs and booze are powerful and they're powerless. They really believe it, and they act it out. And that ain't the worst of it.

"They go through absolute hell when they're hurtin', 'cause they're so shit scared of gettin' addicted that they won't even take pain killers. Not even aspirin. . . . Don't ever break a leg around 'em. Those stupid fuckers won't give you pain meds, even if they've got 'em, which they don't. And they'll feel self-righteous about it, like they're doing you a goddamned *favor*—forcing you to face your pain, to 'grow' through your pain.

"That's the way it works on Earth. Here, it seems different. Kuru? Seems like they think it's the same as tobacco and coffee, a fucking sacrament: it ain't booze, and it ain't a drug 'cause Will B. never talked about it, there's no law against it, and they've bullshitted themselves into believing that it provides 'direct communion with God.' So it must be okay."

Kel stopped walking, looked at Chuy while raising one eyebrow, and asked, "Come on. You saw how fucked up they got on that shit. They're supposed to be so damned straight and spiritual and they do that? How can they?"

Chuy shook his head. "How can they not do it? It's pretty damn simple. They love to get fucked up. Tobacco and caffeine they've had forever, they love 'em, they ain't booze, and they ain't drugs, by definition. They say they ain't, so they ain't. It's the same with the Kuru: they say it ain't a drug, so it ain't a drug."

Kel paused and then asked, "So they chain smoke, slug down gallons of coffee, get fucked up every night on Kuru, and feel righteous about how much straighter they are than everybody else?"

"You got it, man. What's really funny is what happens to 'em back in New M. What they preach is such bullshit that almost nobody wants to join 'em, except for folks who were into it back on Earth and never figured it out, and they don't arrive all that often. So, since they only rotate their New M staff when they get new recruits, they end up staying there for months. They watch each other like hawks, but a lot of 'em crack, figure out that it's a bunch of shit, or they just have to get fucked up. And there are plenty of ways to do that.

"The Kuru goes bad in a couple of days, and it won't grow down there, so that doesn't work for 'em. But they still believe that they're totally out of control, totally powerless, and they *want* to get fucked up. So they do the really bad shit in New M: dust, spike, or whatever new nightmare the chemists have come up with. When they drink or do that other shit, they believe they have no control, so they don't. It's real common for 'em, even the old timers with tons of time, to go out and drink, shoot up, or snort themselves to death. Most of 'em come crawling back to 'the program,' but some of 'em really do manage to kill themselves.

"Back on Earth, some of 'em even fuck themselves to death. If they're 'addicted' to VR sex, they just clamp on the 'trodes and groinal attachment and then hump nonstop in that goddamned chair until they pass out—and then start all over again when they come to. The damned machines can tell exactly what they want. They read their brain waves and then give those sick fucks exactly what gets 'em hard. If there's nobody else around, some of 'em just keep humping until they die. Usually from dehydration."

"Jesus. I heard some shit about that, but I thought it was a load."

"It ain't. They've been bullshitted into believing they have no control, that if they leave the program they'll die. And then they go out and prove it. It'd be funny if it wasn't so tragic."

Kel turned away from Chuy and started back down the path. A few minutes later he turned and asked, "How long until we get to New Harmony?" He didn't give Chuy a chance to answer before adding, "I don't know how much more of this shit I can take."

<u>21</u>

WILDERNESS, n. A pristine, spiritually inspiring place—preferably not
experienced directly, especially overnight
or in inclement weather.

—Chaz Bufe, *The American Heretic's Dictionary*

About a klick later the path made a U-turn as it rounded the
southern end of a ridge; two klicks to the north it intersected the
main road's rutted, overgrown tracks. Kel had barely stepped onto
it and started walking west when Chuy poked his arm and pointed
to a trail that joined the road a few paces ahead on the south side.
"We should take that. I don't think they'll come after us, but we
shouldn't take chances. It'll be slower, but it'll be safer. We ain't all
that far from Serenity. I think we're pretty near to the turnoff."

Kel didn't feel like arguing, so he followed Chuy down the new
trail. It led southwest for a kilometer before it went around another
ridge and turned back toward the road.

An hour after they'd started down the trail, they were walking
northeast. Chuy was clearly unhappy about this and, when Kel
asked, Chuy said they were heading back almost directly toward
Serenity, and he guessed that they'd come out close to where they'd
started.

As they neared the top of a rise, Chuy looked over it, saw the
main road, and immediately ducked down. Kel opened his mouth,
but Chuy put his finger to his lips, pulled Kel down with his other
hand, and whispered, "It's Jimbo. The motherfucker has a cross-
bow! He has a few of his boys with him. I guess they didn't appreci-
ate us taking all that shit."

"I thought you said they wouldn't come after us!"

"I was wrong."

Chuy scrambled as quietly as he could back down the rise, with Kel following. Three hundred meters down the trail, Chuy stopped, motioned for Kel to be quiet, and listened intently. He whispered, "I don't think they're following us. But we can't go back to the road, and I don't remember any trails crossing this one, so we're gonna have to go cross country."

Kel shrugged, whispered, "Let's do it," and they stepped off the trail and began bushwhacking west through waist-high dry grass and between occasional pine-analogs. As they were stumbling and cursing, Kel said, "This is fucked. But it ain't as bad as back home. I used to really hate hiking through this kind of shit because of the goddamned rattlers."

After too many minutes thrashing through the thick grass, they found a new path heading south into rocky terrain. They switched trails several more times, generally heading west, for the rest of the day, quitting on a north-leading trail while the sun was still an hour above the horizon, so they would have time to build a fire and prepare some food before nightfall.

The next morning, after a simple meal of sausages cooked on the still-hot firepit stones, raw corn, and, for Chuy, a couple of ja-lapeños, Chuy led the way back to the main road. When they hit it, it had a noticeable uphill grade. By late morning, the grass along the side started changing from tall and yellow to green, turning darker and darker as they trod on. By late afternoon, it was heavy and damp, nearly like sod. The trees were changing too; the pines, dome trees, and pine-analogs were growing fewer and shorter, with most bent to the east, with more and more drill trees appearing. As they marched on, the sky to the west grew darker as the wind picked up and the temperature dropped.

The farther they walked the more Kel worried. He'd been looking for a sheltered camping spot for over an hour, but hadn't spotted one yet as the sun sank and the gathering clouds drifted by low overhead.

Just as Tau was flattening on the horizon, the road crossed a shallow stream, not much more than two meters wide. As he was preparing to jump to a flat rock in the middle of it, Kel glanced to his right and spotted what looked like a cave forty meters upstream on the steep west bank. He gestured toward it and said, "What do you think?" The only way to get to it was by clambering along the nearly as steep east bank, and then crossing the stream, but Chuy said, "It'll do," and they began slogging toward it. They managed to stay out of the water until they were opposite the cave, but the stream was still two meters wide and there were no rocks sticking above the surface. Kel took off his socks and boots and waded across in ankle-deep, freezing water. Chuy followed. The "cave" turned out to be not much more than an overhang with a narrow strip of sand between it and the stream. But at least it would protect them if it rained and if the wind didn't pick up too much.

As the last light from Tau faded, they sat in under the overhang. Kel rubbed his near-frozen feet, put his socks and boots back on, stuck his head out, and looked up toward the ridge above them. There were no fallen trees anywhere nearby, and the slope was so steep there was no way to get to the scrub pines and scrub drill trees growing above them. It would be a cold night.

Chuy began to pull out rocks from the floor of the overhang with near-frozen hands, piling them at the front of the "cave." Kel joined him, and within ten minutes they had excavated a pit a quarter-meter deep, almost two meters long, and a meter across, and had built a short wall of stones piled across the front of the overhang. Kel untied one of the food bundles and put the blanket on the bottom of the pit, and they wolfed down their cold fare of bread, cheese, and apples.

Then they untied the other bundle they'd taken from Serenity and settled into the pit. They pulled the other blanket over themselves, placed as much of the food as they could at the back of the overhang, and left out the cooking gear and everything else that could stand the coming rain. They put their matches on top of a rock and then covered them with an overturned cooking pot at the very back of the overhang.

As the light died and the wind picked up, it began to pour. At first, they could see large, individual drops on the grey-white boulders on the opposite bank. Then, as the light faded further, the wind roared and the rain began splattering in sheets on the rocks across the creek.

For the first half hour, the wind blew directly away from them. Then the wind picked up and the raindrops pounding on the boulders on the other side of the stream began to swirl and spatter back toward them, slowly soaking them, as the wind howled. There was no point in talking, and no chance of sleeping. There was nothing to do but lie shivering under the increasingly wet blanket. As the night wore on, staccato flashes of lightning illuminated a strobe-frozen scene: the few dwarf pines on the opposite bank, visible through the nearly horizontal sheets of rain, bent over almost parallel to the ground. Pebbles and even fist-sized rocks ricocheted off the boulders opposite the cave, and when they rebounded, in the brief flashes of lightning, they hung motionless in mid air. The drill trees, in contrast to the scrub pines, stayed nearly upright, their branches closed in tight to their trunks. Between lightning flashes, Kel could hear but not see rocks and the occasional small tree or bush smashing out of sight onto the rocks. As the wind shrieked even louder, some of the smaller rocks began rebounding from the opposite bank all the way onto the blanket that covered his and Chuy's huddled forms.

They curled into fetal positions, back to back, enveloped by the wind, rain and cold. Moments later, huddled under the sopping blanket, Kel thought, "What the hell? Might as well enjoy the show." He rolled onto his back and stuck his head out as a blinding lightning strike hit a dwarf pine on the opposite bank meters away. The near-simultaneous deafening thunder clap and actinic flash sent—too late!—Kel's hands rushing to cover his ears and eyes as he tried to blink away the flashing, pulsating pattern on his retinas. He was miserable; this was one of the worst nights of his life, worse than any night he'd spent in a jail cell. He slipped back in under the blanket, pulled it over his head, and shivered. Finally, toward dawn, the storm slackened, and he lapsed into an uneasy, tortured sleep.

Chuy was the first to rouse himself an hour-and-a-half later, as the sun poked over the ridge above the opposite bank. Kel was shivering violently, even though the temperature was rising quickly and it was noticeably warmer than during the night. When Chuy stirred, Kel stuck his head out from under the sheltering wool blanket. Chuy sat up, reached a numb hand down, and shook Kel's shoulder, saying, "Come on, *ese*. Let's get outta here."

Kel's back, arms, and legs ached, and his hands and feet were nearly numb, even though the sun was shining directly into the cave. After Chuy stepped out from under the overhang onto the strip of sand next to the stream and stretched painfully, he said to Kel, "Hey man, we need to warm up." With that, he started doing jumping jacks. Even though it was the last thing in the world he wanted to do, Kel joined him.

A moment later, as they continued to jump, Chuy huffed out, "Ever wonder why a lot of the buildings here have those weird-assed west walls? Ever wonder about the drill trees? Now you know."

* * *

Most of their food was wet, so they made a breakfast out of what was still edible but would spoil quickly, stuffing down as much as they could stand of the wet bread, muffins, and cookies from Serenity. After they wrung out their clothes and their blankets, and did more calisthenics to warm up again, they packed what food they could salvage into a single bundle, and the cooking pots, silverware, and other gear into the other.

It had been a tough call—whether to wrap themselves in the wool blankets for warmth and carry what little they could in their hands and pockets, or use the blankets to carry all of the food and cooking gear.

Chuy tried the flashlight they'd lifted at Serenity. It was dead. He tossed it back into the cave. Kel looked at him askance. Answering the implied question, Chuy said, "*Un regalo*. A gift to future archeologists."

He tied his boots together by their laces, stuffed his socks into them, hung them around his neck, and scrambled across the stream. Kel followed.

After they'd crossed, they both rubbed their nearly frozen feet with their hands, put their damp socks and boots back on, and clambered along the bank back down to the road. They turned west and began walking abreast, climbing again, shivering in their slowly drying clothes.

After a few minutes of marching uphill, Kel said, "That was fucking awful."

"No shit. But we should be okay. Storms like that are unusual this time of year—"

"This time of year?"

"Yeah. Tau II's orbit is pretty elliptical and we're inbound, so the storms will get worse the closer we get—"

"Worse? Why?"

"Same as on Earth. The more the oceans heat up, the worse the storms. And since this place is almost nothing but oceans, there's nothing to slow 'em down. Anyway, we're okay for now. The worst is still months off, and we're near the summit."

Kel looked questioningly at him.

"This is an east-west range. Only twenty-one, twenty-two hundred meters high, and this pass is the lowest point for a couple hundred klicks on either side, almost all the way to the coasts. You get one hell of a Venturi effect. Once we're on the other side it drops off pretty fast, so we should be okay even if another storm blows in."

An hour later they climbed one last hairpin curve, and suddenly they were looking down on green hills with patches of white boulders and occasional drill trees, and lower, in the distance, a conifer forest that grew thicker and thicker the farther it receded toward the horizon. Except for a few cumulus clouds, the sky was clear. The only sign of civilization was the rutted track they were following, which disappeared, then reappeared, and then disappeared again behind the foreground hills, long before it reached the forest.

Kel's feet hurt, but he was shivering and eager to start down. They stopped a klick down the road at an outcrop of granite boulders, and lay down on their backs on the barely heated rocks. After futilely attempting to soak up almost nonexistent heat for two minutes, they took off their damp boots, wrung out their socks, tied their bootlaces together for the second time that day, and slung their boots around their necks.

Kel stepped barefoot back onto the heavily eroded road, walking gingerly, wincing as he stepped on pebbles and protruding rocks. Three painful meters later, he stepped off the road and onto the grass along the side of it. Chuy followed. The grass was cold and slippery, and the going was slow, but they didn't have much choice. It was too painful to walk on the road; their feet were tender from walking in wet boots, and out here blisters could be a death sentence. So, Kel led the slow. barefoot descent down the side of the road toward the forest.

Three hours later they reached it; at first there were low and sparse, and then medium-height and more densely packed pines. They decided to camp beside a stream fifty meters north of the road next to boulders twice their height. After resting for ten minutes, backs against the nearest west-facing boulder, luxuriating in the heat the boulder radiated, Kel got up, gathered fallen branches, and Chuy lit a fire. As soon as it was going, they draped their blankets over a low branch on a tall pine and placed their boots far enough away from the fire that they would dry but wouldn't bake hard and crack. Kel rooted through the food and grabbed a couple of apples and ears of corn, and what had been dried fish. They ate, and then, so tired they could barely move, pulled their still-damp blankets down from the branches, wrapped themselves in them, curled up in front of the fire, and were asleep before the sun set.

22

CYNIC, n. A blackguard whose faulty vision sees things as they are, not as they ought to be . . .

—Ambrose Bierce, *The Devil's Dictionary*

Late the following afternoon, footsore and weary, they left the road, walked into the woods, found a clear space next to a stream, gathered fallen branches, built a fire, and put two of their four remaining sausages on the firepit stones. After they'd eaten, Kel pulled out the final bottle of brandy from Baghavad, opened it, took a pull, and handed it to Chuy, who said, "I thought we were saving this for a special occasion."

"If surviving that fucking storm ain't a special occasion, I don't know what is."

Chuy took a pull and handed the bottle back to Kel. Kel paused and then said, "I've asked you about this before. But seriously, do you ever think about goin' back to Earth?"

"Yeah, I think about it."

"And?"

"Even if I could do it, I think it'd be a real bad idea."

"Don't you have family there?"

"Not anymore. Even if Earth ain't turned into a dead ball of shit, no. They're all dead. None of 'em could afford Comp Med, so they're all dead. They weren't scumbuckets, so they didn't even get Merit Med. You know how it goes. The rich live forever, their butt-boys live as long as they bend over, and the good die young.

"Everything was falling apart way before I got busted. My family? Jeeezus. . . . My parents worked their butts off their entire lives doing shit jobs. A hell of a lot of good it did 'em. . . . Rest of the family was in the same shape. Work was all they had. . . . We used to go to church on Christmas and Easter, but quit doing that when I was a kid. My sisters didn't even have *quinceaneras*. Couldn't afford it. Both of 'em got knocked up when they were sixteen or seventeen. My folks were real ashamed of it. . . . Of course, they had the kids. Fucked up their entire lives. Fucked up their *novios'* lives too. They all broke up within a couple of years. So, no college. Raising kids as single parents. And a lifetime of shit jobs to support 'em.

"I didn't do that. I was the only one to ever graduate from college. And only because of the GI Bill.

"The rest of my family? No roots. A lot of my cousins don't even speak Spanish. Them and my brothers? Most of 'em ended up in prison or the military. A bunch of 'em ended up dead. It's always the same shit: if you're poor and Mexican, you're fucked. It's still gotta be that way. . . . And you know what's the worst part? Knowing that you're getting fucked and not knowing who's doing it, or even when they're doing it.

"Used to be that racists were racists. At least the motherfuckers were up front about it. Now, they're smart enough to use code words. Smart enough to smile in your face while they stab you in the back. And most of the time you never know it. . . . So, Earth? Why in hell would I want to go back?

"And if I'm gonna die, I'd rather die here. At least there's no surveillance cam on every wall, no drone cams, no cops kicking down your door and putting guns to your head. No bullshit charges about resisting arrest or assaulting an officer after they kick the shit out of you. No one looking over your shoulder telling you what to think and do every fucking moment of your fucking life; and there ain't no 3-D or VR *putos* telling you how free you are and how grateful you should be to live in the greatest fucking country in the history of the fucking universe."

Chuy looked sharply at him, and Kel, jaw hanging open, eventually managed, "You sound pretty pissed off."

Chuy choked off a laugh. "No shit! Aren't you?"

"Yeah, but I never thought that much about it. Just sort of thought things were the way they were. Things were fucked up, but what could I do? What could anybody do? But you're fucking pissed. Don't you want to go back and do something about it?"

"No. Even if I could, I wouldn't. Even if Earth was still there, I give up. When I got sent here I was so disgusted I was almost happy they busted me. When they didn't kill me, throw me in some ultra-max, dismember me for organs, or stick me in cryo, but sent me here instead, I thought I'd hit the fucking jackpot. I'm *happy* to be here.

"Even if there's some good explanation for the radio silence—and there probably ain't—I won't go back. The fucking people on Earth get screwed over generation after generation after generation, and they keep coming back for more. . . . They ought to make hands around the ankles, ass in the air the official national posture. Have people assume the position at ball games . . . It's all so goddamned obvious, and they just don't fucking get it. When they shipped me here, the richest one percent owned seventy percent of the goddamned country, and the motherfuckers haven't done any useful work for generations. Three fucking mega-corps control the entire goddamned media, what people see, feel, and think—if you can call that thinkin'. . . . Most people are just shit terrified of being out of a job, so they'll submit to anything, absolutely anything, and it's 'yes massah,' 'no, massah,' 'whatever you say, massah.' . . . The miserable fuckers won't even stand up for themselves or their kids, and they rat out anybody who does. And will it ever change? Will it ever get better? Ever? I don't fucking think so.

"So, do I want to go back and do something about it? Fuck no. Screw those people. I feel sorry for their kids and for the people who fight back, but most of those fuckers richly deserve what they get."

Chuy stood up and said, "Bend over and grab your ankles. Here comes Uncle Sam!" He mimed grabbing a victim and then thrust his pelvis viciously forward. After two more thrusts, he sat down, took a long hit of brandy and sat staring at the fire, the bottle dangling from his right hand.

Kel stared at Chuy in stunned silence. Eventually, he reached for the bottle, pulled it from Chuy's unresisting fingers, and had a slug. Moments later he took a smaller drink and handed the bottle back to Chuy, who took a long sip and then let the bottle dangle from his fingers. Kel didn't reach for it again.

Five minutes later, Chuy was still sitting stock still, the bottle hanging from his hand, staring into the fire, when Kel curled up in his blanket with his back to the flames and tried to fall asleep.

23

DICTATORSHIP OF THE PROLETARIAT, n. A theological term and an article of faith. It is paralleled by the Catholic belief in transubstantiation and is equally plausible.

—Chaz Bufe, *The American Heretic's Dictionary*

After two more days of walking downhill along the rutted road, Kel and Chuy passed a crude wooden sign reading, "New Havana —100 km."

They walked on for a few minutes before Kel asked, "What's New Havana like? It always sounded like a good idea to me."

"A good idea? What idea?"

"Communism."

"Communism?"

"Yeah. I never believed all that crap in history class, and communism always seemed like a pretty good idea to me."

Chuy stopped and turned toward Kel.

"Well, it is a good idea. But what they've got in Havana ain't communism."

"What do you mean? They say they're communists?"

Chuy didn't answer. He cocked his head and stared at Kel, scowling.

After an uneasy second, Kel asked, "Come on. Why would they lie about that?"

Chuy waited a few more seconds, relaxed, and half-laughed. "They ain't lying. They believe it."

"So, isn't it true? Isn't everyone equal?"

"Some are more equal than others."

Kel didn't get the reference and didn't reply. After a moment, Chuy said, "Look. Do me a favor when we get to New Havana. Let me do the talking. Just shut up and watch. You'll see what kind of place it is when we get there." With that, he turned away from Kel and marched on.

Kel looked at Chuy's retreating back, closed his mouth, and quickly caught up with Chuy.

Several hundred meters down the road, Chuy told him, "New Harmony is only another thousand clicks. You'll see the real thing when we get there. And seriously, let me do the talking when we get to New Havana."

* * *

Three days later, two hours after they'd gotten up, broken camp, and began trudging down what was still a sad excuse for a road, the ruts slowly began to disappear; and then, almost imperceptibly, mud with occasional patches of gravel gave way to gravel with occasional patches of mud.

Kel was so beat that he didn't notice. Neither did Chuy. When Kel spotted a convenient log by the side of the road, Chuy was happy to stop and rest. They were too tired speak; they just sat and stared in exhaustion at the road's improved surface. After staring at it for what seemed like hours, Kel's eyes widened; he pointed at the road and said, "Check it out."

Chuy looked dully at it for several seconds, and then said, "Holy shit!"

Kel said, "Yeah. I think we're there."

He raised his eyes from the road and took a closer look at their surroundings. Even though they were still in the midst of meadows and forest, one signs of civilization was unmistakable: a clearcut hill to the north with a silted-up, muddy brown stream flowing off it.

Fifteen minutes later, as they were trudging westward, crossing a wooden bridge above a coffee-colored creek, they saw huge smokestacks belching black smoke near two decapitated hills to the south of the road. As they gradually drew parallel to them, Kel growled in disgust, "Jesus! A goddamned cement plant! Looks like that ancient piece of shit in Marana." Chuy didn't bother to respond, except to grunt.

Half an hour later they came to a wooden bridge spanning another muddy stream. They crossed it, rounded a bend, and abruptly faced a two-meter-high, barbed wire-covered barricade blocking the road, with an equally high fence stretching off on either side of the barricade into the distance in a cleared strip. Five meters farther on, in the middle of the cleared strip, there was an unpainted, cinder block building with antennas on its roof, a gate across the road, and a second, higher fence abutting it. Beyond that, a third fence, interrupted by a gate, extended into the distance. All three fences were topped with razor wire, and all three were marked with red warning signs every twenty meters bearing lightning bolts and the words "Danger!" and "¡Peligro!" beneath the bolts. Two hundred meters to the south, in the cleared strip, a crew was digging a pit, evidently some type of trap.

Kel took one look at the nearest warning sign and shuddered. *Jesus Festering Christ! Three goddamned electric fences!* He tried to hide his reaction as two pimply faced, clean-shaven policemen emerged from the cinder block building and approached them.

The cops stopped two meters away from Kel and Chuy, inspecting them wordlessly. After a few seconds, the younger cop stepped forward and addressed the bedraggled travelers.

"Who are you? And what do you want?"

The two cops looked Mexican, so Chuy switched to Spanish.

"*Nos llaman Jesús Andrade y Kel Turner. Somos refugiados. Pedimos asilo. Nos escapamos de Serenity hace una semana.*"

The younger policeman looked closely at their grimy, wrinkled clothing, stubbly cheeks and matted hair, as the other cop gripped his truncheon with both hands, twisting it slowly. The younger cop replied in English: "Asylum? You claim that you escaped from Serenity a week ago? That you're refugees?"

Chuy, more than a bit irritated, replied, "We *are* refugees. From Serenity."

The cop turned away without saying a word and walked back into the cinder block building. His partner continued to stare silently at Kel and Chuy, and continued twisting his truncheon in his hands. Kel and Chuy stood and waited . . . and waited.

Two hours later, after the cops confiscated their cooking gear, blankets, and remaining food, Kel found himself bouncing next to Chuy in the back of an electric jeep, heading toward the center of the surprisingly large town that was New Havana. After being marched through a maze of five-meter-wide corridors in a soul-deadening, neo-Mussolini-style building with high white ceilings, white tile floors, and what were probably fake, but might have been real, marble walls, they found themselves sitting in straight backed wooden chairs before an imposing, painfully neat, highly polished wooden desk—the unmarked blotter on its spotless surface lined up at precise 90-degree angles to its sides, as was the rectangular wooden penholder to the side of the blotter—in a large, dark, almost empty room with no windows. A policeman, arms folded, stood behind them. Huge portraits of Fidel Castro, Che Guevara, Hugo Chávez, and another hispanic man Kel didn't recognize, all in idealized, heroic poses and wearing military camouflage uniforms, hung on the wall, two meters behind the desk. The lighting in the room was dim, but floodlights pointed up at the portraits of Castro, Che, Chávez, and the other military man. It reminded Kel all too much of the lighting used in Catholic churches to illuminate statues of Jesus, Mary, and the saints, and at Baghavad to illuminate Byung Hyung Fuckwad's portrait.

There was nothing else to focus on, so Kel closely inspected the portraits, pondering the technical details, thinking in disgust, "What a fucking cliché! What shitty technique!"

Chuy, in contrast, had closed his eyes, and was breathing deeply. He'd known what to expect.

After several uncomfortable, silent moments, while Kel contemplated the icons and Chuy appeared to be in a zen-like state, Major Asahi, a thin, bald-headed Asian man of indeterminate age, wearing a starched brown military uniform and wire-rimmed glasses, walked stiffly into the room through a door to the right of the desk. He carefully pulled out the plush executive chair behind the desk, sat down, painstakingly and needlessly straightened the blotter and penholder, looked up at Kel and Chuy, and waited just long enough before speaking that the silence became nearly unbearable.

"Our comrades in Serenity confirm that you are indeed refugees."

They both started.

Asahi smiled. "Yes, we have ways."

His smile abruptly vanished as he continued, "It is entirely understandable that you would wish to escape the spiritual fascism of worshipping powers greater than yourselves. But, tell me, why did you come here?"

Chuy answered quickly. "We couldn't go back to Baghavad—we just escaped from there—and we were on foot. We had to come here."

"You escaped from Baghavad before escaping from Serenity? Tell me more."

Chuy hesitated for a few seconds, and then he did tell Asahi more, carefully omitting all references to politics, and especially anarchism, while vividly describing, with some embellishments, their escape from racist, criminal elements in New M and the emotional tyranny of Baghavad and Serenity.

He finished by telling Asahi of the danger Bud would face if and when he returned to Baghavad, and asking Asahi to warn Bud. Kel, looking slantwise at Chuy, hoped that Chuy's ulterior motive, informing Bud of their whereabouts, wasn't as obvious as it seemed.

Asahi listened carefully, his hands resting on his chest with his fingers steepled, his glasses perched on the end of his nose, and his eyes staring over their tops at Chuy. When Chuy had finished, Asahi waited a few seconds and pushed his glasses back up his nose with his index fingers. His eyes darted back and forth between Kel and Chuy, before fixing on Chuy. He paused, straightened, and said, in a surprisingly mild voice, "Welcome to New Havana, comrades."

He pushed his glasses, which had already slid down his nose a centimeter, back into place, and looked up at the policeman.

"Comrade, take these workers to the People's Construction Cooperative."

Chuy asked, "What about Bud? The fascists will kill him when he returns to Baghavad."

"That is Bud's problem. But I will discuss the matter with my superiors."

"Please! Bud could be on his way there now!"

Asahi's voice hardened. "As I said, that is Bud's problem. I will discuss the matter with my superiors."

Asahi motioned to the policeman to take Kel and Chuy away. Chuy began to speak again, but the policeman nudged him in the back with the tip of his truncheon at the first syllable. Asahi looked down at his desk and restraightened the blotter and the pen holder as the cop herded Kel and Chuy out of the room.

Once through the door, the cop stepped in front of them, said, "Come with me," and began marching them through the maze of corridors. As they followed, struggling to keep up, Kel whispered to Chuy, "Who was that other dude beside Che, Hugo, and Castro?"

"The other guy on the wall?"

"Yeah."

"Modelo, *el líder máximo*."

The cop turned his head and glared back at them, and they shut up. They emerged from the corridor into the ten-meter-wide entrance hall, with the sun casting long pools of light onto its white, hexagonal-tile floor through a bank of high, narrow windows. Thirty seconds later the cop pushed open the three-meter-high front door, walked through it without holding it open for them, and after Kel pushed it open again they walked down the building's granite steps, following the cop onto the street. Their boots crunched on gravel as they marched off to the north in the mid-afternoon sun, avoiding the occasional muddy puddle.

They tromped silently through a city of three- and four-storey, unpainted, rectangular cement buildings, laid out in a strict grid, with 20th-century-style power poles, transformers, and electric lines hovering over the streets and sidewalks. Huge portraits, all in bold primary colors, of Modelo, Mao, Lenin, Stalin, Che, Pol Pot, Kim Il Sung, Kim Jong Il, Enver Hoxha, Avakian, Fulani, Silo, LaRouche, Reibenbach, Castro, and several others that neither of them recognized, faced them from both the east and west sides of the cement buildings. On the north and south sides, where there were no portraits, lines of laundry hung from postage-stamp balcony after postage-stamp balcony.

The people they passed on the street came in all shapes, sizes, ages, and races, but all were shabbily dressed, with the exception of a few cops and men in military uniforms. All of the civilians avoided eye contact with the cop who was herding them along. Kel reflected that Chuy had been right. This did seem to be an equal-opportunity society: black, white, brown, red, yellow, male, female, gay, straight, young and old—all seemed equally cowed.

As they trudged on, Chuy motioned subtly upward with his head. Kel raised his eyes and saw surveillance cameras mounted on the power pole above him, and then on every other one. They continued walking for another twenty minutes, occasionally passing queues lined up before the stores that occupied the ground floors of some of the apartment blocks.

Abruptly, the apartment blocks ended, and they were on the outskirts of town passing a shuttle landing pad surrounded by razor wire, with spotlights on poles along its edges. Even though no shuttle was present, several guards lounged around the pad. Three hundred meters beyond it they arrived at the Construction Cooperative, a one-storey, frame building badly in need of a paint job. The cop gestured at the door with his truncheon and immediately walked off without speaking and without looking back.

As the cop's footsteps faded, they hesitated for a few seconds. Kel surprised Chuy by being the first to walk into the building. Once inside, Kel found himself facing a nondescript, balding official wearing a rumpled brown uniform identical to Asahi's, but bearing far fewer medals, sitting behind a desk and looking down at a sheaf of paperwork. His brass name plaque proclaimed, "Comrade Molson." Without saying a word, Molson reached into his top desk drawer, pulled out pens and clipboards thick with dozens of forms, looked up far enough so that he appeared to be staring at their navels, and handed the clipboards to both of them. He motioned for them to back away and sit on two rough wooden chairs against the wall.

Kel started to speak, but Molson looked down immediately, and Chuy tugged on Kel's arm, pulling him toward the seats.

Two hours later, Chuy was almost finished, and Kel had filled out the last of his forms. He got up out of his chair, walked across the room, and attempted to hand the forms to Molson. Molson stared at the papers without accepting them, turned his head, and looked back at the clock on the wall. It was one minute after five. Molson turned back toward Kel, looked up, stared at him for several seconds, and then shook his head. After a few more seconds, he spoke: "Come back tomorrow."

Kel's jaw dropped.

"What!?"

"Come back tomorrow."

"What!!? Come on! We're done!"

"Come back tomorrow."

Kel slammed the papers down on the desk and shoved them toward Molson. Molson pushed them back and glared at Kel.

"Go! Come back tomorrow!"

"You told us to fill these out and give them to you!"

"Go! It is after five."

"After five?!"

"After five! Too late!"

"Too late?!"

"Too late! Go!"

"Go where?! Where can we go!? Where can we sleep!?"

"That is your problem. Come back tomorrow. Go!!" He pointed toward the door.

"No!"

Molson reached for the telephone on his desk, looking up out of the corner of his eye at Kel. As Kel opened his mouth to protest, Chuy grabbed his arm and pulled him away, silently and frantically mouthing the word, "No!"

After a moment, Kel regained his voice as Chuy dragged him toward the door.

"Okay! Okay! We're going."

Still, he hesitated as Chuy pulled him. Molson, his hand on the telephone, glared at Kel and rose from his desk. Chuy pulled harder on Kel as Molson began to lift the receiver. They were already going through the door when Molson shouted, "Out!"

24

Arbeit macht frei.

Precisely at eight the next morning, Molson unlocked the door. Kel and Chuy, hungry, dead beat, unshaven, and shivering, with leaves and grass in their hair, entered the office and walked to the petty functionary's desk. Molson, in his still-rumpled uniform, pointedly ignored them, sat down, and pulled out what were apparently the same forms he'd spent all afternoon staring at, and occasionally scribbling on. Without saying a word, and without looking up at them, he reached into one of the drawers, brought out pens and clipboards thick with dozens of fresh forms, and handed them to Kel and Chuy.

Kel looked at the first form and tried to hand the clipboard back to Molson. He snarled at Molson's bowed head, "We filled these out *yesterday*!"

Molson looked up, staring over his coke-bottle glasses at Kel. "Those forms are no longer valid. Forms must be submitted on the day they are filled out." He looked down again.

"But—"

Molson looked up directly at Kel, locked his eyes on Kel's, and emphasized every word.

"Those Forms Are No Longer Valid." Molson pushed the form-filled clipboard back at Kel. "Fill these out!"

As Kel stared at him, speechless, Molson returned his attention to the paperwork on his desk. Kel hesitated, fists clenched, looking down at the light glinting off the top of Molson's scalp, wanting to beat his head in; but he forced himself to walk to the chairs along the wall, where Chuy was already filling out the fresh forms.

Two hours later, they handed their completed forms to Molson, who detached them from the clipboards, slammed a large rubber stamp down on them, and laid them atop his overflowing "in" basket without giving them a glance.

Molson picked up the telephone, and a few minutes later Kel and Chuy were following a cop to the Construction Cooperative barracks, which turned out to be all too much like those in Baghavad and Serenity: bare rafters, a concrete floor, rows of bunks with (as in Serenity) individual footlockers, and in the common area at one end a number of wooden tables and chairs, with chess sets on two of the tables, and a ping pong table off to one side. The work crews were already gone for the day, so after they were given new clothing they showered and headed for their bunks. They fell asleep immediately, despite their hunger.

Kel was still napping when the work crews returned. After a few moments of semi-consciousness, the noise finally rousted him as his new barracks mates exited, heading toward the mess hall. He sat up, rubbed his eyes, and shook Chuy awake; the few other workers left in the barracks eyed them warily. No one spoke to them and no one joined them as they followed the last stragglers out the door.

The mess hall was much like the ones in Baghavad and Serenity: long wooden tables with benches on both sides, arranged in rows, with a serving line at one end. After five minutes of standing in line, they discovered that the chow was better and more plentiful than at Baghavad, but not as good as at Serenity: black beans, corn tortillas, rice, salsa, watery beer, and fried and pickled jalapeño and serrano chiles. After wolfing down a huge plate of beans and rice, Kel, who had been poking with his fork at the fat green, fried jalapeños on his plate, picked one up gingerly between his thumb and forefinger and looked inquiringly at Chuy. Chuy smiled. "They're good, man. *Múy suave. Múy sabroso.* Really good. Really mild."

With that, Chuy stuck an entire serrano in his mouth, pulled the stem off, tossed the stem onto his plate, chewed the chile up, and swallowed it, finishing it off with a long swig of beer and a sigh of satisfaction. Kel tried to do the same. He got as far as biting down on the chile and starting to chew before his eyes bulged and his face turned red. He spat out the half-chewed chile and started choking before he jumped up and ran toward the restroom. Chuy and several others at the long table laughed, some almost doubling over, but no one came closer or spoke with Chuy. He looked slowly around, then up, noticed a security camera pointing straight at him, and looked away from it, acting as if he hadn't seen it.

A few minutes later a shaken Kel returned.

"You asshole! Why the hell didn't you warn me!?"

"About what?"

"Fuck you, Chuy."

"Why? What'd I do?"

"You know, asshole."

"Cool it man, you got off easy. A few years ago I was eating those damned things and drinking beer, and I got a hay fever attack and rubbed my eyes. That fucking hurt. I had to wash 'em out with soap—three times. Another guy I knew was doing the same thing. He was at this party and was totally *borracho.* He'd been drinking all afternoon and eating serranos fresh off the vine, and he forgot to wash his hands before he took a piss . . ." Chuy started laughing. "He was hopping up and down like this"—Chuy got up and started hopping, grabbing his crotch, mock screaming and laughing uproariously—"and he ended up jumping in the goddamned swimming pool!"

He sat down, picked up another chile, stuck it in his mouth, pulled off the stem, raised his glass of beer toward Kel, mumbled "¡*Salud!*" through a full mouth, and downed his beer and the chile in one gulp. A few seconds later Kel, who had been slugging down beer to quench the fire, put down his empty glass and muttered "Jesus Festering Christ!" as his mouth started burning again; he jumped up from the table frantically searching for more beer. The surrounding workers roared.

The next morning at 6:00 a.m., Kel and Chuy pulled on heavy dungarees, hard hats, and goggles, which they rested on the brims of their hard hats. After a breakfast of fried eggs, tortillas, salsa, and bitter black coffee, they climbed onto the back of an electric flat bed truck with a gang of fellow workers, and within minutes were bouncing up a hill through a beautiful stand of fir trees. They rounded a bend without slowing and ground to a halt in a flat, partially cleared area several acres in size, studded with stumps. It was even uglier than the fir stand had been beautiful.

After the truck stopped, everyone got off. The other workers ignored them, and Kel, looked at Chuy, who seemed equally lost, and then stood around feeling stupid while the others were busily rushing about preparing to do god knows what. Finally, a few minutes after everyone else had wandered off, Stakhanov, who they thought was the foreman, noticed that they were still standing around and walked up to them.

He was an intimidating presence: powerfully built, blond-haired, blue-eyed, and 190-cm tall, a buzz-cut bricklayer in his late twenties with tobacco-stained teeth and fingers, who spoke decent English, and who was puffing on a stogie.

"Comrades! Come with me!" He turned and strode off without waiting for a reply.

They followed him to another truck, and Stakhanov unlocked a compartment on its side. He pulled out two dozen sticks of dynamite, blasting caps, and fuses.

"You know how to use these. Yes?"

Kel and Chuy looked dumbly at the explosives. After an awkward silence, Kel spoke: "No." This was too low tech. He'd never used anything as crude as this.

Stakhanov, chewing on his cigar, said, "Do not worry. Is easy. Is nothing. Is just stumps. That is all. Just stumps. This is fast fuse. Watch." He set down the explosives, cut off a piece of fuse, pushed its end into a blasting cap, and, to Kel's amazement, took his cigar out of his mouth and bit down on the blasting cap, crimping the fuse into its end. He then inserted the cap into the dynamite. He pulled the stogie from between his lips and lit the fuse, displaying it so that they could see how fast it burned, cutting it only when it was less than twelve centimeters from detonating the stick of dynamite, laughing at the petrified looks on Kel's and Chuy's faces.

He tossed the still-burning fuse to the ground, picked up the explosives, handed them to Chuy, and pointed to a shovel on the truck. Kel picked it up, and Stakhanov led them into the stump-studded clearing. As they walked, the whine of chainsaws filled the air, rising and falling in pitch as saws started, stopped, screeched, smoked, revved, and bit into living wood, with workers felling tree after tree at the edge of the clearing and other workers cutting off branches from the fallen trees. In counterpoint, a grinding, metallic sound came from the treaded tractor that was hauling off the logs. Fifteen minutes after work had begun, the entire clearing was swathed in a haze of blue smoke from the two-stroke saw motors.

Kel, Chuy and Stakhanov stopped as they came to a large stump at the edge of the clearing, well away from the other workers. Stakhanov pointed to it.

"Start here, comrades. Dig under. Then place dynamite. One stick. For socialism!"

And he walked off.

Kel looked at Chuy in disbelief, hesitated for a few seconds, and then started digging, gradually shoveling out a cavity beneath the stump.

Five minutes later, Chuy nervously inserted a fuse into a cap, crimped it with his teeth before inserting the cap into the stick of dynamite, stuck the dynamite under the stump, and packed mud around it. As Kel gaped, he lit the fuse, jumped up, and began running like hell. After a fraction of a second, Kel followed him.

They huddled behind another stump as the dynamite went off with a loud whump!, sending the stump and clods of mud flying into the air. The stump landed with a dull thud a few meters from them, while dirt and pebbles rained down on top of them. Seconds later, after the ringing from the blast had died away, the rising and falling whines and screeches of the chainsaws faded back in, and they got slowly to their feet, brushing off the dirt that had fallen on them.

They were still gawking at the hole the blast had created when Stakhanov reappeared.

"Well?"

Chuy, clearly irritated, replied, "Well, what?"

"Well get to work! Haul off stump!" He gestured toward a snag pile fifty meters away. "There is rope in truck. Haul!"

He stalked off, and Kel walked off in the opposite direction, returning a couple of minutes later with a ten-meter length of thick hemp rope. They wrapped it around the stump and pulled it over the rough ground to the snag pile. Then they took the rope, shovel, dynamite, blasting caps, and fuses, and moved on to the next stump.

At the mess hall that evening, and later in the barracks, the other workers continued to keep their distance, watching them with distrust. It didn't help that two nights later security troops arrived in the middle of the night and hauled off Caguama, one of their barracks mates. What was almost worse than the intrusion was that the victim didn't struggle, didn't scream, just slumped and walked off dejectedly, his arms pinioned by his captors, as Kel, Chuy, and the other workers watched from their bunks, pretending that they were still asleep.

* * *

Three days later, the stumps were burning along with the rest of the debris in the snag piles at the edge of the clearing, and a thick grey haze hung over the work site. But the ground was leveled and the first footings had been poured for what looked to be a massive structure. Kel was hod carrying for Stakhanov, who was setting bricks at a frenzied pace on the west wall of a partially finished outbuilding. Stakhanov had just run out of mortar and was frantically looking for his hod carrier, Kel. But Kel was exhausted, and disgusted—the wheelbarrow he was using had a partially flat wheel, making his job agonizingly difficult. He had just gotten a fresh batch of mortar and was staggering around the outbuilding's corner when Stakhanov saw him and began yelling from a dozen meters away: "Mud! Where is my mud?!"

Kel yelled in return, as he was approaching, "Here! What's the rush?!"

Stakhanov yelled back, louder than ever: "Socialism, comrade! We build socialism! A rush there always is!"

Kel gaped at the crazy Russian and almost dumped the eighty kilos of mortar he was pushing along the uneven path as he strained to push the barrow over the minute rises impeding its nearly flattened front wheel. He set it down next to Stakhanov, sighed with relief, and without saying a word took the empty wheelbarrow Stakhanov had been working from and began running with it back toward the cement mixer.

As he was rushing, handles in hand, toward the mixer, he muttered to himself, "Socialism. . . . Building fucking socialism!"

As he said this, another hod carrier who had overseen the entire episode, and who could apparently read lips—a salt-and-pepper-haired, bearded, heavily muscled man in his early fifties, but going to fat, and with long, curly gray hair and a wild beard—approached pushing a wheelbarrow of mortar up the path. He looked closely at Kel, looked up at Stakhanov, and started to laugh. When they were nearly parallel, he slowed and said, in a heavy Russian accent, "I see you have met my friend, comrade blockhead!" He laughed hysterically and trudged on, not waiting for a reply and not looking back.

25

Only fools can believe that Communism is possible in Russia," was
Lenin's reply to opponents of the new economic policy.
As a matter of fact, Lenin was right. True Communism
was never attempted in Russia, unless one considers thirty-three
categories of pay, different food rations, privileges to some
and indifference to the mass as Communism.

—Emma Goldman, *My Further Disillusionment in Russia*

Kel, Chuy, and Mikel, the hod carrier Kel had passed the day before, and who had invited himself to join them, were taking their
lunch break the following day, sitting on stumps and a downed
log at the edge of the clearing; they sat silently for several minutes,
eating chorizo and onion sandwiches, and drinking coffee, before
Kel asked Mikel, "What's up with Stakhanov? You guys seem real
friendly, but you call him a blockhead. What's up with that?"

Mikel smiled, but looked around before replying. "Stakhanov?
Is not obvious? He thinks I am his friend, and in way I am. But the
man is blockhead. He means well, but is blockhead.

"I see you first day here. Stupid ass shows you how to blow off
head." Mikel mimed inserting a fuse into a blasting cap and crimping it with his teeth. "Is stupid. Very stupid. Here is how to do." He
began miming again, inserting the fuse and then putting his hands
behind his back, making squeezing gestures. "Crimp with . . .
how you say?" He made the squeezing gesture again and looked
imploringly at both of them.

Kel ventured, "Pliers?"

"Yes. Pliers. Like this." Mikel mimed putting a fuse into a cap,
putting a pliers around the end of the cap, and then stuck his hand
behind him and mimed crimping with the imaginary pliers. "Will
blow off ass, not blow off head!"

He laughed, and so did Kel and Chuy.

"The, how you say, poor asshole shows you how to blow off head." He laughed again.

After a pause, Chuy asked, "What about Caguama? What'd he do? Some political shit?"

Mikel looked at him slantwise for a few seconds before replying. "No. Stole building materials. Sold on black market." He hesitated a few seconds. "Political talk, they tolerate, but they watch. As long as no action, no organizing, they watch. But more talk, more they watch. Talk okay as long as no effect, no action. Gives illusion of freedom. Is way for people to blow off steam. Also way for state to keep track. So, talk they tolerate. But action? Organizing? RPF, if lucky."

They both looked questioningly at Mikel.

"Re-education Project Force."

* * *

The next day they were taking lunch again, following a harangue by Stakhanov on the need to build socialism more quickly.

Chuy looked at Mikel and asked, "Does comrade blockhead ever let up? Is he always like this?"

"Yes, is always like this. Dumb ass really thinks we build socialism."

Kel replied, "We're not?"

Mikel's smile faded, and he looked closely at Kel, and then shifted his gaze toward Chuy. Chuy, who in turn had been closely studying Mikel, chimed in quietly, "No. We are not. This is not socialism."

Mikel, who had been unconsciously holding his breath, let it out as Kel asked, "Then what are we building?"

Mikel smiled maliciously, looked to his left and right, gestured toward the unfinished building with his outstretched hand, and said, "The people's palace! The palace that is a shrine to the people! The new palace for Comrade Modelo!"

* * *

After a less than enthusiastic afternoon of building socialism, Kel, Chuy, and Mikel were sitting on the back of a flatbed as it bounced and ground away from the construction site. Stakhanov was sitting a few feet away from them, his back to the cab, on a coil of rope. He pulled out a quarter-liter bottle of vodka from his back pocket, took a long hit off it, shook his head, shuddered, took another, and handed the bottle to Kel.

Kel was about to take a slug when the truck hit a bump as it passed a line of men clumsily running along the side of the road. They were dressed in dirty blue coveralls and were carrying shovels, picks, and sledge hammers. The bottle clinked off Kel's teeth, and vodka splashed on his chin and shirt. Kel sputtered and then did a double take as he noticed that the men had ankle chains, were shackled together at the wrist, and were being herded by grey-uniformed minders with bullwhips. One of the prisoners was Caguama, the worker who had disappeared in the middle of the night a few days earlier.

Kel gestured with the bottle toward the blue-clad men, who were already receding in the distance, enveloped in the dust the flatbed had kicked up.

One had lost his footing, and upon stumbling to the ground pulled the rest of the line down with him. One of the minders immediately hit the prisoner who had fallen with a single lash to the man's back. He screamed. And then the other guards began cracking their whips in the air until the prisoners were back on their feet and had started running again. Even at a quarter-kilometer's distance, Kel easily heard the snap of the whips and the struck man's scream of pain over the road noise. Kel looked uneasily at Stakhanov and asked:

"What the fuck!? Who are those guys?"

Stakhanov answered, "Members of RPF, Re-education Project Force. Level Two. Deviationists and criminal elements. Re-education through honest labor and study of techno-scientific socialism. Parasites and destructive elements they were, but productive members of society they will be, productive members building socialism!"

"But why the whips? The shackles? The running?"

"To remind them that they have much time lost, that they have much ground to make up. Is for own good."

At this, Mikel, who had turned away from Stakhanov, almost choked. He lifted his fist to his mouth and bit it to stop himself from laughing out loud.

Kel turned his attention back to the bottle. He wiped off the lip with his hand, took a long slug, shuddered, wiped his mouth with the back of his sleeve, took another hit, and feeling the warmth spreading through his body said, "Damn I'm glad this week is over!"

Chuy replied, "I'll be gladder when you pass the goddamned bottle."

Kel handed it to him and Chuy said, after a long slug, "I'm dead beat," as he handed the rapidly dwindling bottle to Mikel.

Stakhanov, smiling and energetic, piped up, "Yes, tonight we rest. Tomorrow we hear speech of Comrade Modelo in Moncada Square!"

Kel snuck a sideways glance at Mikel, who lifted his eyebrows just before Kel said, "I'm too damned tired for that."

Stakhanov's face tightened as he replied, "Everyone goes. Is revolutionary duty!"

Mikel, not entirely managing to suppress a chuckle, added, "Duty and privilege, comrade! Duty and privilege!"

Chuy reached for the bottle, took a hit, raised it, and echoed Mikel: "A duty and a privilege, comrades! A duty and a privilege!" He handed the bottle back to Mikel, who in turn took a long slug from it, raised it above his head, and said, "Probst! To building of socialism!" A second later, he took another slug, which almost instantly came shooting out of his mouth and nostrils, as he choked and sputtered while trying to keep himself from laughing out loud.

* * *

Saturday morning, Kel was lying on his bunk after breakfast as the barracks emptied. Soon, he and the equally sacked-out Chuy were almost the only ones left in the building. The clock on the wall read 9:20 as Stakhanov entered and walked purposefully toward them, exhorting them as he approached, "Comrades, hurry! Comrade Modelo speaks in less than hour! Hurry we must!"

Kel, hungover, his head and body aching, groaned as he sat up on the side of his bunk. Chuy grunted and pushed himself off his mattress like an old man whose every move hurt, as Stakhanov hovered anxiously over them. As soon as they had put on their boots, Stakhanov said "hurry" and headed for the door. No footsteps followed, so he stopped in the doorway and looked back to see them still sitting on the sides of their bunks. Stakhanov raised his voice and said, "Must come! Follow! Take water!" He waited impatiently as they slowly rousted themselves and grabbed their canteens.

As Kel went through the barracks door, a blast of heat slammed into his face. He nearly staggered backwards. It was the hottest day since he'd arrived on Tau II.

He and Chuy trudged after Stakhanov, and soon were staring at his rapidly receding back as he rushed through block after block of nearly identical grey cement apartment buildings, distinguishable only by the portraits on their sides, the streets empty but for other stragglers doing their best to avoid standing out, scrupulously avoiding looking up at the cameras. When Kel and Chuy arrived at the parade grounds, workers, bureaucrats, party members, and police were all frantically aligning themselves in evidently pre-arranged order.

Kel would have been totally lost but for Stakhanov, who had waited at the edge of the crowd, nervously pacing back and forth, and who knew exactly where they should be. Soon, they found themselves standing in an almost military formation with the other members of the Construction Cooperative. Workers from the other industries were standing in rank upon rank of similar formations, behind ranks of lower echelon party members, police, and bureaucrats. The upper echelons were sitting on unshaded bleachers on either side of the elevated, covered speaker's platform. It was only mid-morning, but it was already 35 degrees, and those standing in place were sweating heavily.

The crowd was humming with whispered conversations as ten o'clock approached. When it arrived, the murmuring gradually died out until the huge crowd was nearly silent. And then they waited. Until 10:05. Until 10:10. Until 10:15. Even though the minutes were only 49 E-seconds long, it still felt like forever to Kel. His head was pounding, and he was already longing for his bunk. At

10:20, Modelo, bearing only a passing resemblance to the idealized portrait in Asahi's office, a grotesquely fat man in his 50s, sweating profusely, with a pencil-thin black mustache, pock-marked complexion, and wearing baggy fatigues, waddled onto the shaded speaker's platform. He rested his sausage-like arms and a fair amount of his body weight on the lectern, and beamed out at the crowd. At his appearance, the crowd began applauding and cheering wildly. They continued to applaud and cheer for fully five minutes, with Kel and Chuy reluctantly joining in, until Modelo raised a pudgy hand to quiet them. After a dramatic pause, he began to speak in Spanish: "*Estimados compañeros*" . . . He paused and then continued in only mildly accented English, still the international, now the interstellar, *lingua franca*:

"Comrades, workers, and we your servants, the people's police, and the people's services administration, we are very proud of the great works we have accomplished through our heroic sacrifices for socialism. In the last year alone, production of electricity has risen twenty-seven per cent; production of timber nineteen per cent; production of potatoes seventeen per cent; production of bricks twenty-three per cent; and carrots a full thirty-three per cent! And all this in the face of the opposition of not only the imperialist controllers of this planet, but also the opposition of internal fascism. Despite these obstacles, we have seized all these gains for this, our socialist homeland, La Nueva Habana!" He swept his right arm from right to left and waited expectantly until the crowd realized it was supposed to applaud, and did so. When the applause died down, he continued, "We did this not only in the face of imperialist opposition, but also the opposition of the religious obscurantists who surround us and their agents who bore like termites into the healthy heartwood of our society! But these vermin are swept aside like the insects they are by the revolutionary fervor of our heroic people, a fervor which has never wavered! Because of this, we have exceeded production quotas in cement by thirty-two per cent this year alone . . ."

After a few minutes of this, Kel zoned out. He focused what was left of his attention on stopping himself from swaying or, worse, collapsing, while he paid attention to Modelo only as one would to the drone of an insistent mosquito. Occasionally, Kel's ears registered bits of Modelo's monologue, floating in and out as un-connected, stream-of-consciousness fragments: "This objectively counter revolutionary, decadent, petit bourgeois, so-called freedom of speech . . ." ". . . blood-sucking *capitalistas, imperialistas* . . ." ". . . we must unleash . . ." ". . . smash . . ." ". . . hands off . . ." ". . . workers party . . ." ". . . deviationist running dogs! . . ." ". . . white privileged bourgeois middle class . . ." ". . . liberated zone . . ." ". . . continue to build socialism in the face of . . ."

* * *

Three hours later the temperature was over 40 degrees and Kel was swaying, close to collapsing, his canteen long emptied, almost too dazed to notice the dozen or so workers in the surrounding ranks who had fallen to the ground. Their fellows ignored them, focusing their attention—or at least trying to maintain the appear-ance of doing so—on The Beloved Comrade.

Modelo took a long drink of ice water and continued droning on as Kel, and the rest of the wobbling, dehydrated ranks attempt-ed to maintain the appearance of interest: ". . . decadent, counter-revolutionary puppets . . ." ". . . revisionists . . ." ". . . enemies of the people . . ." ". . . stooges of the objectively reactionary ultra-left deviationists . . ."

Modelo paused and emptied his glass of ice water, which was immediately refilled by a cringing man dressed in a brown uni-form identical to that of Modelo, minus the five-star epaulets and the chestful of medals. Kel didn't notice. It had all become a blur, words floating in and out, totally divorced from any meaning. It was like listening on bad drugs to a bad jam band hammering an endless two-chord riff into the ground.

As Kel swayed, nearly blacking out, Modelo found his second wind and began nearly shouting what were by now, to Kel, inco-herent phrases: ". . . smashed by the people's heroic vanguard, the people's liberation police . . ." ". . . the party and the people, as one . . ." ". . . we, your servants . . ."

More members of the audience collapsed as Modelo, becoming ever more heated, and gesturing ever more emphatically, continued: ". . . this infantile concept, this product of trade union consciousness . . ." ". . . these stooges, these puppets, these running dogs of inter-stellar neo-colonialism . . ." ". . . these deviationist stooges . . ." ". . . when the still-oppressed peoples rise against these bourgeois parasites . . ." . . . until, with his voice rising and his gestures becoming ever more emphatic, as the sun hung in the afternoon sky, he concluded: "The revolutionary justice of the people's democratic dictatorship will smash to pieces the fascist insect which sucks the blood of the people! *¡¡Venceremos!!*"

Modelo stopped, waited expectantly, and those still standing applauded as vigorously as they could. For five full minutes, growing louder as they regained full consciousness, no one daring to stop, with some of those who had collapsed staggering to their feet and rejoining them in the applause. They continued until Modelo graciously waved his hand for them to cease, bowed his head, and pumped his fist in the air. After holding that posture for what seemed like a full minute, while the applause swelled again, he lumbered off the platform, down the steps, and into his air-conditioned limo, a heavily modified farm truck.

Chuy, who was still standing, helped Kel get up, and they tottered off the field, back toward the Construction Cooperative barracks, leaning on each other. The rest of the audience wasn't in much better shape. The one apparent exception was Stakhanov, who had joined Kel and Chuy. He was beaming. He turned back, his eyes fixed on Modelo's retreating vehicle until it vanished. He pulled out the ever-present bottle from his back pocket, raised it and shouted: "*¡Viva el líder máximo! ¡Viva el socialismo! ¡Un discurso magnífico! ¡Salud!*"

26

Work is the curse of the drinking class.

—Oscar Wilde

On Monday morning, as the sun was rising, the wake-up bell rang. Kel was lying on top of his bunk, still in his clothes. Since he'd quit drinking early the previous evening and had slept for nearly ten hours, he felt good, but he was ravenous. Chuy was still in his bunk, one boot-clad foot sticking out from under his blanket and over the side of his bunk, and one arm clamping his pillow over his head.

Kel sat up, reached over, and shook Chuy's arm, cheerfully announcing the day with, "*¡Levantate compañero!*," which came perilously close to using up his stock of multi-syllable Spanish words.

Chuy, who had stayed up way later, and so had drunk way more than Kel, growled sleepily, "*¡Chupa la verga!*" Kel pretended not to know what that meant and shook Chuy's arm again, adding brightly and a bit maliciously, "Come on! Get up! *¡Levantate!* Time to eat! It's a beautiful day!"

When Chuy still didn't move, Kel lifted the pillow, and Chuy looked out at him with a half-open, bloodshot eye. Kel insisted, "*¡Levantate cabrón!*" to which Chuy managed a weak, "Fuck off," before pulling the pillow back over his head.

When Kel shook him yet again, Chuy lifted the pillow off his head, glared at Kel, and said, "Get the hell out of here, asshole! Lemme be!" and clamped the pillow back down.

Kel tried again, this time without shaking Chuy. "C'mon! You're gonna miss breakfast. You need to eat. We have to be at work in an hour."

"Fuck off!"

As Kel was getting up, he gave Chuy's arm a squeeze; Chuy told Kel to go fuck himself, and Kel was off. He was sitting alone in the mess hall, with no one else near, halfway through his plate of chilaquiles and his second cup of coffee, when he heard a bus pull up outside. Mikel was the first through the chow hall's door. Several other workers who had caught a ride from town followed him inside. As Mikel grabbed a tray and glanced around, Kel waved at him, and he joined Kel after he was served.

Mikel, as usual, was in good humor. As he was sitting down, he asked, almost bubbling over, "A great speech? No?"

"Yeah. Almost as good as these chilaquiles." Kel looked down at his plate of stale, fried corn tortilla strips covered with the local versions of cheese and salsa.

"A true paving stone on path to socialism," Mikel chuckled. Without waiting for a reply, he scooped up and began munching a huge pile of chilaquiles, washing them down with mouthfuls of black coffee, the slopover trickling down through his beard.

Kel asked, "What's on the agenda today?"

Still chewing, Mikel replied, "What else comrade? Building socialism!"

"Seriously."

Mikel snuck a swift upward glance up toward the camera. He swallowed and wiped the back of his hand across his mouth. "We finish foundation for main building this week. Is good. Means, maybe, bonus and half-day off."

* * *

They finished the foundation on Friday, a half-day before schedule. The only damper was that security had shown up at noon and had hauled away in handcuffs one of their coworkers, Olaf, who had been notable only for his extreme reticence to discuss anything.

On the way back from the site, Mikel pulled out a half-liter bottle of vodka as the flatbed bounced down the road.

"To job well done! Probst!"

He took a long hit and handed the bottle to Stakhanov, who took an equally long slug.

"Probst!"

He handed it to Kel, who raised it toward his mouth. The truck hit a rut, and Stakhanov and Mikel laughed uproariously as the bottle clinked against Kel's front teeth and vodka splashed over his face and shirt. Kel wiped his face with his sleeve, took a hit, and passed on the bottle.

As it came back to him, Stakhanov said, "Tomorrow we work half day. Then Mikel and I show you good time. You work good. You work hard. You deserve good time."

* * *

Early the next afternoon, still sore after unloading all of the timber for the framing of the people's palace, the crew piled onto a flatbed and headed back toward the barracks.

After they had showered, eaten, and drunk a few beers while playing penny-ante poker, Kel, Chuy, Mikel, and Stakhanov took a shuttle bus to the center of New Havana. It was less than an hour before dark as Mikel mumbled an excuse and got off at the fourth stop. Kel and Chuy looked quizzically at each other, and then at Stakhanov, who was chuckling as Mikel stepped off the bus. "His wife! Mid-level comrade! Must report!" Stakhanov mock saluted and laughed out loud.

The bus rolled on. Ten minutes later it arrived at the ramadas and benches that comprised New Havana's bus terminal, which sat on the bank of the city's ten-meter-wide "river." From there, it was a short walk to an apartment-block basement that had been converted into a bar. At the entrance, a slab of beef with a sleeves-removed T-shirt and buzz cut took their money and ushered them inside. The interior was vast. The bar took up the entire basement.

In contrast to the drab, unpainted exterior, the interior was a riot of colors. There were full-color posters of Modelo, Castro, Kim Jong Il, and other revolutionary heroes, murals depicting the battle of Stalingrad, the attack on the Moncada barracks, and the liberation of Tegucigalpa. One wall was even devoted to an aviary, an enclosure easily six meters wide by fifty meters long, lit by warm, fluorescent lights, and filled with plants, small trees, and parrots. Green parrots with yellow heads and napes; huge blue parrots with gold breasts and massive black beaks; grey parrots with red and maroon tails; and white parrots with wicked looking grey beaks and fanning head crests. How in hell had they gotten parrots here? Gene banks and favors called in? Who knew?

Most of the parrots were screaming, and the noise was so intense that Kel wondered how a band could be heard over it. Then he looked toward the front wall and saw the stage and the racks of speakers.

The band was just beginning to set up as he, Chuy, and Stakhanov moved near to the front and sat down at a round wooden table. As soon as they were seated, a waiter approached.

Kel tried to order a rum and coke, but the waiter recoiled.

Stakhanov quickly ordered for all of them—"¡*Cervezas pa' todos!*"—and then explained to Kel, "Coca-Cola is bourgeois deviation. Do not again order. Creates wrong impression, and we do not even have. No rum. No coke. Sugarcane does not grow. Wrong climate. On coastal plain, yes. Here, no."

Chuy looked at him. "Tequila?"

"Tequila, yes. Beer, vodka, whisky, rye, yes. Rum, no. And wine? Bourgeois bullshit. Could grow, but do not."

Their beers arrived, and Stakhanov was downing his when Kel asked him, "Why did the founders come here? To this cold climate?"

"Cold? Is warm."

Chuy chimed in, "No choice. Earth-gov put all of the settlements down more or less in a row about equal distances apart. At least a hundred, two hundred klicks between 'em. Wanted to minimize conflict. Some got lucky, like Baghavad, which is warm, on the coast, and east of the mountains. Some weren't so lucky, like New Havana. Twelve hundred meters high and on the windward side. So no rum, but plenty of pines and rain."

While they were slugging down their second beers, Mikel arrived. Stakhanov smirked and asked, "The boss, how is she?"

Mikel exploded. "¡*Vete a la chingada!*" and they were off and running, shouting at one other in Russian, Spanish, and English, then laughing, and then shouting some more.

While they were chewing on each other, Kel turned his attention to the stage. The set-up looked solid enough, but even more antiquated than the gear they'd used in New M: huge, black-grilled

speakers—no flat radiators here—and rectangular monitor speakers tilted back, aimed upward, resting on cinder blocks. There were
also a guitar amp and a bass amp of unknown make, both of which
were large and looked heavy. Plus a drum kit on a short riser at the
back of the stage: a 22-inch kick drum, a snare, two mounted toms,
two floor toms, and more cymbals than anyone should rightfully
have: a hi-hat, two rides, two crashes, a splash, and even a sizzle,
with rivets popping through it. To top it all off, there was a cowbell
on a bracket on one of the cymbal stands, a pair of timbales off to
the side on another stand, and it looked like the guy even had a
foot pedal hooked up to a pair of claves. After he checked out the
drum set, Kel nodded at it and said to Chuy, "We'll see."

They were on their third beers when the band members began
wandering on stage, desultorily took out their instruments, and
began experimentally blowing and plucking notes as they tuned
up. It was a large band: bass, drums, guitar, keyboards, two sax
players, a trombone player, two trumpet players, and a conga player with a table full of hand percussion instruments next to him,
which he was arranging carefully: claves, güiro, maracas, cuica,
cowbell, flexatone, and a couple of others that Kel didn't recognize. When everyone had tuned up and it was relatively quiet, one
of the sax players stepped out in front for the sound check. He
said, "¡Moncada!," and the band broke into a fast version of the
standard descending Am-G-F-E Latin riff, with a piano montuno
pattern driving the whole thing. After eight bars, the guitar player,
who stood facing the band with his back to the crowd, flattened
his hand horizontally and emphatically drew it across his throat in
the universal "cut" gesture, and then yelled, "¡*Corta!*" He walked
over to the control board at the side of the stage and adjusted two
of the sliders.

While he was walking back to the front of the stage, Kel, after
signaling to the waiter for more beers, observed to Chuy, "Can't
hear the guitar and the keys are too loud."

The guitar player, facing the other musicians, said, "¡*Otra vez!*,"
counted "*un, dos, tres, cuatro*" and the band broke into the same
tune. This time the keys were still too loud, and the guitar player
made the "cut" gesture after only four bars. The band stopped, and

he went to the control board. When he returned and had them start again, the mix was right. He signaled "cut!" for the third time after another four bars, walked back to his place on the side of the stage, adjusted the position of his vocal mike, leaned into it, and said, "*¡Homenaje al materialismo dialéctico!*"

He counted off four again, "*Un . . . dos . . . Un, dos, tres, cuatro,*" and the band broke into a fast, horn-driven tune. The band was so loud that Kel couldn't even hear the parrots, much less Stakhanov and Mikel, who were now nearly in each other's faces, still shouting at each other and laughing.

After the song wrapped up, Chuy leaned over and said to Kel, "What was that, a Guaganco?"

"How should I know? I was never into that Afro-Cuban shit."

"Never mind. These mothers can really pl—"

The guitar player bent over his mike and cut off their conversation with a loud, "Our next tune will be another original. It's called, '*¡Muerte a los contrarevolucionarios!*'"

* * *

The next morning, Kel woke shortly after dawn, still fully clothed, on top of his bunk, his head pounding. He glanced over at Chuy and saw that Chuy, also fully clad, had managed to pull the pillow over his head, but that he was stirring fitfully. Kel crawled back in under his blanket, pulled his pillow back over his head, closed his aching eyes, and spent most of the day in his bunk, alternately sleeping and suffering.

He and Chuy emerged only after sundown for some hair-of-the-dog action in the barracks rec area before returning to their bunks and blessed oblivion. It could have been worse. Thanks to the weeks of hard work and decent food, they were both in the best shape they'd been in since they were in the army.

* * *

On Monday morning, they were up, bright and chipper, eating a local favorite, *huevos fritos con papas fritas*, in the mess hall, when Mikel joined them.

"*¡Buenos días! ¿Como estan?*"

Kel replied, "Better than yesterday."

Mikel laughed. "A fun night, no?"

"What I remember of it."

Mikel laughed again as Kel asked, "What was with the music? It sounded great, but what was with those stupid titles?"

Mikel arched an eyebrow toward the surveillance camera overhead and said, "We need to eat. Work is soon. We talk of other things later, when is more time."

They finished breakfast ten minutes before the trucks were scheduled to leave, so they refilled their coffee cups and walked outside, heading down a trail behind the mess hall. Twenty meters down the path they sat down on a grouping of rounded stones.

Mikel was the first to speak. "Yes, the music is good. But it does not challenge Modelo. That is why he tolerates it. No vocals. And ass-kissing titles: '*Los martires del Partido Comunista Cubano*,' '*¡Che!*' '*¡Fidel!*' '*Raúl—el simpático hermano del pueblo*,' '*Himno al líder máximo*,' . . . *¡Que mierda!* . . . What shit! . . . '*¿Los comités en defensa de la revolución?*'" He wrinkled his face in disgust thinking about the network of neighborhood spies, and spat out. " '*¡Los comités en defensa del régimen!*'

"The musicians, they want to play. So, they give their songs these stupid titles. These ass-kissing titles. Some think that music itself is revolution. They really think music itself wakes people up. What *pendejos*!" He shook his head.

Kel wasn't through. "Why the hell do they put up with it!? For that matter, why do people put up with all the cops, cameras, and fences? We're in the middle of nowhere. What's the point!?"

Mikel laughed. "Is for own protection! From deviationists, spies, reactionary elements who would crush peoples' revolution. Is danger. Always danger. And always fear. And people *want* to believe."

27

No, Well, Not Much of an Exit

The following evening after work, while waiting for the chow line to open, Kel was sitting on a fallen log and Chuy was sitting on a rock in a clearing off one of the paths leading into the woods behind the barracks. They were talking in low voices as a figure, unheard and unnoticed, stepped off the path into the shadows a few feet from them, and stopped to listen.

Chuy's voice was low but emphatic: "There's no way. You've seen that electric fence—make that fences!—and there're probably booby traps between them. Maybe even mines."

"Give me a break! They don't even have guns. Is the fence even electrified? And they're gonna booby trap what? A hundred klicks of fence?"

"Maybe they did. Maybe they didn't. Maybe there aren't any traps. But we don't know that. And if there are, where are they? Maybe they don't electrify the fences. But do you want to bet your life on it? And, assuming they do, how are we gonna get through three electric fences?"

"Insulated shoes, gloves and bolt cutters?"

"You want to bet your life on it?"

"There's gotta be a way out of here! It's worse than living in Phoenix! Always looking over your shoulder. Always being careful about what you say, who you say it to."

"Yeah, it sucks. But let's wait. We'll find a way out. Let's not do something stupid and get ourselves killed or stuck in the RPF."

"We're living in a goddamned barracks, working more than full time, and building a palace for that asshole Modelo . . . How much worse can it get?"

"A lot worse."

"There's gotta be a way out of here. Maybe Mikel knows something."

"Mikel?"

"Yeah, Mikel."

"Can we even trust him?"

Before Kel could answer, the figure in the shadows stepped into the open. Kel and Chuy looked up, their mouths hanging open, as Mikel sat down on a rock next to Kel's. After a deliberate pause, he said, "Yes, you can trust. And yes, there is way. Stakhanov is on watch duty at yard tomorrow night. As you know, vodka he likes. Here is what we—"

Chuy cut him off. "What's with this 'we'? You coming with us?"

"No."

"Why not? If you hate it here so much, why not?"

Mikel grunted. "Is fair question. When I was young, I believed. I believed really. My wife, she believes still. Very much. I love her, so I stay." He shrugged.

After a long pause, Chuy asked, "So what do we do?"

* * *

The next evening, Kel, Chuy, and Mikel were sitting at a table in the construction barracks' rec room, an addition still under construction with bare studs and bare rafters—so no surveillance cameras—and with a two-liter bottle of vodka and half-full shot glasses before them, playing penny-ante poker. Kel had just won a hand of seven-card stud, and had raised his glass in salute as Stakhanov walked into the barracks. Chuy waved his drink and motioned for Stakhanov to join them. "¡Compañero, juntanos!" Stakhanov smiled and said "Da! I do watch duty in hour. But one does not hurt!" He walked over and sat down. Mikel got up, walked to a cabinet along the nearest wall, and made a show of looking for another shot glass. He returned with a water glass, which he set on the table before Stakhanov. Stakhanov looked at it in surprise, and then in satisfaction, as Mikel poured four fingers of vodka into it.

Stakhanov held it up to the nearest light, stared at it a second, lowered it, and said, "One only. Tonight I do guard duty." He slugged half of it down in one gulp, looked at his comrades, and spoke. "Is good to finish people's palace, no? He raised his glass again in a toast and said, "Chtob vse byli zdorovy!" and clinked his glass against Mikel's. Mikel returned the toast in Spanish: "¡*Salud!*" Stakhanov nearly drained what was left in his glass as the others downed their half-full shot glasses.

Stakhanov reached into his pocket and pulled out a handful of change. He dropped it onto the table, took a long sip of what was left of his drink, and then carefully separated his coins into piles. Mikel dealt a hand of five-card stud, which Kel won.

Mikel passed the deck to Kel. Chuy picked up the bottle and started to add a bit to Stakhanov's glass, as Stakhanov waved him off and said, "No more." Chuy, bottle still in hand hovering over Stakhanov's glass, said, "Just *un poco más*," and when Stakhanov said, "Okay, *un poco*," Chuy added almost three fingers, and then filled his, Kel's and Mikel's shot glasses three-quarters full. He raised his glass and looked at the others.

"To comrade Modelo!" Mikel, Kel, and Chuy chugged their 20-cc shots as Stakhanov downed half of his 100-cc shot. Chuy immediately called out "¡*Otro!*" and refilled the glasses.

Kel called a game of four-four-four with an ante of four, and as he was dealing Mikel asked, "What in hell is this?"

Kel replied, as he rapid fired cards, "Four up, four down, fours wild." Stakhanov won the comparatively large pot, raised his glass, said "¡*Salud!*" and took another slug.

Chuy poured two fingers into his, Mikel's, and Kel's shot glasses, and poured another two fingers into Stakhanov's water glass. Chuy raised his shot glass and looked at the others at the table and said, "¡*Salud!*" They downed their slugs of vodka almost simultaneously.

Mikel, obviously enjoying himself, filled their glasses again, turned toward Stakhanov and said, "Imperialism lives comrades! Imperialism lives! As does the need for permanent revolution! Institutional, permanent, state revolution! ¡*Muerte al imperialismo!*" He raised his glass and toasted, "To the people's state! To the people's state that is the will of the people! To the party that is the will of the people! To transubstantiation!" Kel, and Chuy, trying not to laugh, spilled their drinks and sputtered out what they hadn't spilled, as Stakhanov, who was already so far gone that he took the toast at face value, chugged the rest of his vodka. He looked at his comrades and smiled woozily, raising his now-empty glass. Mikel immediately refilled it nearly half full and nudged Kel, who in turn nudged Chuy under the table. Mikel looked at Stakhanov, raised his empty shot glass and said, "*¡Salud!*" while pointing with his eyes toward the door.

Chuy took the hint and, after "downing" an empty glass, looked at Stakhanov and said, "Comrades! *Volveremos pronto.*"

Stakhanov, looked up at them with a dull smile on his face, lifted his glass, and downed most of its contents in a gulp. He shuddered before looking at the half-full bottle sitting on the table. He said nothing more as he fumbled for it and filled his glass to the brim.

* * *

Boris and Arkady were already up, providing enough light for navigation. Kel led the way, semi-blitzed and stumbling, through the pines along a narrow path from the barracks toward the construction yard, a barbed wire fenced enclosure of sheds and metal barns, with a guard shack at the gate. Chuy was carrying a food pack wrapped in a sheet, containing food they'd saved from their dinner plus some that Mikel had brought from town that morning. When they reached the yard, all of the lights in and on the guard shack were off, and the barbed-wire gate next to it was chained at its end to the last post in the fence. But whoever had chained it shut had been sloppy, and there was some play in the chain. Kel pushed on the gate, and it moved twenty centimeters. He pushed harder and it moved a few more. While still straining against it, he said to Chuy, "Come on. Let's go."

Chuy, barely able to see the gate and the fence post, tried to inch his way through the gap without ripping himself on the barbs as Kel pushed on the gate. Chuy didn't succeed. A barb gouged into his abdomen, and he said, "Shit!" Then he was through and pulling hard as Kel squeezed through, gouging himself on both his back and stomach.

As they walked across the gravel-covered yard, Kel felt blood soaking the front of his ripped shirt, put his fingers on the stain, and whispered, "Fuck!" He was drunk enough that he wanted someone else to blame for his pain. Mikel, drinking vodka with Stakhanov back in the barracks, immediately came to mind. While wiping his bloody hand on the back of his pants, he said hotly, "Fucking Mikel! Did that asshole set us up?"

Chuy hissed "Shhh!" and added, "No, he didn't. Mikel's a good guy, and he has a good reason for staying here. He has a wife. Family."

"Have you ever met her?"

"No."

"Jesus Festering Christ!"

"Cool out! It's okay, man. Seriously. We haven't been set up."

"I don't like it. I don't like this plan much eith—"

"It's a little late to think of that now."

Kel wasn't deterred. "Even if we can get one of these stupid-ass flatbeds started, can we make it to the perimeter without being stopped? Will it make it through the fences? And even if it does, will it make it across open country back to the main road?"

They arrived at the trucks, and Kel checked the first one. No luck: the keys were missing. The same with the others. All of the drivers had evidently followed s.o.p. and turned in their keys.

After they finished checking the trucks, they walked across the yard toward the tool shed that held the key cabinet. Kel pushed the door open and peered inside. Dim shafts of light from Boris and Arkady slanted down toward the floor from the building's one small window. He walked across the threshold and onto the dirt floor, felt to the right of the door and found the key cabinet. It was secured by a padlock. Kel said, "Shit! We need a bolt cutter or a crowbar," and walked farther into the shed with Chuy close behind, feeling around the free-standing, two-meter-high metal shelves for the tools they needed. A half-dozen meters into the building, they still hadn't found what they were searching for, and were feeling their way blindly into the ever-blacker interior. After another minute of nervous fumbling in the ever increasing dark, Kel found a bolt cutter. He turned, tripped, and stumbled into Chuy, sending both of them slamming into the nearest shelf. It tipped and came down on the next shelf, setting off a cascade. The noise was deafening. They scrambled to their feet, Kel dropped the bolt cutter, and they clambered across the downed shelves and spilled tools toward the exit.

They were out the door and halfway back toward the guard shack, and Chuy had just slung the food pack over the fence and into the pines, when every light in the yard came on.

28

Deja vu all over again

It was painful. Kel lay on his back, staring at the institutional-green ceiling, thinking of the last time he'd found himself on a jailhouse bunk—back on Earth after Mig set him up. His head was pounding and the gashes on his back and stomach hurt like hell. He rolled painfully onto his side and stared at the graffiti-strewn wall a foot before his face, wondering how it had come to this: lying bruised and battered, waiting to be press ganged into the Re-Education Project Force. If he was lucky.

He leaned over the edge of his bunk, looked down and started to speak to Chuy, who was occupying the lower bunk. Before he got a word out, Chuy put a finger to his lips. Of course. Every word they said was being listened to, probably recorded.

Chuy raised himself on his elbows and said: "Jesus Christ! Why did we drink all that fucking vodka? And why in hell were we even in the yard?"

Kel caught on and said, "Trying to help Stakhanov. He was even more fucked up than we were. Somebody had to cover for him."

Chuy said, "Fuck me!," sank down on his wafer-thin mattress, and covered his eyes with his arm.

* * *

The next day at the hearing, Major Asahi was not impressed. "Helping Stakhanov? Covering for him? You didn't even have his keys! You went into a tool shed and knocked over a dozen racks of tools!" He sat back, pushed his wire-rim glasses up his nose, steepled his fingers, and stared at them. After several seconds he leaned forward, gripped the edge of his desk, and barked, "Well? What have you to say for yourselves?"

Chuy was the first to speak. "We're sorry, sir. We were just trying to cover for Stakhanov. We were all drunk. What else can I say?"

Asahi slouched back in his chair and resteepled his fingers, as if carefully considering his next words.

"And all of the noise? Knocking over all of those tool shelves?"

"We were drunk! I don't *know* what we were doing! We were *drunk!*"

"Yes, you were drunk. Apparently very drunk. You made an incredible amount of noise. The *guardia* heard you nearly half a kilometer away. After they apprehended you, we found Stakhanov passed out in the barracks rec room. So your story is consistent with the facts. But still . . ."

He pushed his glasses back up his nose and paused. A moment later, he said, "Your behavior was admirable in that you were attempting to help a comrade. But it was also undisciplined and individualistic." He sat down, leaned forward, and said, looking over the top of his glasses, "You are remanded to the Re-Education Project Force, level one."

Despite expecting this, Kel gasped, "For how lon—"

Asahi cut him off. "As long as is necessary!"

"But—"

Asahi cut him off again. "Do you want level two!?"

Chuy kicked Kel before he could say another word. Seconds later, a guard led them from the room.

* * *

The RPF barracks were as primitive as those at Bhagavad. The food was lousy: rice, beans, tortillas, and raw—not even pickled—jalapeños. No beer, just water. And no eggs, cheese, meat, fruit, or vegetables, other than the jalapeños. And to call the routine mind numbing was understatement.

Up at the crack of dawn, the same shitty, boring breakfast, being shackled together at the wrist, running a half kilometer to the quarry, being unshackled, breaking large rocks into small rocks with sledge hammers until noon, the same shitty, boring lunch—exactly the same as breakfast, but served cold at the work site—breaking up more large rocks until three, then spending the rest of the afternoon wheelbarrowing the small rocks off to the gravel piles at the other end of the quarry. Then the same shitty, boring dinner, the same as breakfast and lunch, then, finally, relative relief: study hour. This month, the required reading was *The Collected Works of Enver Hoxha*, Volume 13 (of 23). While reading the first paragraph from Chapter 36 of the fist-thick book, Kel felt his head begin to swim—how could anyone write this shit? Let alone 23 volumes of it? What sort of person could *do* that!? The worst part was that he had to pay at least minimal attention to Hoxha's leaden prose, as there was always a discussion at the end of the reading hour.

After that, the real fun began: the nightly, hour-long self-criticism session.

A week after they were sentenced to the RPF, Chuy was required to speak. Kel was unsurprised to hear him launch into a highly edited, revised version of the drunkalogue he'd given at Serenity. Two nights later, Kel was forced to publicly humiliate himself. He had plenty of his own material, but he also borrowed freely from his master-teachers at Serenity. He ended his confession with: "I was down on my knees in an alley, all fucked up, vomit all over my beard and shirt, my pants down around my ankles, and trying to fuck some orange cat I'd grabbed, when I heard some chick screaming, 'No! No!! Not Tinkerbell!! Not Tinkerbell!! You bastard!!!' A couple minutes later I looked up, saw flashing lights, and some cop standing over me with a club. I let go of the cat, and my head caved in.

"I woke up in jail the next day. I felt like shit warmed over, head pounding like someone was banging it with a framing hammer, blood and vomit all over my face and shirt, scratches all over my arms and dick, and shit in the seat of my pants. I'd hit bottom in the capitalist hellhole, and I was taking it out on myself. I wasn't fighting back. I was wallowing in individualistic self-pity. I had hit bottom. I had not yet found socialism and the path of self-renunciation! Now I have! Thank you, comrades!"

Kel held up the Hoxha volume to the applause of the other prisoners.

29

Waiting for Leatherface

Six weeks later, Kel and Chuy were back in the Construction Cooperative barracks rec room, sitting at a table, drinking beer, playing penny-ante poker with Mikel and Stakhanov. Stakhanov was winning and was in an expansive mood.

"*Da!* Is good you are back. I very sorry about RPF. I know you try to help. And me? No RPF. Mikel's wife, she helps. But reduced grade. Watch duty at construction yard three nights week, three months. No vodka ration. Beer only." He looked with distaste at the bottle in his hand. "But is better than nothing. Is better than RPF!" He laughed and slugged down half the bottle.

* * *

On the job the next day, while blowing up stumps preparatory to laying the foundation for another monument to socialism, Kel whispered to Chuy, "There might be a better way out of here than driving a truck through the fence. Maybe we can get out through one of the border posts."

Chuy gasped, "The border posts? They're filled with cops!"

"Yeah, cops without guns. They just have clubs, knives, and shock batons. That's all. And if we hit 'em late enough, most of 'em will be asleep. And there are vehicles there. . . . We wouldn't have to chance getting busted again at the yard, getting stopped before we hit the perimeter, or getting stuck in the fence or going cross country before we hit the road. We either get out that way or we're stuck here. . . . Come on, what have we got to lose?"

"Other than our lives? . . . And how in hell would we get through those posts and grab a vehicle?"

Kel cracked a crooked grin. "You ever see an old 2-D called *The Texas Chainsaw Massacre*?"

* * *

The next day, Kel bought two downers from Ruíz, the shrimp/weasel barracks dope pusher, and carefully ground them up. The following night it was Stakhanov's turn to do watch duty at the construction yard.

Stakhanov was drinking beer that evening while playing poker with Kel and Chuy prior to his shift. While Stakhanov was taking a piss break, Kel palmed the powder, made a show of refilling Stakhanov's glass, and dumped the ground-up downers into Stakhanov's beer. Stakhanov came back, downed his beer, made a face as if puzzled by the taste, threw down his losing hand, scraped what was left of his change off the table, got up and walked to the construction yard.

An hour later, Kel and Chuy walked into the circular pool of light surrounding the yard's entrance. Chuy had a mostly full liter bottle of vodka in his hand, and Kel had three shot glasses in his, carrying them with his fingers stuck down into the tops of two of them, his thumb in the third, and pressing all three together so he wouldn't drop them. When he saw Stakhanov in the guard shack, he raised the glasses in the air and slurred, "Hey comrade! Hows 'bout a drink?!" Stakhanov was woozy, but reluctant.

Kel filled his and Chuy's glasses half full, and they downed them. He half-refilled them, as Stakhanov reached toward the third glass. He took it, ignoring the thumb print near its top, as Kel filled it for him. Forty-five minutes later he was out cold and snoring heavily, and Kel and Chuy were heading for the nearest tool shed, Stakhanov's flashlight in hand, in search of bolt cutters and chain saws. Five minutes later, as they were leaving the yard, Kel made sure that Stakhanov was lying on his side so that he wouldn't drown in his own vomit in case he puked.

Ninety minutes after that, Kel and Chuy were breathing heavily, sweating, their backs against the wall on either side of the rear door of the western border station. The guards had done them a favor and left the gate in the inner fence open. The station was silent but for occasional drunken grunts. Kel crept silently along the side of the station to the middle gate across the road. It was secured with a two-cm-thick hardened chain and massive padlock. Kel didn't even try to use the bolt cutters on the chain or lock. Instead, he put down the bolt cutters and crept back toward the entrance to the border post. He quietly picked up his chain saw and put his back to the wall. Chuy already had his saw in hand.

Kel gestured with his head toward two jeep-like vehicles that were parked on the gravel behind the building. His heart pounding, he motioned with his head toward the vehicles and whispered, "Do you know how to hot wire those things?"

Chuy shook his head. "No. Do you?"

"No. And I don't think they could spring the gates even if we could get 'em started."

Kel nodded his head toward the post's door, wondering if he really wanted any part of this. He held the saw upright in suddenly heavy arms, breathing shallowly, and looked at Chuy until Chuy said, "Let's do it!" Chuy grabbed his saw's rip cord and mimed counting to three. They pulled their cords simultaneously. The saws screeched, Chuy kicked in the door, and they charged in to screams and crashes as the cops pulled themselves out of their bunks or grabbed for their weapons. Holding their chain saws bars up, Kel and Chuy revved the motors and ran toward the screams, the saws shrieking.

* * *

Fifteen minutes later, after Kel trashed the electrical system of the jeep nearest the building, losing his saw in a blinding arc that fused the chain to the bar, they were riding silently in the other jeep. Kel was driving as fast as he dared along the main road a few kilometers to the west of New Havana, cursing the fact that both jeeps had been carrying less than a half charge, that it was raining like hell, and that they'd be lucky if they made it much over two hundred klicks.

They were bouncing up and down, back and forth in their seats, heading down the rutted buckboard switchbacks into a gorge that plunged three hundred meters in a little over three klicks. Their headlights revealed a contracted universe of deep, muddy ruts, ghostly images of rock walls flashing by on one side, through sheets of rain, and a black void on the other.

The darkness loomed nearer as they skidded toward the edge before the wheels grabbed and they were back in the ruts. Heart pounding, Kel did his best to push the brakes through the floor. The jeep fishtailed in the mud, sliding again toward the void. It stopped less than half a meter from the edge. Kel sat breathing hard, his foot pressing on the brake; he reached over to Chuy for the bottle of vodka they'd ripped off at the border post. He took a slug, handed the bottle back to Chuy, eased off on the brake, and tentatively pressed down on the accelerator. A moment later, as they inched down the incline, Chuy handed him the bottle again.

Kel took another swig, shuddered, and hit the brakes to check their increasing speed. He passed the bottle back to Chuy, who took a slug, capped it, and stuck it under his seat.

A moment later, Chuy said, "I hope that *cabrón* is okay."

"Who fucking cares? I didn't cut him that bad. The stupid moth- erfucker shouldn't have come at me like that. He probably won't lose his arm. I barely hit the bone."

Kel snuck a quick sideways glance at Chuy. The guy definitely had some *cojones*, but why in hell should a little blood bother him so much? He'd been in the Central Asian wars, too. He had to have seen worse shit—much worse shit—than that.

Chuy reached in under the seat, grabbed the bottle, uncorked it, and took a swig. He offered it to Kel, who pushed it away. After Chuy recapped it and put it in under the seat, he leaned back into the sparse padding and closed his eyes. Kel, hands gripping the wheel hard, stared straight ahead, riding the brakes down the steep muddy grade as the rain pounded down.

* * *

The gorge and rain were long past, and it was even darker. Bo- ris's jagged crescent was descending through the pines on the west- ern horizon and Arkady was already down. Kel's only reality was the ever-shifting, jiggling, blinding cone of light from the jeep's headlights. As Boris sunk below the horizon, Kel hit a pothole that jolted Chuy awake. When it was obvious that he was alert, Kel asked him, "You want to drive for a while?"

Chuy grunted, "Yeah." Kel hit the brakes, the jeep came to a stop in the middle of the road, and they changed places. Chuy pushed down on the throttle, the jeep bucked, picked up speed, and they rode on, bouncing in their seats, the only sound the hum of the wheels on the washboard road. Twenty minutes later, a crude wooden sign on the side of the road flashed into Kel's view. He yelled, "Stop!" Chuy flinched, hit the brakes, and the jeep skidded to a halt.

Chuy backed up clumsily, the wheels popping in and out of the ruts, until the sign was in the penumbra of the headlights. Chuy maneuvered until the lights pointed directly at the sign. They both strained to read the faded lettering: "Xenadu—53 kilometers, Iron Dream—245 kilometers."

Kel asked, "Which way? What the hell is Xenadu? And which one is closer to New Harmony? The Iron Dream?"

"Yeah, but we ain't goin' there. We're either goin' to Xenadu or we're gonna go as far as we can in this thing, dump it, and then go overland and around The Dream. My vote is Xenadu. It's the Mind-Head compound, but it beats the goddamned Nazis. This damned jeep will die in another hundred klicks or so, if we're lucky. So it's Xenadu."

Kel almost jumped out of his seat.

"MindHead?! Do you know what the fuck that is? Do you know what those fuckers do to people?!"

"Come on. From what I've heard, they're weird as hell, but they ain't all that bad. And we don't have much choice. This thing ain't charged enough to go more than another hundred klicks at the most, and we don't have anywhere near enough supplies to walk around The Dream and then another three or four hundred to New Harmony. We'll play along while we're there, and we should be able to catch a shuttle within a week. Bud told me they're in and out of there all the time."

Kel took a deep breath. Chuy really didn't get it.

"Remember my pal Ernie, the sort of half-assed keyboard player we used to play with in Desperate? He was into that shit. Never played loud enough, never stepped out front, always sort of hid in the background? Remember him?"

Chuy didn't reply.

Kel continued, "You never wondered why he was so beat? Never wondered what happened to him?"

Again, Chuy didn't reply.

"They got ahold of him, cleaned out his bank account, clamped one of those helmets on him, and within a month they had the poor fucker confessing that he had sex with dogs."

"What breed?"

"Very funny, Chuy. But seriously, this is dangerous shit."

"I'm serious too, man. What breed? And males or females?"

"Jesus F. Christ! They destroyed the poor bastard—you fucking *knew* him! You played with him—and you're makin' fun of him!"

Chuy had drunk enough that he was really enjoying messing with Kel, who had begun to intensely irritate him. "It's 'Hey-soos,' not 'Jeezus,' and my middle name isn't 'F.' And yeah. I am makin' fun of him. He wasn't responsible for any of it? Give me a break. He walked in there with his eyes wide open."

Kel shook his head in disgust and looked away into the darkness.

They rode on for several moments until Chuy said, "Seriously, we're going to Xenadu."

"You goddamned moron! Are you out of your fucking mind? Have you ever read *Diuretics* or any of the other shit that that sick fuck Grossberg wrote?"

"Yeah, that is some fucked up shit. But Grossberg's dead, and like I said, what choice do we have? Do you want to walk four or five hundred kliks to New Harmony and take a chance on the damned Nazis catching us while we walk around them? Or starving while we do it? If you want to try, be my guest. I'm heading for Xenadu."

After a few more moments of bumping along the rutted mud road, Kel looked over at Chuy and said, "You really wanna know about the dogs? Ernie told 'em Dobermans. . . . Male Dobermans. . . . It was a lie, but that's what they wanted to hear.

"And if they don't hear what they want to hear, they don't stop. Ernic told me about some real grisly shit. The sick part is that he bought into it, thought it was 'necessary.' That they were helping him.

"Here, it's probably even worse. They don't have access to any modern tech, so god knows what kind of barbaric shit they're doing. Think about that before you haul our asses in there."

Chuy stared straight ahead into the ovals of light oozing from the headlights, his hands squeezing the wheel.

Forty-five minutes later, they were approaching the turnoff to Xenadu, the jeep was noticeably slowing as its batteries ran down, and the sky had begun to lighten. Another sign appeared with an arrow to the left toward Xenadu and a straight arrow pointing toward The Iron Dream. Xenadu was only 30 klicks away, while The Iron Dream was still 222.

Kel glanced up at the approaching dawn and said, "We'd better get rid of this thing."

"It's only thirty klicks to Xenadu. Let's ride. It's still forty-five minutes until dawn, and this thing will probably make it."

As Chuy took the turnoff to Xenadu, Kel said, "Come on. If we drive in there, we're fucked. How in hell are we gonna explain this jeep?"

Chuy kept his eyes on the road, his hands upon the wheel, and muttered "Fuck you, Kel." Ten minutes later they were still bouncing down the road to Xenadu, a rutted track even more primitive than the road to The Iron Dream.

30

The subordination of a nation to a man is not a wholesome but
a vicious state of things: needful, indeed, for a vicious humanity.
The instinct which makes it possible is any thing but a noble one.
Call it 'hero-worship' and it looks respectable . . . From ancient
warrior-worship to modern flunkeyism, the sentiment has ever
been strongest where human nature has been vilest.

—Herbert Spencer, "Representative Government"

Chuy pulled to a stop a few meters before a dilapidated wooden
bridge. Even in the half-light from the approaching dawn, they
could see gaping holes in the bridge's deck. Kel got out and walked
gingerly onto the overlapping planks running in raised parallel
tracks the length of the deck. He shook the flashlight he'd taken
from the jeep's glove box and pointed it down into the darkness.
His heart pounded when he saw the steepness of the ravine and the
creek running along its bottom, a good thirty meters below where
he was standing.

"Damn!" He walked carefully on the wooden tracks back to the
jeep and said, "Let's ditch this thing and walk. This ain't safe to
drive on."

He walked to the back of the jeep and began searching, increasingly frantically. He looked accusingly at Chuy and said, "Shit! You
must have left the food at the border post."

Chuy snorted disgustedly. "Me? . . . Let's see if there's anything
in this damned thing."

Chuy got out of the driver's seat, pushed past Kel, and shortly
found an emergency pack half-crushed beneath the spare. He
grabbed the pack and hefted it onto his back. Kel reached into
the cab, removed the canteen from beneath the seat, and also the

nearly empty bottle of vodka. He downed half of what was left and passed the rest to Chuy, who emptied it and flung the bottle down into the gorge. Kel walked to the back of the jeep, bent his shoulder into it, and began pushing while Chuy both pushed and steered. When they'd almost reached the bridge, Chuy turned the wheel to the right and sent the jeep plummeting into the ravine. When the crashing sounds had died away, they stepped onto the bridge's raised tracks and began gingerly walking across it. At its middle, Kel took the flashlight from his pocket, shook it to energize it, and pointed it down. "Shit!" A half-meter of the jeep's rear end was sticking up out of the creek.

Chuy sighed and said, "Don't sweat it. Unless they stop and look down—or unless it has a transponder—they'll never find it. Screw it. Let's get outta here."

Kel led the way to the other side of the bridge and up a densely wooded hill, stopping and shaking the flashlight every few dozen meters, walking on until it died, then shaking it again. When they stumbled into a small, flat clearing immediately before a steep ridge, they stopped, and Chuy said, "Let's crash." He put down the emergency pack and reached inside it. They were in luck: they had an emergency blanket and a tarp.

Three hours later, well after dawn, the sun peeked over the crest of the ridge above them. It was still cold. Kel raised his hand to shield his eyes, sat up, and quietly opened the emergency pack that was lying next to him. There was a flint and steel, a knife, a plastic pouch with monofilament line and fishing hooks, two steel sporks, two crushed cartons of hi-pro biscuits, a two-liter canteen, and half-a-dozen hot-food packets, two of them oozing brown juice from rips along their sides, where the spare had crushed them. Kel was still poking through the pack as Chuy stirred. As Kel put down the pack, he looked at the blanket and discovered that one corner of it—the corner covering his leg—was smeared with the brown food ooze. So were his pants.

Chuy sat up as Kel was wiping the fouled corner of the blanket on the ground and trying futilely to clean his pants. After a few ineffective wipes he gave up, took out two damaged hot-meal packets, folded the fouled blanket, and stuck it back in the pack.

He handed one of the packets to Chuy; they pulled the strings, hurriedly set down the rapidly heating foil packs, and before his was cool enough, Kel started to shovel down its bland, mushy, over-heated contents. He yelled and almost spat out the first bite. Chuy, who had held back, laughed. When Kel dug his spork back in two minutes later, strips of skin were hanging down from the roof of his mouth. After eating, Kel walked into the woods to bury the re-fuse as Chuy tore off some low hanging branches and covered their tracks in the clearing. He stepped off the path, said "Come on" to Kel, and spent half an hour leading the way, bushwhacking to the top of the ridge. Once there, he found a trail heading downhill in the general direction of Xenadu.

Five hours later they were crouching behind some bushes near the edge of the woods on a hill above the settlement—no gates, no fences—gaping at a three-storey English manor house with manicured lawns and well-tended topiary, with people rushing to and fro between it and dozens of smaller brick and frame build-ings. A large number of greenish, ant-sized people were visible in the distance, working in fields and orchards. It looked much like a 19th-century, English-gentry version of Baghavad.

In the foreground, people—a lot of people—were walking hur-riedly on the paths from building to building, but many others were running. Those that were walking, in fact, strutting in a forced gait, were dressed in bright green, military style uniforms, medals and epaulets gleaming brightly in the sunlight, some wear-ing snappy white space force officer hats. Those that were running were dressed in dull, lime-green, pajama-like uniforms. Many of them, both the walkers and the runners, were sporting what looked like World War I-era leather flight helmets, with wires run-ning from the backs of the helmets to packs clipped to their belts. A kilometer south of the main building, in another clearing, more pajama clad workers were loading crates onto small flatbed trucks at a shuttle pad, with no shuttle in sight.

Chuy looked at the clearing and said, "Shit. We must have just missed one." He gestured toward the settlement. "You want to check it out? It looks harmless enough." He pointed toward what seemed to be the mess hall, judging from the pleasant odors wafting up the hill. "Let's get some grub. We can bullshit 'em. It worked at Serenity and New Havana. It'll work here." He started to get up, but Kel pulled him back.

"It *won't* work here! Didn't you hear *anything* I said to you? Look at those helmets!"

"So?"

"So!? Mind control! I wasn't shitting you about Ernie. They really did that to him. In a lot of ways, it's like Baghavad. The same lectures, over and over. Father worship. Every moment of every day. For months! For years sometimes! And you wouldn't believe some of the other shit they do. We need to be fucking careful."

Chuy slowly settled back on his haunches.

Twenty minutes later, a siren went off and people streamed out of the outbuildings, heading for the mess hall. All of the pajama-clad figures were running, while their gaudier cousins were walking stiffly but quickly, in a corn cob-inserted strut. In the distance, the agricultural workers marched robotically to field kitchens.

After Xenadu's residents entered the mess hall and field kitchens, there was no movement for half an hour. Then, the process reversed itself, and the dull-green and neon-green figures streamed out of the mess hall and field kitchens on their way back to the outbuildings and fields. It was impossible to tell men from women, although it should have been easy, despite the distance, uniforms and pajama suits. The robotic movements all but erased the usual telltale differences in motion. When it was apparent that nothing more would happen, Kel, who was dropping from fatigue, glanced questioningly at Chuy, who looked equally tired, and said, "Let's crash. You want to eat first?"

"No man, we've only got six more MREs."

Kel grunted agreement and reached into the pack for the dirty tarp. They spread the tarp on the ground, and were asleep within minutes, shielded from the still-high sun by the bushes and overhanging trees. Four hours later, as sunset approached, they stirred and sat up. Chuy looked at the emergency pack next to him on the ground, and then at Kel, who nodded and said, "Let's do it."

Chuy pulled out one of the hot-food packs and said, "We'd better split one. There are only four more of these things and those crushed dog biscuits." He handed the packet to Kel, who waited more than the recommended full three minutes before diving in. Minutes after they'd finished sharing the MRE, they nodded off again, with the sun nearing the horizon, and the field workers streaming back into the compound.

Peeling bells woke them when it was already deep twilight. Even in the gloom, they could see hundreds of figures running or walking toward the second largest building in the compound, a long, one-storey brick hall. After waiting until the sky was almost totally black except for a faint glow on the western horizon, Kel said, "Let's go. Imitate what I do."

He led the way down the hill, creeping through the bushes, and once in the cleared area began strutting on the nearest path toward the hall, acting as if he knew exactly where he was going. None of the very few self-preoccupied stragglers noticed his or Chuy's odd clothing in the near-total darkness.

Three minutes later they were crouching beneath one of the hall's open, wood-casement windows, cautiously peering in. The Xenadu drones were sitting rigidly in rows, facing a podium on a short riser. Those in neon green uniforms were sitting in the front part of the hall on padded wooden chairs, while those in dull green pajamas sat behind them on unpadded benches without backs. A late middle-aged white man with hard, pig eyes, a triple chin, gin blossoms bursting on a nose so wide it looked like a crushed strawberry, and a heavy five o'clock shadow shading pendulous jowls, wobbled onto the slightly raised platform at the front of the hall.

He was dressed in an immaculate white space force uniform with wide epaulets bearing six huge silver stars, his chest festooned with dozens of medals and ribbons. On what Kel bet was a bald head, he wore an oversized admiral's hat set at a jaunty angle.

He rested his arms on the podium, looked out over the assembled crowd, stuck his index finger into his collar, pulled down, and jerked his head violently to the right, his wattles lagging behind the rest of his head by a fraction of a second. He turned back toward the crowd, cleared his throat, threw his head back, and began to roar, saluting them with "You the elect! You the Clean! . . ."

Kel stared slack jawed at the grotesque figure at the podium. He gasped, in a strangled whisper, "Holy fucking shit!," grabbed Chuy by the arm, and pulled him down from the window.

Chuy protested. "What the—"

"It's Grossberg! They cloned the motherfucker! It's Max Fucking Grossberg!! We've got to get out of here! Now!!"

He started pulling on Chuy's arm. Chuy resisted, and whispered back heatedly, "No man, I want to hear this!"

"No man, you don't. And you don't want to be around when those morons come marching out." He tugged on Chuy's arm again.

This time Chuy pushed him away and whispered, "Fuck you, man! I want to hear this!"

They crouched while Grossberg's voice boomed through the open window. He was talking about an alien mothership nose-diving 65 million years ago into the Yucatan, with the explosion implanting alien subminds in the early mammals and the dying dinosaurs. He joked about who was luckier, the dinosaurs, who couldn't handle the alien subminds and died, or the mammals who could, and who carried the alien mind parasites to this very day. He paused, and the audience took its cue and laughed in unison at his lame attempt at a joke. Chuy turned toward Kel, eyebrows raised. Kel shrugged.

Grossberg spoke about the heroic efforts of his previous incarnation on Earth, who had attempted to cleanse humans of the alien subminds through pure mental teq, and of the near-destruction of him and his work by subductive alien minions who had nearly obliterated his movement and persona, save for a few skin cells from his nose, a single copy of his holographic personality profile, and a few hundred dedicated Cleans who had made the hard decision to emigrate to this chosen world rather than face continued persecution on Earth. (Kel smiled as he recalled that this was the only one to which they'd been given access.) Grossberg nodded at his second in command, Tom Wayne Gracy, and then continued, acknowledging that they were all here thanks to Commander Gracy, who had somehow managed to smuggle Grossberg's holo profile and nose cells to Tau II in his naked, frozen body.

Grossberg smiled at the comfortably seated neon-green ranks in the front rows, who puffed up and sat straighter. A few in the back, in their pale green, penitential pajamas also started to puff up, but quickly thought better of it and shrank back down.

Grossberg was still building. He urged the cleans and near-cleans to look around them, to see all that they had built. He urged them to think about how far they had come, from near extinction at the hands of subductives to being on the verge of cleansing an entire world! And, yes!, now they had the real Teq for it, not the pallid mental disciplines that took years of hard work to master, but real, hard-wired, physical Teq! Real hardware! Real *headware* to clean an entire planet! He held up one of the electrode-helmets in his right hand and its control pack in his left, waving the apparatus in the air.

Grossberg set the rig down on the lectern and waved his arms, urging the mob to its feet. The entire crowd rose as one and began waving their arms in the air in imitation of their leader as he began to bounce up and down, his jowls and gut weirdly lagging behind the rest of his body. Grossberg finally stopped bouncing, jerked his head to the right, his jowls gradually settling, clenched his jaw, put his right index finger inside his collar, pulled down, swallowed, jerked his head, looked back at his followers, and began chanting:

"An entire world—"

The crowd responded in unison: "Clean!"

"An entire world—"

"Clean!"

The call and response continued for several minutes. Kel tugged on Chuy's arm, and they slunk away from the window and started walking, then running, unconsciously crouching, as fast and as quietly as they could back to their refuge on the hill overlooking the compound. The call-and-response followed them all the way back.

31

CULT, n. 1) An unsuccessful religion; 2) A pejorative term employed by members of religious bodies to refer to other religious bodies.

—Chaz Bufe, *The American Heretic's Dictionary*

As the call and response faded in the distance, Kel climbed the last few meters to their hiding spot, with Chuy close behind. It was getting cold, so they laid down back to back on the tarp, and pulled the dirty emergency blanket as best they could over themselves. It helped, but not enough. It took Kel a full hour to fall asleep, all the while longing for his son and a place to call home—even his pit of an apartment in PhoenixMetro, as long as he could see Folky—or even Chuy's promised anarchist Valhalla, which sounded too good to be true, and so probably was.

Eight hours later, Tau poked its orangish head above the horizon. Kel protectively covered his eyes with his arm, but a few moments later admitted defeat, stretched, and sat up, unshaven and feeling grimy. Chuy was already awake, sitting up, staring straight ahead at nothing. They sat numbly until Chuy reached into the emergency pack, and pulled out the canteen and took a long slug. He handed it to Cal, who finished what little was left in it. Then Chuy pulled out the sporks and one of the last three food packs. He tilted his head and raised one eyebrow in question toward Kel, who grunted agreement. Chuy pulled the string, handed the packet to Kel, who consumed half of it as soon as he dared, handed the rest to Chuy, and within minutes they had devoured the steaming mush.

It was barely a half hour past dawn, and the now-familiar running and walking figures were already scuttling across the compound in all directions. All but one. On the far left, Kel noticed a single, green, pajama-clad, electrode-helmeted figure, his head bowed and his hands clutching his helmet, shuffling slowly, almost staggering away from a large brick building near to the far end of the hill that was their temporary home. The building was very near to where the hill curved down and petered out at the edge of the compound, and it was one of the few two-storey buildings. Strangely, it had no windows and was set well apart from the other structures.

A second dull-green clad, helmeted figure was approaching the building, jogging, but haltingly, and at a much slower pace than the other running drones. His dread, even at a distance of over half a klick, was palpable. No one else was anywhere near the place.

Before he had a chance to comment, Kel heard footsteps and thrashing in the distance from further up the hill. He put his index finger to his lips, and they both listened. The noise was growing closer. No one who was stalking them would make that much noise, but still . . . it was time to go.

* * *

They stopped at the bottom of the hill and hesitated until they heard footfalls from above them on the hill coming closer. To their left, there was nothing but a hundred-meter clearing between them and the large patch of woods at the edge of the shuttle pad. On the right, the only refuge was the brick building, which blocked the line of sight from the manor house and the other structures. They ran for its side, away from the rest of the compound, and stopped at its only door. Kel put his ear to it, heard nothing, and tried the handle. The door opened onto a brightly lit, antiseptic corridor with overhead recessed lights set in white tiles, balancing a white ceramic floor and glossy white-painted walls.

He stepped inside, after Chuy, and they began walking down the corridor, their every step echoing down the hall, as indistinct voices gradually floated in from a side corridor a few dozen meters behind them. Chuy tried a door. It was locked.

A deep male voice, coming nearer, rising above the others, resolved into a lecturing, upper-class British monotone: ". . . uncover the repressed memories and alien sub-routines. Then we can begin . . ." A muffled scream from somewhere nearby drowned out the

professorial lecture. Chuy grabbed the next door handle and twisted hard. It was locked. He ran to the next and tried. Again, locked.
As the voice droned on, becoming louder and louder, and as the
screams increased in intensity, he tried a fourth door, twisting the
knob violently. It turned, and he pushed in. The heavy door swung
open so easily that he barely managed to stop it before it slammed
into the wall.

They were in a small, dark room, a one-way mirror taking up
an entire wall, with seats behind a mixing console that extended
the wall's entire length, but for a rack of recording gear at one end.
The one-way mirror looked out on a white, brightly lit room. The
room's centerpiece was a shaven-headed, near-naked, ball-gagged
man in a hospital gown strapped to an operating table. The bound
man lay trembling, his eyes darting wildly from side to side, his
body straining against his restraints. As he lay there shivering,
three middle-aged men dressed in surgical garb entered the room.
Their badges identified them as doctors Benway and Petiot, and A.
DeLarge, RN.

Doctor Petiot, assisted by DeLarge, attached wires to the man's
head, clipping electrodes to short studs protruding from his skull,
As they did this, Doctor Benway was staring intently at a computer
array.

Once Petiot had finished attaching the electrodes, he began
talking to the strapped-down man. Kel and Chuy couldn't hear a
word Petiot was saying.

Chuy glanced down at the control board and gingerly pushed
up a slider pot on the far right. Petiot's lip movements immediately became synchronized with the rich baritone voice they had
heard in the corridor: ". . . edit out more of the sexual perversions
implanted by the alien subminds, and replace them with healthy
attractions. You must realize that it is not *you* who feels these per-
verted attractions. You only *think* that you feel them. But it is not
you! It is the subductive omegans that have infested your mind
and body! And we will defeat them! *You* will defeat them! You
will be free! You will be clean of these unhealthy attractions." He
squeezed one of the man's bare, trembling arms. "There is nothing
to be afraid of. We have done this dozens of times with others who

had problems too deep seated to be cleansed via normal exposure to Father Thought, and every time it was a success. You did not respond to normal aural therapy, so we must provide you with direct, cortical contact with Father."

Petiot looked over at Benway and nodded. Benway typed in several commands as Petiot walked over to join him, and they stared at the screen before them. The screen was turned away from them, so Cal and Chuy had no idea of what Benway and Petiot were seeing.

Petiot frowned, and Benway typed in a command. The man on the couch convulsed in agony for several seconds, his eyes almost bulging from his skull, as he tried to scream. Benway typed in another command, and the man's body stopped straining against the restraints and slumped back to the couch.

Benway glanced at Petiot, who in turn keyed in another command. The naked man began grunting with pleasure, thrusting his pelvis and now rock-hard member as much as his restraints would allow. After a good two minutes of this, and immediately after the naked man had started jerking preparatory to orgasm, Petiot typed in another set of commands.

The naked man abruptly stopped jerking. Benway boomed: "Are you man enough to become Clean, or do you want to remain infested with alien subminds!?" When the man began to get hard again, Petiot shocked him so hard he almost bit through the ball gag.

Chuy jumped to his feet, grabbed the door handle, pulled it open, without checking to see if anyone was outside, and rushed down the hall with Kel close behind him. Chuy pushed open the outside door, dropped to his knees, and vomited while Kel anxiously watched the now-closed door, his gaze alternating between it, the hill, and the area in front of the building. Chuy shuddered, wiped his mouth on the back of his sleeve, and looked accusingly at Kel.

Kel asked, "Do you still want to hang around here and 'get some grub'?"

32

ADVENTURE, n. A disaster in retrospect, especially one
involving the pain and suffering of others.

—Chaz Bufe, *The American Heretic's Dictionary*

Kel crouched in the woods at the edge of the shuttle pad. Chuy was squatting two meters away, his fist to his mouth, fighting off the dry heaves. Kel watched silently as two helmet-clad repairmen worked on the brakes of one of the electric trucks that hauled cargo to and from the shuttles. The wind was blowing, and they were far enough away that Kel couldn't hear what the techs were saying to each other. One of the techs puckered his lips and apparently began to whistle. The other gave him a stern look, and the man stopped, looked down at his helmet's control pack, adjusted its settings, and went back to work, sans whistling. He started to whistle again, but caught himself, looked nervously at the other man, and realized with obvious relief that his partner hadn't heard him. As the green-clad drone bent back over the vehicle, Kel looked toward Chuy, who had recovered from his spasms and was sitting with his back against a tree, staring into space.

Two hours later the lunch bell rang and the techs crawled out from under the cargo truck and walked back toward the compound. Kel reached into the emergency pack, poked around in it, pulled out one of the smashed-up hi-pro "dog biscuit" packs and looked questioningly at Chuy, who nodded assent.

That evening, after the bell rang and the pajama-clad drones disappeared, Kel and Chuy, hungry and thirsty, left their hiding place and walked over to the nearest of the cargo trucks. Chuy stuck his head into the cab, looked at the controls, pulled the lever in under the dash, walked to the front, and lifted the hood. He looked down at the motor and batteries. He withdrew his head.

178 ◆ Zeke Teflon

"Fuck. Even if we could get back to the road without them notic-ing, this thing probably won't go more than forty klicks an hour, and the batteries don't look too good."

"So, what do we do, wait for a taxi?"

Chuy ignored the sarcasm. "Yeah, pretty much. That's all we can do. We can't go back, and New Harmony is another six or seven hundred clicks. But this place gets a lot of shuttle traffic, I know some of the pilots, and even the ones I don't know think these ass-holes are whacked. Most of 'em would probably help us. We should be out of here in three or four days, max."

"Three or four days? On these two MREs and what's left of these dog biscuits?" Kel looked at the cargo trucks. "Is there any food or water in these things?"

In the third one, Chuy found a four-liter jug of water and a very stale cheese sandwich. After they both slugged down several gulps of water, Chuy split the sandwich carefully in half, handed one part to Kel, kept the other for himself, and said, "Bon appetit."

The next morning, they split the next-to-last last MRE. Late that afternoon, Kel was keeping watch as Chuy sacked out. Kel looked covetously at the pack and the last MRE and biscuits, but he re-sisted the temptation. Just before it was dark enough to roust Chuy and head for the nearest orchard, wheels crunched on the gravel path from the main buildings. Kel shook Chuy gently and mo-tioned for him to be quiet when he opened his eyes.

A moment later, pajama-clad drones driving produce-laden trucks approached the shuttle pad and stopped at its edge. Kel looked up and saw a gleam in the sky. A descending shuttle. Five minutes later, the workers approached it as its cargo ramp de-scended. They began trundling produce into the shuttle's hold, and unloading barrels and crates. In the midst of this, the pilot, a large man moving stiffly, wearing sunglasses and a helmet, emerged from the cockpit.

Kel whispered to Chuy. "Recognize him?"

"Maybe. It's hard to tell in this light."

Chuy crept through the brush toward the pad, crawling on hands and knees between broken-down crates and weather-beaten pallets. When he was about twenty meters shy of the shuttle, and crouching behind a dilapidated crate, he stuck his head up to see if he recognized the pilot. He did. The pilot had taken off his helmet and sunglasses—and it was Miller! Fucking Miller!

Chuy dropped behind the crate, and Miller stared for a second at where Chuy had been, as if he'd seen something, but then sat down on the cockpit steps and lit a cigarette. He tossed the match into the dry weeds and exhaled smoke through his nose.

Chuy waited several breathless moments before creeping away, thankful for the noise of the workers banging up and down the shuttle's loading ramp. Forty-five minutes later, he and Kel watched as Miller's shuttle, laden with produce, ascended vertically and then accelerated up and off in the direction of New M. Two minutes after the last cargo truck had departed, Kel said, "Let's head for the orchards. We need to stretch what we have left."

When they got to the nearest trees, Kel fumbled in the darkness, searching blindly for fruit through the leaves and branches. He bit into the first piece he found, a rock-hard pear. Both he and Chuy were so hungry they gnawed down two pears apiece before heading back toward the brush surrounding the shuttle pad, where they pawed around in the darkness until they found their gear. Kel pulled out the emergency blanket and tarp, and they wolfed down the remaining shreds of biscuit before spending a miserable night shivering, bent into fetal positions by the cramps induced by eating green fruit. Sleep came eventually, but too near to dawn.

When Kel awoke the next day, he was cold, stiff from sleeping in an awkward position, half-dead with fatigue, still suffering from cramps, and hungry and thirsty; the water was almost gone, and the cramps were so bad that eating the final MRE didn't even seem appealing.

There was nothing to do, so they waited and suffered. The drones were already in the fields and orchards, and there was no way to steal food or water without being detected.

At noon, when the cramps had finally subsided enough that eating the last MRE was starting to seem like a good idea, the shuttle pad workers and trucks reappeared, and a few minutes later another shuttle landed. As its cargo bay dropped, its cockpit door opened and the pilot, wearing sunglasses and helmet, stepped

down and wandered off into the bushes, putting the shuttle between himself and the loading crew. Chuy crept through the weeds
to get a better look at him. When he was within ten meters of the
pilot, but still hidden by the tall grass and brush, the pilot took off
his helmet and started to unzip his fly. And, yes! Chuy stuck his
head up and whispered loudly, "Bud!"

Bud gave a start, his hand suspended. "Chuy?"

"Yeah!"

"What the hell are you doin' here?"

"Don't ask. We need to get out of here."

"Hold on a minute." Bud turned his back to Chuy. Thirty seconds and a half-liter of relief later, he wiped his hand on his pants,
turned around, and said in a low voice, "Why the hell should I help
you? Those assholes almost killed me at Baghavad."

"That wasn't our fault!"

"It wasn't?"

"No, it wasn't. You knew what you were doin' when you dumped
us there. You had to. Don't bullshit me. And then you didn't show
up. What the hell were we supposed to do?"

"I didn't show up?! I showed up *before* I said I was going to! And
you took off two fucking days before then! You couldn't wait two
fucking days?"

"How the fuck could we have known what day it was? How the
fuck were we supposed to keep track of time? Every goddamned
day is the same at that goddamned place! Come on, Bud. We
thought you abandoned us. Give us a fucking break! We'll die if
you leave us here."

Bud scratched the back of his head, apparently pondering
whether or not that would be a good or a bad thing. Finally, he
said, "What the hell. I'll drop you at my next stop."

Chuy tried to hide his relief.

"Where's that?"

Bud didn't answer. Instead, he smiled, put his index finger to his
lips when Chuy started to speak, and motioned for him to keep down
and remain silent as he turned and walked back toward the shuttle.

A half hour later, the incoming cargo had been shuffled out and
the outgoing cargo had been shuffled in. As the last of the retreat-

ing trucks was two hundred meters down the path and trundling toward the compound, Bud emerged from the still-open tailgate and motioned for Chuy and Kel to join him. They ran through the weeds, crouching, more out of fear than reason.

Bud said "C'mon" and led the way to the cockpit. He sat down in the pilot's seat, strapped himself in, and flipped the switch to bring up the tailgate. It stopped halfway up, and he banged his fist on the panel next to the switch. On the third whack, the tailgate jerked loose and rose the rest of the way.

He checked the bewildering array of readouts before him, pulled back on the joystick and the shuttle began to rise as Chuy strapped himself into the co-pilot's seat and Kel squatted between Bud and Chuy.

As the shuttle continued to rise, Chuy asked, "Come on, Bud. Where are we goin'?"

Bud was concentrating on the readouts before him, his free hand flying back and forth over the controls. "Shut up! I'm busy."

When they were a hundred meters in the air, Bud turned his head and said, "You don't listen too good, Chuy. I'm droppin' you at my next stop."

"Bud, come on."

"Like I said, you don't listen too good, and I don't owe you no favors. Not after that shit at Baghavad and all that shit with Bonnie. I'm droppin' you at my next stop."

Chuy slumped in his seat. "Okay, Bud. Where?"

Bud stayed silent long enough, screwing with the controls, that Chuy began to squirm. Finally, Bud said, "Baghavad!"

"Shit!"

But turned away, focused on the controls. "Yep, Baghavad."

"You can't be serious!"

"No?"

Bud turned his head, hiding a smile. He pretended to make more adjustments, while studiously avoiding looking at Chuy. He finally turned toward him and laughed.

"Come on. Me, serious? I was just fuckin' with you. We ain't going to Baghavad." He paused for dramatic effect as Chuy squirmed again.

Seconds later Chuy couldn't take it any longer and blurted out, "Where are we going?!"

"The Iron Dream."

"No!"

Bud didn't reply.

"You're fucking with me. Right?"

After watching Chuy fidget for several long seconds, he said, "No. I ain't fuckin' with you. We're goin' to The Dream."

Chuy turned white.

"Can't we at least hide in here and go on to your next stop?"

"Not this time. It'll still be daytime, they'll be unloading almost all of the shit in the bay, and once it's out there's no place to hide. They can see right up into the cockpit.

"What if I kill you right now?"

"Can you fly this thing?"

Chuy didn't reply.

"I didn't think so."

Ten minutes later the shuttle shuddered violently, then started flying smoothly again. Bud swore, switched on the autopilot, unstrapped himself, and mouthed "Shut up!" when Chuy opened his mouth.

He'd pushed Kel out of the way and had taken a step back toward the engine compartment when the shuttle juddered, the engines sputtered off, and it plummeted down. Bud grabbed a strut on the back of the pilot's seat and maintained a death grip on it as his body straightened nearly horizontally to the floor.

Kel shot backwards into a pile of burlap sacks filled with apples, and began clutching desperately at the cargo netting attached to the side of the shuttle, the straps biting into his fingers.

They dropped sickeningly, until the engines slammed back on and the autopilot kicked in a hundred meters above the ground. The shuttle shot up violently. As it was climbing, Bud clawed his way back into the pilot's seat, grabbed the stick, frantically punched at the controls, and a moment later set them down on the nearest flat spot.

The shuttle bounced and came to rest. Bud sat breathing hard before getting up and walking back to the engines, pulling out a tool kit from a locker along the way. Kel, bruised and battered, his cramped fingers still locked in the cargo-bay netting, was amazed that Bud, while walking past, actually asked him if he was okay. And he basically was; he had a cut on his forehead, an aching shoulder, aching hands, and more bruises than he cared to count, but no broken bones and, he hoped, no concussion.

Half an hour later, they rose smoothly into the air. Bud was ignoring them, concentrating on the displays and readouts.

Kel, crouched again between the pilot's and co-pilot's seat, this time seated on an emergency pack he'd pried from the wall behind the pilot's seat. He glanced at Bud, and then spoke in a low but urgent voice to Chuy: "If we're actually going to that shit hole, you can pass as white. Use Floyd Anderson. It's just unusual enough that it'll work. Remember, you're Floyd, Floyd Anderson."

A look of disgust passed over Chuy's face before he relaxed and replied, "Floyd!? Jeeez-us. H. Christ! Thank you Kelvin!"

Kel didn't manage to suppress a smile. "Very good, Floyd."

"You're fuckin' enjoyin' this, ain't ya, ya fuckin' shit sombitch."

As Chuy slipped seamlessly into redneckese, Kel broke up; Bud, who was trying to stifle it, started half-hiccupping half-laughing. Still choking, he turned toward Chuy, who had also started to laugh.

"Okay, Chuy. We ain't goin' to The Iron Dream. And we ain't goin' back to Xenadu or Baghavad. We're goin' to New Harmony. That's where I was goin' anyway. I was just fuckin' with you."

He laughed again. Neither Chuy nor Kel joined him; they just stared at him.

Bud pulled out a full-liter Mason jar from under the pilot's seat, took a swig from it, and passed it to Chuy. Chuy took a long hit and shuddered at the horrible, metallic taste. He passed the jar to Kel, who in turn took a hit, recoiled, and passed it back to Bud.

After the jar had gone around twice more, and Bud had put what was left of it back under his seat, Chuy said, "Man, I'm sorry about Bonnie. That was low."

Bud replied, "Yes 'twas," without looking at Chuy. He pulled out the jar again, unscrewed the top, took a hit, passed it to Kel, and said, "Have another," before lighting a fat joint.

They flew on in a haze of *mota* smoke, as the Mason jar dwindled and Chuy fed Bud an embellished version of their adventures. Then the shuttle shook again, as if being hammered by hail the size of softballs. It screeched and began pitching crazily from side to side. Bud fought to maintain control, muscling the control stick contrary to the shuttle's lurches, as Kel flew toward the ceiling and then the walls, and Chuy jerked against his seat's restraints.

The stick went dead and the shuttle dove toward the earth. Just before it slammed into the ground, the controls kicked back in. Bud pulled up the nose, and the shuttle hit tail first and then flipped, coming to rest upside down, its cabin half crushed. A few seconds later, a flame burst from its tail section.

33

LOVE, n. 1) The recognition of another's ability to increase one's happiness; 2) A form of temporary insanity. The cure, as Nietzsche points out, often costs no more than the price of a new pair of eyeglasses.

—Chaz Bufe, *The American Heretic's Dictionary*

Kel looked up. A hazy white figure towered over him. He tried to speak, but couldn't. He tried to move his head, but he couldn't do that, either. He felt pain in his shoulder and pain in his head and chest, but it was dull, somewhere in the background. He had a vague memory of being slammed around, and feeling blinding pain, but he couldn't make sense of it. And he felt peaceful. It only hurt when he moved. So he didn't. He closed his eyes and slept. He woke while it was still dark, and screamed in agony until the figure in white appeared over him, muttering soothing words, and he began to float again.

Three days later, Kel woke up and looked at the white figure entering the room. It hurt too much to move almost anything but his eyes, but he was awake, and she looked good: blonde hair, green eyes, and a figure that pushed against her uniform in all the right places. He tried to sit up, but a burst of pain in his head and chest stopped him a few centimeters above his bed, gasping.

She put her hand on his shoulder, and he allowed her to gently push him back. She looked down at him, smiled and said, "Easy cowboy. Relax. You're still hurt." When he had settled, she said, "I'll give you something to help you sleep."

Kel tried to speak, but he couldn't; all he could do was gasp as she slipped a hypodermic needle into a small glass bottle, and then into a tube leading into his right arm.

* * *

The sun slipped behind the hills in the distance, the window darkened, and Kel awoke. The pain was still there, but not as bad—tolerable. And his head ached. But he was conscious of his surroundings: white walls, white floor, white ceiling, white bed, white sheets, and a picture of a blond-haired, blue-eyed Christ on the wall facing him, hand raised in greeting. The nurse walked into the room, leaned over him, and asked, "How do you feel?"

"Alive."

He had to be, to be so aware of her body only inches from his face, her aroma, and the warm feeling of her hand pressing two fingers against the skin over his carotid artery. After looking at her watch for fifteen seconds, she pressed the back of her fingers against Kel's forehead, and withdrew them.

He was definitely feeling better. It was all he could do to prevent himself from reaching up and grabbing her. It had been a long time. Too long. But he was still too weak and in too much pain. The nurse straightened, looked down at Kel's wide eyes, and smiled, recognizing the power she had over him. She injected the dose she'd prepared, turned, undulated toward the door, and slipped through it without looking back as he slipped into semi-consciousness.

As he was going under, Kel stared after her. Velky. Velky Popovice, RN. That was what the name tag above her left breast had said. The name tag had also borne a symbol that seemed vaguely familiar: three green lightning bolts flying away from each other toward a red circle.

34

WHITE SUPERIORITY, n. The fondest dream of those whose existence is the strongest evidence against it.

—Chaz Bufe, *The American Heretic's Dictionary*

A week and a half later, the morning he was released, Kel walked into the sub-commandant's office. He was functional but still hurting, wearing the grey wool uniform he'd found carefully folded on the chair by his bed, and now all too aware of the meaning of the lightning-bolt symbol stitched to the uniform's arms.

The office was oddly familiar: rough hewn lumber walls, buffed pine floors bearing an occasional throw rug, and a fireplace made from rounded river stones set into one wall. It looked like the hunting lodge his family had rented on his dad's splurge-vacation when he was seven. All that was missing was the dozen or so mounted deer heads; here, there was only one, a far-from-impressive six-point buck.

The short, pudgy man in the black uniform behind the desk noticed Kel gazing toward it, looked up, and smiled silently in triumph. Kel, trying to hide his sarcasm, smiled back and said, "Nice buck." It went right over the guy's head. He beamed as Kel gaped at the head and then at the office's furnishings. There were bookcases, display cases with trophies, plaques and other mementos, a huge lightning-bolt flag, a nearly as huge black velvet portrait of the blond-haired, blue-eyed Christ he'd seen in his hospital room, poster-sized framed photos of Hitler, Goebbels, Smithers, Chicalito, Schoenmutter, Rippard, and Davison, faux-Maxfield Parrish paintings of cold, scantily clad, sexless Nordic beauties, and an amazingly realistic acrylic of the grinning chimp-like figure on Tau II's funny money, surrounded by what Kel presumed were his house slaves.

The short, fat weasel of a man motioned for Kel to sit down in the wooden chair before his huge desk as he sank into a leather swivel chair that almost swallowed him. He looked to the right, away from Kel, and began absent mindedly tapping a wooden pointer into the palm of his left hand. He kept this up for a good thirty seconds, as Kel grew increasingly nervous. Finally, the man put the pointer down on his desk, removed his wire-rim glasses, and carefully cleaned them with a handkerchief before delicately placing them back on his nose.

When at last he turned toward Kel, Kel had to force himself not to stare at an ugly, curved scar on the man's right cheek. Rather, the Reverend's cheek. The name plaque on his desk identified him as the Reverend Roberto Belette Schwarz. The Reverend didn't deign to speak to Kel; instead, he inspected him, like an entomologist would an insect.

Schwarz was a pudgy, fussily groomed 50-something with a comb-over consisting of five greying, greasy strands. (All implants had been removed from prisoners bound for Tau II, including, cruelly, even hair implants.) To complement his garish black uniform, Schwarz was wearing knee-high black leather boots and black leather gloves. After a few more seconds, he blurted out in a surprisingly high voice, "Do you have any questions?"

"Yes. What happened to Bud and Floyd?"

Schwarz smiled. "Bud was not hurt badly. A shuttle picked him up two days after you were brought in. He was injured; he had broken ribs, but he'll survive. And who is Floyd?"

"The other passenger."

"Oh. And who is he?"

"How the hell should I know? Never met him before."

Schwarz continued smiling, but didn't reply.

Kel squirmed before asking, "Why didn't they take me if they took Bud?"

Schwarz lost his smile. "Do you think the miscegenated mongrels who run this planet care about you? About me? Do you really think the mud people care about us?"

"But why Bud and not me? He's white, too."

"Don't be naive. Bud is their lackey. You, apparently, are not."

Kel didn't reply.

After a few seconds, Schwarz asked, "What kind of work do you do?"

"I'm a musician."

"You don't look it. And do you really consider that work? You look like you've been doing manual labor."

"I was. They made me do construction work at New Havana."

"Good. You can do the same here after you work a few days doing mess hall cleanup. Consider it an exercise in humility."

Kel suppressed an impulse to strangle Schwarz.

The smirking, leather-clad little man added, "Don't worry. You can also play your music here. We have a fine marching band."

Kel looked down at his hands. A marching band. Wonderful. Fucking wonderful. He could almost feel the goddamned glockenspiel hanging from a strap around his neck.

Schwarz chuckled at Kel's obvious disgust. "We also have other types of music: Country. And Western." He laughed. "Even Death Metal. A wide spectrum."

Kel blanched visibly as Schwarz smirked and continued, "No jazz. No blues. No nigger music." He stopped and stared at Kel, who was doing his best to present a blank face, but wasn't succeeding.

"In any event, your story about what you did in New Havana checks out. According to our sources, you made a brave escape.

"By the way, they've already tried you in absentia and pronounced death sentences upon both you and Andrade."

Kel went white.

"Yes, we know his name. *Floyd's* name. . . . And they've already tried and executed your accomplice."

Kel looked up, shocked. "Oh Jesus! Not—"

"Yes. They executed your friend Stakhanov. Our condolences. He was obviously a good man, even though a Slav."

Kel sat open mouthed. Stakhanov!? He was a decent enough guy in his own blockheaded way. And now he was dead . . . And he and Chuy had caused it.

While Kel was sitting and stewing, Schwarz continued. "Tell me one thing. Why didn't you kill the red swine at the border post when you had the chance?"

Kel blurted out the first thing that came to mind: "We didn't have to."

Schwarz smirked. "You obviously have some misconceptions about what is 'necessary.' But you will get over them."

Kel hesitated and then asked, "What happened to Chuy?"

"Chuy?" Schwarz pronounced the name as if it was a curious obscenity. He sneered, "You can go."

"What hap—"

Schwarz lost his smirk. "You can go!"

Kel didn't even ask where.

35

GOD, n. 1) A three-letter justification for murder; 2) An unsavory character found in many popular works of fiction.

—Chaz Bufe, *The American Heretic's Dictionary*

Christians call it faith . . . I call it the herd.

—Friedrich Nietzsche, *Beyond Good and Evil*

The large church was full. Like Schwarz's office, it was rectangular and made of rough-hewn lumber. It held row upon row of identical pews, extending from the back to only five meters from the slightly raised platform bearing the lectern. At the back of the platform, a huge 2-D dominated the wall, featuring the same black-velvet Aryan Jesus as in Schwarz's office, but now with whip in hand and wrath in his eye, driving cringing, hook-nosed creatures out the open front doors of a temple as they snatched at coins. Similar scenes festooned the other walls: Hitler, standing resolute, pistol in hand, defending blond-haired, blue-eyed Aryan children from slavering, subhuman semitic hordes; Rushbo, the man-mountain, slaying the serpent of drug addiction with the sword of truth; a beatific Rippard, staring in wonder at his own raised hand, at the vial of sickle-cell plague it held with which he had temporarily stopped the mud-people takeover of the Earth; and in the back a huge painting depicting the blessed nuclear fires that had cleansed the Earth of the terrorist heretics in Riyhad, Mecca and Tehran, and Satan's spawn in Tel Aviv.

Directly above the church's back door, a camera pointed over the crowd toward the lectern. Three others along the walls also pointed toward it, while a fifth mounted behind the pulpit panned the crowd sitting neatly in the pews. The church was far too small to hold The Dream's entire population, but those who couldn't attend could at least watch.

The pews were packed. The first twenty rows were filled with men in black uniforms and their women, also dressed, modestly, in black. The fifty rows behind them were filled with men and women dressed in grey, but for a few women in white nurse's uniforms. Kel was in a row near the back. He was dressed in the same plain, grey, military style uniform as all of the other men in the back pews. His armpits and upper back were already drenched with sweat, and the collar of his wool uniform itched. But he barely noticed.

Velky was sitting next to him, her white nurse's uniform spotless, her leg pressed against his. He reached over, without taking his gaze from the lectern, and put his hand on her thigh, and squeezed. While looking straight ahead at the man who had just stepped behind the lectern, and who had yet to speak, she moved his hand off her thigh, and onto his, but continued to hold his hand, squeezing it. They were both gazing straight ahead, breathing hard, as the tall, well-built man behind the lectern prepared to speak.

Conrad Held, the founder of The Iron Dream, a grandfatherly man with a shock of white hair and sparkling blue eyes, straightened, waited several well-calculated seconds, and began to speak in a deep, resonant voice.

"White brothers and sisters. Ever since freedom loving, God-fearing people uncovered the truth about the Jews, the Communist faggot Zionists have been denying God's plain truth. Yes, they've been denying it. Denying the truth. For centuries. Denying it. Denying it. Denying it. Year after year after year, decade after decade—and, yes, century after century!

"They've been denying it forever, and they thought that they got away with it. But they didn't!" He paused. "They didn't get away with their lies! They didn't get away with it because freedom fighters like Henry Ford, Adolf Hitler, Richard Smithers, and Bill Schwarz, the ancestor of our own assistant pastor, didn't let them! These freedom fighters have been telling the truth about the Jew conspiracy for hundreds of years! And brave people acted on that truth. Some. But not enough!

"And what happened!? God's mighty rod smote faggot, Jew-loving America, and that same mighty rod smote faggot, Jew-loving Europe!" He paused again. "Why? How? How did it happen? Tell me! How did it happen? How did the world deliver itself up to Jew avarice and Jew faggotry?!"

He swept his gaze across the sweaty faces. He looked down and hung his head, gripping the sides of the lectern, his knuckles growing white. After several seconds he relaxed his grip, inhaled, looked up, and roared:

"You already know why! The white race was too stupid to listen! They crucified the one man who had the guts to do something about it, and now the entire Earth is under the New World Order! All of the homelands of the white race are gone, overrun by the Jews and their mud people puppets. Do you want to know why?!!

"I'll tell you why! It's the same damned reason we're under their jackboots here! The white race was too gutless, too stupid to fight back! We came here to escape the Jews, niggers, gooks, spics, and the race traitors who lick their boots! And what have we got?! Jews, niggers, gooks, spics, and race traitors!!! They control this entire"—he smashed his fist into his open palm—"miserable!"—the fist smashed again—"damned!!"—the fist smashed yet again—"planet! They do!! You know it and I know it!"

"Long before freedom-loving Aryans discovered the Protocols of the Elders of Zion, the Communist-faggot Jews were lying. But we knew the truth then, and we know it now! There have always been heroes who have stood up to the New World Order! They paid a terrible price, but they stood up to it!"

Held reached down into his pocket, pulled out a tattered paperback, clutched it to his breast, and raised it high above his head.

"In the 1920s, over two centuries ago, this little book told the truth, and it helped lead to the great cleansing. That's why we're reproducing it today, here and in New M!

"It's called *The International Jew*. It was written by one of the great men of the twentieth century, Henry Ford. *Before the führer rose to power!* Henry Ford loved the white race so much that he not only wrote this book and used his own money to print it, but he also gave our beloved *führer*, our original beloved *führer*, tens of thousands of dollars.

"Why?! Because he loved the white race! Because he loved the *führer*! Think about it! He did it simply because he loved the white race! Simply because it was the right thing to do!" His voice dropped and he lowered his head. "The right thing to do. . . ." He jerked his head up. "And the *führer* understood! Do you think it was an *accident* that the *führer* had Henry Ford's portrait on his wall in Munich?!"

He paused, and after a few seconds continued in full voice: "Think about this!! Henry Ford not only wrote this wonderful book, *The International Jew*, but he used his own money to print millions and millions of copies of it in America and Germany! Think about it!! One of the world's richest men loved the white race so much that he used his own valuable time and money to save it!" He paused and let the silence drag on. "Well, he *tried* to save it!!

"Freedom fighters like Hitler, Ford, Goebbels, Irving, Chikalito, The Order, Aryan Nations, New White Resistance, and the Eco-American Nationalist Party have been telling the truth about the Jew conspiracy for over two hundred years. And there were twelve glorious years, twelve years of heroes, twelve years of a clean, healthy social order. But now the entire Earth is gone! Gone because the Jews manipulated the white race into fighting itself!"

His voice dropped and he lowered his head. "The white race *was* fighting itself. And no one would listen!" Held kept his head down, but his voice was rising. "No one would stand up for the white race! No one!!"

His head rose slowly. "Well, *almost* no one!!" He paused, and when he continued his voice was still rising, quivering with emotion. "Irving, Smithers, Matthews, McVey, Dave Turner"—Kel jerked to attention at that—"Wilson, McLaughton . . . They were heroes! Heroes who loved freedom! But heroes crying in the wilderness!

"No one would listen to them while the Jews were murdering the Earth! No one would listen while the Jews sent their infected mud-people puppets streaming across America's borders, across Europe's borders, like a wave of filth!!" His voice rose even further. "And they destroyed America! They destroyed Europe! Just like they destroyed their own homelands!!" His voice dropped, and then began rising again. "They fouled their own nests. Then they fouled our nests. And then they fouled the entire Earth!

"They bred like maggots. They destroyed the Earth's climate and brought on the floods, droughts, and hurricanes. And they lied about it! They lied!!"

Held gripped the sides of the lectern harder and clenched his jaw before thundering, "And now, the entire Earth—what's left of the Earth!—is under the new world order! Do you know what that means!? The *New Jew Order*! That's right! The *New Jew Order*!! America is gone! Britain is gone! South Africa is gone! New Zealand is gone! Australia is gone! All of the strongholds of the white race are gone, overrun by the mud people!! By the Jews and their vermin mud-people puppets!

"They flooded out like cockroaches and they overran the white world! . . . And why did it happen? *Why*? . . . The white race was too gutless to fight back! Too stupid to fight back! . . . Yes! The white race was too gutless and too stupid to fight back! They should have killed them. Killed them all! Killed them like the vermin they are!!"

Held raised his head, closed his eyes, and let his arms drop to his sides, his hands palms out toward the crowd. Kel, whose hand was tightly grasped in Velky's, snuck a look at her. She was transfixed, her gaze locked on Held.

Held opened his eyes, grasped the sides of the lectern, and fixed his gaze on the congregation. He spoke quietly at first, but gradually raised his voice.

"Do you remember your arrival? Naked, shivering, like cattle, before those mud beasts?! Do you remember what that was like? Waking naked in those pods with the mud beasts running their hands over you? *Into* you?! Knowing what they were doing, but being unable to move? And then rolling around sick, clutching your guts, on filthy mattresses? And when you could barely move, being kicked to your feet, prodded along like cattle, herded into rows, and having Corona or some other spic, nigger or gook strut around screeching at you, like he was better than you, better than a white man or woman!?" . . . He lowered his voice to a whisper. "Do you remember?"

He looked down for several seconds before lifting his head, and gradually raised his voice from a near-whisper to an outright shout. "Yes, it's painful. But you need to remember. You need to remember! You need to remember what they've done to us! To our children! To our families! To our women! To our white race! To *you!* . . ."

Ten minutes later Kel and everyone else in the church—when had it happened!? And what was he doing? And oh god did Velky's swaying hips feel good against his!—were on their feet as Held was slamming his fist into his hand, over and over and over, in time with the words: "It's time for the white race to rise! It's time for the white race to rise! It's time for the white race to rise! . . . "

The seething congregational herd swayed as it cheered Held's words, and Kel was gone again, as he bumped and ground into Velky. Minutes later, as he and Velky were still grinding against each other, he was dimly aware that his hand was still in hers, which was tightly, almost painfully clutching his, as Held built to his climax.

"Yes, the Jews and the mud people control this planet! Or they *think* that they control it! But things are beginning to change! And it's starting here! And it's starting now!"

Held lowered his voice again. "When they sent us here, it was so bad that the few real whites left on Earth could do only one thing: escape! That's right! They came here! Here! They paid to come *here!* *You* paid to come here! *You* paid to escape the Jews, niggers, gooks, faggots, commies, anarchists, atheists, spics, and the pile of dung they made of the Earth!

"We were the first ones here! And this place wasn't much. But it was ours! This was our new homeland, the new homeland of the white race! We were the first ones here, and it was ours!!

"And what have we got now?! They sent the scum of the Earth here, and now we have exactly the same damned thing we had on Earth! Exactly the same! The mud people control New M! They control Earth-gov! They control every other god-forsaken settlement on this god-forsaken planet! The Jews and the mud people control *everything*!!" He paused for effect and dropped his voice. "Almost" He lowered his voice even further, to a whisper. "Almost . . . . ."

He began gradually raising his voice. "But they don't control us. They don't control *us*!! And we're not going to take it anymore! Things are going to change!! And it's starting here! And it's starting *now*!! . . . And *you're* going to do it! . . . That's right, *you*!!" He pointed his right arm at the crowd, index finger extended, sweeping from left to right, jabbing for emphasis at individuals. "You're going to do it!! Yes you!! You!! You!! You!! And you!!! You're going to do it!!!"

He looked out in challenge at the undulating mob, lowered his head, lowered his hand to the side of the lectern, and paused several seconds before raising his head and screaming:

"Do you believe in the white race?!"

The crowd thundered back, "Yes!"

"I can't hear you! Do you believe in the white race??!!"

"Yes!!"

"I still can't hear you!! Do you believe in the white race???!!!"

"Yes!!!"

"I still can't hear you!!! Do you believe in the white race????!!!!"

"Yes!!!!!"

Held stopped suddenly, his hands gripping the sides of the lectern, and he waited, until the entire crowd, still on its feet, gradually stopped swaying and lapsed into near-silence. Then he waited some more, staring out at them, until a few in the crowd couldn't stand it any longer and began to fidget, some muttering incoherently. Held looked icily at each in turn, until their neighbors silenced them. When all was quiet again, and the tension so heavy it could shatter under the weight of a pebble, he took a breath, straightened, and began to pound his fist into his hand rhythmically, slowly and softly at first, and then faster and harder, and then he was slamming it on the lectern. Many in the crowd joined him, stomping their feet in time to his pounding rhythm. The unseen sound man turned up the volume on Held's microphone so that, when he spoke again, he nearly drowned out the deafening stomping. He boomed out, in time with the rhythmic footfalls:

"The white . . . race . . . is rising! . . . The white . . . race . . . is rising!! . . . The white . . . race . . . is rising!!!" He paused again, as the crowd stomped in unison, and then shouted, still in sync with the stomping, "Tell me!"

The crowd chimed back in near-perfect time, "The white race is rising!"

"Tell me!"

"The white race is rising!!"

"Tell me!!"

"The white race is rising!!!"

"Tell me!!! . . ."

After a full minute of racial-pride call and response, he held his right arm straight out, hand straight up, and screamed, "Stop!" Almost the entire crowd did, hands in mid-air. And then Held screamed: "Do you believe!!?"

The congregation screamed back, "Yes!"

"Do you believe??!!"

"Yes!!"

"Do you believe???!!!"

"Yes!!!"

Almost simultaneously with the final "yes!!!," Held flattened his hand and began to thrust it repeatedly forward, while screaming the same words over and over, receiving a single-word response from the crowd: "Yes!!!" The entire congregation was imitating Held's gesture, violently thrusting their arms out and forward, while screaming back their response to his call. They were fixated on Held, their eyes glassy. Kel, in a near dream state, began thrusting his arm forward, screaming in response to Held's call while still grinding against Velky. He noted, as if from a distance and to his horror, that some part of him—a large part of him—was enjoying his immersion in the herd, was enjoying being swallowed up by it. He fought it, but he couldn't hold out; he went under again. The wave of emotion rolled over him, and he was no longer an individual, but a part of the orgasmic, screaming, thrusting mass.

After perhaps the fiftieth "Do you believe?!" the man behind Kel accidentally jabbed his saluting arm into Kel's shoulder, and Kel became abruptly aware of his surroundings and himself. He was still grinding against Velky, and he was still rock hard. Kel turned toward Velky and saw her glazed eyes, rhythmically thrusting right arm, quivering body, and her mouth forming the word, over and over, "Yes," as she ground against him. He stared at the rest of the enthralled congregation, and resisted the near-overwhelming conflicting desires to fuck Velky on the spot or run out of the church as far and as fast as his legs could carry him; instead, he forced himself to thrust his arm forward while mouthing the word he had already begun to hate, "yes!," while continuing to grind against Velky. He stole another glance at her. She was screaming "yes!" over and over again while thrusting her right arm outward and grinding her hips into his. Over and over. And over.

36

HUMAN BEING, n. One who makes mistakes repeetedly . . . repetedly . . . repetedley . . .

—Chaz Bufe, *The American Heretic's Dictionary*

The next Saturday was beautiful: 25 degrees C, low humidity, clear skies, and just a hint of a breeze. Kel looked down at the compound. It was impressive, bigger than Baghavad or Serenity, its boundary marked by guard towers and barbed wire fences extending in both directions as far as the eye could see. Not that that mattered. He was lying entwined with Velky on a blanket in a clearing on the hill above the chapel. His hand was massaging her scalp, her long blonde hair flowing between his fingers. Her eyes were closed and she was purring with contentment. He continued kneading while gently pulling her toward him, and then leaning forward and kissing her, open mouthed. After waiting, deliberately holding back, he felt her tongue tentatively flick his. They sank into a prolonged kiss, their tongues gently teasing each other. While they were still kissing, he pulled his hand loose from her hair and slid it down to her waist, and then her butt. He felt her tense, sensed that he should stop, but continued anyway. He slid his hand up across her thigh and then under her blouse. As he reached her breast, she broke off the kiss, grabbed his hand, pulled it down, put her other hand against his chest, and pushed him away. She rolled away and sat up. Kel grasped after her, but she grabbed his hand, holding it tightly, glaring at him.

Kel said, "What's wrong? You want me! I want you! Come on! What's wrong!?"

"You're pushing me! That's what's wrong!"

After a few seconds of open-mouthed gaping, he tried to pull his hand away, but she held it tight.

He saw her angry glare, and said, "Okay! I'm sorry! I'm sorry!"

She grasped his hand for a few more seconds before almost throwing it at him. Kel looked at her slantwise through half-closed eyes as she readjusted her clothing. She waited for him to speak, but, not knowing what to say, he didn't. Eventually she continued:

"Don't you understand? It's wrong. You're pushing me. I know that you can't help it, but I don't like it. I know what men are like. But you're too fast. And I don't like it. I just don't like it."

Kel tentatively reached toward her again, but she pushed his hand away.

She got up and stalked down the hill, almost stomping her feet as she put distance between herself and Kel.

Kel lay still, resting on one elbow, and looked after her, his jaw hanging open. Why in the hell did this or something equally off the wall always seem to happen? Were they all out of their goddamned minds? Or was he? And was it his imagination or had she been grinding her hips into his just days ago, for what seemed like eternity?

After a few moments of bitter reflection he shook himself out of it and said, "Fuck it!" He looked down with renewed interest at the guard towers, the fences stretching out into the distance, and the shuttle pad near the edge of the settlement at the base of the hill. Discouragingly, it was set behind two rows of razor wire and had a guard shack by its gate, with floodlights on the shack's roof and on poles set back from the pad at its corners. So, no escape there. No way to get to New Harmony, let alone back to Earth. No way to find out what happened to Folky. Probably ever.

37

MURDER, n. One of the most heinous crimes, and one for which there is never an adequate excuse. Not to be confused with the noble and necessary practice of killing upon government command.

—Chaz Bufe, *The American Heretic's Dictionary*

On Monday, Kel was back at his construction job. It had been tolerable the previous week; the work was so mindless that he could fantasize about Velky and not miss a beat. Now it wasn't tolerable. No fantasies, just bitter disappointment, and work didn't get much worse than this: form setting—lugging into place back-breakingly heavy plywood forms, wrestling them so that they snuggled up against each other, then knocking wedge-shaped steel shims with a heavy framing hammer onto protruding, bulb-ended steel wires laced through the forms, and then filling the forms with concrete. After that, walking back to the forms they'd set the previous day, knocking the shims off, and pulling the forms away from the hardening concrete. The finale was always the same: hauling the stripped forms and shims back to the flatbed, so that the seemingly never-ending cycle would resume the next day.

Exhausted, Kel jumped off the tail of the flatbed, walked the few hundred meters to his barracks, put on his camo unform without showering, and was soon rushing along with several dozen other camo-clad men, most at least a decade younger than he was, through The Iron Dream's obstacle course, climbing over fallen tree trunks, crawling under barbed wire, clambering up netting, and over walls.

After an hour of watching the recruits silently, but for an occasional shout of rebuke, Murphy, the master sergeant drill instructor, blew his whistle and yelled, "Dismissed!" Kel, exhausted and filthy, fell in beside two of the other recruits, Andre, another member of the foundation crew, a tall, muscular, blond man in his early twenties, half a head taller than Kel, and Zed, a skinny, greasy-haired semi-literate from Oklahoma in his early thirties, who had the comparatively cake, though much less macho, job of dishwasher. Zed had been in The Iron Dream longer than either Kel or Andre, but hadn't risen above being shit man on the kitchen crew.

As they walked from the obstacle course to the showers, Kel was huffing and puffing, almost gasping as he spoke.

"That almost killed me."

Zed, panting harder than Kel, said "That warnt shit! Ya think that's bad?!?"

Andre looked contemptuously at Zed, put his arm around Kel's shoulders, and said, "Do not worry. You will get used to it."

Zed smirked and said, "Yeah, sure."

Andre didn't even bother to reply to Zed, before turning his attention back to Kel. "It will become easier, comrade. This week is worst. Next is better. Then, we begin firearms training."

"Firearms?"

"*Ja!* You did not know?"

"No! I thought that only Earth-gov had weapons."

Andre laughed. "Not true. Very soon we teach the Jews and their mongrel puppets a lesson they will not forget." He smiled, but Kel didn't. Zed forced a laugh, but Andre didn't even glance in his direction. Andre said to Kel, "Let's get a drink," to which Zed added, "Shee-it yeah!"

* * *

After six more agonizing days of form setting and enduring the obstacle course, nightly 2-D vids featuring Jewish, black, Asian, and Mexican vermin raping white women, before meeting their well-deserved gory ends, and another weekend enduring Velky's cold, well cool, shoulder—at least she was talking to him again—Kel was back in the locker room, drying himself after showering. Andre had fucking jived him about it getting easier. It had gotten harder. And he still hadn't discovered a way out of this racist hell-hole.

As Kel was rubbing his hair dry with a towel, Murphy walked into the room and stood hands on hips for a moment, looking around the room, taking in the recruits' naked and half-naked bodies with a bit too much interest, before assuming his full DI persona. He pulled his eyes away, put his hands on his hips, and shouted, "Listen up, ladies!" Everyone stopped dead. Murphy waited an instant and pulled a key from his pocket.

He held the key up long enough that Kel wondered what in hell he was doing. Murphy turned, put the key in the padlock securing the locker immediately before him, opened the lock and removed it, and then put the key in the lock securing the locker next to it, opening it and removing that lock, too. Then he wrapped a meaty fist around the vertical bar separating the two lockers and pulled up. Both lockers swung out into the aisle, one to the left, one to the right, revealing a passageway leading downward. Murphy bowed and said, sweeping the way with his hand, "This way, girls."

Kel hurriedly pulled on his clothes. As soon as the first of the excited recruits entered the passageway, still buttoning up and zipping, Murphy put his hand on their backs and guided them in, not quite pushing. Kel, following an excited Zed, was almost the last down the steps to the firing range.

* * *

Five days later, Kel still had no idea how in hell he was going to get out of the Dream, and it was time for another firearms session.

Kel stepped through the hidden door and walked down the steps into a large room with bare concrete walls. It had a walk-in locker at one end and a firing range at the other. Andre, who had entered before Kel, motioned for Kel to join him near the end of the firing bays.

When the last of the militia men-to-be had stepped out of the passage, Murphy emerged. He pushed past the recruits toward the walk-in locker that took up the back wall. His assistant, corporal O'Keefe, walked into the locker as Murphy turned toward the recruits and said, "Form a line facing me."

As the recruits queued up, the corporal emerged pulling a cart laden with racks of assault weapons. Murphy said, "March forward, receive your weapon, and continue to the firing bays." Kel and Andre waited, and then filed past Murphy. O'Keefe handed them, and all of the others, AK-97s, projectile weapons which had been old on Earth when Kel left, but which had a muzzle velocity nearly twice that of the original AK-47, and which used shred-on-contact rounds. When a 97 slug hit a limb or a torso, it would simply explode.

Kel walked the few meters to the nearest unoccupied firing bay, and put on the ear protectors hanging on a peg. The weight of the weapon was familiar. Too familiar. He stared at the AK, holding it loosely in his hands. It was the same kind he'd used in Uzbekistan, back when he won his bronze star. Back when the ten-year-old Uzbeki kid's head had exploded like a watermelon. He'd played that scene back in slow motion, over and over. Not every night, but on too many.

Alcohol helped deal with it, but not enough. He hadn't had much choice—no choice at all, really—the kid had a bomb strapped to his chest. But his finger pulling the trigger and—always, always in slow motion—the kid's head exploding and his brains and skull fragments splattering against the wall, still woke Kel up screaming.

The first time he'd come down to the firing range, five days ago, he'd been able to numb out. But not this time.

"Kel! . . . Kel! . . . Are you okay?" Andre was shaking him.

Kel couldn't hear a word Andre was saying. He took off his ear protectors as Andre repeated, "Are you okay? Are you okay?"

"Yeah, I'm okay."

"You sure?"

"Yeah, I'm sure."

Murphy was staring at them and had started walking in their direction. Andre walked to his bay and put on his ear protectors; Kel lifted his rifle to his shoulder without putting on his protectors, flipped the switch to put it on semi-auto, and began firing single shots as fast as he could pull the trigger, hitting the man-shaped target every time, with the shots clustering on the center of the target.

Minutes later, as he was about to squeeze off another shot, a siren wailed and Kel stopped firing. As the firing range was engulfed in silence, Kel became aware of a persistent ringing in his ears. Murphy was speaking, but he couldn't hear him.

The targets rose simultaneously toward the ceiling, revealing a stained, bullet-pocked wooden post at the back of the range. Two grey-uniformed guards, their heads in black hoods with only their eyes showing, walked onto the stage from the right, dragging a smaller, gagged, hooded figure in baggy coveralls between them. They tied the figure to the post and walked away, as the prisoner shuddered violently, and strained outward, trying to scream or break free. Murphy walked out onto the firing range and stepped in front of the hooded, struggling figure, and began speaking, as Kel's hearing gradually faded in over the ringing in his ears.

". . . race traitor . . . Corona . . . mud . . . . . . stooge . . . Give him what . . . deserves. . . . One shot . . . . my . . ." Murphy strode back behind the firing line and yelled, "Raise weapons!" A few of the recruits half-heartedly raise their guns; most didn't. Murphy shouted, "Well, ladies!? Raise weapons!!" A few more lifted their guns. Murphy shouted again, his face bright red, "Well???!!!" After a moment's hesitation, almost all of the rest raised their weapons. Murphy bore in on the few stragglers, including Kel, and yelled at the nearest one, "You, Olson! K.P. and cleaning the latrine for a month! With a fucking toothbrush! And three times through the obstacle course tonight!!!" He screamed, "Raise weapons!" Olson, Kel and the other stragglers raised theirs, and Murphy shouted, "Fire!!!"

Kel was tempted to turn his gun on Murphy. But he aimed slightly above the prisoner's left shoulder, instead. Several others, including Andre, also deliberately missed. But Kel didn't feel any better about it. And he guessed that the others who had missed didn't, either. The shots from the rest of the squad had ripped the tied figure's body to shreds, streaks of gore splattering in all directions against the earthen back wall.

After the firing stopped, Murphy walked back onto the range, then up to what was now little more than a mass of gore tied to the pole. He loosened what was left of the bloody hood and pulled it off. Half of the prisoner's head was blown away, but she was still recognizable as a woman, her red hair caked with blood and brains, and with a ball gag drooping from her shattered jaw.

Seeing what he had done, the recruit in the bay to the left of Kel vomited. Kel barely managed to stifle his own gag reflex. Several others didn't. When the sound of retching had faded, Murphy asked the recruits, "Feeling a bit squeamish, ladies? Well don't!! This bitch was fucking mud people! She gave birth to a mixed-race abomination!

"And I lied. She wasn't working for Corona. She came here three days after she arrived in New M. But that was long enough for her to fuck a nigger. Said she was raped, but what real white woman would let a nigger fuck her? . . . She asked for it!" He lowered his voice. "And get used to it, you pussies. This is war. The survival of the white race is at stake. You did your duty to the white race!" He stared at them for several seconds, then pointed to the recruit next to Kel and to one of the others who had vomited. He scowled at the puke-covered floor and said, "Get a mop and bucket and clean this shit up you gutless faggots! Now!" As the two were heading up the stairs for the mop closet, he turned toward the rest and said, "Clean your weapons, then place them on the cart and get the hell out of here!"

Kel, ashen, looked toward Andre. Andre stood silently for several seconds before he began mechanically stripping and cleaning his gun. Kel was still cleaning his as Andre trudged leadenly up the stairs. Kel watched him disappear, and then saw Zed, who upon catching Kel's glance came over, punched him on the arm, and said, "What's the matter, bro? . . . Come on! That was fuckin' great! I ain't had so much fun since I stuck a firecracker up a cat's ass!"

38

NASHVILLE SOUND, n. Hank Williams on Prozac.
—Chaz Bufe, *The American Heretic's Dictionary*

The next afternoon, Schwarz walked into the barracks as Kel, hair wet from the shower, was finishing dressing. Schwarz beckoned for Kel to follow him outside. Kel, breathing slowly to calm himself—what the fuck did Schwarz want with him on his day off?—pulled his belt tight and followed Schwarz out the door. A few meters past it, Schwarz stopped and turned to face him.

"Murphy informed me of your performance yesterday. If you hadn't cut up those Reds at New Havana, you'd be cleaning the latrine, like Olson . . . But you did. So you get off with an extra hour every afternoon on the obstacle course and participating in the marching band. I remember how thrilled you were when I told you about it and our other bands at your intake interview. We also need a guitarist in Death and Glory, and Family Values."

Kel tilted his head and squinted at Schwarz.

Schwarz answered the implied question: "Our best über-metal group and our traditional country group. It's one of them and the marching band. Choose."

Kel, wondering if Schwarz was fucking with him, hesitated and said, "The marching band and Death and Glory."

"Fine. The marching band and Family Values it is." Kel feigned looking upset. Schwarz smirked and continued, "You'll still have to work construction and still have militia duty."

Kel sighed. That was fine. Doing anything other than form setting and watching every word he said would be a blessing; even the marching band might be a relief. And thank god he'd been right about Schwarz bullshitting him. Über-metal was unthinkable. He just couldn't do it—shrill, overdriven guitar, racist, sociopathic lyrics, painfully simple chord progressions, repetitive rockabilly and borrowed-punk rhythms, the blast beat, endless, repetitive guitar solos that were little more than distorted scale exercises, and banshee vocals. All at ear-shattering volume.

For decades before he'd been deported, it had been the Eco-Nazis' primary recruiting tool back on Earth. And it had worked. Give the people what they want: mind-numbing shit. Shit that would jack them up into a sadistic fury. Ages ago, he'd wandered one night into an unfamiliar but okay-looking no-cover bar in the Sedona sector of Phoenixmetro and heard the band break into the first song of what was probably their third set, the leaden ballad, "Aryan Mystic Maiden." As the song screeched into the air, he'd muttered "Jesus Festering Christ!" at what he thought was so low a volume that no one could possibly hear him. One of the assholes who'd blindsided him and then kicked the shit out of him must have been a lip reader.

So, no, he wouldn't play that shit. Ever.

Schwarz led him to an A-frame a good kilometer from the barracks, and almost out of the settlement, set against a hill beneath what looked like Douglas Firs. Schwarz walked in first, waited for Kel to enter, looked at the two skinny guys who were lounging on a broken-down, stained couch, gestured toward Kel, and said, "Your new guitar player." Schwarz didn't wait for a reply and turned to address Kel without missing a beat: "Marching band. Eight a.m. The square." Again, Schwarz didn't wait for a reply. He was already walking out the door before Kel could utter a syllable.

Kel turned to his new bandmates and unconsciously drawled, drawing on his Southern Arizona background and years among rednecks in the military, "Howdy y'all, I'm Kel." The two skinny dudes muttered "Howdy. Ernie." "Billie." Billie added, "I'm the bass player," after which Ernie said, "I'm the singer. Play some guitar too," pointing to a funky looking acoustic leaning against the wall next to a small, crappy looking drum set—crummy plywood drums with a funky looking red finish, shaky-looking, too-thin stands, tarnished no-name cymbals, and a three-legged wooden stool rather than a throne behind it all. The crowning stroke was a filthy pillow lying inside the bass drum, which didn't even have a front head.

Then there was the p.a., a four-channel head plugged into single-10" speaker cabs with no horns, torn grill cloth, and no stands; the cabinets were set up on crates. But at least there were mikes for Billie and Ernie, a mike hanging from a stand above the drum kit, and one set on the pillow inside the bass drum. So, no mike for Kel, no vocal mike for the drummer, and no monitors. Live, this set-up would sound fucking great. With this type of no-monitor p.a., the best he could hope for was that he might be able to hear the bassist and drummer, and they might be able to hear him if they all set up close enough to each other.

The guitar gear was as primitive as the p.a. and drum set: a no-name Telecaster copy plugged into what looked to be an ancient Bassman head with a 2X12 bottom. The head's front panel was even black. Could it be? No, it couldn't. They hadn't even made copies for forty years before he'd been exiled. Kel walked behind the amp and looked into the head, hoping against hope. But no. No tubes, not even any transistors. Fake as all hell. Just the ubiquitous plug-in black box familiar from every consumer product in the world, in this case almost certainly lobotomized to sound like the power circuit in a 1960s or 1970s transistor amp. The worst sound in the world. No doubt about it, it'd sound like shit, even overdriven all to hell. And no reverb or other effects.

Kel picked up the fake Tele. He tried to tune it. The harmonics at the 12th fret wouldn't come out quite right against the notes on the 7th fret, so he checked the bridge. Already adjusted to the max. So it'd be way out of tune in the upper registers. The higher he went on the neck, the worse it would sound. Wonderful. Fucking wonderful.

Topping it all off, the drummer walked out of the bathroom, still zipping his fly with one hand while gripping the front of his pants with the other. He finished zipping, pulled his belt tight, and looked up at Kel and the others. Kel started to grunt disgustedly, but caught himself. It couldn't be, but it was: Zed. Fucking Zed.

Zed glanced at Kel, didn't notice Kel's momentary look of dismay, and walked behind the drums, sat down, picked up his sticks, did a roll on the snare ending with a simultaneous rim shot and foot kick, and said, "Hey bro. Good to see ya. Let's play some fuckin' country! How about 'Nigger Fucker'? Ya know it?"

Kel said, "No," even though he'd heard it and could have faked it. He'd never figured out why David Allen Coe—who as far as Kel knew wasn't a racist—had ever recorded that fucking thing.

Kel pulled the fake Tele off its stand and flicked the switch on the back of the fake Bassman. He looked at Zed and asked about another Coe tune: "What about 'Cum Stains on the Pillow'"?

Zed laughed and said, "Hell yeah!"

Ernie picked up a no-name, fake P-bass, and Billie, after saying, "Yep! I know that one too!," grabbed the funky looking acoustic, strapped it on, and stepped behind the mike.

Kel adjusted the strap holding up the fake Tele and said, "Let's do it! Key of G?" Billy said "Yeah," counted out . . . One . . . two . . . one, two, three, four," and within seconds he was chunking out chords and singing about cum stains on the pillow in the middle of the bed.

Kel tore through a solo on the lower frets. After a final verse they finished, and Kel and Zed almost simultaneously said, "Shee-it yeah!"

After they ripped through two more Coe classics Kel had suggested, "Pussywhipped Again" and "I'd Like to Fuck the Shit Out of You," Billie reached down, opened a beat-all-to-hell, brown briefcase, pulled out a sheet of paper, and handed it to Kel. "Here's the set list. Let's add those Coe tunes." He grinned, "Well, at least sometimes, in certain see-lect venues."

As Kel gaped at the list, Billie put his acoustic on its stand, walked over to the 'fridge, grabbed four bottles of beer, opened them on the handle of one of the kitchen cabinets, laced them between his fingers, walked back, and handed one to Kel, one to Ernie, and one to Zed.

Kel took a long hit, looked the set list over, and suppressed a shudder. It led off with the Toby Keith anthem, "Boot Up the Ass," and went on from there. Charlie Daniels, Oakridge Boys, Alan Jackson, Brooks and Dunn, Lee Greenwood, Adam Einbar, Rupert Burley, Heber Overgaard, and a bunch of shit he didn't recognize.

After he'd slugged down half his beer, Zed proudly announced that two of the most odious-sounding tunes were his originals. The only hint of relief during the first set was "Okie from Muskogee," which Zed, Billie, and Ernie obviously took at face value. But Kel, who knew better, didn't. The only Hank Williams number was, of course, "Kaw-Liga," arguably the only racist number Hank ever wrote. And even then, given Hank's time and place, you had to give Hank a break; he hadn't meant anything by it.

Kel took a slug from his beer and said, "Let's do the first one. One . . . two . . . one, two, three, four . . ."

Then they were off and running into "Boot Up the Ass"—which Kel internally translated to "Tongue on the Boot"—with Kel subtly fucking it up rhythmically. When they ended, Kel chirped enthusiastically, "That was damn close! Let's try it again! What a great fuckin' tune!" And he fucked up the comping again, while overwhelming them with torrents of sixteenth and thirty-second notes during his solo, deliberately playing most of it in the high, out-of-tune register. At the end of the second attempt Kel said, "Let's try it one more time, that ain't quite right!" And they did. And then three more times, until Kel said, "Somethin's wrong with that. Y'all have any idea what? I sure don't." Nobody else did, either. Kel suppressed a smile and said, "Let's set it aside and move on to the next one."

When they came to "Kaw-Liga," Kel forced himself to play it straight, and it sounded great. While he was playing it, he kept reminding himself of his bass-player friend Randy, a six-four, ex-Mormon Apache, who had played it over and over in country bars—while keeping a straight, wooden face—and who had killed himself with booze, ice, and dust two years before Kel had been deported. And yeah, it fit. He could play that. It reminded him of Randy. He didn't know whether to laugh, cry, or both, but yeah, he could play it.

Since he was thinking about Randy, he asked if they knew Randy's favorite country song, "East Bound and Down." They did, and it sounded great. They added it to the set list. Two hours later Kel said, "Phew! I'm done," and set down his guitar.

They had knocked out fifteen or so songs, but, curiously, none of the Alan Jackson, Lynyrd Skynyrd, Rupert Burley, Charlie Daniels, Brad Paisley, and Oakridge Boys numbers that Schwarz and Held loved. It was basically down to Hank, Hank Jr., Hank Jr. Jr., Hank Jr. Jr. Jr., Hank Jr. Jr. Jr. Jr., Patsy, Buck, Merle, Willie, George Jones, Dwight Yoakam, Mickey Gilley, and Junior Brown, singers whose livers had, mostly, sued them for separate maintenance, and whose songs had not a hint of political awareness or lack thereof.

So, life was good. Well, at least tolerable. Schwarz, Held, and the other Nazi shitheads didn't have a clue. And neither did his dickhead bandmates.

39

The only thing that hurts now is the pain.

—Al Perry, song title from the CD "Losin' Hand,"
by Al Perry and the Cattle

Kel's uniform chafed. And it was no fun carrying a three-quarter-meter bass drum strapped to his back and resting on his chest. And it really sucked being restricted to playing "one" and "three" on almost all of the songs, most of which sucked as bad as only playing "one" and "three."

Kel continued going through the motions: marching in a straight line, his body bent backward under the weight of the drum resting on his chest, turning in unison with the rest of the marionettes, and hammering out his two-note mantra. Within minutes, Kel was desperately wondering when the torture would end.

The marching band specialized in songs that had been ancient when Kel had been a kid, including, without a hint of irony in The Dream's ultra-homophobic atmosphere, the Queen anthems "We Will Rock You," "Another One Bites the Dust," and "We Are the Champions." Those songs were prehistoric, but they were still popular as marching band songs, at least at The Iron Dream. As were "Crocodile Rock," "Rock and Roll (Part 2)," and several other moldy oldies too vile to contemplate. To make matters worse, these abominations were interspersed with truly dreadful arrangements of "Flight of the Valkyries" and the rest of Wagner's and Sousa's greatest hits.

It didn't help that Zed was marching nearby, playing a strap-held snare drum, and taking obvious pleasure in the militaristic rhythms and choreographed thrusts of the band. It almost made it worse that the band was playing all of this shit reasonably well.

At 10 a.m., after two solid hours of marching and beating "one" and "three" until Kel's mind reeled, it came to an end. Despite his fatigue, he put down his drum, walked over to Zed to keep the peace, slapped him on the back, and said, loudly, "Hey bro! Great fuckin' job!" Zed hammered a rim shot in reply, causing everyone in the band, including the director, to look up. Kel put his hands to his ears in mock horror, and staggered theatrically back to his bass drum. He looked at Zed, gave him the thumbs up, picked up his drum, and headed toward the band room, which was a good hundred meters away.

Weirdly, in relative terms, the music had sounded good. Zed was actually a pretty good drummer, and had been spot on with the snare. Kel had been, too, with the bass drum, and so had Billie on the cymbals. The woodwind and horn players had been right there, too. It almost felt good, in a skin-crawling, closeted leather-gay sort of way. Kel was glad it was over.

He plodded back into the locker room. Time to get out of his miserable goddamned uniform. And time to go talk to Velky. Talk to her? Talk? That wasn't what he wanted to do. But what else could he do?

Head Number Two, The Wrong Head, had one thing, and one thing only, in mind—and Velky wasn't going for it, at least not on Head Number Two's terms. And Head Number One, although under the influence of Head Number Two, didn't want to do what she wanted—marry her and stick around—but didn't want to cause her any pain. So what to do?

It reminded him all too much of his childhood Catholic visions of a black devil on one shoulder, whispering bad thoughts into one ear, and a white angel on the other shoulder, whispering good thoughts into the other. In this case, there was no angel and no devil, just a throbbing, engorged Head Number Two quivering on one shoulder, spurting bad ideas into Head Number One's ear. Kel laughed out loud, envisioning the grotesque conversation:

Head #2: "Come on! Whatever it takes! You know what you want! And you know what she wants."

Head #1: "No! She said 'no' and that means no. I'm not going to push it."

Head #2: "You're not? Oh please! Who do you think you're kidding? Do you want to fuck her or not?"

Head #1: "Yeah, of course I do."

Head #2: "So?! Do you think she wants to fuck you!? Of course she does! So tell her what she wants to hear. Anything! Tell her you love her. She'll fuck you in a heartbeat."

Head #1: "No! That'd be a terrible thing to do! She'd be hurt. Bad."

Head #2: "So?!"

Head #1: "So!!??"

Head #2: "Come off it. Do you want to fuck her?"

Head #1: "Yeah, of course. But I won't lie to her. I'm not that kind of asshole."

Head #2: "You're not?! What kind of asshole are you?"

Head #1: "I am *not* a fucking asshole!"

Head #2: "Oh really? What about Jeanie? Tony's girlfriend? Remember what you told her?"

Head #1: "Oh Jesus!"

Head #2: "Yeah. Oh Jesus. See??"

Head #1: "See what?! I almost got killed! That was a fucking disaster!"

Head #2: "A disaster?! Wasn't she good? One of the top ten?!"

Head #1: "Top ten? . . . Top five! . . . Oh Jeezus!"

Head #2: "Yeah. Oh Jeezus. Come off it and tell her what she wants to hear. Tell her you'll marry her."

Head #1: "No! I'm not gonna do something that stupid again, and I'm not gonna act like a goddamned scumbag!"

Head #2: "Come off it! Do you want to fuck her? Tell her what she wants to hear."

And so on.
After a lengthy argument, Head #1 won. Barely.

40

EAGLE, n. A large, carnivorous bird which swoops upon smaller, unsuspecting animals. Once its prey is in its clutches, the eagle proceeds to tear apart its still-living victim limb from limb.
When live prey is unavailable, the eagle will happily feast upon carrion. Thus, the eagle is the natural—some would say the only— choice as the official symbol of the U.S. government and other authoritarian regimes, which shall go nameless for fear of belaboring the obvious.

—Chaz Bufe, *The American Heretic's Dictionary*

It was Friday night, hoedown time at The Eagle's Nest, a hunting lodge-themed bar on the outskirts of The Iron Dream that reminded Kel all too much of Schwarz's office, but on a grander scale: pine floor, pine walls, pine ceiling, bare pine rafters, and a few pathetic four-point buck heads mounted on plaques on the walls, along with Eco-Nazi posters, flags, and photos of Held, Smithers, Rippard, and other racial heroes.

Kel, Zed, and company had set up their gear at the back of the hall on the slightly raised, slightly too small stage before a great lightning-bolt flag hanging down from the rafters to near the stage floor. Without monitors, the set up had been tricky, even with only four pieces. Kel had angled the guitar amp, bass amp, and p.a. speakers so that they could all hear each other, but it had been hell getting Billie's mike placed so that it hadn't howled with feedback, like a dog having its nuts crushed in a vise.

Even so, they'd had everything set up and had done a sound check a good half hour before the first set—it sounded like shit, as Kel had expected, but it was as good as it was gonna get—and they'd been hammering down beers ever since. One good thing about The Iron Dream, Kel had to admit, was the beer. They really knew how to make the good shit here. What he was drinking was close to an IPA—light, bitter, smooth, and very alcoholic. The dark beer, as he'd already discovered, was just as good.

The Nest was gradually filling up with fine specimens of the Aryan genotype, but Kel, who was searching eagerly, didn't notice the one blonde he'd hoped to see. She'd been cool to him since the incident on the hill, but she had to be aware of this gig. It had been prominently mentioned on the Dream's inescapable FM station and in its daily scandal sheet, *The Storm*.

She had to come. But she hadn't, and it was nearly show time. And then it was. They opened with one of their quieter numbers, "City Lights," went on to "It Just Don't Get It No More," and then, without stopping between songs, went into overdrive with "Orange Blossom Special." The crowd went nuts, and they were off. Half an hour later, when they closed with Junior Brown's mutated, Hendrix-quoting version of "The Sugar Foot Rag," the dance floor was full of swinging, swaying bodies—and Velky's wasn't among them.

An hour later, following the second set, they put down their instruments after closing with a killer, extremely fast version of Jerry Reed's classic, "Texas Bound and Flyin'." They grabbed their drinks, walked off stage, sat down at a table near the front, and continued to pound down beers. Velky still hadn't shown, but at least the beer was good. Damned good. And their coworkers and militia mates were more than happy to keep it coming.

Then, as Kel was starting his third beer of the break, Zed was tugging on his arm, pulling him back toward the stage. Kel shook off Zed's hand, and walked, more or less upright, to his amp. After he pulled his guitar strap over his shoulder, flicked the amp's "on" switch, and checked that he was more or less in tune by hitting harmonics at the 12th fret and checking them against notes on the 7th fret, he looked out over the crowd. Still no Velky.

They began by book-ending the previous set with "East Bound and Down." Then it was on to nothing but fast dance tunes. Forty-five minutes later, She walked in. And She looked up at him, smiling. He looked down at her, and lit into the final song of the set, a rocked out version of the Mickey Gilley classic, "The Power of Positive Drinking."

When they were done, Kel put down his guitar, managed to get off the riser without tripping, and stumbled toward Velky. He reached toward her, and she backed away. He reached toward her again, "Come on baby. I love you! Come on! Wha's a matter?"

She backed further away from him and said, "You're drunk!" before turning and walking toward the front door.

He stumbled after her, saying, "Baby! Come back!"

She kept walking, without a backward glance, as he lurched after her. He stumbled and would have landed face first on the floor, except that Zed grabbed him and managed to break his fall. After he hauled Kel upright, Zed steered Kel back toward the table where Ernie and Billie were sitting. He sat Kel down in a chair and put a beer in his hand, saying, "It's cool, bro. Shit happens. They're all like that. Fuck 'em!" Fifteen minutes later, he hauled Kel back on stage.

Kel pulled it off. He managed to stay upright, his higher brain functions mostly shut off, while his hands were on automatic pilot. He made it through the set, but after the final number he tripped over the edge of the stage and nose dived to the dance floor.

He woke up late the next morning on his bunk, fully clothed, dried gore caked around his nose, and the sickening metallic taste of blood in his mouth. He had no idea how he had gotten there or what had happened to him. His only reality was a viciously throbbing head, noises that were way too loud, lights that were way too bright, and a world of loneliness and pain.

That afternoon, Murphy rousted him. Hungover and feeling like death, Murphy forced him to run the obstacle course.

41

GLORY, n. An exalted state achieved through participation in
military operations, often by having one's guts blown out
and dying in agony amidst the stench of one's own entrails.

—Chaz Bufe, *The American Heretic's Dictionary*

Kel shot up from his bunk when the klaxon sounded, pulled on
his uniform and boots, and headed for the assembly area. Murphy
and the other noncoms were already there, herding militia members through lines where enlisted men were handing out weapons.
Kel received an AK-97. A separate line was dedicated to RPGs and
more exotic weapons.

Kel shuddered as he looked over and saw a militiaman shoulder
a Ciegadera, one of the burning/blinding laser weapons he'd seen
used in Central Asia. He was glad he just had the AK. He didn't
think he could stand firing a Ciegadera at another human being.
They could burn through body armor at thirty meters and blind at
three kilometers. And their power packs were bulky and extremely
heavy.

Once he'd received his weapon, Kel lined up with the other recruits in stiff ranks, like bullets in a magazine, before an empty
platform. Twenty minutes later, once the final man had stepped
into place, the Reverend Held strode onto the platform, stepped
behind the podium, and spoke.

"Thanks to race patriots"—he gestured at a slowly rising shuttle
heading east—"we know that in two hours the enemy will land
here. And we will annihilate them. The mud people and their race-
traitor stooges will attempt to defile our community, will attempt
to enslave us—again. This is the day we have been preparing for,
the day we have awaited for decades. This day is the beginning of
the renaissance of the white race on this planet. Earth gov, Mud

gov, is in its death throes. Loyal elements have informed us that Mud gov will land many of its remaining troops here and will attempt to imprison our leaders and deport the colony en masse to the western islands, as they did the Muslim scum. We will give them a welcome they will long remember, if any of them live to remember it!"

He smiled, savoring his witticism, and continued: "This day will be consecrated in the history of this planet, and in the history of the white race, as the day God's chosen people began their march to victory, their march to their rightful place as rulers of this planet. You will be the shock troops of that march. . . . Victory or death!" Held saluted them with a rigid arm held out straight, and, after receiving their eerily silent salute and clicked boots in return, lowered his arm, stepped down from the lectern, and marched toward his headquarters without looking back.

Murphy barked, "Follow me!" to Kel's squad, and marched them to the main square, where he spread them out in an irrigation ditch on the open side of the square in ones and twos, hidden behind bushes or other cover. He also put troops hidden by camo-netting on the tops of buildings on the adjoining sides of the square.

Murphy assigned Kel to a slight bend in the shallow, dry irrigation ditch, behind low bushes. As he was leaving, he told Kel, "Don't shoot until all of them have their cargo ramps down and are unloading. We don't want to give any of them a chance to get away! Good hunting!"

As soon as he settled into a reasonably comfortable position, Kel checked his weapon, and then turned his attention to his surroundings. He was surprised by how few militiamen were guarding the square. But then he realized that The Iron Dream had, probably, only 1,500 soldiers, 2,000 max, the powers that be didn't know where Earth gov would land, and that there were at least a dozen logical places; so, the militia would necessarily be spread thin. Still, this was one of the most likely places, as it was central and had a large area where shuttles could set down.

Kel settled down to wait.

The stillness was broken by a truck pulling a microwave fryer into place beneath a large conifer further down the ditch. As soon as it was uncoupled, its crew strung camo nets over it and its flat front plate. Then there was silence. Again, Kel shuddered as he looked down the ditch and saw, twenty meters away, a militiaman with a Ciegadera sitting on his haunches, the power pack resting against the side of the ditch. Where in hell had Held gotten ahold of those goddamned things? From the shuttles that landed once or twice a week at the secluded, heavily guarded shuttle pad? And how in the hell would shuttle pilots get that shit unless someone in Earth-gov was heavily on the take or a "race patriot"?

For that matter, what the hell was he doing here? In a place where people would get blown to bits, broiled alive, or blinded? Or, more to the point, where *he* could get blown to bits, broiled alive, or blinded. And for what? And what would he do once the shooting started?

He just prayed that the landing would be somewhere else, so that he wouldn't have to make any hard choices. Somewhere else, so that he wouldn't have to kill or be killed in a battle in which both sides deserved to die.

Kel waited, not moving, his heart pounding. After several minutes he realized that even the birds had stopped singing. Even the birds had stopped trumpeting their joy of life.

Then it happened. Specks in the sky. Growing larger, rapidly. No one broke discipline. No one fired a shot. Then the shuttles were descending in dreamlike slow motion in front of him, setting down in the main square. As the last one had barely settled to earth, and the first few had lowered their ramps and had started unloading—with only a few dozen troops and maybe three a.p.c.s on the ground—some dickhead began spraying the nearest shuttle with an AK. Then it was on. And Kel was frozen. He couldn't fire.

Three of the shuttles hadn't lowered their ramps, and jerked upward. RPG fire downed two of them when they were no more than ten meters off the ground. Kel saw the RPG shaped-charge rounds spray out their sides in white-hot fountains of molten metal seconds before the shuttles crashed heavily. The third shuttle took off west, back toward New M, in a hail of small arms fire, leaving a trail of smoke, as balls of fire enveloped two of the shuttles still on the ground.

Soldiers streamed out of the other shuttles, some being cut down before they were even off the ramps, and some flinging themselves to the ground and scrambling for cover. Then, from the largest surviving shuttle, four armored personnel carriers rushed down the landing ramp and turned their .50 calibers toward the building from which they were drawing the most fire.

It was a frame building, the library, and they shredded it, their armor-piercing rounds tore through it like darts through a spider web: .50 caliber slugs ripped the snipers and their cover apart, showering the ground below with shattered wood, glass, and a rainbow of blood. Kel almost puked when he saw the body of one of the victims crash to earth. He wasn't sure, but from a distance he thought it was Andre.

A fusillade of slugs tore through the bushes to his left, and Kel's training kicked in. He was back to gut-level survival, and he was firing his rifle at the enemy, feeling savage exultation as his bullets ripped the arm off an Earth-gov soldier advancing toward him, hurling the man to the dirt, screaming, fountaining blood.

The microwave fryer purred to life, and a dozen Earth-gov troops twenty meters in front of it screamed, their skin bubbling, their eyeballs bursting, as they sank to the earth. Before the fryer could turn toward the troopers on either side of its victims, an infantry man to the left spotted it and sent an RPG round into it, shredding it and sending its crew to the ground screaming, bleeding, and dying from shrapnel wounds. Kel breathed deeply, almost hyperventilating, inhaling the stink of chordite, blood, piss, and shit—the stench of every battlefield since the employment of gunpowder in warfare. But now with another odor thanks to the fryer and the Ciegaderas: burnt meat.

Kel saw a flash, and another Earth-gov soldier screamed and dropped, the flesh on his jaw incinerated by the Ciegadera. Then another flash and another scream. And then the blast of a hand grenade twenty meters away from him. Even though it was already too late—the shrapnel would have hit him by the time the sound arrived—Kel instinctively dove into the dirt. When he raised his head, he looked down the ditch and saw a smoking crater in place of the militiaman with the Ciegadera.

More rounds whined in the air above him. Kel forced himself up and began firing at the advancing Earth-gov troops. One of the surviving a.p.c.s turned its machine gun toward him and sprayed the bushes a bare ten meters to his left, sweeping toward him. He dove face down into the ditch and stayed there, trying to sink through its muddy bottom as .50-caliber slugs burrowed through the mud at the top of the trench, passing barely above his body, kicking dirt onto his back and head.

The noise was deafening, overwhelming—a cacophony of machine gun fire, explosions, and screams. Kel heard a storm of machine gun bullets as the other a.p.c.s turned their guns on his comrades further up the trench. While he was still face down in the dirt, breathing in the stench of death, bullets slamming through the trench top, he heard two huge explosions, and the hail of machine gun fire raking his hiding place abruptly stopped.

He waited a few seconds, raised his head, and saw two of the a.p.c.s burning and another explode in an orange-white glow as an RPG round tore through its armor, and then out the other side in a shower of white-hot shredded metal and vaporized human flesh. It joined the a.p.c. next to it that was burning white hot, the one that, judging from the direction its guns were pointing, had been firing at him. Three of the remaining a.p.c.s were rushing headlong toward the militiamen along the open side of the square, a hundred meters down the ditch from Kel. They breached the perimeter, firing at fleeing defenders as they passed, and rushed down Horst Wessel Strasse toward the center of The Dream, expending ammunition at a prodigious rate, firing at anything that moved and almost anything that didn't. Almost all of the remaining Earth-gov troops were running behind the a.p.c.s.

Kel was dumfounded. He couldn't figure out why they were heading in that direction. It was suicide. They should have retreated into the remaining shuttles and attempted to take off, or they should have headed in the opposite direction toward the main gate. At least that way they'd have had a chance. Not much of one, but a chance. Their command structure must have totally broken down.

Then he noticed the last surviving a.p.c. moving quickly, in a hail of small arms fire, toward the infirmary at the far end of the square, raking the building with machine gun fire. A half-dozen Earth-gov troops were following it, and as soon as they were near the building one tossed a grenade into a ground-floor window. Kel aimed at them, flicked the lever to its full-auto mid-position, held down the trigger and watched two of them jerk and fall as he fought the gun's tendency to pull up and to the right. The other troops continued running behind the a.p.c., firing at anything that moved.

The grenade exploded in the infirmary. Seconds later, a nurse staggered from a side exit, fell to the earth and lay twitching, before lying still. Then a second nurse stumbled through the exit—Velky—dazed, hair hanging down in disarray, her face streaked with grime. Kel jumped up, gun in hand, and started running toward her across the square, dodging burning a.p.c.s and dead and wounded Earth-gov troops, and ignoring the random fire and slugs whistling by him.

When he was near the infirmary, he shouted, "Velky!"

She didn't hear him. Kel continued to run toward her, as she stumbled along the side of the infirmary away from the square. She stopped as she reached the corner of the building and leaned against it, as bullets ripped into the ground before her.

Kel reached her, grabbed her with one hand, and spun her around. She beat on his chest and screamed. He grabbed her with both hands and pulled her to the ground.

She tried to push him away as bullets ricocheted off the wall a few meters to their rear. When one hit near their heads, and a wood fragment pierced her cheek drawing blood, she screamed even louder, but then stopped resisting as the gunfire ceased. Kel looked up and saw fire. The infirmary was burning, smoke pouring out its open windows.

He got up in a crouch and pulled Velky toward the first cover that he saw, a shot-up a.p.c. stalled out and silent along the wall of the building across the road, its doors ajar.

They were crouching behind the a.p.c. as Earth gov soldiers ran past the corner of the building a scant ten meters in front of them without casting a glance in their direction. As soon as the troops were out of sight, Kel crept around the side of the a.p.c., poked the rider's side door fully open with the barrel of his gun, and ducked back. There was no response, no movement, just the sickening smell of death. He stepped forward and simultaneously pointed his AK through the door, ready to fire, and found the source of the stench.

The two-centimeter "bullet proof" glass in the driver's-side half of the windshield was shattered, splintered streaks radiating away in all directions from a jagged three-centimeter hole directly in front of what was left of the driver. He was splattered all over his seat and the floor. There was no one else, dead or alive, in the vehicle.

Kel pushed Velky through the door and then into the aft compartment. He climbed in, reached across the corpse, pushed the driver's-side door farther open, and pushed the corpse out of the seat and onto the ground. He clambered into the driver's seat, despite the gore coating it, and pulled the door shut. He smashed out enough of the remaining shattered glass on the driver's side of the windshield with the butt of his gun so that he could see, even though that meant that he'd have almost no protection from head-on fire. The right half of the windshield was pocked and streaked with break lines, but it would probably hold if nothing heavy hit it.

He looked down at the controls and breathed a sigh of relief. It was one of the ultra-low-tech hybrid models that had transported him from burning village to burning village in Central Asia—a small, lightly armored type that had a single external .50 caliber mounted immediately forward of a pop-up hatch.

He tried the electric drive. Nothing. Then he flipped the switch to engage the combustion motor. It kicked, then died. He waited, and started counting to thirty. He reached twenty and said "fuck it!" He hit the ignition again. The motor turned over slowly, but didn't catch. He counted till twenty and tried again. It ground even slower. So he waited. And sweated. He counted to sixty, tried to push the clutch through the floor, and hit the ignition again. This time the engine turned over slowly, roared to life, backfired, and then roared again.

He was putting the vehicle in gear when a squad of Earth-gov troops came spilling around the intersection facing them, in full retreat. The last man was slammed in the back by a burst of machine gun fire that hurled him to the ground. Two of the surviving troops turned back and fired blindly.

Kel gripped the blood drenched wheel, floored it, and steered straight toward the Earth-gov troops. One managed a shot at him, which barely missed his head. One of the other troopers wasn't so lucky, falling beneath the a.p.c.'s studded tires as it rounded the corner on two wheels.

Kel headed down Irving Strasse, parallel to the Dream's barbed wire fences, in the general direction of the main gate. He cursed as the a.p.c. jerked as it accelerated. The Earth gov soldiers behind him unleashed a hail of rounds that ricocheted harmlessly off the rear armor. Kel noticed a red glow and turned his head; one of the tiny rear windows was turning red and beginning to melt; someone nearby was toasting it with a Ciegadera or some other beam weapon. He averted his eyes and hunched over the wheel.

A bullet tore through the hole in the windshield past Kel and ricocheted around the interior as Velky, huddling on the floor, shrieked. A second round seared its way through the skin on the bottom of his left forearm. He screamed, dropped his arm, and clutched it to his chest, instinctively cradling it with his right arm. The a.p.c. jerked to the right as he frantically grabbed the wheel with both hands through the white hot pain and regained control, as he rounded a corner and headed toward the main gate a quarter of a block in front of him.

Kel looked through the hole in the windshield as the gates' barbed wire rushed toward him. As he was crashing through the first of the three gates, a militiaman on the walkway above—Zed!—was looking him straight in the face, aiming an AK directly at him, his jaw hanging open in shocked recognition. Time stopped. And the a.p.c. smashed through the outer two gates and was speeding away from The Iron Dream. Zed hadn't fired.

Five klicks up the road toward New M, Kel, breathing hard, still totally jacked on adrenaline, pulled the a.p.c. off the road at the top of a rise overlooking The Dream. He left the motor running, and held down the brake. He lowered the window and looked back. Smoke. Shots. Flashes. Explosions. The sound of gunfire was still heavy, but faint. He pawed through the a.p.c.'s front compartment and found a pair of binoculars with polarizing filters—some, but not enough, defense against a Ciegadera. He closed one eye and looked through the binocs with the other. All of the Earthgov shuttles were on fire; all of the a.p.c.s he could see were either burning or motionless; and no one had followed them. He put the binocs back where he'd found them.

The wound to his left forearm was only a crease, but it was still bleeding, burning, and it hurt like hell; his clothes were covered with mud and the gore from the dead driver; and his hands were covered with blood from the wheel.

Velky raised her head above the seats, looked at his bloody visage, and then at the horror show in the distance, and sank back to the floor. Kel put the a.p.c. in gear, and reached down behind the seat toward Velky, attempting to find her with his bloody hand. She grabbed it and held on. He was glad that she did. And, even covered in gore as he was, he began to get hard.

He drove on, clutching Velky with his right hand, the wheel with his left. As he rounded a curve at too high a speed, he glimpsed a sign by the side of the road. He slammed on the brakes, and the vehicle skidded to a halt. The caption to the left of an arrow pointing up then bending at a 90-degree angle read, "Serenity II 257 kilometers"; the caption next to an arrow pointing straight up read, "New Harmony 461 kilometers, Novaya Moskva 649 kilometers." He kept his foot on the brake as Velky got up, clutched his arm, and climbed into the shotgun seat. She shifted her grip to his hand, which made shifting difficult, but he managed it.

Twenty minutes later, Kel pulled off the road into a thicket of conifers at the edge of a stream, the ground thick with native purple ice plants. He turned off the motor to sudden, shocking silence. He got out, walked around to Velky's side, opened the door, and as soon as she was out she grabbed him, kissed him, and pulled him down with her onto the smooth sand along the bank of the stream. He ran his hands over her body as she tugged off his bloody shirt and pants and pulled him into the water. They touched bottom a meter down, got to their feet, and Kel pulled Velky's uniform over her head.

Kel cupped one of her wet breasts, bent down, and ran his tongue around its nipple. She shuddered. He slid his other hand around her hip and cupped her ass, pulling her toward him, and then out of the water and down on the bank. He put her breast in his mouth again, circling her nipple with his tongue as she shivered. She was moaning as she grabbed his shoulders and began to knead them. He drew his head back, pulled his hands along her beautifully smooth thighs, bent forward and began kissing her stomach, and then sank slowly down. She grabbed his shoulders, but didn't stop him.

She clamped his head in a vise grip as he began circling her labia slowly, up one side and down the other with the tip of his tongue. She shuddered and spasmodically gripped his shoulders as he circled her clit with his tongue.

She grabbed his hair, opened her legs wider, pulled him up to her; grabbed him and guided him in. After two minutes of hard thrusting she gasped, "Let me be on top." They rolled over, and he came out. She pushed him backward onto the ground, straddled him, held him with one hand, and sank down on him, squeezing him as she enveloped him. She looked down at him, into his eyes, rhythmically gripping him. He gasped, trying desperately not to come. She squeezed again and he thrust up into her. She gripped him hard and sank down, not letting him move.

She squeezed his body with her thighs, bent forward, grabbed his hands and held them down, immobilizing him. She relaxed her hold on his dick and then gripped him, hard. Held him. Relaxed. Gripped him. Held him. Relaxed. Gripped him hard, and held him there, right on the edge. She relaxed her hold.

She released one of his arms, grabbed his hand and guided it to her clit, as she started to rhythmically squeeze him again, stopping when he was on the edge. He leaned up, she leaned forward, and he took the nipple from her left breast in his mouth, sucking rhythmically as she continued to squeeze. A minute later Kel was on the edge again, and so was she. Her mouth was open and she was panting as he began thrusting harder and harder. But she didn't stop him this time, and as he arched his back and screamed, she was right on the edge. As his body spasmed for the final time, she started screaming, too. She came for far longer than he had, as he lay spent but still hard beneath her, marveling yet again at how much better sex was for women, and how much less they seemed to care about it.

Two minutes later, they were lying on the bank, naked, holding each other. Kel finally spoke: "Jesus! I thought you were a virgin."

"I've been wanting to do that for weeks." She gestured with her head in the direction of The Iron Dream. "But not there."

Five minutes later they put on their soggy clothes and walked back to the vehicle. Kel climbed in and began searching the lockers beneath the benches. He pulled out AK-97 ammo from the first one. Good. His gun was still functional but needed ammo. From the next locker, a box of UV grenades. Weird. They were crowd-control weapons. Nasty, round little things—they'd temporarily blind anyone within thirty meters who looked at them—but still crowd-control weapons that had no place in an assault vehicle. The first locker on the other side held an RPG launcher and a single RPG round. That was odd, too. Why would there be only a single round with the launcher? He inspected the round and the launcher for a few seconds, then put both back in the locker from which he'd taken them.

In the last locker he found two blankets, some other survival gear, and what he'd been looking for—a 20-liter water cube and a dozen MREs. He hauled out the water cube, and when they'd finished drinking he climbed behind the wheel, breathed a sigh of relief when the motor turned over, and backed onto the road. It wouldn't be bad going. It looked as if the afternoon would be clear, warm, and he'd be able to drive as fast as he dared. Maybe as much as 35 or 40 klicks an hour. They ended up averaging a little over half that.

* * *

The next afternoon, as Tau sank toward the horizon, Kel was driving slowly, one hand steering, one on Velky's thigh. An hour after it was fully dark, and after he had almost driven the a.p.c. into a tree, Kel pulled off on a short track into the pines and parked where the track ran out. Velky started to get out, but he said, "Let's not," and squeezed her leg. He got up and went between the seats into the back, put down the much too thin sleeping pad, and fell back onto it. Velky lay down next to him, slid her hand across his chest, and then reached down. But he didn't—couldn't—respond. He was too exhausted. After a few minutes, she gave up, and nestled under his arm. They talked for a few minutes, drifted off, and then Tau was up again.

Kel rose on one elbow, looking at Velky's peaceful form, smiled, and then lost his smile. What the fuck had he done? No protection, not even a condom. And it was too much to ask that she had any of the common implants that protected against pregnancy and most STDs. Not at The Iron Dream. So . . . What the fuck had he done?

He lowered himself back to the floor of the a.p.c. and contemplated the still-asleep Velky. Some of the things she'd told him last night had surprised the hell out of him. One that didn't was that she'd been married to some low-ranking asshole at The Dream, who'd thought it perfectly normal to drink himself blind every night and to sometimes beat the shit out of a woman. Kel had never done that, couldn't conceive of it, and simply said, "Jesus Christ!" when Velky mentioned it. He'd heard it often enough, though. It was the same shit as in every abusive relationship: "You made me do it!" Her ex would beat the crap out of her and then the motherfucker would come crawling back, swearing it would never happen again. But of course it did. The worst part was that Velky still half bought it, still half-blamed herself. But at least she'd had the strength to get out. After she'd ditched that abusive asshole she'd sworn off men. No surprise in any of that.

It didn't surprise him, either, that both her dad and granddad had been low-ranking cops, who had funneled her into a traditional female occupation: nurse. So, she'd decided to show them. She'd gotten involved with a Shield of Odin cell, which committed the organized racist violence the cop patriarchs in her family had only committed in a limited capacity in the line of duty. Again, no surprise. Nor was the fact that they hadn't been able to save her ass from deportation.

What did surprise the hell out of Kel, even though it shouldn't have, was that because she was a cop's daughter she'd been on Merit

Med her entire life until she was deported, and she was five years older than he was, even though she looked five years younger.

Velky opened one eye, and a second later slid her hand up his thigh. He was hard instantly. As they began rhythmically grinding against each other, his last thought before his body took over was "In for a penny, in for a pound."

42

RACISM, n. A sign of idiocy indicating that an individual believes that other racial groups can be even worse than his own.

—Chaz Bufe, *The American Heretic's Dictionary*

It was hot that afternoon. Kel had taken off his shirt, and they were driving slowly down the mud-track road in the late afternoon, the a.p.c. chugging, sometimes missing, as they came to another road sign. New Harmony, straight ahead, was only 240 kilometers, and the turnoff to Serenity II was only 95.

Kel blew through pursed lips and let out a relieved sigh. "It looks like we'll make it to New Harmony."

"Serenity would be a lot safer."

"Safer?"

He looked at her out of the corner of his eye and said, "Come on. The peace and love crowd at New Harmony should be cool."

"Peace and love? They're anarchists! All they want is chaos! To kill people for the fun of it! Rape any woman who comes near them!"

"That ain't what Chuy told me."

"Chuy!?"

"Friend of mine. Lives there. At least he used to."

"That's a weird name."

"Chuy? It's short for Jesús."

"Your friend is a spic?"

"A spic?! Jesus! You tell me you were dying to get out of there, couldn't stand it, and then you lay this racist shit on me?"

"In some ways they're right at The Dream! I just don't like the way they treat women!"

Kel didn't reply, and she looked away, crossed her arms, and gripped her elbows.

Twenty minutes later, as the vehicle bucked and lurched along the road, Velky unlocked her arms, reached over, and put her left hand on Kel's thigh.

"Let's go to Serenity. I'd feel safer. Please."

Kel took one hand off the wheel and covered Velky's with it.

"I was at Serenity One a few months ago, and I have a pretty good idea what we'd find at Serenity Two. And I ain't up for it." Velky pulled her hand away. Kel looked sideways at her and then continued. "Everybody calling some asshole 'Father' and asking 'How high?' when he says 'Jump.' Or, more likely, 'How wide?' when he says 'Spread 'em.' The anarchists can't be worse than that."

Velky snorted, settled into her seat, pulled her arms back across her torso, and looked straight ahead as Kel worked to control the a.p.c., its wheels dropping into and bouncing out of suddenly deep ruts. An uncomfortable four hours later, they were approaching the turnoff to Serenity II. Velky, her feet up on the seat, her arms wrapped around her knees, turned toward Kel.

"Do you really want to surrender to the anarchists?! Think about me! Think about what they'll do to me!"

Kel kept his hands on the wheel, stared straight ahead, his jaw clenched, and growled, "They won't do *anything* to you!"

Five minutes of painful silence later, a battered metal sign appeared on the side of the road with an arrow pointing straight up , beneath the inscription "Serenity II Junction—5 kilometers." Velky pulled on Kel's arm and said, "We can't go to New Harmony. It's full of mud people! Spics, ki—"

"Can the racist horseshit. They're just people like you and me. What the hell else could they be!?"

"But—"

"Can it! If you go saying that kind of shit when we get there, somebody'll hand you your ass."

"And you wouldn't do anything about it?!"

"If it was a woman, no."

Velky turned away from him and stared out the side window, and was still staring out it as he drove past the turnoff and into the near-blinding light from Tau, low above the western horizon.

Neither of them reached out to the other until they'd stopped for the night. Kel didn't even try to find a secluded place off the road. He simply waited until he was on a downhill stretch, stopped, put the vehicle in gear, and put on the brake. That night, he slept wrapped in one blanket, Velky in the other.

Minutes after Tau came up, Kel was back in the gore-caked driver's seat. Velky climbed into her seat without speaking to him as Kel tried to start the a.p.c. It didn't. It just ground over slowly. Two minutes later he tried again. No dice. He said, "Fuck it," left the ignition on, put the transmission in third, released the brake, and pushed in the clutch.

The a.p.c. began rolling downhill, gradually picking up speed. After fifteen tense seconds, equally fearful that the a.p.c. wouldn't start or that it would hit a rut and careen into the rocks, he popped the clutch. The engine caught, backfired, caught again, and he hit a deep rut. The vehicle lurched to the right, and its right side slammed into a tree trunk. Velky shrieked as he fought to regain control.

Half an hour later, Kel's hands were still locked tight on the wheel, almost strangling it, as he muttered under his breath, "Oh fuck. Oh fuck. Oh fuck." The engine was sputtering and the a.p.c. was managing barely twenty klicks an hour on the deeply rutted road. Velky was icily silent. When they finally hit a smooth stretch and he unlocked his right hand and reached over to squeeze her leg, she didn't take his hand. She didn't respond at all. Just continued to sit there, arms locked, staring into the distance. Kel removed his hand and put it back on the wheel. When they pulled to the shoulder for the night, on a downhill stretch, she wrapped herself in one of the blankets and wouldn't even nestle up to his back.

The next morning, twenty minutes after Kel had again started the a.p.c. by popping the clutch as it rolled downhill, a head-sized rock slammed into the windshield in front of Velky. She screamed at the sound as the rock bounced off. Another rock shot through the hole on Kel's side, barely missing his head as he put the pedal to the floor and sank down into the seat. Animal-like shrieks and whoops filled the air as another rock ricocheted off the windshield. Then another crashed through the shards in front of Kel, spraying both him and Velky with tiny fragments.

Kel ducked his head and the vehicle hesitated, spurted forward, then hesitated and spurted again, barely gathering speed amidst their attackers' shrieks. As the a.p.c. spasmed, Kel glanced between the dashboard and the top of the wheel and saw the rock throwers: grungy figures with long, matted hair wearing animal skins. Except for the beards, it was almost impossible to tell the men from the women.

As he tried to push the accelerator through the floor, another rock zoomed through the broken-out left side of the windshield, missing Kel's head by centimeters. More rocks smashed into the sides, top and back of the a.p.c., creating a terrible din as their ringing fused with the screams of the attackers and the engine noise. Kel was sweating blood, desperately clutching the wheel, scared shitless that some of the faster attackers might even be able to catch them on foot. Then life imitated art—a snarling savage was staring Kel in the eye, his fingers bleeding profusely as they clamped down on shards of broken glass in the windshield frame, and their bearded, screaming owner tried to pull himself off the left fender and onto the hood of the vehicle.

Kel saw a pine looming next to the road on the driver's side, swerved, and held on as the pine trunk scraped along the side of the a.p.c. There was a sickening thud, like a sledge hammer slamming into a side of beef, and the attacker was gone. All that was left of him was bloody strips of skin sticking to the glass shards embedded in the windshield frame.

Then abruptly there was near silence, only the sound of the wheels and the tortured engine. The bombardment had stopped, and the shrieks were fading into the distance.

Kel sat up in his seat, snuck a glance at Velky, and looked up just in time to duck a spear that sailed past him into the rear compartment. Another hurtled directly toward him. It barely missed his head, but as he ducked to the right and jerked his left arm up, the spear ripped through the skin along its bottom, and buried itself in the back of the seat, its staff jutting out through the shattered windshield. Kel screamed and tried to pull his injured arm down to his side, but it hung up on the spear and he lost control of the vehicle. The wheel jerked, and they headed straight for a tree ten meters off the road. They had nearly crashed into it when Velky grabbed the wheel and wrenched it back toward the road.

Kel jerked his left arm free, stifling a scream as his skin ripped loose from the spear. He pressed his left arm against his side, put his left hand back on the bottom of the wheel, and continued pushing down on the accelerator.

And then it was done. No more rocks. No more spears. No more savages.

Velky let go of the wheel and squeezed Kel´s shoulder as he was holding his bleeding arm tight against his side, blood gradually soaking his shirt.

They drove on without speaking for several minutes before Velky asked, "Who was that? Who—*what*!?—were those people?!"

Kel grunted, "Let's just hope they aren't Chuy's anarchists."

43

INFLUENTIAL MILITANT, n. Anarchese for "leader" (a term best avoided because of its tendency to induce hand tremors, heart palpitations, and night sweats among the faithful).

—Chaz Bufe, *The American Heretic's Dictionary*

Fifteen klicks past the ambush, the left side of Kel's shirt was soaked with blood. He was on the verge of passing out, and it was taking more and more effort to keep from drifting off the road. At the point where he knew he had to stop, he drove over a rise, and there it was—fields, orchards, a small river, and dozens of buildings scattered amidst a carpet of trees. He hit the brakes, and at the bottom of the rise he pulled off on the first dirt road to the right, and came to a stop before a one-storey green building.

Kel cut the ignition, started to get out, and fell back into his seat. He clutched his arm, eyes unfocused, as blood soaked his shirt and pants. Velky squeezed his right arm above where he'd been wounded at The Dream, got out, walked around to the driver's side, opened the door, and reached in.

She helped Kel out of the vehicle while he continued to press his bleeding arm to his side. A moment later, several figures emerged from behind the building, most holding shovels, picks and other farm tools. The one in the lead, a short-haired white woman in her 40s, wearing a work shirt and work boots, snarled at Kel and Velky, "Who are you, and what the hell are you doing here? And where did you get this thing"—she eyed Kel's uniform and gestured at the a.p.c.—"you pieces of shit?"

Kel and Velky stared at her dumbly, shocked by her overt hostility. Kel emerged from his fog long enough to say "Who the hell are you?"

"My name's Ann." She waited.

Kel, clutching his arm, shaking from the pain, said, "Give me some help! Please! I'm fucking hurt!"

Ann ignored his obvious pain. "Where are you from?"

"We just escaped."

"From where?"

Kel gasped, "The apes up the road."

"Apes? The primitivists?" She chuckled, eying the spear still protruding through the window. "But who shot this thing up? And where is it from?"

Velky stared at Ann and growled, "What is *wrong* with you?! He's bleeding!"

When Ann didn't reply immediately, Velky turned to the loose group behind Ann. "We need help! Bring me some bandages and anti—"

Ann interrupted Velky as if she hadn't even heard her, as two of the hangers-on retreated around the corner.

"Where are you from? And where did you get this damned thing?"

Kel managed, "Earth gov. We were lucky to grab it."

"Where?"

"The Iron Dream."

The crowd murmured, and some pulled back. A few, Ann among them, stepped closer.

"So, you are fucking Nazis. What do you want here?"

Kel, his anger rising, found his voice. "Help. Unless you intend to kill me by letting me bleed to death. We're not fucking Nazis."

"You're from The Iron Dream, you're wearing that fucking uniform, and you're not Nazis? Give me a fucking break."

Kel, now really angry, adrenaline overriding his pain, grimaced. "We're not Nazis. We *escaped* from the goddamned Nazis."

"Then why are you wearing that goddamned uniform?"

"They conscripted me." He snarled, "Sorry for the duds. There wasn't a men's store on the way."

Ann ignored the sarcasm. "Then who the hell are you, anyway?"

Kel, feeling light headed again, said, "Look . . . I need help."

Ann stood gaping at him until Kel gasped out, "Do you know my friend, Chuy?"

Ann flinched. "Chuy!?"

"Yeah, Chuy An—" Kel passed out, almost pulling Velky down with him.

Velky knelt over Kel as Ann gestured at the shot up a.p.c., telling the onlookers, "Let's get this piece of shit out of here and get him patched up."

* * *

Kel looked up. The figure hovering over him said, "Go back to sleep." He did, for nearly a full day. The next afternoon, he was still woozy when Velky came to collect him, taking him, with the help of Julia, one of the nurses, to the apartment Ann had arranged for them to use. He immediately fell into a deep sleep once they lowered him to the bed.

When Kel awoke, there was an apple-sized maroon spot on the bandage on his left arm, and the arm hurt like hell. He sat up, reached for the glass of water next to the bed, and downed it in several long swallows, along with two pain pills. As he was pulling on the clean clothes he found laid out at the foot of the bed, there was a knock on the door. He forced himself up and went to answer the knock.

"Chuy! What the fuck!?"

"Hey *ese*. Yeah, I made it. Tell you about it over breakfast." He gestured at Velky, who was yawning, resting on one elbow. "Your lady friend want any?"

Kel looked questioningly at Velky.

"Go ahead. I'll be ready in half an hour."

Chuy replied, "Cool. We'll be back for you."

Kel pulled the door shut, and as they were walking away Chuy nodded back toward the apartment and asked him, "What's with the chick?"

"It's a long story."

Five minutes later, Kel followed Chuy into The Open Arms, a straw-bale cantina with off-white stucco walls, saltillo tile floors, a stone fireplace in one corner, and too many chairs and tables crowded into too small a space. Kel, who wasn't hungry at all, said, "I'll just have coffee."

Chuy wasn't buying it. "Hey man, you've got to eat. You've got to."

With Chuy prodding Kel, they walked to the buffet, plates and cups of coffee in hand, and served themselves eggs, toast, hash browns, and slices of melon, Chuy taking twice the amount Kel did. As they sat down at one of the plank tables on The Open Arms' patio, Kel, feeling a bit light headed, asked, "No bacon or sausage?"

Chuy laughed. "Fuck man, we're lucky to have eggs, what with the fascist vegetarians around here."

Kel, now that food was before him, discovered that he actually was hungry. He dove in. The food and coffee staved off the sleep-inducing effects of the pain pills, and he was halfway through his meal before he asked, "How in the hell did you get here?"

"It took a while. After we crashed, you and Bud were out cold and looked pretty messed up. I had to haul both of you out through the windshield. After I got you out I looked across the meadow and saw maybe three or four klicks away a fence and a guard tower by a gate, and realized where I was. Then I saw a bunch of guys running out of the gate, and I had to get out of there. I knew they wouldn't fuck with you too much because you're both white."

Kel asked, "How the hell did you make it all the way here?"

"I wasn't hurt too bad, and I lucked out. The windshield popped when we hit, and I had enough time to crawl back into the cockpit, pull both of you out, and then go back to grab that pack you were sittin' on. It had enough high-pro bars that I only ran out less than a week out of here. Had a bunch of other useful shit, too: a flashlight, knife, blanket, flint and steel, even a gun."

"A gun?! Earth-gov can shoot you for having one of those!"

"Yeah, I know. I figure Bud must have put it in there."

"Jesus! Mikel told me that they raided New Havana a couple of years ago after they found out they were making AK-47s. They blew up the plant, with all the people in it, and Corona promised to personally castrate Modelo if they ever did it again."

"I heard that, too. . . . Bud has some balls."

"Yeah. But for how long?"

Chuy didn't answer, and Kel blew out his breath before asking, "So you just walked here?"

"Pretty much. Not much happened until I was only twenty klicks out of here on the road and the primitivists jumped me."

"The same assholes who jumped us?"

"Probably. I know the scumbags who jumped me: Thinks Like a Mountain and his asshole buds, Peaceful Meadow, Wisdom of the Earth, and Spirit of the Earth." Chuy chuckled. "They're real big on 'Earth.'"

"But why'd they jump you?"

"They were pissed off that I was carrying a pack."

"A pack?"

"Yeah, a pack. Technology. They're real puritanical. Claimed I was invading their territory with oppressive technology—a fucking pack!—as if they own the goddamned place. The motherfuckers actually had the balls to threaten me with spears."

"That's nuts."

"Yes, it is. Sanity is not one of their strong points. Ask Ann about it the next time you see—"

"That goddamned dyke?"

"Yeah, her. She's got a good side. She arrived here the same time they did, and she's had to deal with 'em ever since. Talk to her. You might even end up liking her."

Kel snorted.

"Anyway, I humored 'em for a while. Let 'em destroy the pack and all the shit in it, 'cause I was so close to New Harmony it didn't matter. I backed away from 'em while they were doing it—all four of 'em were slashing at it and whooping like crazy—and I ended up pulling the gun on 'em when they started coming at me again. I damned near shot all four of 'em. I fucking wanted to. But I shot at their feet and yelled at them to get down. Surprised the hell out of 'em. Thinks Like a Mountain pissed himself, and I'm pretty sure Spirit shit himself. If I hadn't a been so hyped on adrenaline, it woulda been funnier than shit. What a bunch of goddamned assholes."

Chuy paused. "But hey man, you should go get your lady friend, or you should bring her a plate."

Kel, his head starting to swim as the pain pills kicked in, thought about it for a minute, filled a plate and a mug of coffee, and followed Chuy back to the apartment.

As he left Kel at the door, Chuy said, "Hey bro, let me know when you're up for playin' some music."

44

PRIMITIVISM, n. A millenarian ideology whose distinguishing
feature is religious zeal. Like its near cousin, "deep" ecology, primitivism
is a very useful ideology in that it lets the corporations
and governments responsible for environmental mayhem off
the hook while providing its advocates with a satisfying feeling
of moral superiority over the rest of humanity.

—Chaz Bufe, *The American Heretic's Dictionary*

The next morning, Kel and Velky were sitting with Chuy and
Ann on the patio of The Open Arms. Ann was acting as if absolutely nothing had happened three days before, and Kel was tired
and still in pain, but lucid and feeling quite a bit better.

Velky, looking uneasily at all of the black, latino, and Asian
people walking in and out of the cantina—and at Ann—said, "Kel
told me about it, but I really don't understand. Why would those
people attack us? They don't even know us."

Ann smiled, sipped her coffee, and began: "Other than that you
were driving that piece-of-shit vehicle? . . . It all began twenty-five
years ago when Earth-gov dropped us off down by the river, along
with enough tools, food, and gear to fend for ourselves. The primitivists and their head honcho, this asshole called Burgie, tried to
destroy the tools and equipment while they thought everyone else
was asleep. We stopped 'em without too much violence.

"When we asked 'em why, it was pretty much the same line of
shit I've heard from every damn one of 'em who's ended up here
since then. In boiled-down form, here it is:

She shifted to a high, whiny voice: "'There's nothing like this
left on Earth! Unspoiled nature! We can spend our days singing,
eating, and making love! No work! We can lead a real human existence.'"

Ann snorted and dropped to her normal tone of voice. "What a bunch of shit! They're a bunch of goddamned romantics. Religious believers. No connection to reality. I always tell 'em the same thing, and it never has any effect. I practically have it memorized. Here's how it goes:

"Make love, sing and eat? Right. And shiver in the dark and die at thirty from starvation, dysentery, TB, or giving birth to ten children."

She shifted her voice up, again, and began alternating between high and low voices in an imaginary conversation.

"You don't know that!"

"Yes I do. That's what happened with every goddamned primitive tribe back on Earth. Just look at the fucking evidence."

"What evidence?"

"'Anthropology! Learn to read!'"

"Read!? Reading is inherently oppressive!"

"Oppressive? You call knowing what the fuck is going on oppressive?"

"Yes! Hunter-gatherers were free! We're not!"

"Dying at thirty? Huddling around a fire in a cave worrying about thunder and lightning, about what pissed off the storm gods, and what you can do to appease them? That's a 'real human existence'? That's freedom?"

"More freedom than you domesticated bootlickers will ever know!"

Kel cocked his head and asked, "They're really that nuts?"

"Yes, they are. And I haven't even gotten to the good part."

Kel raised an eyebrow, and she continued. "I've heard this shit dozens of times. It's always the same." She began shifting back and forth between tones of voice again.

"Technology is inherently repressive."

"Tell me, what do you mean by 'technology'?"

"You know, the machine. Science, technology, reading, writing, language, mathematics, industrialism, capitalism, dead rational thou—"

Kel interrupted: "You're shitting me?"

"No, I'm not. I wish I was. They're reductionistic cretins. They really think that language is the same as capitalism. It always ends up the same way":

She began alternating voices again.

"You're crazy!"

"No! You are!"

"No you are!"

"And so on. I always end up saying, 'Okay. You guys do what you want. We'll do what we want. We'll 'oppress' ourselves with houses and hot tubs. You guys can fuck off and do whatever you want. Go hug a tree. Go fuck a tree! Do anything you want. Anywhere you want. But not here! We don't fuck with you and you don't fuck with us. Fair enough?' And they never go for it. They always say:

"No. If you use technology it oppresses us."

"Fine. Then go away."

"No! Wherever we go, your technology will oppress us!"

"How?"

"It will!"

"How?!"

"It just will!"

Ann laughed. "The first assholes who showed up, Burgie and his followers, left our 'domesticated' community to start a hunter-gatherer community—really, a *hunger*-gatherer community—a few klicks upstream, where there are caves near the river. Within two weeks, most of 'em dragged their sorry asses back down here. It was one thing to fantasize about a primitive existence, it was another to actually live it.

"But Burgie and a couple dozen die-hards stuck it out, even though they were pissed that they had to plant crops. They had committed the original sin: agriculture. It's totally obvious that there ain't enough to live on in the wild around here, but they were pissed off anyway.

"For a good year, the assholes who'd drifted back to camp snuck food to 'em. We overlooked it, even though things were pretty marginal. We didn't want anybody to starve, not even Burgie.

The next summer, when they brought in their first crops, those of 'em who'd survived were close to being self-sufficient. Twenty-five years later, Burgie is still out there—a 'wise tribal elder'—and we still funnel every new primitivist up to him.

"Nowadays, other than showing up when they need medical attention, Burgie and his bunch pretty much keep to themselves in their 'neolithic agricultural community,' Camp Kaczynski."

Kel asked, "Are any of the ones who came back that first year still here? And do any of the newer ones get fed up and come back?"

"Some, yeah, but not many stay. Most of 'em can't hack it. They ain't up for the work and the responsibility. When the reality of a primitive existence sinks in, most of them head back here, but they can't hack it. Twenty hours of work per fucking week, and they can't hack it.

"Most of 'em just want to feel superior and have somebody to follow. A lot of 'em end up at Baghavad or Serenity. Some even end up at Xenadu and The Iron Dream, including that asshole Sneath."

Kel looked puzzled. "Sneath?"

"Yeah. Call's himself Schutz or Schitz nowadays. Runty little fucker. He's a wheel at The Dream now. He tried to rape some girl here, and she nailed him in the face with a shovel. Must have left one hell of a scar."

Kel exhaled loudly. "It's Schwarz. And he has a 'dueling scar.'"

45

MONOGAMY, n. A common misspelling. See "Monotony."
—Chaz Bufe, *The American Heretic's Dictionary*

Four days later, Kel was feeling well enough that he and Chuy were setting up musical gear on a small riser in one corner of The Open Arms, along with their drummer for the night, Leroy. The place was packed, and Velky was sitting at a round table with Lorenzo, a thin, clean-shaven black man in his late thirties, who was an expert mechanic, Omar, one of New Harmony's doctors, a stout Cuban man in his late fifties, who doubled as a mechanic, and Elvia, a very pretty Mexican nurse in her early forties.

While he was finishing setting up, Kel was surreptitiously watching Velky, who kept giving sideways glances at the other people in the bar. She seemed to be doing her best to ignore the other people at her table, which was fairly easy as Omar and Lorenzo carried on an apparently private conversation, and Elvia was leaning back, conversing with a woman at the next table. Elvia ended the conversation and glanced toward the stage, where she caught Kel's eye and held it long enough that he started to smile.

She looked away and Kel leaned toward his mike. He was rewarded with a howl of feedback. After Chuy made a quick adjustment to the p.a. head, Kel announced, "Good evening. We're gonna start with an old one. It's for all you folks who ever had a job or a boss you hated. It's called 'Postal.'"

He began playing a slow, repetitive, jazzy intro. After four bars the drummer and Chuy kicked in, and Kel began comping just behind the beat, inserting fills around the comping pattern. When they'd finished the instrumental first verse, Kel began singing.

Every day, same old story
Got no love, got no glory
Workin' hard, every day
Workin' hard, not much pay
Want so bad, to get away
Workin' hard, not much pay

Stupid boss, stupid rules
Stupid job, stupid tools
Follow orders, every day
Follow orders, what they say
Every day, is filled with strife
God I hate, my damned life

(Kel took a solo)

Death on the, installment plan
Is this work, for a man?
Follow orders, made by fools
Just like kids, in some damn school
Want so bad, to get away
Want so bad, to make 'em pay

Got a gun, big AK
Got a gun, watch 'em pray
As I walk, through the door
Watchin' them, hit the floor
All I want, is my boss
Rest of them, won't feel no loss

(Kel took another solo, repeated the first verse, and faded out with)

Let's go postal . . .
Let's go postal . . .
Let's go postal . . .
Let's go postal . . .

Kel pulled his guitar strap over his head, put his guitar down on its stand, turned off his amp, and walked to the large round table where Velky was sitting. She was still giving sideways glances at the other people in the bar, especially at several interracial couples.

Kel sat down in an empty seat next to her. She didn't take his hand when he squeezed her leg. Ann, who had squeezed in next to Lorenzo, and who had been watching Velky closely, asked, "Something wrong, honey? You look like you've seen a ghost."

Lorenzo, who had also been observing her, couldn't resist adding, "Or a spook."

Velky didn't react to the jibes. She stared down, looking at neither Ann nor Lorenzo, and said, "I'm fine. Thank you."

When Lorenzo said, "Are you, really?" Kel snapped back, "Give her a break! She can't help it! What the hell do you expect? She lived in that racist cesspit for years. You guys are acting like a bunch of fucking assholes."

Before Lorenzo or Ann could reply, Velky shot back at Kel. "It's not a cesspit! At least people there don't go around fornicating like animals with—!"

She cut herself off in midsentence. There was dead silence at the table, but for the bar noise in the background, until Lorenzo asked quietly, "What's moral about racism? What's moral about killing people just 'cause you don't like how they look?"

As Velky was searching for an answer, Ann leaned toward her and asked, "And what's immoral about sex? . . . And I suppose you've never fucked a *guy*?" She shot a knowing glance at Kel. "I'm sure you never fucked a *woman*, but not even a guy?"

Velky blushed a deep red and started to stammer. "Tha . . . That . . . That was—"

Ann sneered. "Different?" She snorted. "And you really think you need permission? Face it honey, we're all animals and we all like to fuck. White, black, brown, red, yellow, female, male, gay, bi, straight. We all do it. Get over it."

Velky blushed an even deeper red. Ann's rudeness had struck everyone at the table dumb. After an uncomfortable silence, Elvia squeezed Velky's hand and said, "I think that what Ann's trying to say is that sex is a natural part of life, and that we all want it. As long as we're honest about it and it's between consenting adults, it's a good thing. You don't need to be ashamed of it."

After a few seconds, as Ann, still spoiling for a fight, fumed, Kel tentatively reached under the table for Velky's hand. This time, she let him take it and gave him a hard squeeze.

Since no one else was going to, Elvia broke the tension by saying to Velky, "Tell me about your friends at The Iron Dream. What are they like?" Lorenzo, as soon as Velky had started talking and it became apparent that nothing of interest was going to follow, just b.s. about people he didn't know, turned to Omar and resumed their conversation. Ann got up and sat down at the next table. Two minutes later Kel managed to escape, in search of Chuy and Leroy. A moment later they were back on stage.

Chuy introduced the first song: "Here's another old one. It's called 'Chupacabra Blues.' For all you *gabachos* out there, *chupacabra* means 'goat sucker.' It's from the folklore of the dark ages, back in the twentieth century, not that times are much better now." Without further comment he nodded toward the boys, and they launched into a medium-tempo standard blues tune.

When the song ended Kel leaned into the mike and, putting on his best hick accent, said, "Here's a change o' pace. It's another old one. We used to do this in a band called Bubba's Toxic Breakfast. It's an old one, I don't even know who wrote it." He looked over at Chuy and Leroy, counted "one . . . two . . . one, two, three, four," and launched into a country rock tune.

We're very patriotic
And you know that it's true
And that gives us the duty
To tell you what to do
Now all we really want from you
Is to do just what we say
Go on and lick a boot boy
It's the American way
We're the world's biggest bullies
Don't get in our way
And it's one two three sieg heil y'all
Über alles, U.S.A.

Forty-five minutes later, after they finished the set and came off stage, Kel approached a table filled with empties. Omar was still engaged in a friendly argument with Lorenzo, and Ann was putting the moves on a woman at the next table. Elvia, who seemed pretty lit up, passed a spliff to Velky, who had drunk enough that she didn't blanch in horror. Instead, she puffed tentatively, before coughing spastically as she passed it to Lorenzo. He took a deep hit and passed it on to Omar, who in turn passed it to Kel, across the table, as Kel was pulling up a chair between Velky and Elvia.

As soon as Kel sat down, he felt Elvia's hand sliding up his thigh. He looked at her in surprise, and she smiled. Then he looked at Velky. She was also smiling, but glassy eyed. There was a half-full wine glass in front of her, as there was before Elvia. And there was a near-empty two-liter wine bottle on the table in front of them, nestling amidst Omar and Lorenzo's empty beer bottles. It looked like Velky and Elvia had been keeping pace with each other.

Kel, now on his sixth beer, reached down and squeezed Elvia's hand while he tried to address Omar and Lorenzo, who were arguing about what to do with the a.p.c. As Elvia started to massage his thigh, he managed, "Why in the fuck won't you guys listen to me. This is serious shit. You saw that a.p.c. The goddamned Nazis might be coming . . . "—he paused, trying to maintain his focus as Elvia slid her hand up further—"this way. . . Soon. I've been tryin' to tell you guys . . . this shit . . . ever since I . . . got here!"

Velky's wine-dulled radar went off and she shot suspicious looks at both Kel and Elvia. Omar, ignoring the strange shit going on between Kel and the two women, said, "After what happened at the Dream, Earth gov will be all over them. Don't sweat it *compañero*."

Kel replied, "Don't bet on it. At least check it ou—"

He was interrupted by Elvia. Velky had reached under the table, grabbed Elvia's hand, and squeezed it hard enough that she hoped she would break bones. Elvia gasped and pulled away her injured hand, looking in astonishment at Velky. Velky, except for a hard glance, ignored her, as she slid her hand up and squeezed Kel's balls hard. Way too hard. He jerked as he choked back a scream.

Lorenzo looked open mouthed at Velky, Elvia, and Kel. After Velky relaxed her grip and Kel straightened and took a halting breath, Lorenzo replied to Kel. "Uhhh . . . Check it out? The Nazis will never beat Earth gov. There ain't enough of 'em and they're hundreds of klicks away from here. The comsat was back up today and there was nothing about them heading this way on the news channel."

Velky shifted her grip and began a slow, rhythmic massage, as Kel, trying to focus on the conversation, snorted, "That's rich." He caught his breath as Velky's hand, now squeezing, wonderfully softly, forced him to pause, again. "Anarchists trusting Earth gov news. That's . . . fucking rich—" He stopped as Velky squeezed a little harder, and then began lightly rubbing her thumb in a circular motion around the head of his dick. Kel gasped and straightened. Omar and Lorenzo looked back and forth at Kel and Velky, and started to laugh. Kel managed to continue, barely. "Look at that a.p.c." Velky's thumb continued its circular motion. He gasped, "If that doesn't tell you something—"

As Elvia was rubbing her injured hand, and Kel was gasping, Ann leaned over from the next table and said, "That tells me you two are trouble." She laughed. "And you ought to get a room."

Kel squeezed Velky's hand to get her to stop—temporarily, he hoped—turned toward Ann, and said, "Go fuck yourself!" She continued to laugh and turned away. Kel looked toward the bar and yelled, "Barkeep! *¡Más cervezas!*"

46

HANGOVER, n. The most pedestrian form of self-punishment.
—Chaz Bufe, *The American Heretic's Dictionary*

Kel's skull felt like a vise was crushing it, but an insistent knock on the door managed to rouse him. Velky didn't stir. Kel got up and stumbled to the door. It was Lorenzo, who appeared none the worse for wear. He suppressed a chuckle as Kel, bags under his bloodshot eyes, peered around the edge of the door.

"Hey man. Let's go check out that a.p.c. We might be able to use it for something."

Kel said, "Okay. Give me a minute," and shut the door. After he squeezed Velky's ass, with no response except a grunt and a hand pushing his away, he put on his clothes, and pulled the blanket back over Velky, before stepping into the bathroom. He brushed his teeth, swilled a cheek-swelling chug of herbal mouthwash, spat it out, and pulled a brush a dozen times through his hair, wincing as it caught the knots. He put down the brush, splashed some water onto his face, straightened his shirt, and strode to the door. As he was pulling it shut behind him—weird! no lock; it would take a while to get used to that—he glanced back at Velky. She had pulled her pillow over her head, and would probably be out for the count for a few more hours.

As he stepped outside the door, Lorenzo asked him how he was feeling, with what Kel thought was disguised amusement masked as concern. Kel didn't reply directly, but just said, "Let's go." Lorenzo didn't push it, and started walking down the path that meandered to the north. Kel fell into step next to him. They trod along tree-shaded gravel paths that passed between rounded, stucco-coated buildings—not a 90-degree-angle in sight—painted in bright, primary colors, with solar-electric panels and solar hot water heaters dotting their roofs. Almost every building had a garden; some had flower gardens, some had vegetable gardens with tomatoes, mel-ons, squash, eggplants, beans, corn, okra, garlic, herbs, and chiles. To Kel, it was all a blur. His head was pounding, he couldn't make sense of anything; all he wanted to do was get it over with and go back to bed.

They crossed several small bridges spanning meter-wide irriga-tion/drainage ditches. Some, but not all, of the people they passed said "hi" or "good morning" to them. Others just nodded. When Kel asked, after the third woman in a row had just nodded, "Don't all of you know each other?," Lorenzo replied, "No, we don't. It's one of the problems with a community this size."

"This size?"

"About three thousand people."

"So who calls the shots? How do you decide on anything?"

Lorenzo laughed. "It's easy. Nobody calls the shots. We have work groups that handle the day-to-day shit—what color the paint'll be on new buildings, that kind of shit—and general assem-blies for the major shit."

Kel asked, "Come on. Does that really work? You've gotta have leaders, and you don't seem to have any except Ann."

Lorenzo snorted in amusement. "Leaders? Ann? Jesus H. Christ . . . C'mon. You'll see," and he stepped up his pace. Kel followed, absorbed with the simple task of walking without stumbling on the gravel path between the weird-looking buildings.

To make things worse, there were birds flitting from tree to tree in the near-canopy that hung above them, chattering in a high-pitched cacophony that made him cringe. And want a drink. If his head wasn't pounding so badly, he'd have loved the sound of the birds. Now, it just made him long for a cold one.

They finally left the trees and stepped into direct sunlight. Kel winced and closed his eyes to slits. A few dozen meters into the clearing Kel's eyes adjusted and a single-storey wood structure, with gaps in its walls that screamed neglect, dry rot, or insect damage, came into focus. As they neared the building, Kel nod-dedtoward a damaged area and asked, "Termites?"

Lorenzo laughed. "No. Not even the religious nuts would have brought them in. Well, probably not.

"Some of 'em tried to sneak in freakin' rattlesnake eggs. Injected 'em in glass tubes under their skin. But Earth-gov got all of 'em when they landed. Would have shot the stupid motherfuckers to make examples of 'em, but realized it wouldn't do no good. How could anybody on the way here know 'bout it? So they beat the shit out of 'em, harvested one kidney apiece from 'em, and let 'em go.

"But termites? I don't think they're in the Bible, and they ain't dramatic enough . . . And there ain't no termite-handling sects, so no. Nobody was crazy enough to bring 'em in." He shot a suspicious glance at the building's damaged boards. "Well, probably not."

They stepped through the doorway. Omar was already inside, looking over the a.p.c. with a long, metal, very bright flashlight, which helped despite the overhead lights and the two small windows along the south wall. He opened the driver's-side door and gazed at the spear, still buried in the seat, with dried blood caked on its shaft, and on the wheel and seat. He chuckled.

"I see you had a close encounter of the fourth kind with our primitivists. Actually, 'neo-primitivists.' That's what they call themselves. 'Primitivists' ain't classy enough."

Kel looked at him quizzically.

Omar glanced at the spear. "Those fucking *bobosos* ain't exactly humble, and they hate anybody who disagrees with 'em. If you disagree with 'em, you're evil incarnate, and they do not believe in live and let live. Same as every other bunch of *pinche* fundamentalist *putos*." He paused, but neither Kel nor Lorenzo jumped in. "We try to do things as simple and eco-friendly as we can, but it doesn't matter to 'em. Doesn't mean shit to 'em.

"Check out our sewage system. We separate out the solids, let 'em sit for a year and then compost 'em along with vegetable waste. Use 'em for fertilizer. With the liquids, we run 'em through a series of sand and reed beds, and when the effluent runs out of the last one, before it runs back into the river, it's clean enough to drink. Literally. It really is. But that doesn't mean shit to 'em. It's The Great Satan: technology. We use it, so *we're* The Great Satan. They think it's all oppressive, that *we're* oppressive, that everything we use is oppressive, even things like soap, toothpaste, tampons—"

Lorenzo broke in, chuckling, "Trust me. You don't want to date one." After he stopped laughing, he continued, "They think we're domesticated, and we think they're nuts. We treat our sewage and recycle it, and the fucking idiots shit a few meters from the river upstream from us 'cause it's 'natural.' I think some of 'em even shit right in the river." He shook his head. "We use wells now, because we have to. . . . But they despise us so much we don't see much of 'em—"

Omar interrupted him. "Except when they're sick or hurt. Then, they come in to be oppressed by *me*."

Lorenzo added, "Or when it gets too damned cold. Last winter, when we were out on the far end of our orbit, during the ice storm, a bunch of them came in to get oppressed by warm beds."

Omar and Lorenzo were both chuckling, obviously enjoying the exchange. It almost had the feel of the banter between an old married couple who like each other.

Omar continued, "Yeah. And we had to burn the beds and fumigate the rooms after they left."

"Fumigate them? We had to use a fucking flamethrower!"

They burst out laughing.

Kel was less amused. He felt miserable and was thoroughly puzzled. "Why would anyone live that way? What's in it for them? It doesn't make sense!"

Omar replied, "Oh yes it does. And you just hit on it. It's all about them. There's a real attraction in despair. It relieves you of responsibility. You don't have to do anything. All you have to do is say how stupid everybody else is and feel superior about it. Just sit on your ass, snipe at everybody else—especially anybody who's doing anything—and feel superior about it."

Kel, bored by the conversation, walked to the a.p.c., opened the engine compartment, and asked Lorenzo, "Do you think you can fix this thing?"

Lorenzo, without bothering to look at the engine, said, "Of course. I'm way too familiar with these things. It was running when you got here, so there's probably nothin' major wrong with it, and we can fabricate a lot of the mechanical shit in the machine shop if we need to. So yeah, I can fix it. But why bother? What's the point? The only use this has here is if you could pull a trailer behind it."

Kel sighed. "You don't get it. Those Nazi assholes might be on their way here now. If they are, unless you have a shitload of arms buried around here somewhere and you're way more organized than you seem to be, you'll get massacred."

When neither Omar nor Lorenzo replied, Kel asked, "You really don't care? You really don't care if we all might die?"

Lorenzo responded, "Yeah, of course we care. But look man, all we got is your word, your speculation, and why would those Nazi assholes come here anyway?"

"Other than that they hate your guts and this place is on the only road to New M?" Kel gestured at the a.p.c. "They're at war with Earth-gov. And look at this! How the hell do you think this damned thing got this shot up? C'mon. How do you think it happened? Face it. You've got a situation here."

Omar replied, "It all comes down to this *socio*: *confianza*, do we trust you? And even if we do, are you blowing things out of proportion? Earth-gov says nothing is happening. Why would they lie about that? If there was any major shit going on, they'd want to recruit help."

Kel said, "Why would they lie? When has the government ever needed an excuse to lie about anything? Think about it! You're anarchists and you want to trust the government?" When Omar and Lorenzo didn't reply, Kel switched topics: "There's got to be a shuttle through here sometime soon. Ask the pilot."

Omar shook his head. "We're pretty self-sufficient, so there's not much shuttle traffic. I think the next one will be here in a week."

"You might not have a week. At least send out a scout party to check it out. They could be most of the way here already."

After a painful silence, Kel turned toward Lorenzo and asked, "You really think you can fix this thing?"

"Yeah. I already said so."

"Let's do it."

Lorenzo bent over the engine, surveyed it, and headed for the tool chests along the wall. As he was fumbling through the chests, Kel, trying to break the tension, asked Omar, "How'd you end up here?"

Omar seemed taken aback by the abrupt shift in topic, but it was a fair question, so he paused only briefly before answering. "I was stranded here like everybody else. Couldn't go back to Earth, New M was a hell hole, and I had to get out of there. It was even worse than back on Earth. There, they have three med-service levels, and the people on the bottom get screwed. But at least they get some coverage.

"Here? Sell my services to make money? Make as much money as I could off of sick people? Let 'em die if they can't pay? No. Too fucking evil. I couldn't do it. . . . There are docs in New M that do that, but I couldn't have lived with myself. I heal people. Not let 'em die if they can't come up with the cash. Making money off human misery?" He spat on the dirt floor. "I couldn't do that. . . . And this place seemed like the best thing going."

Lorenzo, who was now on his back on a wheeled mechanic's tray, flashlight in hand, sat up and addressed Omar. "That's you. You could pass for white and you're a doctor. You had *options*. You could have made it back on Earth or in New M. I couldn't. I'm here because there's no racist bullshit and no assholes ordering me around."

Omar snorted. "Give it a rest. You know what bullshit the 'who's more oppressed?' game is. You can always find somebody more oppressed than you are. Think about the ten-year-old hookers on the John Galt orbital back at Earth's L5 point. You do remember that, don't you? The assholes who reamed those poor kids, or pimped them out, claimed the kids were doing it out of *choice*! Who do you think was more oppressed? You or them? Give it a fucking rest!"

Lorenzo said, "Yeah. And how many of them were white? How many were black or brown?" Without waiting for a reply, Lorenzo disappeared under the vehicle. Omar snorted in disgust and stalked away. As Omar walked out the door, Kel lay down on the wheeled mechanic's tray next to Lorenzo's and pushed himself under the a.p.c.

47

MONOGAMOUS, adj. Preferring to have affairs in secret.

—Chaz Bufe, *The American Heretic's dictionary*

The next morning Chuy knocked repeatedly before giving up. Fifteen minutes later, after much prodding, Kel got Velky out the door. He reached for her elbow, but she jerked away. He turned to face her, but before he got a word out she nearly screamed, "No! Absolutely not!"

"Velky, please."

"No! I will *not* humiliate myself like that!"

As they were arguing, door open, a man and woman walking along the gravel path between the buildings slowed and stared at them. Kel glared at the gawking passersby, who turned aside their gaze and moved on.

After they were out of hearing, Kel said, "We need to talk. Let's go back in." He gestured with his head toward the apartment, and tried to take her arm.

Velky shook him off and said, "No!" She turned her back to him and stalked off. He pulled the door shut, and went after her, hurrying to catch up. Moments later they were standing on the side of a path near the road to New M, facing each other. Velky had shaken off Kel's hand when he'd reached out to her after she'd stopped, and had crossed her arms.

"This place is disgusting. We need to go now!"

"No! Where can we go? The Dream? They'll shoot both of us. New M? How in hell will we get there?"

"A shuttle."

"Yeah. In a week or two. And what would we do once we got there? If I go there, Miller and his asshole buddies will kill me."

"Miller? Who's Miller?"

"Miller! That Nazi piece of shit I nearly ki—"

"Oh! 'Nazi piece of shit?' So I'm a piece of sh—"

"Stop it! I wasn't talking about you!"

When she didn't respond, just kept glaring at him, he continued, "Please! We've got to play along here. Please babe, do it for me! Do it for *us*!" Velky didn't respond, other than flaring her nostrils and snorting. After a painful pause, Kel lowered his voice and said, "C'mon, please, we're already late."

"No! I will *not* go to that circle! I will *not* talk about our private affairs in front of strangers."

"Please!"

"No! And don't think I don't know what you're up to! You're dying to have sex with that woman."

"That has nothing to do with it!"

"Oh! So I'm right!"

Kel blew it by choking down a laugh.

Velky's eyes grew wide, and her face tensed; when she spoke again her voice was even higher, her words squeezed out between nearly clenched jaws.

"You bastard! You lying, cheating son of a bitch!"

She glared at Kel, her fists now on her hips.

They were so absorbed that they didn't notice a group of twenty people approaching them on the path. When the group was nearly upon them, they turned away from each other toward the new arrivals. Roberta, a short, energetic German woman in her fifties, with long grey hair in a ponytail and piercing green eyes, stood in front of the others.

"Since you did not come to circle, circle comes to you."

Velky looked at Roberta in horror. "No! I am not going to do this!"

Roberta replied, carefully, "Please, be calm. We do not want to hurt or embarrass. We know you are frightened, and this we do not want. We are friends. Or if you allow us, we will be."

"No!"

Roberta didn't reply. Just kept looking at her.

After a deathly pause, feeling the eyes of the entire group upon her, Velky broke down and started to sob. "Please, no!!"

Roberta walked close to her and stood with her until Velky calmed down. A moment later she led Velky and the rest of the group to a patch of grass next to the path.

"Sit down, please. We will meditate in silence to clear our minds. Please sit, close your eyes, and hold the hands of those next to you."

Two minutes later, Roberta let go of Velky's hand and said, "Peace. Please, move back and form circle." After everyone had shifted position, Roberta continued, "Let us begin." Roberta rose, moved to the center of the circle, and stood, facing Kel and Velky.

"We have new people. They know not the circle. How it goes is this. You are case study. Do not judge. Do not yourself judge. Do not others judge. All have problems. Here, we deal with them. The person with issues, I help them. We help them. They get up, walk, speak. While they walk, only one person, I ask them questions. Them I direct, them I touch; me, they do not touch. The others in circle are silent. They do not get up or speak while someone is in circle. I tell person in circle when to sit. They do not sit when uncomfortable. They do not sit to avoid dealing with issues.

"If person has issues with others in circle, they do not look at them. Ever. Others they look at, or at object. To others they speak, or at object, as if they speak to person they have problems with. When they are done, next person, before getting up, waits at least three breaths.

"Circle of this size lasts for one hour, normally. I determine if over it goes. But hour is normal. Do not expect issues raised at circle to resolve. That comes later."

Roberta permitted herself a smile and looked from side to side. "Does anyone have issues?"

Leroy, a veteran of the process, started to rise. But Aurilio, a guy in his early twenties, got up first.

Aurilio began walking quickly in a clockwise motion around the circle. Roberta joined him. She asked, "What is issue?"

He responded, "I'm angry at my work group."

"Which work group?"

"Sewage system."

"Everyone in group?"

"Everyone."

Roberta, walking next to Aurilio, with her hand on his back, asked, "Why? What comes up?"

"They fuck off. They don't care!"

They walked without speaking for several seconds.

"What do they do?"

"Not filling out forms. Only recording some readings."

"You have talked with them?"

"Yes."

"What do they say."

"That I'm anal."

"Are you?"

"No. I'm responsible."

"And they are not?"

"No."

"On time, do they not show up?"

"Yes."

"Their hours, do they not work them all?"

"Yes."

"The release schedule, do they not follow it?"

"Yes. . . . Most of the time."

"Most of time? You have seen them miss schedule?"

". . . No."

"So, is no danger?"

Aurilio didn't reply as Roberta continued to walk with him.

After another turn around the circle, she asked again, "Is no danger?"

"Maybe. . . . Maybe not."

"And you are only one responsible?"

"Yes."

"The *only* one responsible?"

"Yes!"

Roberta raised her hand higher on his back and began to push down, as she said, "Bend over, put arms above back, and carry weight of the world. The entire world! Feel the weight. It is all on you. Crushing you! Walk! Carry globe! It is all on *you*! Incredibly heavy! Feel the weight! Feel it!!"

Aurilio crouched and continued to walk around the circle, bent over, doing a credible impression of a man bearing the weight of the world on his shoulders.

As they walked, Roberta continued, "You cannot trust anyone! Feel the weight! You cannot trust anyone! The responsibility, it is all on you!" She pushed down harder on his shoulders, and he bent even lower. "On you! Feel it!" She pushed down again. "Feel it!" He continued to walk with her hand pushing down on his back.

She relaxed the pressure slightly, but not enough to allow him to straighten. "Tell us. What have you prevented?"

He didn't reply.

"Tell us. Has come to anyone harm?"

Again, silence. She pushed down harder.

"Are you responsible for actions of co-workers?"

He remained silent. She pushed down even harder.

"Are you responsible for actions of co-workers?"

When he finally said "no," she let up slightly.

"Say it again!"

"No."

"No what!?"

"No! I am not responsible for the actions of my co-workers!"

Roberta suddenly released the pressure on Aurilio's back. He shot upright as they continued to walk.

"Who are you responsible for?"

"Me!"

"And who else?"

"Only myself!"

Roberta pushed down again and asked, "*Only* yourself?"

They continued to walk around the circle, Roberta's right hand pushing down on Aurilio's back.

"*Only* yourself? No one else?"

"To the community."

"So, do it! Your co-workers are members of community. Speak truth to them. Your responsibility is to speak truth. If they do not respond, you all need circle. Call one. I help or Stig or Katrina help as facilitator."

She guided Aurilio to his seat. After a pause, she went over to Velky and reached down. Velky shrank back, shaking her head.

Roberta looked down at her and asked, "You are in pain. You do not want help?"

Velky softly said, "No," burying her head in her crossed arms.

Roberta looked down at her for a few seconds before saying, "Okay. Here we do not force. Perhaps later." She looked around the circle. "Does anyone else have issues?"

Forty-five minutes and six participants later, Velky still didn't want to get up, and the circle ended.

48

OPTIMISM, n. The doctrine, or belief, that everything is beautiful, including what is ugly, everything good, especially the bad, and everything right that is wrong. It is held with greatest tenacity by those most accustomed to the mischance of falling into adversity, and is most acceptably expounded with the grin that apes a smile. Being a blind faith, it is inaccessible to the light of disproof —an intellectual disorder, yielding to no treatment but death. It is hereditary, but fortunately not contagious.

—Ambrose Bierce, *The Devil's Dictionary*

The following day, a new storm hit. Kel loved it. The drumming of the rain pounding down on the roof and the howling of the wind was comforting. The Iron Dream shitheads wouldn't be able to move. If they were already on their way, they'd be bogged down and miserable. If they were still back at The Dream, they'd have to wait out the storm and then wait for at least another day or two, and even after that the mud would delay them.

Kel and Velky spent the day in their apartment, drinking, while the wind shrieked; shortly after dusk, they fell asleep on the bed, still fully clothed. In the middle of the night, Kel was pleasantly surprised when he felt Velky nestling into him. As they were still spooning the next morning, Julia, one of the nurses at the community infirmary, knocked on the door with a small carafe of coffee in her hand.

A quarter of an hour later, Velky and Julia were making small talk as they walked to the kitchen that was en route to the infirmary; once there, they grabbed croissants and more coffee. They were still nibbling at the last bits of pastry as they walked into the clinic. Once inside, Velky asked Julia about pay. And Velky was outraged by Julia's reply. She was going to be paid exactly as much as a sewage worker. Her, a nurse! An hour worked for an hour worked! The same as for a plumber! For a ditch digger!! A dishwasher!!!

Julia wasn't having any of it. She acidly observed that on New Z, as on Earth, there seemed to be an inverse relationship between the usefulness of work and pay for it, citing the pay differential between bankers and garbage men, and golf pros and farm workers. Who the hell was more useful?

Velky was still sputtering as Jobe, a fruit picker/visual artist, who had fallen from a ladder and fractured his left arm, came in. Julia broke off their conversation, and, with Velky assisting her, set the bone, put Jobe's arm in a splint, and sent him on his way with a bottle of pain pills.

After he'd ambled out, there was nothing for them to do other than chew on each other. As Jobe's shadow faded, Velky took up her refrain, "It's not fa—"

Julia turned toward her, scowling, leaning back against the wall, arms crossed, legs crossed at the ankles, interrupting her. "Get over it! Where do you get off thinking that your time is worth more than other people's? Thinking that just because you're more educated than most of them that you shouldn't have to work so hard? That you deserve more than they do?"

"That's not it!"

"No? You're not more deserving?"

"Well . . . yes I am!"

Julia shook her head.

Velky continued vehemently, "Yes I am! I deserve it! I worked *hard* to get my RN!"

"You think they don't work hard?! You think that everybody else is lazy?! That everybody who couldn't afford to go to nursing school is lazy!? That you're the only one who's deserving? Look at them. Look at everybody else. What choice did they have? For that matter, what choice did you ha—"

"I chose to work! To make myself better!"

"Yeah. With mommy and daddy supporting you."

"That's not fair!!"

"That's not *fair*!? How much money you have determines what you can do. Your parents had some money. So did mine. They could afford to send us to nursing school, so we're nurses. If they had less money, we'd be secretaries or waiting tables. If they had more money, we wouldn't be stuck here and might be MDs. And if they had even more money, we'd be teaching in some university back on Earth. Or doing nothing, living off the work of others."

Velky stared at her, open mouthed.

Julia continued: "Do you really think that the people who spend their lives picking fruit, harvesting crops, pouring cement, doing laundry, and washing dishes are lazy, stupid!? . . . That they *choose* a life like that, a life of hard labor because they're lazy? . . . Do you really think that we're better, smarter than they are?"

"Yes!"

"Jesus Christ! Come to the spokes-assembly tonight. You'll see how stupid they really are."

* * *

At the assembly, five dozen people—the active participants, the representatives of all of the work groups—were sitting in chairs in a circle roughly twelve meters in diameter, with another three hundred nonparticipants sitting in a wider circle behind them.

Omar introduced Kel: "Our new *compañero*, Kel, believes that we're about to be attacked by The Iron Dream. Please listen to him carefully."

Kel rose, expecting to speak plainly, easily—he'd played to far larger crowds—but found that he was nervous. He breathed shallowly as he began, speaking too quickly, forgetting his prepared words.

"Look, come on, look at that a.p.c. we drove in on. It's shot all to shit!" He gestured in the direction of the repair shed. "Who do you think did that!? I was at The Iron Dream for three months! I was part of their militia! I was there when Earth-gov attacked! That's where that damned thing came from!" Several faces looked at him in horror. "Not voluntarily! . . . I was on a shuttle that crashed and they grabbed me! I didn't have any choice!"

Most, but not all, of the visibly shocked relaxed.

"Check out that a.p.c.! They were ready. They cut Earth-gov to shreds when they attacked. Look at that vehicle! Go over to the shed! Look at it! Look at the blood on the seats! Look at the shot-out window and all of the bullet marks on the armor! Spears and rocks didn't do that. You're right on the road to New M. If they're headed this way, and they probably are, you're gonna get fucking slaughtered!"

Kel, still breathing hard, sat down to silence.

Alan, a mechanical engineer, and currently a member of the painters' group, rose. "Comrade Kel raises a good point. But do we have any independent confirmation?"

Tom, New Harmony's slim, South Asian communication director, said, "No. But Earth-gov says they have the situation in hand. They probably wouldn't lie abou—"

Kel interrupted him. "They wouldn't lie?! Earth-gov??!! Have you ever seen that son of a bitch Coron—?"

Elvia, who was acting as facilitator, cut in: "Wait. Let Tom finish."

Tom continued, almost too calmly, "They'd tell us. It'd be stupid of them not to. Self-defeating. As bad as he is, Corona isn't a racist."

After two more hours of maddening, exhausting discussion, Kel pleaded, "At least send out a scout party to see if they're on their way! . . . Please!!"

After another hour of discussion, and two hours of hurried preparation, as dawn was breaking a hybrid solar/bio-fuel truck, with a backpack radio, two AK-47s, and Eddie and Shaundray, two Central Asian vets, manning it, took off toward the east.

* * *

When Eddie and Shaundray's radioed report came in two days later, there was jubilation, first in the radio shack and then in the rest of New Harmony. A flight of shuttles heading east had passed over Eddie and Shaundray as they crested a ridge, and very shortly they'd seen fireballs in the distance. They'd waited half an hour before proceeding cautiously toward the column of smoke, stopping three klicks short at the top of a ridge, where they pulled out binoculars, and then radioed back to New Harmony.

When he heard the rest of the details, Kel was aghast.

"All they saw was one burned-out a.p.c. and two burned-out trucks? No more than three or four dozen corpses? It was a fucking *scout party*."

Chuy nodded in agreement. "No shit."

"Don't these guys realize that?"

Chuy replied, "No they don't. Some of the vets might, but even they want to believe that it's over. They really want to believe that Earth-gov saved our butts."

* * *

Three nights later, the general assembly was a disaster. Kel, Chuy, and Kel's curious new ally, Ann, were dismissed as alarmists. Shaundray and Eddie—notwithstanding the fact that they agreed with Kel and Chuy—had seen the evidence that the racists had been stomped into the ground. Earth-gov would take care of any remaining problems. End of story.

But when the "alarmists" persisted, no one objected to Chuy, Ann and the minority who agreed with them digging up the community weapons cache and setting up a defensive perimeter, although the strict pacifists couldn't resist asking them if they weren't becoming what they feared. Chuy's reply, that there was a difference between using violence to murder innocent people and using it to defend them, left the pacifists shaking their heads.

* * *

Kel wasn't impressed. New Harmony's arms cache was pathetic: maybe a hundred and fifty AK-47s, only four with drum clips, the rest with standard thirty-round banana clips, and thirty or forty thousand rounds total—barely two hundred rounds per weapon—

and not much else: only the RPG launcher with a single round, Kel's AK-97, the flash grenades they'd found in the a.p.c., and the a.p.c. itself, which wouldn't be of much use since it's .50 caliber was almost out of ammunition. Kel voiced his frustration at the ad hoc resistance assembly after they'd dug up the arms.

"This is a fucking joke. They have at least fifteen hundred militia members, they're better armed than we are, and they'll probably send most of 'em this way. Do the math."

No one responded. "Come on. There are some decent defensive positions on the way in here, but we'd never hold 'em. So, what do you want to do?"

Ann rubbed the skin at the top of her nose between her thumb and index finger. When she looked up, she said, "You're right. If they're on the way, we're fucked. We can't stop them. The best we can do is delay 'em. And who wants to die for that?"

Kel repeated his question: "So what do we do? Most of these dumbshits won't even evacuate. Won't even prepare for it. So what do we do?"

The question hung in the air. After a pause, Lorenzo said, "Look man, we can't stop 'em, but at least we want to give the people here some warning. There's a ridge about one-and-a-half, two klicks east of here above Fabbri Creek. At that distance, they should be able to hear weapons fire. They'll panic and take off like chickens with their heads cut off, but it's better than nothing. We'll set up a picket there. Then let's talk at the next general assembly about evacuation plans. Who knows? Some of 'em might even listen."

Chuy asked, "What about Earth-gov?"

Ann replied, "Tom finally managed to get a more or less straight answer out of them this morning: 'We have everything under control, but you're on your own.'"

* * *

The discussion at the next general assembly was unusually bitter. In the end, just over half opposed doing anything about the "imaginary invasion" other than passive resistance; just under forty percent wanted to prepare evacuation plans; and ten percent favored armed resistance coupled with evacuation preparations. There was nothing close to consensus.

The pacifist bare majority was opposed to using any communal resources for armed resistance, but in the spirit of compromise agreed that the armed-resistance faction could use two of New Harmony's farm trucks and the a.p.c.

Following the general assembly, at the resistance faction's smaller assembly, Chuy made a proposal: "We can't hold them, and all we want to do is make some noise so that our people will start to evacuate. It doesn't make a hell of a lot of difference if all of us are up there or only twenty or thirty of us, which is all the trucks can carry anyway. What we want to do is prepare to evacuate, start shooting when they come into view, keep 'em pinned down for as long as we can, and then take off. We're not trying to inflict casualties or die, just give warning."

Omar grunted assent. "Makes sense."

Lorenzo shook his head. "There are only thirteen trucks. Total. We can't evacuate anywhere near everybody. Jesus . . ."

Ann answered, "That's why we want to take those who have some guts and common sense. Let the rest of them see where they get with passive resistance with the fucking Nazis."

After a heavy pause, Kel brought up the obvious question: "Who'll be in charge?"

Since he'd had the most military experience, and because he was a trusted, long-time community member, Lorenzo was the nearly unanimous choice.

49

COLLATERAL DAMAGE, n. A military term
referring to dead and maimed civilians.

—Chaz Bufe, *The American Heretic's Dictionary*

The attack, when it came a week later, minutes before sunset, was surprisingly long in developing. Lorenzo spotted the first camouflaged, advancing troops in his binoculars as they emerged from the woods half a klick from the ridge. There were no vehicles in sight, and there were only fifty of them. The Dream troopers, spread out on both sides of the road, were advancing slowly, unaware of their observers. No one was advancing behind them. So, the plan to shoot and run was out. It would be a turkey shoot. Ten minutes later, when the Dream troopers were within fifty meters of the ridge, Lorenzo ordered the militia to fire. The Dream troops dropped in bloody shreds, the survivors wildly returning fire at foes they couldn't see.

Two minutes later the ridge erupted. Lorenzo, shouted, "Out!! Now!!!" as mortar rounds slammed down.

Ninety seconds later the last of the ambushers were still scrambling downhill when a mortar shell took out one of the farm flat beds, spraying torn bodies in all directions. As more mortar rounds plowed into the ridge, sending geysers of mud and rock into the air, the other truck tore away.

Kel, Chuy, Lorenzo, and Ann scrambled into the a.p.c. as shrapnel ricocheted off the rocks above it. Eddie was behind the wheel, waiting for stragglers. Lorenzo, sweating, said, "thirty seconds," as mortar rounds pounded down to the north. He looked at his watch and waited as the seconds crawled by, and then roared, "Go!" as a round hit less than ten meters away, sending shrapnel and gravel pinging off the a.p.c.'s armor. Eddie put the pedal to the floor and was pulling onto the road, when Lorenzo screamed, "Stop!"

A limping straggler had emerged from the trees thirty meters to the south. Eddie jammed on the brakes and started to drop the rear gate as the earth erupted where the man had been. Lorenzo dropped through the hatch and yelled at Eddie, "Go! Go!!" Eddie floored it as shrapnel ricocheted off the a.p.c.'s sides.

* * *

There was chaos in New Harmony. The resistance faction was lining up the eleven remaining farm trucks on the main road, with members at the wheel and others already sitting in the back. The trucks filled almost immediately, and began to pull away. But desperate people began climbing up the sides as they moved out, and the resistance-faction fighters crouching in the backs of the trucks couldn't bring themselves to club down their friends and neighbors. Instead, they helped them aboard as the firing came nearer, amidst screams, bodies clawing over each other, and pulling each other down. Still other shrieking, begging, men, women, and children ran futilely after the trucks, some hanging onto the back gates until they were hauled aboard and flung on top of the others already in the truck beds, or they lost their grip and fell into the gravel.

* * *

The a.p.c. swerved sickeningly on the loose road surface as Eddie floored it. Three minutes later it was in New Harmony. Mortar rounds slammed down as the a.p.c. veered off the road. Kel shouted at Eddie, "The infirmary! The infirmary!" Eddie jerked the wheel and headed down the path to it, crushing the vegetable beds along the sides and the solar lights which illuminated the path, while forcing panicking, cursing people off it.

When they reached the clinic, Kel got out of the passenger's-side door and ran inside as the tailgate dropped. A moment later he emerged with Velky, Julia, Elvia, and Omar, all laden with medical supplies, and half-a-dozen patients, Roberta among them

The tailgate rose as explosions echoed from the center of the village. Eddie turned the a.p.c. around, trashing a flower bed, and headed back toward the road in the deepening twilight. As they lumbered forward, mortar rounds pounded a building to their right as women screamed.

* * *

They skidded back onto the main road and Eddie hit the accelerator. A hundred meters on he swerved around a stalled farm truck in the middle of the road, the last of its passengers running madly into the gathering darkness.

The resistance faction members who had chosen to stay and lead the evacuation ran, guns in hand, through New Harmony's maze of paths with their unarmed friends and neighbors following, some with packs they'd prepared, but most with nothing but the clothes they were wearing. They were still melting into the fields, orchards, and hills when the first Dream troops stormed in, amid screams, random shots, and the grinding noise of an a.p.c. with freshly painted lightning bolt symbols on its sides. Its spotlight focused on the fleeing civilians. Slugs tore into the bodies of men, women and children who weren't fast enough getting away from the road and into the shelter of trees and buildings.

Matthew, one of the remaining resistance faction members, crouched behind a thicket, AK in hand, and began to creep toward the Dream a.p.c., now fifty meters away. It had stopped on the road, floodlight flaring from side to side, occasionally locking onto a victim. A fat, weasel-like figure was standing upright through the a.p.c.'s forward port with a gun in hand. Matthew's mouth opened in shock as he looked more closely at the a.p.c. Two human heads, bearded and with long dreadlocks—primitivists!—were mounted as ornaments above its headlights.

Matthew pulled down the lever on the side of the AK to its middle position and took aim. On the other side of the road, Dian, one of the vets, hidden in another thicket, gripped the RPG launcher bearing its single round.

Matthew, who had no military training, was a terrible shot, and his first rounds ricocheted off the side of the a.p.c., and the rest went wide as the weapon jerked up and to the right. The weasel standing in the port ducked down inside at the exact moment

Dian fired the RPG. The weasel's vehicle exploded. His shredded body flew through its hatch like a cork from a champagne bottle. Murphy and company, in the truck behind the a.p.c., fired blindly toward their unseen attackers, tearing Dian's and Matthew's bodies apart.

* * *

Kel's a.p.c. was tearing down the road. It hadn't received any fire since leaving the community, so Kel rose through its port and looked back toward the red glow that had been New Harmony, as gunshots and barely discernible cries faded into the distance.

The vehicle rounded a bend and screeched to a stop. There was a woman ahead on the right, outlined in the headlights, sitting on a boulder by the side of the road. The woman took no notice of them, but continued sitting, shaking, her head in her hands, rocking backwards and forwards.

Kel yelled at her, "Get in! Damn it! Get in!"

When the woman didn't respond, Ann released the rear gate; ran to the woman, lifted her to her feet, and shepherded her up the ramp and into the vehicle. It was Maria, one of the apolitical, terminal-addict types who had gravitated to New Harmony because they thought it was the softest touch on Tau II.

It wasn't. As soon as Maria had arrived, the newcomer committee had taken one look at her sunken, nearly toothless face and had given her an ultimatum: work or get out. Maria was among the few addicts who had chosen to work. Almost all of the others had hopped the first shuttle out and returned to a life of petty crime and parasitism in New M, or Father-worship and reprogramming in one of the other communities.

* * *

Ann held Maria as she broke down and wept. The ramp closed and Eddie began to inch forward again, holding down his speed until the ramp was in place.

Before the ramp was all the way up, a fireball blossomed behind them. Seconds later, submachine gun bullets ricocheted off the vehicle's back and sides. Kel ducked down through the port as camo-clad troops streamed out of the woods. Eddie floored it and turned the lights off, steering only by the dim light of Boris and Arkady. More bullets found the closing ramp and careened off it as a trooper with a rocket launcher aimed at the retreating vehicle and fired.

The a.p.c. shuddered, and a white-hot glow half blinded those looking back through the final few open centimeters of the tailgate. The rocket had exploded on a boulder two meters behind the a.p.c., rocking it and sending shards ricocheting off of it. One piece made it through the narrow opening, tearing straight through the center of Julia's hand.

Julia dumbly stared at her pitted, bleeding palm before she started to scream. Velky pulled open the a.p.c.'s med kit, beating Omar by a heartbeat. She climbed across the close-packed bodies and gave Julia a shot of synorphine as Omar bandaged her hand, joking, as he wound gauze around her wound, that she now had one of the signs of sainthood: stigmata.

Another blast sent more shards and shrapnel slamming into the a.p.c. Even as it rocked from the explosion, Eddie, sweating profusely, kept his eyes on the road, his hands upon the wheel, and kept going, doing his best to keep the vehicle on track in the pale, grey moonlight.

* * *

Maria came out of her near-shock as the a.p.c. bounced and juddered down the road, with ever-more-distant shots and explosions fading into nothingness, giving way to the hypnotic purring of the vehicle's wheels and motor. She sobbed. They had caught up with the severely overladen farm trucks and had fallen in behind them, at no more than twenty kph, much to Eddie's and Kel's annoyance. Eddie was growling, "Shit! Even on this road they can go faster than this!"

But they ground on, a bit too close to the final truck and its human cargo.

As Eddie fidgeted, fighting to keep his foot off the accelerator, Maria asked Ann, "What happened?"

"The Iron Dream. The fucking Nazis."

"What happened to everybody else? What happened to Tobi?"

"Tobi? McGriff? I don't know what happened to him. He might be in one of the trucks."

"Might!?" She began to wail.

* * *

Arkady had set, and the a.p.c. and the trucks were crawling down a narrow mountain road with a steep drop off to one side, their headlights on. Omar had taken over driving, with Chuy riding shotgun.

Omar cast a sidelong glance at Chuy, then in the mirror at the dozing, shell-shocked passengers, and asked, "*¿Que pienses?*"

"Let's speak English." Chuy glanced back at the sleeping/slumping forms in the dim red light. "They're paranoid enough already."

"Okay. What in hell do we do when we hit New M?"

"Go to the house. They'll know what's going on."

"Let's hope so."

* * *

Dawn was fast approaching as Omar rounded a bend and saw the lead truck plunge down a hundred meter-deep ravine, bodies spewing from it, bouncing from boulder to boulder until they came to rest on the slope or were carried away by the rushing stream at the bottom. The truck behind it ground to a halt at the brink. The others behind it stopped and the drivers and some of the passengers climbed out and looked down. Even in the early half-light, it was obvious there were almost no survivors, only broken bodies on the rocks far below, two of them writhing feebly.

Chuy got out and walked forward past the remaining trucks and gawkers to the washed-out, vee-shaped break in the road. The washout was major—two-and-a-half meters long, two meters deep, and over a meter wide at the edge.

There was no way to get down to the victims, short of a winch and a hundred meters of cable. Chuy turned to the onlookers and said, "We can't do anything for them. And we need to get out of here."

Anya, one of the kitchen crew, said, "We can't just—"

Chuy cut her off. "Yes we can! They're dead. Or they will be, soon. We can't get down! We can't do anything for them!"

Anya spoke again: "We can't just—"

"Yes we can!"

He turned away from her, pointed to a barrel-chested teenaged kid at the brink of the chasm, and said loudly, "Can you get some good-sized stones and some branches?" He looked toward the others on the road near the kid and, without his asking, some of them, mostly teenagers and guys in their early twenties, climbed the muddy slope and began tossing down rocks and branches they ripped from the small piñons clinging to the bank.

Anya grabbed Chuy and began to shake him. He broke her grip, grabbed her by the arms and shook her violently, shouting, "Stop it! If you want to die, do it! But don't take anybody else with you!" He released her, and she stood looking at him, murder in her eyes. She turned away from him and stared grimly down at the broken bodies on the slope below. One of the survivors had stopped moving. The other continued to writhe.

Five minutes later, Chuy yelled for those tossing down rocks and branches to stop, and a pair of workers from the construction group began fitting the rocks into the breach, using the branches as struts, and mud as mortar. Twenty minutes later they slopped the final shovel of mud onto what looked to be a serviceable patch.

The first truck, with only its driver in it, slowly crossed the newly bridged gap. The driver made it, with only a few rocks shaking loose and plummeting into the chasm. He stopped a hundred meters down the road. His passengers followed him across the repair, sticking as close to the uphill side as they could.

The ten remaining trucks repeated the process, with Anya still standing on the brink of the chasm staring down, refusing to go on. As the last of the trucks crossed the repaired section, it gave way under the truck's right rear wheel. Rocks, mud and branches tumbled into the ravine as the driver frantically gunned the engine and the wheels spun, kicking debris into the gap.

Lorenzo, who had been on the side of the road beyond the patch, ran to the truck's cab and yelled at the driver, "Cool it! Hit the brakes!"

The panicked driver did. The truck's right rear wheel sagged into the gap and then stopped, with the axle resting on the brink. Lorenzo surveyed the horrified passengers standing behind him, picked out the four biggest guys, walked to the back of the truck, and said, "Come on! Push!" When they'd joined him, he chanted "one, two, three" and yelled at the driver, "Go!" The wheel turned slowly, agonizingly inching its way up the side of the gap as they heaved, backs and legs straining. The truck lurched up onto the roadbed spraying its rescuers with mud and rocks.

As it did so, Lorenzo screamed and began hopping up and down on his left leg, holding the back of his right leg above the ankle. The two guys next to him grabbed his arms and helped him back to the a.p.c. They laid him on the ground, near the back of the vehicle. Omar felt Lorenzo's lower leg as Lorenzo grunted out between clenched teeth, "What the fuck was that? It feels like I got chopped with a fucking machete."

Omar replied, "This isn't good, *compañero*. You ruptured your Achilles tendon."

"What the fuck does that mean?"

"It means you can't walk anywhere near normal, and you can't run at all. The standard drill would be for me to open up your leg, reattach the ends of the tendon, put you in a cast for a month, and a few months after that you'd be back to near normal. Now, all we can do is put it in a cast and hope for the best."

"Shit! You're sayin' I'm gimped? And there's nothin' you can do about it?"

"It's not quite that bad. If we cast it now, it might reattach if you don't abuse it too much."

"Might?"

"Might."

Omar looked toward the nurses. "There is casting material, isn't there?"

Elvia disappeared into the a.p.c., and a moment later reappeared with cotton batting and fiberglass wrap in hand.

Omar wrapped Lorenzo's leg in the batting, then wrapped the batting with the fiberglass strip which he had dipped in a basin of water Velky had supplied.

When he'd finished wrapping Lorenzo's leg, Omar asked Julia and Velky, "Crutches?" They both shook their heads. Omar gazed down at Lorenzo. "Let's get him across the gap first, and then put him inside."

* * *

Moments later, branches and rocks rained down on the road from the slope above, and Chuy looked up and yelled, "Enough! Let's get the hell out of here!"

As their helpers scrambled down the slope, back to the waiting farm trucks on the other side of the gap, most of the survivors they'd picked up in the a.p.c. walked across the gap and climbed on board the already-overladen trucks. Anya refused to join them. Two minutes later, the a.p.c., its crew, and its few passengers were alone, the sound of the farm trucks dwindling in the distance.

Ann took one of the AK's and pointed it downward toward the final twitching figure on the rocks at the bottom of the ravine. It was Edgardo, one of her friends on the kitchen crew—and one of Anya's occasional lovers.

Upon seeing Ann aim at Edgardo, Anya rushed her. Ann slammed the gun's butt into Anya's chest, sending her toppling backward. Ann aimed down again toward Edgardo and fired until a shot slammed into his torso, he jerked convulsively, and finally was still. Ann turned, pulled Anya to her feet, and pushed her into the back of the a.p.c.

* * *

After Kel and Chuy hastily completed the repair job on the washout, Eddie climbed behind the wheel and said to those still inside, "Get out." After everyone was, he put the a.p.c. in gear, angled the left wheels as high as he could on the uphill slope, and began inching across the patch. As he felt the right rear wheel start to sag, Eddie gunned it, and the a.p.c. shot onto the other side of the gap, as stones and mud shot down into the gorge and back toward the a.p.c.'s passengers on the other side of the repair.

Kel hadn't stood far enough back. One of the rocks hit him squarely on the shin of his left leg, and he went down writhing from the pain of a bone bruise.

While Omar was helping Kel up, they heard the faint sounds of shouts and rocks cascading into the ravine higher up the canyon, toward New Harmony. Kel grimaced, then clambered across the gap and into the vehicle.

A klick later they stopped just past a particularly tight, partially washed out turn that they had barely negotiated. Kel, Chuy, and Eddie got out at and dug frantically at the roadbed with the two shovels and one axe they had, digging the washout deeper.

They stopped and sabotaged the road four more times before they caught up with the farm trucks near the outlet of the gorge. They were at a dead stop. Kel and Chuy got out and walked forward a hundred meters to the leading farm truck. Some of its passengers had just cleared away a small slide that blocked the road and were climbing back on board. The last truck was already moving by the time Kel and Chuy got back to the a.p.c.

Eddie stopped short after going past the point of the slide. Kel, Chuy, and Eddie got out, walked back, shovels and axe in hand, and surveyed the slide. Ann joined them, looking up at the crumbling hillside above. She said, "I think we ought to go. It's too risky." Eddie replied, "Nah. If we're careful it'll be okay. We can start an avalanche. We just need to get above where the slide started." He didn't wait for further discussion and began climbing the slope, shovel in hand. Kel and Chuy exchanged nervous glances and started after him.

Before they caught up to Eddie, he put too much weight on a loose rock and went screaming down the slope, across the road, and down into the ravine, along with the avalanche he had wanted to start. Kel and Chuy stopped dead as the ground in front of them roared downhill, with the edge of the slide stopping a bare half-meter before Kel. When the slide was over, they carefully retraced their steps down the slope. The road was now completely blocked. Eddie had given them at least half a day.

Kel climbed into the driver's seat, and within minutes they caught up with the convoy as it was emerging from the gorge onto the plateau that overlooked the New M plain. Two fallen-tree delays later, the forest was thinning to the right, and sunlight was streaming through the trees. The road was almost at the brink of the plateau's rim, skirting it by no more than five meters. The dropoff was dizzying.

Then they were out of the trees, heading down a precipitous decline on a too narrow, rocky dirt road that hugged the side of the cliff. And going too fast. Kel hit the brakes and a.p.c. skidded toward the abyss. He regained control centimeters from the edge. Breathing hard, he rode the brakes until they were just past the most heart-stopping hairpin turn. His hands were locked on the wheel, his foot stomping on the brake pedal, as they came to a stop. Chuy didn't need to be told what to do. He and Omar got out, and soon their shovel and axe were sending a cascade of rocks and mud down onto the plain below.

While they were working, Kel looked west toward New M and saw a plume of smoke rising from a village in the foreground.

50

Pacifism is simply undisguised cowardice.

—Adolf Hitler, Speech at Nuremberg, August 21, 1926

Animals do not destroy their own species;
it takes a militarist to do that.

—Charles T. Sprading, *Freedom and Its Fundamentals*

They hit the bottom of the decline and were on flat, treeless ground, where they soon caught up with the last of the trucks. Kel turned the a.p.c.'s wheel to the right, drove on the shoulder past the trucks, and stopped in front of them. He walked back to the lead truck, and told the driver to hang back at least two hundred meters in case of trouble. While he was talking to the truck driver, Julia and Velky managed to get the still-angry Anya out of the a.p.c. and into the back of the truck.

The a.p.c. took off and the convoy followed, on what had become a good gravel road, toward the pillar of smoke. Five klicks on, they were nearing Watchtower, a farming village founded by Jehovah's Witnesses. Most of the Witnesses were now at least middle aged, having been imprisoned and then deported to Tau II after conscientious objector status had been abolished during the Central Asian wars; their "terrorist enabler" families had been deported along with them.

The a.p.c. pulled into the village. The small, scattered houses along the road all showed signs of violence. Some were burned entirely, others trashed, their windows broken, doors smashed in, furniture and clothing strewn about their yards. None were untouched. The only signs of life were a few dogs and barnyard animals wandering aimlessly across the road and through the yards.

Kel stopped the a.p.c. before one of the dwellings and got out. Chuy reached behind the seat and grabbed two AK's, handing one to Kel. They crouched and approached the door at a half-run. Broken furniture, trampled clothing, and trampled toys lay scattered along the path.

At the wrecked door, Kel leaned against the wall to its right, and Chuy leaned against the wall to its left. Kel, his heart pounding, kicked the door open and rushed through, weapon at his shoulder. But there was nothing. The front room was empty except for broken furniture. Chuy followed Kel in, and they began methodically inching along the walls, searching the house room by room. The bathroom was empty. The bedrooms were empty. And then they reached the kitchen. Kel burst in, weapon at the ready, pointing at a bearded man slumped over the table, a Bible before him. Kel said, "Oh shit!" The man had been shot in the forehead. The back of his skull was gone, and his brains were spattered against the white plaster wall behind him.

Chuy poked his head around the corner, saw Kel staring at the dead man, and said, "Come on. He's dead. If the assholes who did this were still here, you'd be dead. Let's go." He grabbed Kel by the arm and pulled him away.

When they reached the a.p.c., Chuy started to get into the driver's seat, but Kel stopped him, saying, "I'm okay to drive." Kel got back behind the wheel, put the vehicle in gear, and concentrated on driving as Chuy explained to Omar and the others, ". . . killed execution style."

As they reached the crossroads at the center of the town, Kel saw the main source of smoke: the only large building in the village, the Witness Hall. It was in ruins, smoldering.

Kel stopped. He, Chuy, Ann, and Omar got out and began walking toward the burning building. There were three dead civilians in the street, two men and a woman, with a Chow-mix burying its jaws in the woman's shredded torso. The dog raised its bloody muzzle and charged Kel. He pulled the trigger as the Chow-mix started to leap. It dropped to the gravel a bare two meters from Kel, still growling, still pulling itself forward. Kel cursed and shot the dog again. He'd always hated Chows.

Ann said, "Shit! If they didn't know we're here, they do now!"

Chuy sighed and said, "Cool it. What else was he gonna do? And I don't think there's anybody around here anyway."

They found dozens of dead civilians around the shattered, smoking hall, most along the paths leading from the exits. Several had been killed by shots to the head after falling wounded.

As they were walking back to the a.p.c., Kel asked, "Why would they do this? This is just a farm town."

Ann snorted. "It's pretty fucking obvious." She gestured toward the highest ground between Watchtower and New M, a two-hundred-meter-high hill three or four klicks to the southwest of the village. A TV tower stood atop it.

Kel didn't see anything obvious about the massacre. "Why not just take the transmitter? Why kill all of these people? Most of them are white."

Ann snorted again. "You really don't get it, do you? This was a target of opportunity. It's so damned near the TV tower that they couldn't resist. They hate the JW's. Consider 'em 'race traitors.' And they're pacifists and they have some guts. The fucking Nazis hate 'em, just like the all-American mob did back in the twentieth century. They lynched a bunch of the JW's. Even castrated some of 'em during both world wars just 'cause they refused to fight. So, there you go. What I can't figure out is how they got here ahead of us."

Kel thought about it. "Back at The Dream I saw a shuttle take off to the east before the attack. They must have come back, loaded up, and set down here."

Ann was skeptical. "Then why in hell didn't they use it at New Harmony?"

"Too much opposition. They must have known we had guns, and most of those shuttles can only hold fifty or seventy-five troops. Probably figured it'd be easier to overrun us on the ground. My guess is they landed here, massacred these poor motherfuckers, and went for the transmitter on the hill. Maybe met up here with a bunch of the Nazi assholes from New M. Probably gave 'em a shitload of guns."

When they were nearly back to the vehicle, Omar heard a whisper and turned his head, trying to pinpoint the sound. Seconds later he started walking west. The others followed, with the whisper growing louder as they walked.

Thirty meters down the street they found the source, the general store. Its front windows were shattered, and most of its racks had been turned over or smashed, but it was still more or less intact. And there was a small black-and-white 2-D shining at them from a shelf facing the checkout stand.

They stepped into the building and picked their way through the broken glass and spilled cans and boxes. Kel was the first to the TV. A black-uniformed announcer was reading the news. Kel said, "Shit! It's O'Doul."

Ann frowned and twisted her head toward Kel.

"The Dream's information minister."

Omar found the remote control next to the cash register, pointed it at the TV, and pressed the volume button. O'Doul's words gradually became more audible: ". . . destroyed the terrorist training center known as New Harmony yesterday evening. The Iron Dream's McVey, Matthews, Butler, and Hess columns have risen in New M and will liberate the city within two days. Earth-gov's mongrel troops are deserting their Jew masters and fleeing like rats from a sinking ship." The 2-D cut to footage of Earth gov troops in full retreat with Eco-Nazi militia in pursuit. The voiceover continued: "We urge all race patriots to cooperate with—"

Ann shot the TV; it exploded in a shower of sparks.

Chuy said, "What the fuck!? What did you do that for? We might have learned something useful!"

Ann laughed. "Right."

Chuy shook his head and started to walk away from the store, when Ann said, "Wait! We can use some of this shit."

Chuy walked back in and, along with Ann, began searching through the rubble. The others followed, and five minutes later they walked back to the a.p.c. carrying medical supplies, canned and bulk food, clothing, matches, and anything else that might prove useful.

As they were loading what they'd scavenged, Ann walked back to the trucks, which had, after an agony of waiting, ignored the two-hundred-meter-back order and were lined up behind the a.p.c. People immediately began streaming out of them, heading for the wrecked general store. Kel cocked his head and raised an eyebrow as Ann returned.

She said, "I gave them half an hour."

Kel sighed loudly.

Ann scowled and said, "Really. It won't be more than half an hour."

Inside the store, makeshift groups searched through the chaos. Twenty minutes later, the trucks were ready to roll, laden with what the search groups could carry off; Chuy climbed behind the wheel.

Kel was amazed. "Holy shit! I thought we'd be here for hours."

Ann snorted. "What did you expect? We're anarchists. We're organized."

Kel gaped at her.

Ann said, "Think about it. If you don't have anybody telling you what to do, you'd damned well better be organized. And cooperative." She continued, "Where to now?" She gestured at the hill bearing the TV transmitter and asked, "Want to drop in on those assholes?"

Chuy said, "No. If they have even one RPG we're fucked. We need to keep going to New M. They'll know what's going on at the house and might be able to give us some help."

Chuy stepped on the pedal and the vehicle surged forward, with the trucks following. Three klicks later, after the road turned south, they arrived at a tee. The road to the right continued toward New M, the one to the left led up the hill to the TV transmitter.

They stopped, with the engine running. Ann climbed between the front seats. She gestured toward the hill and said, "Let's get those bastards!"

Omar replied, "There have to be a dozen places where they could pick us off. We only have this one a.p.c. . . . And you want to get us blown away just because you're pissed? Think about the people in the trucks. Without us, no protection at all."

Chuy, who had been watching Ann in the mirror, waited until she sighed disgustedly, moved back, and sat on one of the side benches before he pressed down the pedal and turned to the right.

51

They wrote in the old days that it is sweet and fitting to die for one's country. But in modern war there is nothing sweet nor fitting in your dying. You will die like a dog for no good reason.

—Ernest Hemingway

The a.p.c. sped on, rocks clanging off its undercarriage. Ten klicks past the crossroads, it was racing through another farming community at full speed, with the trucks fifty meters behind. Bodies were strewn in the street and buildings were burning as they roared through the village. As the a.p.c. rounded the final corner before hitting the straightaway heading toward New M, there was an up-ended flatbed truck blocking the road with a small group of gunmen behind it.

When he saw the flatbed, Chuy jammed the throttle down and aimed toward the tail end of the overturned truck. The a.p.c. slammed into it, throwing it to the side and crushing two of the Nazis standing behind it, as others hidden in the single-storey frame house to the right opened up with assault rifles. There was no damage to the a.p.c. or its occupants—just bullets ricocheting off the a.p.c.'s sides and rear.

But the Nazis didn't miss the truck that followed them. Chuy pulled the a.p.c. to the side a hundred and fifty meters past the roadblock, as a shot-up, blood-spattered farm truck swerved to the side of the road just behind the a.p.c. Its windshield was shot out, it was spewing smoke from under its hood, and a woman with a shattered arm was lying in its bed screaming.

The other trucks had stopped before they reached the ambush, and their riders were pouring out into the village as the Nazis opened up on them. Chuy spun the a.p.c. around and headed back toward the Nazis as Kel popped through the hatch, grabbed the handles of the .50 caliber, and began firing when they were within a hundred meters of the house and up-ended flatbed. He sprayed both the truck and the building. The sound was deafening within the echo chamber of the a.p.c.

Kel was still holding down the trigger as Chuy braked to a halt. He lifted his thumbs from the trigger, and he could barely hear anything beyond the ringing in his ears. As the ringing faded, he began to hear moans and cries of agony, first faintly then gradually louder and clearer.

Ann, Chuy, and Omar clambered out of the vehicle and, along with Kel, advanced on what was left of the truck the Nazis had used as a barricade. They were all dead. Kel didn't recognize any of them; they had to be from New M.

Seconds later, Chuy, with Ann behind him, kicked in the door to the house. They stepped across the threshold, weapons raised, and found an abattoir: shredded meat in blood-soaked, makeshift Nazi uniforms, with a black-haired, blue-eyed kid in his early twenties lying writhing, gut shot, bleeding out, on the floor of what had been the living room, his gun just out of reach.

Chuy was lowering his gun to finish him off, when Ann put her hand on the barrel and pulled it down, saying, "No. Don't. He'll suffer more this way." Still holding the barrel of Chuy's AK, she kicked the gut-shot militiaman's gun farther away from him.

She and Chuy glared at each other for several long seconds before Chuy said, "I wouldn't do that to a fucking dog." He violently pushed Ann away, jerked the muzzle of his gun toward the man's head, and pulled the trigger.

The medics from the a.p.c. had nearly arrived at the shot-up farm trucks when the final shot rang out. There were dead and wounded men, women, and children in the beds of the trucks, and others rolling in agony on the ground, the medics who'd been in the trucks already tending the worst wounded.

Two hours later, after the medics had finished treating the wounds of those who might recover, and helping those who wouldn't recover reach as easy a death as possible, the convoy prepared to roll on to New M, minus the trucks that were so shot up they couldn't move.

Omar, Velky, Elvia, and Julia, all exhausted, were standing with the other medics looking at the remaining trucks, now overloaded and sagging with the survivors and wounded. Omar turned to the others and asked, "Can those trucks even move? And if they can't, how in hell do we choose who goes and who gets left behind?"

Rocky, one of the paramedics from the farm trucks, replied, "Well, they just might be able to carry everybody. Or we could cast lots. Or we could just ask who's willing to grab a gun and take off into the bush."

Chuy paused before saying, "There's always another choice. I remember this place now. Two or three klicks down the road it splits. One fork goes to New M and one takes off north toward the coast, toward The Strand. There ain't much there, mostly beach bums, snow-heads, and scammers. But it´s out of the way and there's nothin' worth bothering with, so it should be safe for now. And there are boats. And you have guns."

Rocky cocked his head and asked, "And then what?"

"If worse comes to worst, you can just take some of the boats and head out. Go east until you find a place to hide along the coast or walk inland until you find one of the communities, if the Nazis haven't overrun them, or you could sail west a few hundred klicks to the Magón Islands. They're habitable. You'd eat an awful lot of fish and seaweed, but you'd survive.

"But first, we should search this place. See if we can find any more vehicles. Then hold an emergency assembly to see what everybody wants to do."

Rocky still wasn't convinced. "Why don't you just come with us?

Head north?" He gestured toward the a.p.c. "The extra persuasion might help."

Chuy shook his head. "You won't need it. And we need to get to the outreach house to see if any of them are still alive. At this point, I think they need *our* help." He gestured toward New M: an orange haze on the horizon with pillars of grey smoke rising above the glow. "We're going there, but I don't think it's a good idea to have civilians in open vehicles head into that. But make up your own minds."

Three hours later, search crews had found three more trucks in barns on the outskirts of the town, and the emergency meeting had resorted to emergency measures: majority vote rather than consensus, but with those in the minority being free to go their own way, with a proportionate share of the vehicles, guns, and supplies.

About ninety percent of the survivors, including all of the wounded, except Lorenzo, decided to head for The Strand. But about fifteen of the kids in their teens and twenties, and a few in their early thirties, decided to follow the a.p.c. into New M. One of them with a nostalgic bent suggested they adopt the name "The Durruti Column." The assembly gave them one of the newly liberated farm trucks plus AK's and ammo. This was out of proportion to their numbers, but it was obvious that they'd need it.

As the meeting ended, Chuy, Kel, Ann, and the others from their group walked back to the a.p.c. and climbed in. As soon as the doors and hatch were shut and the wounded and most of the civilians had been transferred to the trucks heading toward The Strand, Omar pressed down the pedal.

* * *

It was mid-afternoon as the trucks heading toward The Strand peeled off, and the a.p.c./single-truck "convoy" headed toward the smoky horizon that was New M. Within ten minutes the a.p.c. and truck were passing scattered refugees; a quarter of an hour after that they were pushing aside a steady stream of them. A few Earth-gov troops, some still bearing weapons lazily slung over their shoulders, were among the refugees. The retreating troops didn't even try to challenge them, and they didn't answer shouted questions; they just continued marching numbly away from the pillars of smoke.

The convoy gradually slowed to a near crawl as it moved into utter chaos. People doubled over, their possessions on their backs, staggered toward them in the middle of the road, as others with only the clothes they were wearing pushed passed them, and heavily laden vehicles forced their way through the refugees fleeing on foot. The a.p.c. plowed through them all, like a tug forcing its way against a tide. The refugees flowed around the convoy, and the civilian vehicles driving toward the a.p.c. found themselves forced upon the shoulder until the convoy passed.

As they steadily closed upon New M, the orange glows in the haze resolved into burning buildings and bomb bursts, as shuttles rained down flaming death on the city. It was impossible to tell who was doing the bombing and who was being bombed.

Then the convoy was in New M's outskirts: ugly composite shipping-container "buildings" and adobe and cinder block hovels interspersed with corn and soybean fields.

The refugees thinned as they entered the city proper an hour before sunset; they found themselves in a maze of unburned but apparently deserted one- and two-storey buildings. As the burning structures loomed closer, and the smoke grew denser, they rounded a corner. Everyone except Omar, who was driving, dove toward the floor as bullets ricocheted off the front of the a.p.c. The gunmen were behind an up-ended electric bus blocking the road in a narrow street, evidently chosen to box in victims. Omar did a quick calculation that the a.p.c. couldn't ram aside the bus, and ducked. He couldn't retreat because the farm truck was too close behind. Kel popped the hatch, stuck his hands through it, grabbed the handles of the .50 caliber and fired blindly at the overturned bus until he ran out of ammo a few seconds later. At the same time, Omar grabbed an AK with a drum clip, raised it above his head through the shattered front window, aimed it more or less at the source of the fire, and held down the trigger, spraying from left to right.

In the back of the truck, two gunmen poked their heads over the cab and began firing. One was immediately decapitated by an AK-97 round, his body flung backward, his blood and brains spraying over those still crouched on the bed. Several of them panicked and jumped off the truck. The three who jumped to the left were cut down immediately. The four who jumped to the right hit the ground and returned fire.

Between the four, Omar, and the gunman still standing upright shooting over the cab, they riddled the overturned bus. A few seconds later, they stopped shooting after the fire from the overturned bus abruptly ceased. Omar spent several long seconds eying the bus, then opened the door of the a.p.c., preparing to head back to care for the wounded. Kel looked up at the single two-storey building on the block, and muttered to Chuy, "Fucking amateurs. None of 'em even went into that—"

A shot rang out from a second-storey window, and one of the women in the bed of the truck flew backward. The return fire shredded the frame building's facade as the survivors scrambled out of the truck bed and took cover along its side. Omar climbed back inside the a.p.c. and ducked down, reaching for the AK he'd been firing, as Kel crouched and went between the seats into the back of the vehicle. Chuy reached into the locker beneath the right-side bench and pulled out six of the UV grenades; he stuck three in his pockets and handed three to Kel. Then he dropped the ramp, and yelled "Cover us!" to Omar and the gunman crouching behind the truck's cab.

As they opened up, Kel and Chuy rushed to the side of the sniper's building. Kel set his gun on full auto, took a step backward, and raked a quick burst along the building's side at waist height. He ran to the front door, kicked it in, and rushed in, weapon at the ready, with Chuy close behind. Nothing. He looked at the stairway at the far side of the room and nodded his head. They walked to it, Kel in the lead, and cautiously ascended the stairs, looking up, guns raised.

At the top of the stairs they faced a short hall with three closed wooden doors on the side facing the street. Kel crept quietly past the first door, knelt, extended his arm and pushed the door inward. A burst tore through the door and wall on the opposite side of the doorway. Chuy, who had been covering Kel, ripped a burst through the wall. Kel tossed in a UV grenade. It went off with a blinding flash as he and Chuy covered their eyes. Kel inched back and peered into the room. The grenade had been unnecessary. Chuy had gotten lucky. He'd hit the sniper in the temple with one of his rounds. After they'd gone through the nerve-wracking routine of checking the other two rooms—empty—they walked back to the a.p.c.

Omar turned the vehicle around, took a right at the corner, took another right, and headed toward the outreach house through the smoke-filled streets, which were empty but for dead bodies, shattered store fronts, and burning vehicles.

The a.p.c. and truck were almost out of the downtown, nearing the outreach house, when they were caught in an ambush from the upper storey of a cinder block building. The ambushers didn't open fire until the a.p.c. was past them. Instead, they concentrated their fire on the truck. It was cut to shreds and ground to a halt a dozen meters past the ambush, its driver dead.

But even as the first shots sounded, Omar raced toward the next intersection, whipped around, and roared back toward the ambush. Chuy, in the shotgun seat, pointed his AK above his head out through the hatch and held down the trigger, firing blindly in the general direction of the ambushers. When they arrived at the truck, Omar screeched to a halt, putting the a.p.c. between the truck and the bushwhackers. Ann dropped the rear gate, and the survivors from the truck, two guys in their twenties and two women in their thirties, scrambled aboard. Lorenzo screamed in pain as one of them fell across his injured leg.

As the ramp was rising and bullets rattled off their armor, Kel yelled, "Anybody else alive?" One of the guys yelled back, "No!" Omar slammed down the pedal and the a.p.c. lurched forward, and then was clear of the ambush as a few final shots ricocheted off the now almost fully risen ramp. Omar took a right at the next intersection, and then took another right.

As Tau set and the orange glow enveloping the city turned hell red, Omar screeched to a stop in front of the New Harmony outreach house. Ann and Chuy jumped out and ran into the building. A minute later they ran back to the a.p.c.

Chuy, struggling to speak, broke the bad news: "They're all dead."

Everyone in the a.p.c. sat stock still until Roberta asked, "What can we do? New Harmony is no more. Our comrades are dead. And if they catch us, kill us they will. What can we do?"

No one replied. Omar gasped and put his head in his hands. Chuy shook him. "Hey *compañero*, let me drive." Omar didn't resist, and Chuy climbed into the driver's seat. He pressed down on the pedal, and they sped away as gunshots rang in the distance. Most, judging by the sound, were at least a few blocks away. But heavy fire suddenly erupted behind them, and several rounds ricocheted off their rear armor. Chuy turned a corner on two wheels, the a.p.c. sped down a side street, and the shots faded. Three blocks later he pulled into a lot behind a two-storey building and stopped.

Kel asked, "Should we head back and join the convoy to The Strand?"

Chuy replied, "I don't think we'd make it. There's no way around town, and we're really lucky that none of the *putos* we ran into had an RPG. If we head back, we'll have to fight our way out at night, and the goddamned Nazis who followed us down the gorge are probably pretty damned close to being here."

Kel asked, "So what do we do? If we stay here, we're dead. If we go back, we're dead. So what do we do? Head west to the coastal range?"

Ann said, "No. It´s not a big range, and there´s only one road in and out. If the fucking Nazis win, we´d be trapped. But we're pretty close to both the Earth-gov compound and the commercial port, so there might be another way. You want to catch a shuttle to The Strand. . . . Or go back to Earth?"

Kel's eyes widened. The mention of Earth was the first good thing he'd heard in days.

Ann continued, "We can't go to any of the other colonies. We show up at any of 'em, the authorities will shoot us. So it's either stay here or go back to Earth. We might be able to snag a shuttle. If it's a VTOL they use for cargo runs, we could head for The Strand.

If it ain't, and it's fueled up, we could head for one of the ships parked around Boris and Arkady. There are a bunch of 'em out there, and we're ex-spacers." She nodded toward Omar and Lorenzo. "It only takes three or four of us to run one of those ships."

Omar blurted out, "Three or—"

Ann cut him short. "It can be done." She looked at the other survivors. "Any of the rest of you have experience?"

Elvia stammered, "I do. . . . But it was a long time ago . . . Low Earth orbit . . . And I was medical, not a real spacer . . ."

"You'll do." Ann looked toward the rest, and waited. One of the Durruti Column women, Emma, said, "I was a pilot."

The other one, Judi, said, "I was a cryo-engineer."

Ann suppressed a smirk. "Cryo-engineer" was a euphemism for "cryo-technician." There was no engineering about it. Just rote-learned routine.

But she'd have to do.

As Chuy drove them away from downtown and the sounds of gunfire and the stink of burning buildings, Ann asked Chuy, "Where to? The commercial port is closer than the Earth-gov compound, but I doubt that there's anything there."

"Let's try it. It'll be way easier than the compound."

Three blocks later, Chuy turned onto Korolev, heading out of town toward the commercial port. As he sped down the street, a red glow blossomed in front of them.

Almost all of the buildings at the commercial port, and its fuel depot, were burning. Chuy rammed through the gate and sped onto the field, where four shuttles were in flames. But one small shuttle was still intact, sitting by itself, away from the other shuttles and burning buildings.

Chuy raced toward it across the runway. A hundred meters from it, he jammed on the brakes as the shuttle exploded in a ball of blue flame. After a moment of stunned silence, Chuy made a 180, headed back toward the shattered gate, and once through it turned toward the burning town and the Earth-gov compound with its shuttle port.

* * *

From half a klick out it was obvious that there was no way through the front gate. A mob of desperate people was trying to get into the compound at the most obvious entry point. But the Earth-gov troops weren't having it. There was no way for them to tell who were legitimate refugees and who were Nazis, and they were repelling all of them. Sometimes with tear and nausea gas, sometimes with low-power fryer waves that hurt but didn't maim, and sometimes with gunfire, when nothing else would do.

Chuy braked to a stop. People were pressing against the gate, and some had set up ladders trying to scale the five-meter-high wall. Soldiers were pushing the ladders over, sending their climbers sprawling to the pavement below.

Tear gas and stun grenades rained down on the crowd, the fryers hummed, and the crowd screamed and retreated temporarily, leaving thrashing victims in its wake. Then it surged forward again, and more tear gas, microwave agony, and stun grenades rained down, and the crowd fell back like a wave on a beach. And then a roar went up and the crowd surged toward the gate yet again.

Kel was transfixed by the spectacle, but finally managed to speak. "We're screwed. How can we get through that?"

Ann said, "We can't. We get in through one of the security entrances. I was in good standing when I stopped working for them. My palm print might still work. Knowing how these dickheads operate, they might never have updated."

Kel stared at her, his jaw hanging down.

"Yeah. I worked for 'em running a forklift for a couple of years before New Harmony was established. What the fuck else was I gonna do? It was before the commercial shuttle fleet was going, and it paid twice what any of the goddamned capitalists here were paying."

Ann gave Chuy directions. He headed down a side street, turned right two blocks later, and continued for six more blocks until Ann told him to make another right, find a place to park, and stop. They were less than half a block from an apparently blank section of the compound's wall.

Ann got out, armed with a machine pistol she'd lifted from one of the Nazis at the overturned-flatbed ambush. She walked carefully along the side of the street, until she came to Korolev, with everyone else behind her. She looked to her right and saw the riot several blocks to the north at the main gate. The street was empty to her left. She looked at the top of the wall directly in front of her, saw no one, and ran catercorner across Korolev to a blank section of wall. She pulled down a hidden panel, revealing a translucent plate. She pressed her palm against it. Waited. Nothing. She tried again. Still nothing. She wiped her hand nervously on her pants and tried a third time. Still nothing. She pulled her shirt tail out and was wiping off the panel when a gate opened two hundred meters farther down the wall, and an electric jeep emerged with two troopers in the front, two in the rear, and sped toward her. Kel fired at it but missed as Ann started running back across Korolev. She stopped, faced them, aimed and fired. She cut down the driver and the man behind him, and Chuy shot the other soldier in the rear. But almost simultaneously a shot from the trooper in the passenger seat ripped through her head.

As Ann dropped, the jeep flipped on its side, and Kel, Chuy, and Omar unleashed a volley, killing the trooper who had killed Ann.

There was silence, but for the distant sounds of the riot.

Kel shouted, "Come on!" and ran toward the overturned jeep. Everyone else hesitated. Kel turned the bodies over, going from one to the next until he found lieutenant's insignia. He removed the lieutenant's large, serrated knife from the man's belt, along with two grenades, which he stuck in his pockets. Then he cut off the lieutenant's right hand. He ran to the panel by the hidden door, pressed the bloody hand against it, and the door started to open.

The others began running across Korolev, with Bari and Kile, the two remaining Durruti Column guys, supporting Lorenzo. They were about halfway across it when the door reached its farthest-open point and five seconds later started to close.

Kel yelled, "Hurry!," and braced his back against the door, trying to hold it open. The door pushed him forward as if he wasn't there. He jumped out of the way as the door closed tightly, just as Chuy and the others arrived. Kel immediately pressed the severed hand against the plate again. Nothing happened. He tried again. Nothing.

"Shit! It has to reset!"

Chuy asked, "How long?"

"Who knows?!"

Ten seconds later, Kel tried again. Nothing.

Chuy looked down Korolev, away from the riot, and said, "Oh shit!" Three silent figures had emerged from the gate the jeep had driven out of and were running down Korolev toward them. They'd almost reached the ruined jeep when Chuy trained his AK on them, put it on full auto, and held down the trigger. The Earth-gov soldiers dropped to the ground and began firing wildly, as Kel and the other survivors opened up on them. It was an uneven fight. The troops on the ground barely had time to scream; they were dead within seconds.

Kel looked at Chuy and asked, "What do we do now?"

"Wait."

Kel was still holding the severed hand as another dark, silent vehicle slipped onto Korolev and pulled into a side street thirty meters behind the smoking jeep. Omar said, "¡Coño!" as he saw one of Corona's finest poke his head around the corner holding an RPG he was preparing to fire. Omar pulled his gun up and fired at him as he was aiming.

Kel frantically pressed the bloody hand against the plate. And the door opened slowly. The soldier with the grenade launcher fired wildly as Omar continued to fire. The RPG round nearly obliterated the overturned jeep as Velky, Elvia, and Roberta pushed through the widening entrance while Chuy and Omar were firing blindly down the street in the general direction of the new Earth-gov troops. Another RPG round exploded on the wall just to the right of the door, sending a shower of fragments spewing away from them. The door shuddered and made metallic grinding noise, but cotinued to open in first and spurts.

As Lorenzo reached the door, a shot ripped through his back. He jerked forward as Kile and Bari nearly lost their grip on him. They scrambled inside, pulling Lorenzo, who was already dead, after them. More shots ricocheted off the wall. Kel continued to fire while Chuy pushed Omar through the door, and it started to close.

Kel yelled at Chuy, "Get inside!" Chuy hesitated and then dove inside as the door juddered. Kel squeezed off a burst and slipped into the narrowing gap. The door shook spasmodically and pinned Kel between its edge and the wall, wedging his torso. He screamed as it stopped then juddered inward another half centimeter, and stopped again, gears grinding.

Hands gripped his arm and leg. He didn't budge. He screamed again as a shot tore through the skin atop his thigh. More hands gripped him. He tore loose as his rescuers toppled backwards onto the floor. Chuy fired a burst through the twenty-five centimeters of the opening, as the gears continued to grind. Kel, nearly hyperventilating, sat up and felt for one of the grenades he'd taken from the dead lieutenant. He pulled the pin and tossed it through the door, and screamed, "Hit the deck!" The grenade exploded, sending a blast wave and a shower of debris back through the gap. Then he tossed a UV grenade out onto Korolev. He yelled, "Shut your eyes!" Chuy and the others who'd pulled Kel through the door didn't hear him through the din, and were just getting up when the grenade went off, leaving them groping.

Kel got up screaming, "Let's go! Let's get the fuck outta here!" He ran to the left, down a dim descending corridor, barely illuminated by emergency bulbs, as the others followed. As they ran after him toward the next intersection, fifty meters on, a grenade flew through the gap in the door.

They had just rounded the corner when the shock wave sent them sprawling, their ears ringing. Fifty meters farther on, that corridor T-boned into one at right angles to it. In the dim light, Kel could barely read the grungy sign directly in front of him: "Revivification" (pointing to the right) and "Docking Facility" (pointing to the left).

Chuy read it too, and charged past him, heading left. Twenty meters down the corridor Chuy arrived at a locked steel door. It was a heavy security door set in concrete, its base fifteen centimeters above the floor.

Kel pushed Chuy aside, pulled out the dead lieutenant's hand from his pants pocket, and pressed the bloody palm against the door's i.d. plate. The door didn't budge. He tried it again. It still didn't open.

The sounds of a blast and collapsing masonry echoed from somewhere behind him.

Bari, one of the Durruti kids, raised his AK toward the locked door and shouted, "Stand back!"

Chuy grabbed his gun and said, "Don't be stupid."

Bari pushed him away and raised his gun. Kel shouted "Duck!" as he dove for the floor and put his arms over his head.

Bari's shots didn't come close to blowing through the door. They ricocheted off it, then glanced off the corridor's walls and screamed into the darkness away from everyone. At least he'd been smart enough, or lucky enough, to shoot at the door from the same side as the rest of the survivors.

They were just getting to their feet as Chuy took off down the corridor to the right, toward the revivication area, yelling "I'll be back!"

After they'd risen, Omar asked if anyone had a grenade. Kel did. Omar took the grenade from him, shooed everyone else thirty meters down the corridor and into the one that abutted it, stood to one side, and fired his AK at the cement beneath the door's gate. Richochets rang down the corridor. After he'd squeezed off a dozen shots he'd excavated a small cavity in the cement. He took the grenade, pulled the pin, set it at the base of the door, ran like hell, dove toward the floor and put his hands over his ears, and opened his mouth, to avoid ruptured eardrums. The grenade blasted out all of the nearby emergency lights.

They were in near-total darkness except for dim flickers of emergency lights farther down the corridor. Kel was getting up, starting to feel his way toward the door, when a monster with blazing blue-white eyes screeched to a stop before him, as a voice shouted, "Don't shoot!" It was Chuy, driving a forklift with mercury-vapor lights.

He maneuvered the forklift toward the door to the docking bay. The grenade had blown out more of the cement beneath the door, exposing rebar and the bottom of the door frame. Chuy maneuvered the forklift's tines beneath the frame and tried to pry it out of the concrete. It didn't budge.

The forklift's rear wheels started to rise. Chuy didn't let up. The door frame creaked, inching gradually outward, as small chunks of concrete popped away from its sides. The frame was groaning, starting to pull away from its concrete home in fits and spurts as the forklift's rear wheels raised higher into the air. When the angle was nearly forty degrees, Chuy lost his nerve. He shut down the forklift's motor, jumped off, and rolled away.

The rear of the forklift was still in the air, the door half pried out of its moorings, when the silence was broken by distant shouts and the sounds of footfalls coming down one of the far corridors. Chuy was the first up. His face looked skeletal, lit by the forklift's lights reflecting off the floor. He yelled, "Let's do it!" He jumped up and hung dangling off the back of the forklift as Omar, Bari, Velky and Elvia joined him, their bodies dangling barely above the floor, lending their weight to the forklift, trying to wrench the door from its frame. They swung in space for two seconds, and then the door groaned and gave way. The forklift bounced down and fell on its side, pinning and crushing Velky's leg. As she screamed, Kel and the others managed to lift the forklift a few centimeters off her as Roberta and Emma pulled her from beneath it.

Chuy stepped through the opening and found a light switch. He gasped. Fifty meters away, down the wall to the left, was a wide open cargo door. They'd found the locked emergency exit.

The room was littered with barrels, empty crates, rags, and other junk, but there was a pneumatic lift against the opposite wall, and an opening above it, doors closed. Chuy shut off the light switch. Dim light filtered around the edges of the opening above the lift. Chuy hit the lights again.

At the bottom of the lift, a large platform waited, empty. Kel raised his index finger before his lips and said, "Quiet! Let's go!" Seconds later, he and the rest of the survivors stepped onto it, as Elvia covered Velky's mouth to smother her screams. Kel pressed the button, and the elevator began to rise toward the closed doors.

As they crouched, the doors retracted, revealing another set of doors two meters above. The elevator continued to rise, the second set of doors irised open, and they found themselves in near total darkness.

The platform came to a smooth halt. A single dim red bulb glowed feebly to one side. They were in a cluttered cargo hold, netting hanging raggedly from eyelets in the walls and ceiling, crates, barrels, and boxes scattered on the deck. Toward the back of the bay there were several racks of cryo-coffins.

Chuy, clutching his gun in his left hand, put his finger to his lips. He and Kel inched their way through the gloom toward the only door. Kel found the control panel, and a second later the door to the cockpit opened silently as he and Chuy pressed against the wall on either side of it. Kel took a cautious peek as the door slid open. The pilot's back was to them; he had on earphones, and the music blaring from them was so loud that Kel could hear it clearly from four meters away. Country. David Allan Coe. Kel shuddered as he thought of Zed and Family Values.

He stepped into the cockpit, Chuy behind him, and tiptoed toward the pilot. He tapped the pilot on the right shoulder. The man jumped in his seat and jerked his head toward an AK at eye level. Kel laughed. It was Bud.

Kel asked, "Howdy Bud. Brown trouser time?"

"Fuck you, Kel."

"Bud, get us out of here."

Bud pushed away the muzzle. "Put that fucking thing down and we'll talk." Kel did, and Bud narrowed his eyes and asked, "Now why in hell should I help you?"

Chuy stepped past Kel and glared down at Bud. He gripped his gun and said, "We're not fucking around, Bud. Get us outta here."

Bud looked at Chuy for several seconds, and finally said, "Well, since you put it that way . . . But how are you gonna get outta here without me? Are any of you qualified to fly one of these things?"

Emma pushed past Kel and Chuy, settled into the co-pilot's seat, and said, "I am. You want me to do this alone?"

Bud stared at her for a moment, trying to decide if she was bluffing. As Emma reached for the ignition switches, he turned his head toward Chuy and said, "You'd better strap into the acceleration couches."

Omar, Elvia, and Julia carried a writhing Velky into the cabin, as the others strapped themselves in.

They were one couch short. Kel gestured toward Velky. "Bring her here. I'll hold her."

Bud replied, "That ain't such a good idea. Her weight'll probably smother you."

"What if we wedge her between my legs?"

"You want dislocated hips?"

"I'll risk it."

Bud shrugged. A moment later Roberta said, "I weigh only forty kilos. She weighs closer to sixty. And she is injured. She needs couch of her own."

Kel opened his mouth, but Roberta interrupted him before he could speak. "Do not argue. Let us strap her in."

Chuy and Omar moved Velky, and Roberta climbed onto Kel's acceleration couch, settled between his legs, and Elvia strapped both of them in.

Chuy called out to Bud, "What about those cryo-coffins? What have we got for passengers?"

Bud said, "Nobody you need to worry about. A bunch of Earth gov desk jockeys. Wanted to go to the colony on Epsilon Eridani after the trouble started." He laughed again. "Or that's where they were going!"

Bud began taxiing. The shuttle roared down the runway and started to rise, barely missing, nearly decapitating, another shuttle taxiing on a cross cutting runway. The G forces built. Kel felt himself crushed into his seat, and would have screamed if the G forces had allowed him to, as he felt the blinding pain of Roberta's now incredibly heavy body slowly dislocating his hips.

After several minutes of agony, he relaxed. And he was weightless. Everyone except Velky released themselves from the acceleration couches. They floated as the sky turned a deep purple, with more and more stars visible every passing second.

After Chuy unstrapped himself, he pushed himself forward and grabbed the backs of the pilot's and co-pilot's seats.

He turned toward Bud. "Know of any available starships?"

"I might."

* * *

Four hours later they were orbiting Boris. A half hour later, they docked with the Rush.

After the docking doors sealed, Kel turned to Omar, nodded his head toward Julia, Elvia and Emma, and asked, "Now what? Can the four of you fly this whale."

Bud smiled. "Could five?"

Kel looked puzzled. "Maybe. But I thought you said you liked it around here."

"You ought to know me better than that. I was just fucking with you."

Kel said, "There's no tellin' what we'll find back on Earth."

"I know. But like a friend of mine used to say"—he glanced at Chuy—"it beats the hell out of the alternative."

Chuy gestured back toward the cargo hold and the cryopods. "What about them? How will they get back to the surface?"

Bud grinned crookedly. "They won't."

After enjoying Chuy's shocked expression for a moment, Bud laughed and said, "We'll take 'em with us. There are only two dozen of 'em. We can revive 'em one by one after we get there. If we want to."

* * *

Two hours later, the Rush hung in blackness against the Milky Way. It began to move away from Tau II, slowly at first, and then ever faster before it vanished in a flash of light.

ACKNOWLEDGMENTS

Thanks to the many individuals who have contributed to this book. First, many thanks to Kathy DeGrave, whose detailed, insightful comments about an early draft of this work were invaluable. Many thanks also to Chris Edwards, Brian Hullfish, Lynea Search, Mick Berry, and David Yerkey for useful suggestions regarding the near-final draft.

Thanks too to my song-writing collaborators and to all of my bandmates over the years, with special thanks to Abe Acuña, Brian Hullfish, and especially Michael Turner for his inspired vocal vamping—reproduced here more or less verbatim—at the end of "Abductee Blues" (Chapter 3).

More thanks are due Abe, Jaime DeZubeldia, and Jerry Díaz for checking the glossary of Spanish-language terms used in the text, to Chris Edwards, who, as well as making useful suggestions, came up with the title for this book, to Primitivo "Festering" Morales, who came up with the primary character's signature expression, and to astronomer Bob McMillan for his detailed answers to questions about planets with eccentric orbits and the characteristics of G8V flare stars. Any scientific errors are, of course, solely my responsibility.

A less personal acknowledgment is well deserved by the web site www.solstation.com, which provided a plethora of useful information on dozens of nearby stars, and the possibility of their being suitable hosts for life-bearing planets.

As for the portrayal of the religious cults, I "thank" the members of the cults with which I've had direct contact, and I sincerely thank the authors of the dozens of books I've read on cults over the years.

Regarding the cults themselves, all of those portrayed in this book are of the "mix and match" variety. In addition to blending characteristics, dogmas, personalities, and practices from many cults, I've also mixed in elements from sci-fi books, short stories, movies, television programs, and too many other sources to cite. There are at least six disparate elements in every cult described in this book.

The portrayal of the New Harmony anarchist community is based in part on time I spent at the Zegg community (which is in no way a cult) in Germany in the 1990s. Most of the members of that community would not characterize themselves as anarchists, and almost all would find my implicit endorsement of violence (in certain situations) repugnant. The material on New Harmony is also based on my experiences with other egalitarian communities and their members, and on anarchist theory and practice.

Finally, any science fiction book draws inspiration from other works both inside and outside of the science fiction field. In the places where I drew from others, I acknowledged it within the text via veiled—and sometimes not so veiled—references to the authors or their works. As well, I couldn't resist adding obvious tips of my hat to my favorite 1970s science fiction novel and to my two favorite Soviet science fiction writers from the same era.

Thanks again to one and all.

—Zeke Teflon

Dear Reader,

With the drastic decrease in the number of reviews published by newspapers and magazines, and the drastic increase in the number of books published annually, reader reviews have become very important.

If you enjoyed this book, please consider writing a reader review for your favorite e-retailer, online bookstore, or book review site.

You'd not only help the author and a small publisher, you'd help other readers discover this book.